HAPPYLAND

THE JACKSON CLAY & BEAR BEAUCHAMP SERIES
BOOK 4

B.C. LIENESCH

JOIN LIQUID MIND PUBLISHING'S MAILING LIST

Follow the link to join our newsletter and stay up to date with Liquid Mind Publishing!

https://BookHip.com/GTQPXSQ

You'll receive a **free** copy of

A Dangerous Game: A Jackson Clay Prequel.

CONTENT WARNING

The subject matter in this novel is intended for mature readers and may not be suitable for children or young adults. Please note this novel contains explicit language, depictions of violence and abuse, and sexual situations including assault.

For everyone chasing a dream.
Keep going.

PART ONE

JOSEPHINE

"You may choose to look the other way but you can never say again that you did not know." —WILLIAM WILBERFORCE

ONE

SPECIAL AGENT JEN BAILEY clenched the cold alloy frame of her service weapon in her hand. Resting her palm on the grip was a habit dating all the way back to her days as a trooper clocking speeders on Interstate 81. Now, she rode shotgun in one of the Bureau of Criminal Investigations unmarked Explorers, a part of a very different operation.

She looked down at the maps app on her phone in her other hand. Seventeen minutes away. The man driving the Explorer, John Pitts. Tall and broad-shouldered with short, salt-and-pepper hair, he looked over at her and grinned at her restlessness.

"Everything still good from when you last checked thirty seconds ago?" he asked.

Bailey ignored his remark. Pitts was a capable agent, but his true expertise was finding ways to get under Bailey's skin. They'd worked together ever since she'd joined the department's Human Trafficking Unit a year ago. In that span, she'd found the number of times she'd wanted to punch him and the number of times she'd wanted to buy him a beer about even. This latest quip might have just put the "punch him" desire ahead by a nose, though.

She was studying their progress on the app when her phone buzzed with an incoming call. She felt her heart lurch into her throat as she read the Caller ID.

Josephine

Bailey tapped the icon to answer the call. "Kristal, what is it?"

Kristal Hardy had unknowingly solicited herself to an undercover special agent in an apartment in Front Royal, Virginia seven months ago. Now, she was known to the Human Trafficking Unit as Josephine — a handle Bailey gave her from Josephine Bakhita, the patron saint of human trafficking victims — in an effort to conceal the fact she was now cooperating with them.

"Bailey! You've got to help me!" Kristal said in between labored breaths. "Something is wrong. Something is very, very wrong. They know!"

Bailey shifted with alarm in her seat. "Okay, just hold on," she said. "We're on our way right now." She motioned for Pitts to drive faster.

"It's not going to be fast enough!"

"It is, Kristal. Just breathe. I promise you, we're coming."

"Listen, you need to know. It's not just Shug. He's—"

Kristal's voice was gone. Bailey ripped her phone from her ear and looked at the screen. The call went dead.

"Shit!" she stammered under her breath. She looked up, thinking for a moment. Her fingers tapped frantically on the armrest built into the door. Maybe Kristal was right. Maybe they weren't going to be fast enough. She looked at Pitts. "Step it up. We're running it Code 3."

"Jen, they'll hear us com—"

"She's blown, John. They already know we're coming. Step it up!"

Pitts shook his head but reached over and flipped two switches. The lights and siren on their car announced their presence to everyone else on the highway. A second later, the convoy of unmarked cruisers behind them followed suit.

Bailey grabbed the radio from the center console and keyed the mic. "Be advised, our source may be under duress. We're going Code 3 the rest of the way. Someone coordinate with the Frederick County Sheriff's Office and have them start us some units."

"Copy, on it." A voice radioed back.

The convoy of a half-dozen cars snaked its way through the light traffic on the interstate before exiting onto the crowded streets of Route 50 in the town of Winchester. Pushing west, they headed for the rural hills just outside of town. Jen looked at her phone once more and clamped her fingers around the grip of her service weapon, unholstering it. They were two miles out.

Their target was the Mt. Olive Motel, a seedy-looking motor lodge that they'd learned through Josephine was being used to exploit trafficked women into sex work. The plan had been to serve a warrant and raid the place, taking Josephine into custody with everyone else and preserving her cover. Now, though, Bailey had no idea what they were rolling up on. As the highway meandered past a sloping hillside, the sign for the motel came into view.

"Here we go," Bailey said into her radio. "Trail cars cover the points of entry. Everyone else, follow us in."

A plot of small cabins, tenuously connected by one roof made up the whole of the motel. Their retro green and orange facade were indicative of the time they'd been constructed, with seemingly little to no upkeep done in the decades since. They were arranged in a crescent around an arcing drive and parking lot that climbed up a shallow knoll.

The fender of their Explorer nosed into the pavement as it shot onto the drive. Pitts led the three cars that followed him to the motel's office, nestled in the center, then jerked the wheel hard. Their Explorer swerved and came to a stop pointing at the office's front doors. The agents driving the other cars followed suit and maneuvered in to form a perimeter around the building.

Bailey hopped out to prepare to lead the lot of them up to serve the warrant when the office door suddenly creaked open.

"Movement! Movement!" one of the other agents shouted.

Pitts and Bailey took cover behind the doors to their Explorer, the other agents doing the same. Bailey waited a minute, her gun trained on the door. It stood half open, with no one and nothing visible inside; just a dark void.

"Virginia State Police!" Bailey called out. "We have a warrant to search the property. I need anyone inside to come out now, slowly, with your hands raised!" The whir of the cars' idle engines was her only response. Reaching into the SUV, she grabbed her radio. "Do we have Sheriff's Office units coming to back us up or what?"

"They're en route now. Couple minutes," an agent radioed back.

Bailey shook her head, frustrated. As she was about to repeat her orders to whomever was inside, the motel office door opened wider. Bailey got even lower behind her door. "You, in the office! This is the Virginia State Police! I need you to—"

Before Bailey could finish, a figure formed in the darkness, slim and feminine. As she stepped out, the rest of her features became visible. Her fawn complexion. Her dyed-blond hair showing its true color at its roots. Her round face inundated with makeup. It was Kristal Hardy. It was their Josephine.

She wore brown cowboy boots and low-rise jeans, but her torso was covered in something bulky and far less stylish. It took Bailey a moment to recognize what it was, but when she did, a chill came over her.

"Jesus Christ!" Pitts said. "Is that a fucking suicide vest?!"

Bailey's eyes focused on the vest. It looked to be something like a hunter's vest, albeit two sizes too big for Kristal. The whole thing hung off her bony frame. Around her abdomen, a wire — or several wires — ran to and from a row of canteen-sized canisters. Bailey looked up at Kristal's face. Her lips were trembling as her mascara began to drag behind the tears running down her cheeks.

"Kristal," Bailey said, taking a deep breath to calm herself. "Is that right? Is that an ... explosive around you?"

Kristal gave an almost imperceptible nod. "I ... I think so. I don't know. They put me in it."

Bailey dropped her head to talk into her radio. "Someone get the local bomb squad rolling *right now*." She looked back up at Bailey. "Okay, Kristal. Do you know if you can take it off?"

"I don't know. They grabbed me and put it on me, and then told me to wait for you all to come or they'd kill me."

"Alright, Kristal. That's okay. We're going to figure this out. I just need you to stay right there."

———

A QUARTER MILE AWAY, a man stepped out of the woods and into the parking lot for the Northwest Assembly of God. His hair buzz cut, he had two upside down revolver tattoos on opposite sides of his neck, framing his jawline. He looked back instinctively but knew he wouldn't see anything. That was the point, after all. Over here, they were hidden away from what was playing out at the motel.

The man reached into his pocket, fetched his phone, and called a number. Half a ring later, a voice answered.

"Where are we at?" asked the voice.

"It's done," the man said. "We left the bitch at the motel as a present for the cops. Your info was right. She tried to make a call as soon as we got to her."

"And the rest of them?"

The man looked ahead at a large Sprinter van sitting idle in the empty parking lot. "Secure, we moved them out before the cops came in. Had a couple of johns we had to scare off, but it shouldn't be a problem."

"What about Liles?"

"Also with us. Secure."

"You bring him to me."

"Understood. And the gift we left back at the motel?"

"Unwrap it." The line went dead.

The man grinned, flashing his yellowed teeth. He opened his contacts, scrolled to a number, and placed another call.

———

BAILEY HEARD sirens in the distance. Backup was coming. She locked eyes with Kristal and put her hand out in a stopping gesture.

"I just need you to stay right there," Bailey repeated. "Can you do that for me?"

Kristal nodded again. "Jen?"

"Yeah, Kristal?"

"I'm sorr—"

The blast kicked Bailey backward like a mule, throwing her the length of the Explorer and onto the pavement behind it. She heard muffled groans and voices, but couldn't make sense of them. Her mind tried to process everything, but it was like running underwater. What had happened? An explosion. The vest. Had it gone off?

Bailey rolled over. Pebbles stuck to her face like tar acne. The pavement was smeared with something slick. Oil? Blood? A combination of both? On the other side of the SUV, she could see Pitts pushing himself to his feet. She grabbed the wheel well of the Explorer and pulled herself upright. Smoke wafted out from somewhere beyond the Explorer. The engine of the sedan next to her was on fire.

Bailey crawled back to her open door, got her feet underneath her, and peered back over the door at the motel office.

Its windows were blown out and more smoke drifted upwards in spectral curls from somewhere inside. Debris was strewn over the pavement in front.

And amidst it all, Kristal Hardy was gone.

TWO

TWO HOURS LATER, Bailey found herself standing over a sink in one of the women's restrooms in the Frederick County Sheriff's Offices in Winchester. Kristal Hardy was dead — blown into a million pieces across a motel parking lot — and now the only keepsake Bailey had of her was the blood on the cuff of her blouse. She stood there, staring at it. Should she try to wash it off? It felt cruel, somehow, given everything that had just happened.

A loud knocking rapped on the door.

"Jen, you in there?" It was Pitts.

Bailey sighed and let her head drop. "Yeah, I'm just washing up."

"The big brass is here. They want to talk to everyone."

Bailey shook her head. Pitts always talked like he only played an investigator on TV. "Got it. I'll be right out."

She slapped off the faucet and looked at herself in the mirror, taking stock. Even by her standards, she looked tired. Her suit was untucked, wrinkled, and dirty, sitting on her athletic frame like hung laundry. The dark rings made her hazel eyes pop better than any expensive eyeliner could hope to, but they also looked like she'd gone twelve rounds with a welterweight boxer, and now the side of her neck was scraped from where she'd hit the pavement. She brushed her auburn hair back and studied the abrasion more closely before shaking her head in frustration. She left to join her team.

Bailey walked down a long, featureless hall to a conference room where Lieutenant Colonel Tom Girard stood waiting at the head of a table. Bailey's team from the motel was seated around the table looking as banged up as Bailey. With gauze wrappings and bandages interspersed throughout the team, they looked more like a motley crew that had been sprung from the local Emergency Room rather than a special investigative unit of the Virginia State Police. Windowless, oil paintings in gilded frames depicting battles from the American Revolution and Civil War adorned the walls behind them. Bailey extended her hand, bloody cuff and all, towards Girard.

"Sir," she greeted. "Jen Bailey, with Human Trafficking."

"Yes, I remember," Girard said with a kind smile. He looked at the blood stain, then up at her scraped neck. "Are you alright?"

Girard was the Director of the Bureau of Criminal Investigation, the Virginia State Police's investigative arm. Bailey didn't interact with him in her normal day-to-day, but she supposed a bomb going off just outside a town of nearly thirty thousand was reason enough to come out and supervise things. At least, until the media attention died down.

"I'm fine, sir," Bailey replied. "A few cuts and scrapes, but I'll live."

"Did you get checked out?"

"A paramedic looked me over at the scene. I refused further medical attention."

"You should probably be looked at by a doctor."

"I'm good, sir. If it's all the same to you, I'd like to get on with it."

His brow furrowed at her brusque response, but he motioned for her to have a seat. "Sure. So, the motel? You all were there to serve a warrant?"

"Yes, sir," Bailey slid into the seat directly to his left. "As you might know, we've been focusing our investigations on the Interstate 81 corridor. Because of its proximity to the inland port outside Front Royal and the numerous distribution centers throughout the Shenandoah Valley, it is a major thoroughfare for truckers, which also makes it a likely hotbed for trafficking activity."

"So, how did the motel play into that?"

"We developed a confidential human source. Kristal Hardy, whom we gave the handle Josephine."

"The woman that had the explosive vest strapped to her."

The image of Kristal mouthing, "I'm sorry" before being murdered shot into Bailey's mind, rocking her for a moment. "Yes, that's ... yes. Hardy was in a stable — or a group of trafficked sex workers — under the control of Sean Liles, also known as Sugar Bee or Shug."

"Liles was their pimp, essentially."

"Yes. Josephine was what is called a Bottom. While a trafficked sex worker herself, she was also a lieutenant of sorts for Liles to help manage the other girls. She informed us that the stable was operating out of the motel. Once we set up surveillance, we gathered enough evidence for a warrant to go in."

"Which brings us to today. So, what went wrong?"

"We're not entirely sure. As we were en route, I received a phone call from Josephine. She was panicked and sounding like they had found out she was cooperating with us. I made the decision to roll Code 3 the rest of the way. When we got there, we moved in and around the motel's office. That's when Josephine came out.

"With the explosive vest on."

Bailey nodded.

"So, they identified her as your source. Any idea how? Or by who?"

"No, sir. Obviously, it just happened and we haven't had time to get into it yet. Speculating, at this point, would be reckless."

Girard pursed his lips. "Still, an explosive vest seems heavy-handed for a local pimp."

"Liles used narcotics as a tool to keep his stable in line. Usually, it was bottom-tier junk, like meth. But Hardy told us a few months ago he started bringing in something new, something she'd never seen before. He called them Pepsis, like the soda. She was able to get us a tablet and we had it analyzed. Chemically, it's a new designer drug related to Pyrrolidinophenones. A psychostimulant similar to cocaine, but more refined."

"Again, this all seems above the pay grade of some dirtbag."

"Exactly, which was an angle we were very much interested in. Josephine said Liles didn't get the stuff from his regular distributors. Designer drugs are big money, so, naturally, we wanted to know if Liles had connections to a larger, more complex trafficking organization."

"You were hoping to flip Liles, expecting a bigger fish out there."

Bailey nodded again. "A bigger fish that was willing to set off an explosive vest to remain unidentified."

Girard put his hands on his hips, taking a deep breath in, then out. "Alright. I want you guys to pursue this. At the very least, it sounds like we now have Liles for Murder 1. That's a hell of a thing to hang around his neck, pun intended. I'm guessing it gets him to start talking." He leaned over and shuffled together his files on the conference table. "Of course, we have to find him first."

THREE

SEAN LILES BANGED his head against the SUV's window as the rocky road it traversed kicked him side to side. Any other time he'd let out a choice, four-letter word — or perhaps a string of them — but not now. Now, he was too scared.

He wasn't sure how long they'd been on the road — the hood over his head didn't exactly make it easy to keep track of time — but Liles figured, by the way he was jonesing for another hit, it had to have been a couple of hours.

The SUV slowed for a moment, then, as it returned to speed, the ground was smooth beneath its tires. *Paved road*, Liles thought.

"There," Nick Graves said from the passenger seat, directly in front of Liles. "Pull up to the doors."

From the moment they'd first met, Graves scared the ever-loving shit out of Liles. Now that he'd taken Liles on this masked field trip, the fear had only metastasized. Still, Liles didn't dare ask where they were or who was with them. Or the real question on his mind: was he going to leave alive?

The SUV came to an easy stop and everyone's doors popped open except for Liles. A moment later, someone opened his for him and pulled him out. They pressed him face first against the body of the car, took his wrists behind him, and bound them.

"Please," Liles now dared to say. "I'm not fightin' y'all. You ain't gotta do this."

"Shut up," said a gruff voice.

A pair of hands grabbed him underneath each arm and start to carry him forward, his feet dragging behind him. As the three of them crossed over some unseen threshold, Liles could make out through the mask that they had come from some place dark — likely outside — and into somewhere brighter. Then, a blend of smells hit him. The most dominant one was the unmistakable smell of horse shit.

The men turned with Liles, bringing him through another doorway before dropping him onto his knees. Someone behind him removed the hood, and for the first time since they left the church parking lot, Liles was able to take stock of where he was. The smells now made sense. They were in a barn, specifically in what looked to be a horse stall.

Liles counted five men in total around him. Nick Graves, with his twin pistol tattoos peeking out over the collar of his workman's jacket, three other men similarly dressed and equally menacing, and then a fifth man standing in the far corner. As he stepped into the single light overhead, Liles could see now he was different than the others. He was older; clean-shaven with hair slicked-back and slightly to the side and was dressed in a full suit save for the tie. The man stepped towards Liles so that he was now standing over him. Liles tried to look up at him, but was blinded by the light overhead.

"Sean Liles," the man said. "Sugar *Bee*." He chuckled. "Interesting nickname. Why do they call you that?"

Liles wasn't sure if he was supposed to answer or not. "I—I don't know, sir. It's just what they call me."

"A man often has nicknames when his own doesn't carry much weight." The man started to circle Liles. "And do you know where you are, Sugar Bee?"

"A ... barn?"

The man chuckled again. "Not quite. No, a barn is for storing farm equipment or livestock. Here, at the *stable*, we house our prized horses." He kept circling. "That's what it's called, no? Your roster of girls. A stable?"

"I—I guess?"

"An apt metaphor, I think. You keep them all under one roof, keep them safe. The only problem is being in close quarters with one another allows the opportunity for disease to spread. All sorts of diseases. Herpesvirus, Strangles. For all its beauty, nature loves to harbor just the nastiest things. The standard practice is to isolate and treat the infected. But every once in a while, you have one horse that is just ... *problematic*. For whatever reason, it can't get right. And then, that horse becomes a liability. That's when you really have some tough decisions to make."

Liles never considered himself particularly smart, but even he could see where the man was going with this. "Sir, I'm very sorry if I caused you trouble. I didn't even know ... about you."

The man stopped in front of Liles and once again stood over him. "That's just it. You don't even know *who I am*. And yet, you're threatening to spread your problems onto me, not unlike an infection." He crouched so that his face was closer to Liles. "Law enforcement are like a virus, *Sugar Bee*. They leech onto the dumbest and most susceptible of us and don't stop until they've gotten to those of us that have gone to great lengths to insulate ourselves."

"I didn't know Kristal was talking to the cops, I swear to god."

"Precisely my point. *You* didn't know." The man poked him sharply in the chest. "*You* didn't keep an eye on *your* stable. If it weren't for my sources, *you'd* be in handcuffs right now, probably singing like a goddamn soprano. Putting all of *us* — the ones you didn't even know about — at risk. So, now it's my problem."

"I'm sorry, sir. I—"

The man stood up. "Do you know how we put down a horse when it comes down to it? These days, people feel the *ethical* or *humane* way is to euthanize them. Drugs." He shook his head and sneered. "Admittedly, that would be fitting for you."

"Please, don't—"

"But I prefer the way my daddy showed me. And his daddy before him." Graves stepped forward and handed the man what looked like some kind of hardware tool. "It's called a captive bolt gun. That's just a fancy way to say it fires a bolt into the horse's skull, stunning it if not killing it outright. Crude? Maybe. But sure is effective. And *cost* effective. Hell, it doesn't even waste a bullet."

Liles began to quiver as tears welled up in his eyes and he released his bladder.

"Unlike you, Mr. Sugar Bee, I intend to look after my stable. And protect it. At all costs."

Liles opened his mouth to scream, but the man pressed the bolt pistol to Liles' forehead and pulled the trigger. In an instant, Sean 'Sugar Bee' Liles' life was extinguished. His body slumped forward before keeling over to its side. Graves stepped up next to the man, looking at the body. The man handed Graves the bolt pistol.

"The next time you sell extra Pepsis to some dipshit for a quick payday, it'll be you with a hole in your head," the man said. "You understand me?"

"Understood, sir."

The man nodded at Liles' body, grabbing a rag off a nearby hook, wiping his hands, and discarding it. "Clean all of this up. And once you get him out of here, I want the whole stall bleached."

"What do you want us to do with the body?"

"I'll leave that to you. But whatever you do, make sure he's found. I don't want any more prying eyes. This ends with him."

Graves nodded as he and the others got to work.

FOUR

IT WAS after midnight by the time Bailey was finally able to leave for the hotel the department was putting them up in while this new investigation unfolded. She and the rest of the team had left the Sheriff's Office sometime in the mid-afternoon and gone back to the Division II Field Office out of which they had initially run the raid. Six hours later, Bailey had pored over so many pieces of paper she could no longer see the forest through the trees and so rendered any more effort useless for the night.

As she took the ramp onto the highway, she cracked her window to allow the fresh air to rejuvenate her just long enough to make it to whatever two beds and a coffee machine lay waiting for her. In the late spring night, the air was so brisk that it felt more like the coming of fall. It made her think of the autumn night several months earlier when Kristal Hardy had agreed to cooperate with them. It was a choice she made to take back control of her life; a life that was unceremoniously snuffed out this morning.

Settling into the ride to the hotel, the memories of that evening washed over her.

Bailey and Pitts sat in their Explorer, parked at the far corner of the vast lot for Charles Town Races and Slots in the panhandle of West Virginia. Pitts dominated the armrest between them. Strictly speaking, the two of them shouldn't have been up there — at least not without liaising with their counterparts in the Mountaineer State — but Kristal Hardy had finally agreed to meet with them again, and Bailey wasn't going to miss the opportunity.

In front of them, the racetrack was awash in a halo of bright light from the towers dotting the infield. Bailey heard an announcement blare from the PA system, but she couldn't make it out. She cracked her window, curious to hear what she was missing.

"Is that our girl?" Pitts asked from behind the wheel.

Bailey looked over to see a woman dressed in jeans and a halter top making the walk over to them. The orange glow of the half-smoked cigarette wedged between her lips coming closer as she followed the long sidewalk that edged the parking lot, her bare arms were wrapped around her midsection for warmth, pinning her faux Chanel purse to her side in the process.

"That's her," Bailey said.

In unison, she and Pitts got out of the Explorer and formed a two-person blockade on the sidewalk just in front of their car. When Kristal Hardy got to them, she sucked a long drag of her cigarette before taking it between her fingers and pointing at Pitts, her eyes narrowed.

"I thought you said it would just be you," she said to Bailey.

"This is John Pitts," Bailey explained. "He's my partner."

"Yeah, well," Kristal took another drag from the cigarette, "I don't know him, so I don't trust him. Shit, I don't trust you, either, but I don't have a fuckin' choice."

Kristal was jittery and Bailey wondered if it was the cold, nerves, withdrawal, or some combination of the three. She was on edge, and Bailey knew she needed to calm her down.

"John," Bailey kept her eyes on Kristal. "Why don't you stretch your legs some?"

Pitts paused just long enough to make sure his protest was

noted, then stepped around Kristal and began strolling toward the casino, hands in his pockets. When he was out of earshot, Bailey continued.

"So, you wanted to talk. Let's talk."

Kristal finished her cigarette and dropped it to the ground before snuffing it out with her stiletto heel. "I haven't got long. I told him I needed to have a smoke."

"Liles? Or a john?"

"A date." Kristal rolled her eyes. "Dumb prick couldn't pick a fuckin' winnin' horse if he tried. The losers always want to take it out on you afterward."

"It sounds like you could stand to make a few changes. I could help with that."

Kristal pulled another cigarette out of her bra. "I'm not a fuckin' snitch," she said as she fetched a lighter from her pocket and lit it. "I want to make that clear right now."

Bailey turned her palms out in an open gesture. "Sure, but for me to help you, you've got to help yourself first. A part of you must want out if you're here talking to me."

Kristal tsked under her breath. "A part of me. That's a funny fuckin' way of putting it."

It took Bailey a minute to understand, but then she put it together. Kristal wasn't holding her midsection because she was cold. "You're pregnant."

Kristal shook her head in disbelief. "Fuckin' a, right?"

Bailey nodded at the cigarette. "You really shouldn't be doing that, then."

"Do you know what a fuckin' shit storm this is for me? It's a cigarette between my lips or a fuckin' gun. Take your pick."

"You can't be the first girl to get pregnant. I'm guessing Liles doesn't know yet."

"You'd think I'd still have it if he did?" Kristal gripped her abdomen tighter.

"If you want to keep it, you can do that, Kristal. It should be your choice. I can help you."

Kristal shook her head as a tear formed in the corner of her eye. "Fuck." She fetched a tissue out of her purse and wiped it away.

Bailey stepped toward her and took the tissue from her. Kristal flinched as she did. Seeing this, a sadness came over Bailey.

"Here," she said softly. "Dab at it or you'll smear your mascara."

Kristal sniffled. "I'd just never thought about it, you know? My mother was an alcoholic piece of shit. I didn't want to have anything in common with her. But when I saw that damn test, a part of me thought, I could do this, you know? For both of us. I could be better than she was." Her arm dropped to her side. "But I can't. Shug would never let me out. He'd fuckin' kill me before it came to that."

Bailey reached out and touched Kristal's arm. "Like I said, I can help you. *We* can help you."

Kristal shook her head again. "Yeah, but for what? To narc on him? I told you, I'm not doing that."

"You would have to cooperate, yes, but nothing you're not comfortable doing. Do you even realize you're a victim in all of this? Life dealt you a shitty hand, Kristal. But you help us put Sean away? And you get out from underneath him? That's a *real* second chance. Those don't come by that often."

Kristal sniffled. "So, what? I'd have to wear a wire or some shit?"

"Not necessarily. Like I said, it wouldn't be anything you didn't want to do. I've seen a dozen guys like Sean. He's going to fuck up on his own. You just need to help us be there when he does."

Kristal looked out at the racetrack just in time to hear the crack of the gun and see the gates open as another race got underway. A dozen fillies tore off down the back straightaway. Kristal could hear their hooves clomping over the smattering of cheers coming from onlookers lined up against the railing. She watched as the horses rounded the first turn, a jockey in a green and gold silk ushering the chestnut thoroughbred he rode into the lead.

Kristal turned back to Bailey. "I think I can do that."

———

AS BAILEY ENTERED the front lobby of the hotel, the convenience shop next to the front desk caught her eye. She'd only eaten a couple slices of pizza since everything turned to shit early that morning, and now her stomach was reminding her of that fact. She walked over and grabbed a small can of pringles and a pack of M&M's. Now inside the little kiosk, she noticed the refrigerator with an array of drinks. On the top shelf were little bottles of wine. She was more of a brown liquor woman, but in the good old commonwealth of Virginia, there was no finding that outside a distillery or state-run liquor store. Bailey reached in and grabbed a mini Merlot, thought about it, and then grabbed two more. She positioned her two hands over top of her bounty like crane claws from an arcade machine and picked everything up.

"On the room, please," she said to the clerk manning the front desk.

Taking the three flights of stairs to her room, she tucked everything under one arm as she reached for her key card, let herself into the room, and locked the deadbolt on the door, finally in for the night. Bailey put her keys, gun, ID, and wallet on the nightstand, shed her work clothes and slipped into one of the cuck chairs — her crass term for the random chairs facing the bed in every hotel room — with her five-course dinner. She had just unscrewed the top to one of the small wine bottles when her phone buzzed from her discarded pants.

Bailey let out a sigh of frustration, then reached over, fished her phone out, and answered it. "Bailey."

"It's Pitts," her partner answered on the line. "Did I wake you?"

"No, I just got in."

"Well, don't settle down."

Bailey straightened her posture, alert. "Why? What's up?"

"Local sheriff's office just called. Sean Liles just turned up. Dead."

————

SEAN LILES' body was found at a large truck stop on the south side of Harrisonburg. It took Pitts and Bailey ninety minutes to drive out that way, and once they'd arrived it was close to three in the morning.

The truck stop itself seemed to be operating normally save for the clot of emergency vehicles clustered at the far back corner. Pitts pulled in and navigated them past the rows of semis and nosed up to the yellow police tape that was anchored to the last motor coach in the lot. Climbing out of the Explorer, Bailey and Pitts showed their credentials to a fox-faced patrol officer and waded into the fray.

Liles' body was face down, tucked at an awkward angle, as if dumped, in the corner formed by the pavement at the cinder block wall that closed off the back side of the lot. As Bailey and Pitts came over to it, a woman was kneeling over the body, studying it with a flashlight. She was trim, with a full head of curly hair, and Bailey recognized her immediately, having worked a case long ago and remaining close over the years. It was Bailey who'd introduced this woman to a man named Jackson Clay.

"Detective Cole," Bailey said. "Long time no see."

Detective Angela Cole pivoted her stance to turn and face Bailey. Her bronze complexion complimented her brown eyes that now crinkled as she grinned. "Jen, hi." She stood up and snapped off the latex gloves she'd been wearing. "They told me state police had someone on their way, but I didn't expect to see you. You're out this way these days?"

"I'm with the Human Trafficking Unit now, so I'm kind of all over."

Cole raised her eyebrows and curled her lips, as if impressed. She looked back over at Liles' body. "This guy tied to something you're looking at?"

"He is. You hear about that explosion in Winchester earlier?"

Cole nodded again, and her eyes narrowed as if just noticing the abrasions on Bailey's jaw and neck. "I did. Jesus, that was you guys? Are you alright?"

"It wasn't the most fun I've had at a motel, I can tell you that." Bailey gave Cole a small, pacifying smile. "But we're fine. We were serving a warrant. Our source walked out in an explosive vest. Before we could do anything about it, it went off."

"Jesus fucking Christ."

"Yeah, well. Sean Liles here was the pimp of our source and the target of our raid."

"Unfortunately, it looks like someone beat you to him."

Bailey cocked her head, ceding the point. "How was he killed?"

"If you flip him over, you'll see he's got a bullet-sized entry wound to his forehead." Cole pointed to her own forehead. "Square between the eyes. Could be a small-caliber pistol, but I don't think so."

"No?"

"No, something like that would've been up close, execution style, but there's no tattooing around it from someone firing a gun point-blank. The medical examiner can confirm, but I don't think you'll find a bullet or fragments there of inside."

"Any idea what it was, then?"

"You're going to think this sounds crazy, but it looks to me like the work of a bolt gun."

Bailey did, in fact, give her an expression somewhere between skepticism and confusion.

"My grandfather had a pig farm in southern Maryland. Growing up, I used to go out there a lot. He'd slaughter and butcher his own livestock. Believe me, it's not something you forget about when you see it at ten, eleven years old. The wound on Liles here looks like the handy work of a bolt gun, similar to something my grandfather used."

"Fucking hell," Pitts murmured.

Bailey shook her head. "Someone put him down."

"There's minimal blood and virtually no brain matter around

him here. I'm guessing he was killed somewhere else and dumped here. So far, no one here saw much of anything."

Bailey didn't reply. The explosive vest around Kristal, the designer drugs, and now their dead pimp. It all spoke to something else at play, something beyond Liles and the girls he worked. For every question Bailey had managed to answer, two or three more popped up in their place. But one big one underscored them all:

What the hell was going on?

FIVE

BAILEY WORKED alongside Pitts and Cole until dawn, processing the scene and taking statements. Everything proved to be a dead end. No cameras covered the far end of the parking lot, only traffic around the truck stop itself. All those cameras showed was that dozens of cars and semis had come and gone in the hours leading up to Liles' body being discovered. They canvassed the truck stop and interviewed almost fifty people — mostly semi drivers — that all said they hadn't seen anything suspicious.

By seven, Bailey and Pitts decided there were no hot leads at risk of going cold if they got a few hours sleep and drove back to their hotel. Just as guests were coming down to the lobby for their free continental breakfast to start the day, the two of them headed upstairs to finally end theirs.

She got all of five hours of shut-eye before her phone buzzed on the nightstand next to her head. Groggily, she reached over for the phone and checked the message. The whole Human Trafficking Unit was to meet with Lt. Col. Girard at the Division II Field Office at three that afternoon. She looked at her phone's clock. It was 2:17. Bailey rolled over and sighed in exasperation.

———

A HALF-HOUR LATER, Bailey was showered, freshly dressed, and downstairs waiting for Pitts. The two of them rode over to the Division II field office together and found the rest of the team already waiting.

The meeting took place in a large conference room that had as little charm and character as one would expect in a government office building. Everyone filed into seats around a large table that dominated the space and, a minute later, Girard came in and took his place standing at the head of it.

"Good afternoon, everyone," he said in his polished, professional voice. "By now, I'm sure all of you know Sean Liles' body was found at a truck stop outside Harrisonburg last night. Bailey and Pitts, you went out to the scene, correct?"

Bailey nodded. "That's correct, sir. We combed over everything out there. There wasn't much we can work from."

"Which is our problem." Girard reached for something behind him and tossed it onto the table. It slid to a stop a few feet across from Bailey. It was the front page of The Washington Post. Bailey looked over at it. A large, full-color photo showed the bombed-out remains of the motel office from yesterday. She read the headline over top.

ONE KILLED, SEVERAL INJURED IN MOTEL BLAST TIED TO
HUMAN TRAFFICKING RING

"Morning news shows also ran Liles' murder, and it won't be long before someone in the press pieces together what we already know," Girard said. "That the two are connected."

Pitts leaned back in his chair with a smirk. "I guess it works in our favor The Post's circulation isn't what it used to be."

Girard ignored the comment. "Whether they piece it together tomorrow, a week from now, or a month from now doesn't matter.

The point is it's going to be another bad headline. I had a call with the Superintendent and the Governor two hours ago. Simply put, the Governor isn't waiting for the bad headlines to continue to pile up. He wants to go on the offensive. Tomorrow morning, he'll be holding a press conference announcing that the State of Virginia is declaring war on human trafficking."

Bailey shook her head. "Sir, the Governor can't *declare war* on anything much less a metaphysical concept."

"What he means, Special Agent Bailey, is that there will be a major policy shift within the borders of the commonwealth on how human trafficking is combated. Among other initiatives, a new specialized outfit is being created: the Western Virginia Human Trafficking Task Force. It will be a multi-jurisdictional partnership compromised of local and federal authorities, as well as us here in the State Police, and you all specifically, the HTU."

"What is the mission of this new task force, sir?" another Special Agent, Mark Foley, asked.

"To investigate and mitigate human trafficking in western Virginia abroad, but specifically the I-81 corridor coming through the Shenandoah Valley. The task force is going to be the tip of the spear for combating human trafficking in the region. This case with the motel and now Liles' murder seems like an ideal place to start."

"I assume some of us are going to be reassigned to the task force?" Pitts asked.

"Yes. The task force is going to comprise investigators from all the agencies involved. At the local level, that means some of the larger counties as well as major cities. Roanoke, Lynchburg, Harrisonburg, etc. The feds will be supplying people from the FBI, DHS, and DEA."

There was an audible groan throughout the room.

Girard spread his arms out. "If we want federal money, everyone needs to be invited to the dance."

"So, who of us are going ... dancing?" Bailey asked.

"Four agents amongst you all will be reassigned to the task force, at least to start. I was hoping, Special Agent Bailey, that you and Pitts would be a part of that as you've been running point on this thing with the motel thus far."

"Can do, sir," Pitts said. "Who will be in charge of the Task Force?"

Bailey shot Pitts a look, displeased that he'd taken the liberty of answering for the both of them.

"An Executive Coordinator. The governor made it clear he wants the state leading this, which puts the ball in our court. Pitts, since you're the senior agent, it's yours if you want it."

"It'd be an honor, Lieutenant Colonel. Thank you," Pitts said.

"Done. Alright everybody, like I said, we'll need two more to join Bailey and Pitts here, so if you're interested, please let me know. Otherwise, that's it for now. Special Agent Bailey, Pitts, if you could hang behind for a second."

Everyone else packed up and filed out of the conference room. When they were gone, Girard took a seat on the table.

"We're still hammering out the final details on this thing but, for now, the task force will be operating out of Roanoke. It's squarely in your area of operation, unlike Richmond, and both we and the feds have offices there. It's a happy compromise for everyone," Girard said.

"That'll work, sir," Bailey said. "When do we get started?"

"ASAP. Return to Richmond, pack whatever you need to be gone for a while and report out that way. The feds have empty office space in the U.S. Attorney's Office down there that they've agreed to loan it to us for a base of operations. You'll need to coordinate with the U.S. Attorney for Western Virginia anyway, so it's a win-win. I'll have someone send you the details. They're expecting you down there the day after tomorrow."

"We'll get on it, sir," Pitts said. "Anything else?"

Girard shook his head as he slid off the table. "Happy hunting."

Bailey walked out with a renewed fire stoking inside her. She hadn't been able to help Kristal Hardy, to get her the life she deserved. But there were thousands like her. In just her couple of years with the Human Trafficking Unit, she'd met dozens of them. They all had different names, different stories, but at their core they were all Kristal Hardy. A woman that had been exploited, abused, and lied to.

She was determined to save the next one.

SIX

AINSLEY JENSEN WAS HAVING the best night of her life. Or, at least, the best night in recent memory. As she sat shotgun in Sophie Ramos' Toyota Paseo, the evening desert air blowing through her honey blonde hair, Olivia Rodrigo crooning from the staticky car stereo, everything that had been weighing on her felt like it existed in a different multiverse.

That was something Ainsley had recently become obsessed about. Multiverses. Ever since she saw *Spiderman: Across The Spider-Verse* with Sophie at the Sawmill Theatres last year, she'd become intrigued by the idea. The idea that there was another life out there for her. Somewhere where Ainsley Jensen had been born on the right side of the tracks.

That was a saying she never understood. The right side of the tracks. There were no railroads in Heber-Overgaard, Arizona, only Highway 260 where it met 277, and truthfully there wasn't a whole hell of a lot of wealth on either side. But as the pine trees of the Sitgreaves National Forest flew by, Ainsley didn't think about that. It was early May. The Senior Prom was in two weeks, and Noah Greene had just asked her out. Two weeks after that, school would be over and she'd finally graduate. And then adulthood. And getting the fuck out of this town.

As they cruised into the main drag through town, Sophie nodded over to her left. "Hey, you want to stop at DQ and grab a burger? I'm starving."

Ainsley looked at the time on her phone. "Okay, but really quick," she said. "I've got to get home. I can't get grounded now."

"Why? Because *Noahhhh* asked you to prom?" Sophie sing-songed Noah's name.

Ainsley rolled her eyes. "Yes, so let's go."

Sophie chuckled as she flicked on her turn signal and cut across the highway.

Having spent the afternoon doing rips from a bong down in Show Low with a couple of others from school, Ainsley was now famished. She ordered a burger, fries, blizzard, and soda to wash it all down. Grabbing their food from inside, Ainsley ran back to the car, where she and Sophie gorged themselves and didn't stop until there was nothing but empty wrappers in front of them.

Ainsley's stomach began to hurt on the drive home, but she didn't care. It seemed like nothing could dampen this high. Not the high she'd gotten off of the weed with her friends, but the euphoria she was now experiencing thereafter.

As they pulled up to her grandma's house, Ainsley sighed with disappointment. The ride — the high — was over. Maybe there was a multiverse where she and Sophie never stopped and headed on for Phoenix. She looked over at the Sophie in this multiverse and smiled.

"I'll text you," she said.

"Mmkay," Sophie replied.

Ainsley opened her door and stepped out onto the gravel road. Her grandma's house was a small, two-bedroom ranch-style, the last "real" house before the double-wides and trailers on the far end of their neighborhood. She watched Sophie drive off into the distance before rounding the fence post and going to the door on the side of the house. Parked out front was her grandma's Kia, but there was another car next to it. It was an old, black F-250. It was her mother's truck.

She felt herself go numb. Slowly, she stepped to it, reaching out and touching it; almost as if to make sure it was real. Ainsley stood there, frozen, her hand on the back of the truck, when the door to the house swung open and the screen in front of it kicked out.

"Ainsley Marie Jensen!" a woman shouted. "Where the hell have you been?!"

Ainsley was dumbfounded. Charlene Williams might've been her mother by birth, but that was the only manner in which she resembled a parent. When she'd been picked up for a DUI three months ago — her third in as many years — and didn't come home after posting bail, Ainsley had moved in with her grandma. It had been so much better than dealing with her mother and her booze-fueled mood swings. Now, Charlene glowered at her from the concrete slab that was her grandmother's front porch. Her bronze skin and thinning black hair wilted in the Arizona heat, her lumpy features melting underneath its desert sun.

Ainsley was trying to piece together what Charlene being here meant for herself when the screen door kicked open once more. A man a head taller than Charlene, with curly brown hair and a bushy goatee pointed accusingly at Ainsley from the open doorway.

"Are you fuckin' deaf, girl?" he said. "You heard your mother. Where the fuck have you been?"

Ainsley felt a pit form in her stomach. Darren Moore was her mother's on-again-off-again boyfriend. The two were like fire and gasoline: dangerous enough on their own, but together they made any situation absolutely combustible. The night her mother had driven off and picked up her DUI, she'd told Darren to pack his things and get out. If he was here, too, then they must be back together. And that would only make whatever this was worse.

Darren stomped toward Ainsley, his doughy features jiggling, and reached out for her. "You get in here, girl!" he seethed. "You got some nerve leavin' your grandma here worryin' 'bout you!"

Ainsley sidestepped his advance, swatting at his outstretched arm. "Get the fuck away from me!" she screamed.

"Ainsley, get in here right now!" her mother shouted from the doorway.

Ainsley started walking backward. "No! To hell with you! Why are you here?"

"I'm here because I'm your mother! Now, come here!"

Tears welled up in Ainsley's eyes. "Fuck that. And fuck you! I'm not going back with you!"

"She's your goddamn mother and you'll do as she goddamn says!" Darren growled.

"The fuck I will!"

Ainsley didn't know what to do. She wanted to see her grand-mother, but she also wanted nothing to do with her mother. And if her mother was here, no matter if her grandma was home or not, *she* didn't want to be here. She loved her grandma and loved living with her, but now Darren and her mother were between her and that real-ity. Ainsley didn't see a way to change that. A voice began to tell her to run, and it got ever louder like an approaching siren. Finally, Ainsley listened to it.

She turned and ran.

Her mother and Darren continued to shout at her, but it was drowned out by her breaths heaving in and out of her chest. She heard an engine roar to life and knew now they were coming after her. She wouldn't let them catch her. Ainsley ran as hard as she could down the gravel road.

When she got to the trailers on the last street, she didn't stop. She sprinted down the open driveway of one, hopped a cattle fence, and continued head-long into the forested hills beyond. Darren or her mother or whoever was in the truck could try to run after her, but she liked her odds. The voice that had told her to run stayed with her.

Keep going, it said. *There's no going back. Not now.*

————

AINSLEY WOKE UP SHIVERING. After running long and far enough that she was sure she'd lost whoever was chasing after her, she cut back to civilization, eventually making her way to the high school.

As she walked, she tried getting a hold of Sophie. When her texts went unanswered, she called her, underscoring just what an emergency it was. Sophie ignored the call and Ainsley burst into tears. It was amazing how many friends you thought you had until you really needed them.

Ainsley tried her grandmother's cell phone. After several rings, she heard her mother's voice, filled with alcohol-fueled rage.

"Just what the hell do you think you're doing you stuck up little shit?!" she growled. "Wherever the hell you are, you come home right now!"

Ainsley hung up, tears welling up in her eyes. She was huddled in one of the baseball dugouts at the school's field, absolutely freezing. All she had on were shorts, a tee, and a hoodie. Her body trembled. In that moment, she realized she was alone in every sense of the word. With her bare legs tucked up inside her sweatshirt, she contemplated her next move.

It was Saturday morning. She couldn't decide if that simplified or complicated things. One thing was for certain, she wasn't waiting out the weekend in this wooden box. And going back to her mother with whatever she had in store for her, was also not an option.

No, she had to go back. It was her only option. But she had to play it smart. She needed a plan. She tried to brainstorm, but all she could focus on were the frigid temperatures. She needed something warmer. She needed clothes, *her* clothes. *To hell with it*, she thought. She was going back to the house. She'd figure everything else out later.

Her grandma's house was a quick twenty-minute walk away, but Ainsley took a circuitous route so she could approach the house without being seen. When she got to the neighbor's fence, she rose slowly. As she did, her heart sank. Her mother's truck was still there.

Whatever her mother was doing, she was sticking around. And that meant Ainsley wasn't. Instead of going to the side with the door, she followed the neighbor's fence line the other way, snaking around to the backside of her grandma's house. Once there, she made it to her bedroom window and peeked in. It was empty, and the door was shut.

Ainsley tried the window. It was unlocked and opened when she pushed it. In one swift heave, she lifted herself up and through and into the bedroom. She bounced onto the bed, rolled to her feet, and stepped to the door, listening quietly. A duet of violent snoring came from the living room. Darren and her mother were asleep and, considering she didn't hear the television on and set to the morning news, she guessed her grandma wasn't either. It was time to get her stuff and get out of there.

She grabbed her duffel bag — the one she'd used to move just three months earlier — and threw in as many clean clothes as she could. Then she grabbed a charger for her phone and the wad of cash she kept in her dresser. In less than five minutes, she had everything put together. She threw the bag out the window, then herself.

With each strap around a shoulder, wearing the duffel bag like a backpack, she left her grandma's house behind. When she got to the highway, she headed out of town, thumbing for rides from passing cars as she did.

She made it a couple of miles when, at last, a car heading in the opposite direction slowed down on the rural four-lane highway. A young guy with a boyish face lowered his window and smiled.

"Hey, where ya headed?" he asked.

It wasn't until that very moment, Ainsley realized she didn't have a clear answer for that. She stared at the guy, slack-jawed, her brain spinning its wheels trying to come up with an answer.

"I'm headed to Holbrook," the guy said. "That help ya out?"

Holbrook! Tessa lived in Holbrook. Ainsley didn't know Tessa's last name, but she and Sophie had hung out once at a bonfire together, and Tessa had said she lived in Holbrook. Or, at least, that she worked at the Safeway there. Tessa was cool; maybe she could help her out. More importantly though, Holbrook fit squarely into the open-ended category of 'anywhere that wasn't here'.

Ainsley smiled back at the guy. "That's funny. That's exactly where I'm headed."

"Well, you know you're walking the wrong way."

Her mind searched for an excuse. "Yeah ... I was headed up to the Circle K. See if anybody might give me a lift."

"I'll save ya the trouble." He slapped the side of his car from the outside and nodded towards the interior. "Hop in."

"Thanks!"

Ainsley trotted across the highway, opened the passenger door, and slid in.

SEVEN

THE WESTERN VIRGINIA HUMAN TRAFFICKING TASK FORCE convened for the first time the following Monday morning. The unit had requisitioned a suite of offices on the tenth floor of a concrete-and-glass office building in downtown Roanoke. An array of cubicles was at the center of a large open space. Along the windows were private offices as well as a conference room with views of the Mill Mountain Star to the South. Inside, a projector sat atop a large veneer table surrounded by computer chairs, throwing the Department of Justice logo onto a screen hanging from the ceiling at the far end of the room. On the wall opposite, a map of the western half of Virginia was thumbtacked to the wall.

Led by Pitts, Bailey walked into the conference room with her laptop joined by the delegacy from the Virginia State Police — Mark Foley and another special agent with the Human Trafficking unit, Samantha Cross, both of whom filled the last two spots. As Pitts came to the center of the room, Bailey, Foley, and Cross filed in amongst their new colleagues.

The Task Force was just as Lt. Colonel Girard had promised: there were detectives from several local municipalities as well as investigators from a whole alphabet soup of federal agencies. Bailey looked across the way and recognized Detective Cole from the Harrisonburg Police. Bailey nodded at her, and Cole nodded back with a grin. Pitts directed everyone to introduce themselves to the group and led off. Halfway through, though, a knock came at the open door.

"Ah, Mr. Weisz," Pitts said, offering the man his hand. "We weren't expecting you."

Chris Weisz was the U.S. Attorney for the Western District of Virginia. Weisz was in his forties but looked younger, bolstered by classic good looks and a full head of sandy brown hair. Bailey had worked with Weisz a handful of times — he'd liaised with them on the motel raid, helping to secure the warrant — and she took him to be a capable, if not ambitious, jurist, hungry to climb the political ladder.

Weisz took Pitts' hand and shook it. "Well, I was around and had a minute," Weisz said, flashing a million-dollar smile. "Just wanted to take a moment to say hello to everyone. We're lucky to have you all here. If you need anything from me or my office, we're just upstairs." He pointed to the ceiling. "I assume this is an opening briefing of sorts. Have we covered the raid outside Winchester?"

"Not yet, sir," Pitts replied. "We were still making introductions. Then I was going to get around to that."

"Oh, perfect. Don't let me stop you." Weisz slid into a seat facing Pitts.

Pitts continued, but not before having everyone start their introductions over again. When they were through, he briefed everyone on the events that had precipitated the formation of the task force: the raid that went sideways at the motel and the subsequent murder of Sean Liles.

"We're going to pursue this thing full-force," Pitts said. "But the fact of the matter is this is not the only thing this task force can and should be working on. And we have a good bit of manpower here, so I want only a handful of you on this. Special Agent Bailey is going to run point for us with this squad. Everyone assigned to this should have gotten an email already. I'd like you all to stay behind. Everyone else will have assignments forthcoming."

Weisz raised his hand. "I'd like to sit in with the team as well, if that's alright."

Pitts nodded. "Of course."

The vast majority of people filed out of the room. When they were gone, Bailey took stock of who was left. There were only nine left in the room, including Pitts and Weisz.

"Okay," Pitts said, "You all, like I said, are going to pursue this thing with the motel and the murder of Sean Liles. We can pull in others if their expertise is needed, but for now, I think you all are a solid squad. Because it would be a little cumbersome to have a task force within a task force, we're going to unofficially refer to you as a team."

"Like what?" Bailey asked. "The A-Team?"

Weisz chuckled. "I like that. Or, what was Hardy's handle? Josephine? Maybe you're the *J-Team*."

"Sure, that's good," Pitts said.

Bailey looked down to roll her eyes. Pitts was all too eager to please the US Attorney.

In total, the J-Team was composed of seven investigators. Aside from Cole, Bailey only knew the other five from their introductions. Investigator Cliff Kavanaugh, a tall, trim gentleman with receding brown hair, was from the Frederick County Sheriff's Office. Detective Ben Brooks was of average height, but stocky and completely bald with striking blue eyes. He was from the Albemarle County Police Department. Special Agent Timothy Wilcox had to be the youngest of the outfit — Bailey couldn't imagine he was older than thirty — and had a full head of close-cropped dirty blond hair. He and his colleague, Sara Ramos, were from the FBI's Richmond Field Office. Ramos had raven black eyes and matching shoulder-length hair that she kept back in a tight ponytail. Last, there was Kevin Nguyen from the DEA's Washington, DC Division Office. He was shorter and in phenomenal shape, with a beige complexion and black hair cut high and tight, Army-style.

Bailey came around to stand in front of all of them and connected her laptop to the projector. The image on the screen changed to show her desktop. "Good morning, everyone," she said, "for those who may have missed it, I am Jen Bailey with the Virginia State Police. Most of you are aware of what has happened in the last seventy-two hours, but I'll give you all the CliffsNotes anyway."

Everyone listened, including Weisz who had first-hand knowledge of the case. The projector showed everyone various images. There were pictures of the motel, both before and after the blast, and then came the picture of Liles' lifeless body at the truck stop, covered in a white tarp. Juxtaposed next to it was his most recent booking photo.

"Liles was a low-level pimp barely capable of running the few girls that he did," Bailey said. "This makes the explosive vest and designer pharmaceuticals very much above his pay grade. Obviously, our main concern now is that there is a much larger actor at play here. One we have yet to identify."

At this, Bailey noticed Wilcox lean over to Ramos and start conversing in an undertone.

Brooks raised his hand. "Do we have any more information on these designer drugs? The Pepsi?"

"We had our labs do some initial analysis, but over the weekend we had the samples we collected sent to the DEA for further analysis. I believe Agent Nguyen can give us some better insight."

Sitting back in his office chair, Nguyen kicked forward toward the table and reviewed some papers in front of him as he spoke. "Pepsi looks to be a new type of Pyrrolidinophenones and acts as a norepinephrine–dopamine reuptake inhibitor. In layman's terms, when ingested, it'll give you a high similar to cocaine."

"So someone reinvented coke?" Brooks asked.

"It's *similar* to cocaine," Nguyen reiterated. "But it is pristinely engineered, so the sensations of euphoria are probably increased several fold. Consequently, it's almost certainly that much more addictive as well. The only apt analogy I can think of is if Cocaine is your average grocery-getter sedan, this stuff is, I don't know, a Maserati."

"Any idea where it's being made or by whom?" Bailey asked.

"Your guess is as good as ours. We haven't seen it anywhere else so far and it is chemically distinct from other designer drugs we've seen like it. Basically, everything about it screams exclusivity and affluence."

Wilcox and Ramos' side conversation suddenly became more animated.

Pitts cocked his head over their way. "Anything you two would like to share with the class?"

"The resort," Ramos said.

"I'm sorry?" Pitts asked.

Wilcox cleared his throat and leaned forward. "It's just this mentioning of a more sophisticated operation and now the designer pharmaceuticals that, as Agent Nguyen said, screams exclusivity. There's a place not far from where Liles' body was dumped that we've had our eye on for some time. Intel on it has been extremely hard to come by but, near as we can tell, it's some sort of hyper-exclusive resort."

"Where specifically is it?" Bailey asked.

At that, Wilcox stood up and came around the table to the map of the western half of Virginia. "Highland County." He studied the map for a moment, then pointed at a spot practically on the border with West Virginia. "Here. Up in this little notch. It's about thirty, thirty-five miles due west of Harrisonburg."

"Why has the FBI had their eye on it?"

"First and foremost, the people coming in and out of there. There's an airfield a few miles away … here." Wilcox pointed to another spot south and west of where he'd been pointing previously. "It used to be a locally owned airfield, by which I mean it was a strip of grass for bush planes. Five years ago it was purchased, and a paved airstrip large enough for private jets was put in. We've been tracking tail numbers of the PJs going to and from the airfield since. They're all owned by very wealthy people and often in positions of power, albeit usually in the private sector. We haven't ID'd anyone who has landed at that airstrip who hasn't had at least two commas to their net worth."

"Contrary to the belief of some, being rich is not a crime," Weisz quipped.

"That's true. But when you dig into the records of who owns the two properties, it becomes a corporate shell game. On top of that, when you dig into the tax records, it shows virtually no employees on salary. It's pretty hard to run a resort that caters to the wealthy without anyone working there."

"At least working legitimately," Ramos added.

"People are picked up from the airfield in private vehicles — almost always black Range Rovers with dark tinted windows. In a rural county with a median income under thirty-five thousand, private jets and range rovers and gated resorts don't go unnoticed. The locals refer to it as Happyland, imagining some sort of retreat for millionaires."

"Like I said, though, being rich is not a crime," Weisz said. "I'll give you the cooked employee payrolls are shady, but we're not the IRS. This is a human trafficking task force. We're not looking to ring anybody up for tax fraud."

Wilcox shrugged. "Real criminals have been brought down for less."

"Just ask Al Capone," Nguyen added.

"Either way," Wilcox continued. "You all were talking about an as-of-yet-to-be-identified, high-end, organized criminal actor in the area. This place, as the local beat cops say, fits the description."

Bailey nodded. "I think it's worth taking a closer look at."

"Even if we wanted to," Pitts said, "the real question is how."

"Same as we did over at HTU," Bailey offered. "We insert one of our own as a john. Or, I guess in this case, a resort-goer. And then see what we see."

Wilcox shook his head. "Like I said, it's hyper-exclusive. Your average Joe can't just take an Uber over."

"What about getting someone in on the other side?" Pitts asked. "Any trafficking operation needs manpower. We identify the group at work and slip someone onto the crew."

"Do any of us have undercover experience?" Kavanaugh asked. "I know I sure as hell don't."

Pitts rubbed his chin. "We could potentially get someone with UC experience."

Wilcox shook his head. "When they ID'd Kristal Hardy as an informant, they strapped a bomb to her and blew her up. If whoever did that is behind this place, I don't want a dead cop on my conscience."

A knock at the door sounded, and a young woman in a pencil skirt stood in the open doorway. She looked at Weisz. "Sir, you have a call with the State AG in five," she said.

Weisz propelled himself out of the chair. "Ah, yes. That's right." He turned back to the group. "Well, again, it was good to meet everyone. I know you'll keep up the great work. I'll be out of the office the rest of the week, but if you need me, just ask Kelly—" he gestured at the woman in the doorway "—here and she'll be able to get a hold of me. Just my two cents ... let's not put all our eggs in this resort basket. We've got enough manpower. I don't want to get tunnel vision on this."

Pitts nodded in thanks and Weisz left, Kelly closing the door behind them.

An idea started to form in Bailey's head. "What if we supplied our own source?" she asked.

"Isn't that what we're talking about?" Wilcox asked.

Bailey shook her head. "I'm not talking about one of us or flipping a source inside. I'm talking about supplying our own. Our own source, outside of law enforcement so he doesn't look or act like law enforcement."

They needed someone that they could trust, someone who had worked with law enforcement before. Someone who could venture into the darkness in search of answers and find out if there was a connection between Liles and his girls and this resort. She knew someone who was good at finding things like that.

"It sounds like you have someone in mind," Pitts said.

Bailey typed away at her laptop. A moment later, the file projected on to the wall changed to an image of a man. He looked to be in his forties, his skin tough and weathered from a life lived harder than most. His hazel eyes complimented his hair and beard, save for where it had started to gray in certain spots.

Pitts read the name next to the image. "Jackson Clay."

"Wait a minute, I've heard of this guy," Brooks said. "He beat his wife's killer to an inch of his life or something."

"His ex-wife. And the guy was a serial killer who also abducted and killed Clay's son," Bailey corrected.

Brooks pointed at the screen. "I remember now. George Alvanitakis. I've seen photos of the guy since. I don't know, Jen. That Clay guy did a real number on him. Alvanitakis is eating meals out of a straw now in a state prison."

"Any of us are lying if we said we wouldn't do the exact same thing if it was our kid," Bailey said.

"Isn't Clay himself in prison?" Pitts asked.

Bailey shook her head. "He was released to house arrest a few months ago. He's at his cabin up north now."

Brooks shook his head from across the table. "I don't know. Do we really want to pin our chances of cracking this thing on a convicted felon?"

At that, Cole, next to him, leaned forward. "I can vouch for Clay," she said. "I've worked with him before. He's ... unorthodox. He's not a badge, but his head and heart are in the same place as ours."

Pitts looked at Bailey. "Would he even do it?"

Bailey thought for a moment. She took a deep breath in and out. "Truthfully, I don't know, sir. We'd have to find out. It would help if we had something to sweeten the deal. Maybe a commutation of the rest of his sentence? A pardon?"

Pitts shrugged. "Anything like that would take getting the Governor's office involved."

Bailey cocked her head to the side. "Well, if he's serious about this new initiative …"

"Wait, are we seriously considering this?" Brooks asked.

"If Bailey and Cole both say this guy is legit, I think we are," Pitts replied. He turned to Bailey. "It looks you have a trip to make in the morning."

EIGHT

THE NEXT MORNING, Bailey made the three-hour drive to see Jackson Clay. His cabin was tucked away on Bull Run Mountain, twenty-five miles west of Washington, D.C. at the far north end of Prince William County. As she ascended the unpaved driveway, her unmarked Explorer cutting a course through the bed of fallen leaves that covered it, Clay's cabin came into view. It was a classic timber-frame cabin with a covered porch that ran the length of its facade and a staircase descending to the yard in front of it.

As she pulled up, she spotted Clay, thrusting what looked to be a post hole digger into the earth at his feet. He stopped when he saw the car and waited, wiping off his brow. Bailey climbed out of the driver's seat and smiled at him. Jackson didn't return it, though Bailey knew not to be offended; it just wasn't Jackson's nature.

She paused for a moment and took him in. He looked a tad older — that much could've been expected, having not seen him for a year and a half — but that wasn't all that was different about him. Bailey wasn't sure, but she thought he looked calmer. The intensity he'd always carried with him had eased some.

"If it were me on house arrest, I'd be inside with my feet up and a glass of Pinot," she finally said, coming around the front of her car.

Jackson smirked. "I've always been more of a beer guy."

Bailey nodded at the hole in front of him. "Building a fence?"

"Is that your investigative skills at work?" He went back to digging.

"What do you need a fence for? Are you going to get a dog?"

Jackson shrugged. "You never know."

"You haven't been making runs to Home Depot, have you? They can bust you back to prison for that, you know."

"I source it myself, if you must know." He pointed his head toward a circular saw and ax next to a fresh tree stump across the yard.

"Ever the woodsman, I see."

Jackson shrugged. "Being on house arrest means being resourceful."

Now it was Bailey who grinned. "How is it, by the way? Being on house arrest?"

"Not so bad." He shrugged. "Quiet. Simpler."

"It must beat prison."

Jackson cocked his head to the side, ceding her point. "My lawyer said your letter was integral in swaying the outgoing governor to commute my sentence. I appreciate it."

"Anyone who knew the truth knew you didn't deserve to be locked up."

Jackson didn't say anything.

"But still," Bailey paused. "You getting along alright out here on your own?"

Jackson thrust the digger down into the Earth, then jostled it. "I make do. Bear comes up about once a week with some groceries and whatever else I might need. Every month, he cuts me a check for my share of the store in Martinsville. It's enough to get by."

Bailey smiled. "And how is Mr. Beauchamp?"

"Same as he's always been."

"I bet."

A quiet came over the two of them and, for a moment, Bailey just leaned against her car, watching him work. As he brought the digger up with dirt in its clutches, he looked over at her.

"So, are you going to get around to whatever this visit's about?" he asked. "Not that I don't enjoy the company."

Bailey took a deep breath in, and steeled herself. "I need your help with something, Clay. For work."

Jackson eyed her as he dropped the dirt in the digger's clutches next to the hole. "You need me to look at something?"

"This is going to be more hands-on."

Jackson shook his head as if he knew that answer was coming. "Sorry, I'm retired." He lined the digger back up over the hole and thrust it back down. "Besides, unless your suspect is lurking somewhere around here, I'm not going to be very useful." He lifted the cuff of his jeans, revealing the monitoring device strapped to his ankle. "Or did you forget?"

"I've already spoken to your parole officer. He'll agree to suspend location monitoring and release you into my charge."

"Is going back to prison an option?"

Bailey ignored the snide remark. "I could really use you, Clay. We're in a tough spot on this one."

"Like I said, I'm retired."

"What does that even mean?"

Jackson stopped digging. Wiping his brow again, he rested his forearms atop the digger. "It's been a long two years, Bailey. I'm not the same guy I was then."

"You don't seem to have slowed down much from where I'm standing. Sure, you're a little longer in the tooth, but we all are."

"It's not that."

"Then what is it?"

Jackson looked around as if an escape from the conversation was somewhere nearby. "That day I chased down Alvanitakis, I was prepared to give everything up." He nodded toward the cabin. "I left a note inside there even saying this much. I was spiraling toward a six-foot hole in the ground, and I was just hoping to take one last monster with me."

Bailey's voice was soft. "I know."

"But you talked me down. That day at the theme park, you stopped me from crossing a line I hadn't crossed before. One that I wouldn't have been able to come back from."

Bailey was silent now.

"I was willing to throw everything away because I thought there was nothing left to lose. But I was wrong. These two years have shown me that. And I'm working on building something here. Not this fence … this is … never mind this. I mean I'm building myself a life here. A life after Nat and Evan. A peaceful one. For real this time. I have a second chance, one that you helped give me, and I can't risk throwing it away again."

Solemn, Bailey nodded, thinking what to say next. "I'm glad you've healed. Or, I guess, are healing. Really, I am. I don't know why life had to deal you such a shitty hand before you could discover it, but you have a gift, Clay. And I'm not the only person who needs your help now."

Jackson hesitated a beat, weighing her words. Then he gripped the pole digger with his hands and thrust it back down into the hole. "I'm sorry. I can't help you."

Bailey stared at him as if her gaze might force him into reconsidering. When it was clear that it wouldn't, she conceded. Pushing herself off her Explorer, she walked around the front of it, headed for the driver's side. But as she got to the door handle, she stopped. A thought came to her. She opened the door, reached for the files she had on the passenger seat, and came back around to Jackson with one in hand. She held it out for him to take.

"Her name was Kristal Hardy. She was a sex worker that wanted out and I was working to help her do that. Give her a second chance and a new life, just like you. Only the last time I saw her, someone sent her to us with an explosive vest strapped to her and set it off. She was five months pregnant."

Jackson didn't stop digging and didn't say anything.

"Do you remember what you said to me the first time we met? The first time you asked me for information? For help? I had asked you why I should give you what you need and let you do what you do. You said because maybe it brings someone home that otherwise wouldn't have. Kristal Hardy didn't strap that explosive vest to herself. Whoever killed her is still out there. Do you think she's going to be the end of this?"

Jackson still didn't say anything.

Bailey dropped the file at his feet. "The next Kristal Hardy is out there somewhere. I'm asking you to help me bring her home."

Then Bailey marched back to her car and left.

NINE

IT TURNED out staying with Tessa was absolutely awesome. Tessa seemed to know everyone worth knowing in Holbrook and was the life of most hangouts. Even better, she was talented at getting many around her to do things for her. Dax, who worked at the Little Caesars, slipped her pizzas free of charge. Sonny, who worked loss prevention at the Walmart in Winslow, would let her walk out with a bag of clothes as long as it wasn't anything too pricey. And whenever Tessa did decide to go into work, she always came home with beer and liquor.

This is the way to live, Ainsley thought.

She'd expected to only crash for the weekend, then find her way back up to Heber-Overgaard for school on Monday and explain to the school what had happened, but Monday came and went and Ainsley didn't feel like leaving. Why should she? Sophie was ghosting her and all that was back there for her was stress and uncertainty and the very real possibility of having to go back to living with her mom. If she was leaving her grandma's place one way or another, it was better she did it on her own terms.

As she and Tessa woke up sometime just after noon, they lay

sprawled out on the one couch in Tessa's living room, watching South Park. Ainsley watched Tessa as she took a hit from her pipe. Her long, slender legs were intertwined with Ainsley's in the middle of the couch. Her braided russet hair came over both shoulders, framing her heart-shaped face. Her verdant eyes became small slits as she smiled at Ainsley through the smoke. She leaned forward and handed her the pipe. Ainsley took it, lit it, then let her head fall back as she blew the smoke upward.

"Hey, you think you could get me a job at your work?" Ainsley asked.

"At Safeway?" Tessa cocked an eyebrow. "The fuck would you want to do that for?"

"I mean, I'm going to need a job eventually to make some money. I could work with you."

Tessa shook her head. "You don't want to work there, trust me. Gil, my boss, is a fucking creep and asshole. I won't be there much longer, anyway."

"Why not?"

"I'm leaving this place, dude."

"This house?"

Tessa laughed as she smiled. "This house, this town, all of it."

"Why? What's wrong with living here?"

"Well, it's a fucking shit hole, for one. Besides, it was never going to be forever."

"So, where will you go?"

Tessa took the pipe back from Ainsley and took another hit. "Out East. My sister, Mackenzie, went out that way about a year ago." She sat forward as if she were about to share a secret. "There's this place out there. You can make stupid fucking money. Like, making in a week what I make in a few months now. And on top of that, this place is crawling with rich guys. I get one to give me a ring? Boom, I'm set for life."

"But ...what if you don't like them? What if it's all just old boomers?"

"Even better. Then he bites the big one and I get all his money."

"But until then, you'll have to …"

"I don't mind letting some old prick fuck me a couple times a week to spend my days poolside. Anyway, it's not much different than it is now."

"What do you mean?"

Tessa popped off the couch and strolled into the kitchen, grabbing a pack of pop tarts before coming back. "Dax? Sonny? Hell, fucking Gil at the Speedway."

"You're sleeping with them? All of them?"

"We don't sleep, we fuck. Or, at least, I blow them. How do you think I get all that shit?"

"I don't know. I thought maybe they give it to you because you're pretty or you guys are friends or something."

Tessa smiled. "They do think I'm pretty. But nothing in this life is free, hon. The faster you figure that out, the better off you'll be."

Ainsley fell quiet. She turned back to the TV, unsure what else to say. She imagined those guys wrapped around Tessa's finger, unable to resist her charm. The idea of it being nothing more than a business transaction was a lot less, well, charming. She'd never known anyone that had done sex work. That was what they were talking about here, wasn't it?

Tessa watched her for a moment, then gave her a playful slap on the leg. "Hey! You should come with me!"

"What?" Ainsley asked.

"East, to this place. You should come with me! Find a guy of your own. In the meantime, we could be roomies with my sister."

"You don't even know if your sister is there."

"She has to be. I haven't heard shit from her for months. Lucky bitch probably already bagged herself a guy."

Ainsley wondered why Tessa didn't fear something may have happened to her sister. "I don't know …"

"Come on, you totally should. I wasn't going to leave until next month, but we could go sooner. Together."

Ainsley was quiet again. Something about all this made her nervous, but wasn't this ultimately what she wanted? She'd always planned to leave anyway. What if this was fate or whatever, handing her the way out? She thought of the other Ainsleys in the other multiverses. There was probably a movie star Ainsley, a big shot CEO Ainsley, even a housewife Ainsley like Tessa dreamed of for herself. There were also probably other Ainsleys, though. Ones that lived and died in piece-of-shit Arizona. Ones that met some loser, got knocked up, and became abusive alcoholic assholes like her mom. What if she had a choice? What if she could choose which Ainsley she wanted to be? Going with Tessa made her anxious, but going back to her mom and never leaving this place downright terrified her. And if there was a third option, Ainsley certainly didn't see it.

"Okay," she grinned. "Let's do it."

TEN

THAT EVENING, Bear came up to Jackson's cabin for his weekly resupply. Well over six feet tall and built like a bourbon barrel, Archibald Beauchamp fit his adopted name perfectly. As he climbed out of his old, firetruck red Suburban, he scratched his bushy beard, then gave Jackson a lopsided grin before embracing Jackson in a hug equally befitting of his name. Once he was free, Jackson grabbed the groceries out of the back of the Suburban and Bear grabbed the dinner for them he'd stashed on the passenger seat — in this case, subs from Sheetz.

Jackson brought the groceries into his kitchen, grabbed a Miller High Life out of the fridge, opened it, and left it on the dining table before starting to put everything away. When Bear came through the front door and saw the brew waiting for him, he growled with pleasure.

"Go ahead and start," Jackson said. "I'll be right there."

But Bear had already dug in. After Jackson finished putting the groceries away, he sat beside his friend. The two of them ate in virtual silence — par for the course when eating with Jackson. When they were done, Bear let out a hearty belch, signaling the end of the meal. As he leaned back in his chair, giving his ample gut more room to make itself at home, he noticed the manila folder caked in a fine layer of dirt on the kitchen counter.

"What's that?" he asked, pointing a thumb at the folder.

Jackson, who until then had been fine with water, got up and grabbed his own beer from the fridge. "Bailey came to see me today," he said.

"No shit? Lady-cop Bailey?"

Jackson wondered how many Baileys Bear knew. "That would be the one."

"You haven't seen her in what, over a year? What'd she want?"

Jackson twisted the top off his beer and took a sip. "Help."

"Yeah, I bet you helped her. Helped her take her top off." Bear let out a breathy chortle.

"Bear." Jackson shook his head.

"Okay, okay. So, what then?"

"She wanted help with a case."

Bear's brow furrowed as he whistled through his jowly lips. "Her *asking* you to get in on a case? That's got to be a first."

"It is."

"What all does she want you to do? Look over that file there?"

Jackson came back to the table and sat down across from Bear. "A bit more than that, apparently."

"How much more?"

"I don't know. I didn't ask."

"Goddamn, jumpin' in no questions asked?" Bear grinned. "That's my ride-or-die Jacky boy right there!"

Jackson took a deep breath in and sighed. "I told her no, Bear." He took a long drag from his beer.

Bear didn't say anything. Jackson studied his friend's face as he processed what Jackson had just told him. The tells were subtle, but they were there. It was how Jackson had always fleeced the man whenever they played cards. Bear could never quite hide when he was sitting on a pocket pair. Now, though, his face told a different story. What started off as surprised transformed into confusion, and then Jackson thought he read a dash of disappointment. In the years he'd come to know Bear, he could count on one hand the number of times he'd truly surprised him. This had become one of those times.

"Why no?" Bear asked at last.

"I have to move on. The person I was, the one I'd become after Evan and then Nat, was someone willing to throw it all away because he thought he had nothing to lose. I know that's not true now. I've spent the last two years rebuilding myself — my *life* — and I can't risk becoming that person that would throw it all away again."

Bear nodded, his face expressionless.

"You disagree?"

"What I think doesn't really matter, brother. This is about you and your choice. Like you said, it's your life we're talkin' 'bout here."

Jackson didn't say anything. He took another sip of his beer.

"Hey, I forgot to mention, though. Bobbie called me last week."

Jackson raised his eyebrows. "Yeah? How is he?"

Bobbie Casto was the nephew of Ray Byrd, Bear's late business partner. A few years back, Bobbie had gotten swept up in a crooked Vice Unit of a Sheriff's Office in West Virginia making illegitimate busts. He'd been wrongfully accused of the attempted murder of a police officer and had been on the run when Bear and Jackson got involved. Trying to right everything had cost Ray Byrd his life. In the time since, Bear had checked in with the kid off and on.

"He's doin' real good. 'Bout to finish his first year at West Virginia after transferring from junior college."

"Good," Jackson said. "I'm happy for him."

"Yup. He's a Criminal Justice major there." Bear snorted. "He told me he'd never much been interested in all that before what happened to him. Now, he's all about makin' sure it doesn't happen to someone else."

"I hope he does."

"Mmhmm." Bear took a long pause. "You did that, you know? You gave that boy a second chance."

"*We* did it." Jackson corrected. "With Maggie and Fraggie and everyone else. Including Bailey. And we did it because it was the right thing to do."

"You got that right. But it doesn't make what I said any less true. About a second chance. That boy could've been rotting in prison and God knows what would've happened to him in there, labeled as an attempted cop killer. But you — *we*, I guess — stopped all that."

Jackson started to see where Bear was going with this. "You're saying taking this case for Bailey is the right thing to do."

Bear shrugged. "That's not for me to decide, brother. I mean that. And it doesn't matter what you do or which way you go. Left, right, I'm on your hip either way. But I will say, some things are undeniable. And one of those things is no one but you could've brought Bobbie home. And same is true for that girl that'd gone missing when we first met."

He was referring to Sara Beth Parker, a teenager that had been abducted in Harrisonburg, Virginia the year before Bobbie's problems. In following the trail to a group of heavily armed militia members, Jackson had met Bear. Together, they'd brought her home.

Bear leaned forward, resting his meaty arms on the table. "You're right that you've built a new life for yourself here and I'm damn proud of you for that. Ain't no one got the right to ask you to risk it for anything, let alone someone you don't even know."

Jackson cocked his head to the side. "But ..."

"But I also imagine no one could ask you to join up with the Army. To become a Ranger, to serve where you did. All that business in Taco Bar or whatever you told me about."

Jackson snorted. "Takur Ghar."

"Right. That. You didn't need to step up and do all that, but you did, anyway. The same way you did with Bobbie and the Parker girl and a dozen others." Bear leaned back again. "It's because you've got that call to serve in you. People can grow, but they can't change who they are at their core. You've got that in you and it will never go away." He shrugged as he rested his hands on his gut. "It's just up to you whether it's time to listen to it again."

––––––––

NOT LONG AFTER THAT, Bear left and headed home to Martinsville. After he was gone, though, Jackson found himself still at his kitchen table with a beer in front of him. What Bear had said was weighing on him. Nothing he'd told Bailey about building a new life for himself wasn't true, but Bear had a point as well. All his life, Jackson felt a call to something bigger than himself. It'd been a natural path to take most of his life. Truthfully, this was the first time since marrying Nat he found those two ideas at odds with one another. Now, he needed to reconcile that.

He got up from his chair, grabbed a fresh beer and the file on Kristal Hardy, and eased into a recliner in his living area. He laid the folder in his lap and began to flip through it. When he got to Hardy's photo, he stopped and studied it. Years in a tough life had taken its toll, but she was very pretty nonetheless. Jackson could see there was a pain behind her eyes, a medley of hurt and regret and sadness. He recognized it from every time he'd looked in the mirror since Evan died.

Jackson thought about what Bailey had told him; about Hardy being five months pregnant and wanting to get out of the life she'd been living. Not for her, but for her child. Someone somewhere had taken that chance from Kristal Hardy, same as a cold-blooded serial killer had taken it from him. The only difference was Kristal Hardy was no longer alive. Not only had she been robbed of a chance at a new life, she'd been robbed of the chance to make those who'd taken it from her answer for what they'd done.

As he dwelled on it, that injustice began to burn inside Jackson. It grew from a few embers to a single flame to a raging salvo. He pulled out his phone and called Bailey. It went to voicemail, so he left a message.

"I'm in."

PART TWO
SAFE HOUSE

"Man - a being in search of meaning." —Plato

ELEVEN

JACKSON WAS SITTING on the steps leading up to his front porch, a cup of coffee in hand, and a large military-style rucksack packed next to him when Bailey arrived just after ten the next morning. Overnight, Bailey had gotten Jackson's message and called him to let him know she would be there first thing. She'd done just that, but Jackson was nevertheless all ready to go. Stepping out of her car, Bailey put on a pair of mirrored aviators and walked over to him.

"You look ready to roll," she said.

"I said I'm in," Jackson replied. "To not be ready would just be wasting time."

Bailey put a foot up on the step next to Jackson's leg and nodded at the monitor around his ankle. "We need your P.O. to take care of that before you go anywhere."

As if on cue, a second SUV rolled up behind Bailey's Explorer. This one, however, was clearly a personal vehicle. The orange Hyundai had the decal for a local little league on a rear window. Jackson's parole officer climbed out. A man of average height, though appearing taller due to his squared shoulders and athletic frame, came over and joined the two of them. Clean-shaven and bald, his swarthy complexion glowed in the late morning sun. Bailey extended a hand.

"Special Agent Bailey," she introduced herself. "We spoke on the phone."

"Marvin Thompson," he shook her hand. "Pleasure. Although, I must say, this is highly unusual. I don't think I've had such a deal called in since I began."

"Desperate measures," Bailey said. "Nevertheless, we greatly appreciate the cooperation."

"Uh huh," Thompson grunted with a leery stare. He fished a ring of keys out of the pocket of his cargo pants before crouching down next to Jackson's leg. "Now, I've told Special Agent Bailey here, but I'm telling you, too: this is not a get-out-of-jail-free card. You are being released into Special Agent Bailey's custody. If she reports you as missing or absconded from her guardianship, you will be considered a fugitive of the state. I don't think I need to explain that we're in a whole different ball game if it gets to that point."

"No, you don't, sir," Jackson said.

"Also, it doesn't matter if you're here or in the care of Special Agent Bailey. The conditions of your early release remain. You are prohibited from drinking excessively, using, possessing, or consuming controlled substances, and using, possessing, owning, or transporting a firearm."

Jackson didn't know the full details of what he was getting into, but he imagined the last condition was going to be hard to follow. "Deal."

"And I have to reiterate my strenuous objection to all this. You've been doing really well, Clay. In my line of work, we talk a lot about bad habits that can trigger old behaviors. For most folks I deal with, that's associating with those who got them in trouble in the first place." He glanced up at Bailey. "I can't say that this doesn't feel like the same sort of thing."

Jackson, too, looked at Bailey.

"So noted," Bailey said. "Anything else?"

Thompson stood up and raised his hands, palms open. "That's it from me. My bosses and your bosses signed off on this, so it damn sure isn't going to be my ass paying for it if it all goes sideways." He looked down at Clay. "Good luck."

Clay nodded in thanks.

Thompson turned and took the couple of steps down to the front yard. He stopped and took in the array of fence posts plotted around the yard. He turned back to Clay. "Are you building a fence?"

"I was. Then this all happened."

Thompson's brow furrowed. "What for? You getting a dog or something?"

"Or something."

Thompson shrugged, got into his car, and left. When he was gone, Bailey took his place standing in front of Jackson.

"So, what's the game plan?" Jackson asked.

"I'm part of a task force assigned to this case," Bailey said. "We're operating out of Roanoke. You'll come with me down there where you'll be brought up to speed with what's going on and how we plan to use your, uh, skill set."

"Sounds good." Jackson stood and grabbed his ruck sack off the porch before fishing his keys out of his pocket. "I'll follow you?"

Bailey gave him an incredulous look. "Did you not hear your probation officer? You're being released into my supervision. You'll be riding with me. Come on."

"I assume whatever plans you have for me involve me going somewhere law enforcement can't go or be spotted. How is that going to work, exactly, without me having my own vehicle? Are you going to drop me off and pick me up from soccer practice every day?"

"*If* you need a vehicle, one will be provided to you."

"What? A rental? Or some car that comes back as a state or federal vehicle?" Jackson shook his head. "Whatever we're about to do, you want everything to look legit. I drive my own truck."

Bailey let out a sigh of frustration. Jackson was being his usual difficult self, but he had a point. She shook her head. Two minutes into his supervised release, and they were already breaking the rules. "Fine. You follow me. But I want you on my ass the whole way. I'm talking, close enough I can see the whites in your eyes in my rearview."

"I prefer to drive with sunglasses on. Better for your eyes."

Bailey turned a shade redder. "Then I better be able to read the fucking brand. Come on, we have a long drive ahead of us."

"You're the boss."

Jackson carried his rucksack over to the black 1985 Dodge D100 pickup parked just outside the array of fence posts. It had previously belonged to Bear before being loaned to Jackson after his own truck was turned into aluminum swiss cheese their first time working together. Jackson liked it so much, he ended up buying it off of Bear.

Throwing his ruck sack onto the passenger side of the bench seat, he climbed in. With the turn of the key, the engine ignited and roared to life. Ahead of him, Bailey was climbing into her car. He waited until she started to back down his driveway before opening up his phone and making a call. Bear picked up after the first ring.

"Jacky boy, you okay?" he asked.

"I'm good," Jackson replied. "Listen, can you get someone to watch the store for a few days? I could use your help."

"Sure thing. What's going on?"

"That thing with Bailey I told you about? I'm doing it. It's time to go to work."

TWELVE

BAILEY WALKED Jackson into the offices for the task force in Roanoke just before three that afternoon. As they walked through the building, almost everyone — including those not working the Kristal Hardy case — stopped to take in the man. For most of them, it was similar to seeing Bigfoot brought to the zoo. Before his trial, Jackson Clay was little more than an urban legend. They'd all heard the stories over the years: abduction victims mysteriously found, all with some variation of the same story of an unknown man having saved them only to disappear as soon as they were safe. When the trial came, Jackson Clay charged with beating George Alvanitakis to within an inch of his life, most of them had followed it. Now here was the man in the flesh, the man who had brought hell to earth for those that had taken everything from him.

Together, Bailey and Jackson entered the conference room where the J-Team was assembled and waiting. Bailey stepped to the side and gestured with an open hand to Jackson.

"Everyone," she said. "This is Jackson Clay, our new confidential human source."

"Thank you, Jen," Pitts said, breaking the momentary awkward silence. "Mr. Clay, it's good to have you with us. Why don't you have a seat and we'll get into how you might be able to help us."

Jackson nodded and slid into a seat at the far end of the table. Pitts briefed him on everything that had happened leading up to the motel raid and after. He finished off with the resort and the airfield on which they were now focusing.

"Ultimately," Pitts said, "our goal is to place you inside the resort where you can gather more intel and evidence."

"I hope you've got an eight-figure bank account in the Caymans and a private jet," Jackson said. "I loaned mine to a buddy."

Pitts flashed a terse smile. "No, we believe our best angle is to place you in this man's charge."

Pitts tapped at the laptop in front of him. The projector in the room turned on and cast a man's mugshot onto the wall. He had brown hair shaved short with a matching beard wrapped around his chin. Beneath it, his neck was tattooed with twin upside-down revolvers. His frosty blue eyes, perched over a frozen sneer, seemed to leer at Jackson.

"Meet Nicholas Graves," Pitts said. "Mr. Graves hasn't found a form of organized crime he hasn't dabbled in. His record begins with assault with a deadly weapon when he was eighteen and goes from there."

"Sounds like a nice guy," Jackson quipped.

"Exactly. But even with his past endeavors, this all seems rather big for Graves to be behind it. Our best guess right now is that Graves is some sort of security or muscle for the place. If he's there, there are undoubtedly more like him. Our hope is you can join up in their ranks."

"Hope?"

Pitts raised his hands. "Poor choice of words, I apologize. We think it's the best play given what we know."

Bailey raised her hand but didn't wait to be called on before speaking. "I thought we hadn't been able to get eyes on and make an ID on anyone specifically within the resort."

Pitts gestured over to Wilcox.

Wilcox cleared his throat. "We were able to reroute one of the Bureau's satellites and we've had overhead surveillance on the area for the last twenty-four hours. That obviously doesn't help with facial ID, but last night we tracked one of the Range Rovers seen coming and going from the resort to a place over the state line in West Virginia."

Pitts tapped at his laptop some more and the projected image changed to an overhead shot of a building nestled off a rural highway.

"This is about a half hour up Highway 220 from the town of Monterey, a couple miles from the resort and airfield," Wilcox explained. "It's apparently a gentleman's club called *Belle Bottoms.*"

"A strip club," Bailey translated.

Wilcox nodded. "On the way back, the Range Rover pulled into a gas station in said town of Monterey. We were able to pull CCTV footage and—"

The projector changed to security cam footage of Graves gassing up the SUV.

"As the footage continues, you can make out at least two more men in the car with him. We're guessing the men either have some sort of business at the club or visit it when they're off the clock. Either way, it gives us a public place outside of the resort for you to make contact and link up with Graves."

"Do we know if the club is owned by the same people who own the airfield and resort?" Bailey asked.

"We do not. As was mentioned the other day, the ownership of everything is a shell game we're still working our way through."

Jackson shifted in his chair. "So, I assume some sort of identity and get in good with Graves?"

Pitts shook his head. "We think that's too risky. The less we give these guys to poke holes in the better. We actually think the right move here is to send you in as, well, you."

"Me?"

"Yes. You have no official affiliation with law enforcement and your conviction for attempted murder plays into our hands. If I can be perfectly honest, Mr. Clay, on paper, you look like you fit right in. A violent ex-con fresh out of prison."

"No offense taken," Jackson said flatly.

Pitts sighed and took a seat on the table. "Of course *we* know you play for the good guys. All we're saying is your current situation works to our benefit. We'd be wise to use it."

"Do you have proof they're trafficking through the resort? Why don't you just move now?"

"We have, as has been laid out, several interesting pieces of circumstantial evidence. We think we're on to something here."

Cole raised her hand to interject. "Or this could all be a waste of time."

"That's right, Cole," Bailey said, leaning forward. "It's possible there's nothing down this rabbit hole, but that's the gig."

A quiet came over the room. Bailey studied Jackson as he looked up at the screen with the CCTV footage from the gas station. She pictured the gears churning in his head.

"So, what's the play?" Jackson asked. "Wait for them to go back to the club, then it's on me to find a seat at the cool kids' table."

"Essentially, yes."

Jackson nodded. "That's got to be two or three hours from here. Are we supposed to sit here and hope they stay that long?"

"No. We realized we're a bit out of the way here, so we started looking and we're able to secure a property nearby. It's a four-bedroom house just off the highway that runs between the resort and the airport."

"A safe house."

"If you want to think of it as that, sure. But it's nearby, and we can monitor highway traffic directly from there. Plus, it's secluded, so there are no nosy neighbors to worry about. You, Jen, Angela, Cliff, and Timothy will operate from the house out there while Ben, Sara, and Kevin work out of the offices here. This thing is Jen's brainchild, so she will run point for the group."

Jackson was quiet a moment longer before he popped out of his chair. "Sounds good, I'll meet you guys there."

"You're under the guardianship of this office, Mr. Clay. You won't be going anywhere without one of us."

Jackson held up his keys, the key ring around his index finger. "I drove separately. There's only room for two, me and my bag."

Pitts face morphed into something between confusion and annoyance. He looked at Bailey.

Bailey raised placating hands. "It's fine. Jackson here got a good talking to from his probation officer before we left his house. He knows what happens if he doesn't behave."

Pitts took a moment, thinking. "Alright, but you drive straight there and wait for the rest of the team."

"Done."

Jackson stepped around Bailey and made his way out of the task force's offices. When he got in the elevator, he texted Bear the address of the safe house.

THIRTEEN

JACKSON ARRIVED at the safe house and took in the sights. It was a single-family detached home with gray wooden siding and matching roof shingles that gave the whole place a dreary monochrome appearance. The main floor parted with the sloping hill around it as it sat atop a walk-out basement beneath. The hill ran down to a large pond with a grassy meadow beyond it. In the front, a garage jutted out from the far half of the house with the roof stretched at a shallow angle to accommodate it. Tucked into the elbow formed by the garage and house was a large slab driveway closed in by a stone pony wall.

Jackson parked his truck in front of the garage door, concealing it as much as possible from the highway, and waited for about an hour when two pairs of headlights came down the sloping, unpaved drive that led up to the house. A moment later, up pulled a dark blue Chevy Impala and black Explorer. Jackson made out Cole driving and Bailey in the passenger seat of the Impala.

He climbed out and stood beside his truck, waiting for them. Bailey and Cole opened their doors and climbed out as well. Bailey held her hand over her eyes to block out the sun coming in at a sharp, late afternoon angle down the lush green valley the house was nestled into.

"Yeah, those vehicles don't scream law enforcement at all," Jackson quipped.

"They have standard state plates and no emergency lights," Bailey countered. "Same as if you bought it straight from Carmax. Besides, we'll be putting them in the garage once we get it open," she raised her eyebrow at him, "and you move your pickup."

"Where should I park?"

Bailey stepped to the trunk and grabbed her bags before heading to the front door. She stopped when she got to Jackson. "Out front. You're obviously worried about being conspicuous. A forty-year-old pickup should fit in nicely in this neck of the woods."

Jackson grabbed his rucksack and followed her in.

The house was everything it was not on the outside. Wood-paneled walls stained a warm cherry oak lined the inside leading up to a vaulted ceiling painted a cream white. Jackson took the stairs down to the lower level. A short hallway branched off into the four bedrooms. Two had a pair of twin beds in them, while a third had a double. The bedroom at the far end had a full king and French doors that opened out to the lawn and pond. As soon as he scoped each one out, he heard footsteps coming down the stairs behind him.

"I've got the master bedroom," he said.

"First of all, it's no longer called that. It's called the primary now," Cole said. "And why do you get it?"

"Because I'm the most likely to get shot at in all this."

He turned and left Cole to come up with a better reason why she should have it. One by one, everyone else came down and picked a bed. Timothy Wilcox, the FBI special agent, helped himself to the double and Cliff, left with no other choice, plopped his suitcase down on one of the twins in another room. Bailey eyed the room he was in, then the last room, empty with a pair of twins itself, and finally Cole in the hallway.

"What do you think? Roommates?" she asked Cole.

Cole looked in on Cliff already spreading his stuff to the second bed in his room. "Sounds great," she replied flatly.

Jackson left his things in his room and came back out to his truck. He walked out to the far end of the drive and took in the countryside. Two sub-ranges of the Appalachians stretched through the area like the backs of massive beasts and formed a hilly valley dotted with trees in between. It was beautiful. Serene, even. Jackson understood how it could play home to an ultra-exclusive resort. He just worried, if their suspicions were true, what terrors these hills hid.

Bailey came out and joined him. "You good?" she asked.

But before Jackson could answer, Wilcox came out the front door, jogging toward them. "Guys, we've got movement," he said. "On the hillside, coming down the drive. Unknown vehicle."

As it came around the switchback on the hillside, Jackson and Bailey saw the vehicle, too. With its headlights pointed at them and daylight fading, it was hard to see the make and model.

Bailey reached for her service weapon on her hip. The vehicle bucked and swayed under a loose suspension on the bumpy drive. Bailey unholstered her gun and held it at the low ready with two hands in front of her. Jackson reached out and placed his hand on her arm.

"That's not necessary," he said.

Bailey looked at him incredulously as the vehicle — and old, fire truck red suburban — bounced onto the paved lot and skidded to a stop. Bear, beaming behind the wheel, rolled down the passenger window.

"Now that's a fine 'how do you do' to the guy that brought everyone dinner," he said.

Bailey holstered her pistol and turned to Jackson. "What the fuck is this, Clay?"

"Backup," he replied.

"That's not funny."

"I'm not laughing."

Wilcox walked over and joined them. "Does someone want to explain to me what the hell is going on?" he asked.

"This is Archibald Beauchamp," Bailey explained, not taking her glare away from Jackson. "Mr. Clay's portly cohort."

"Hey, we can't all be size 0, Slim Jim," Bear retorted from his truck. He looked over at Wilcox. "My friends call me Bear. I guess it's up to you whether we're friends or not, junior."

"My name is Timothy Wilcox," Wilcox chastened. "*Special Agent* Wilcox."

Bear kicked his door open. "Whatever you say, squirt. Where do you want me to put the pies and where should I drop my stuff?"

Bailey ignored Bear. "Can I talk to you for a second?" she said to Jackson, an edge to her voice. She grabbed him by the arm and pulled him to the edge of the paved lot. "Just what the fuck do you think you're doing?"

Jackson's tone remained calm and matter-of-fact. "Bear's here to watch my back."

"Listen to me, Clay." She put a pointed finger to his chest. "First, that's something that has to be cleared. Not just with me, but up the line. And I think you knew that and that's why you kept it to yourself until right now."

"You always were a sharp investigator."

"Cut the shit, Clay. And second, *we're* your backup."

"It can't hurt to have one more."

"It can when that person isn't a part of this task force let alone law enforcement. I mean, Jesus Christ, Clay. Do you understand what we're trying to do here? We're trying to build a case, not you and your buddy running off into the woods to play army. Do you know what a liability he is?"

Jackson shrugged. "He stays. The other option is I go back to my life and you go back to square one. And you get to explain it all to your boss in Roanoke."

"Pitts is not my ... nevermind that." She blew a seething sigh between her lips. "Fine, Bear stays *for now*. But he is only here to assist and advise, nothing hands-on. The second he becomes a problem, he's gone. And I don't care if you leave with him or not. You're not worth my career."

Jackson doubted these rules would last, not unlike what he'd agreed to with his probation officer. "Deal."

The two of them turned and walked toward Bear who was standing by his Suburban.

"Jackson and I will take the pizzas in. Thank you. Bedrooms are downstairs. I think your friend here forgot you were coming, because he opted for one of the rooms with only one bed." She came around Bear and grabbed a stack of pizzas from the tailgate. "I guess you two are going to get chummy here."

Before Bear could load up a comeback, she was across the drive and walking through the front door. Wilcox was standing by the doorway, waiting for her.

"What is going on?" he asked.

"Bear is going to assist us. I'll keep him on a short leash, and I've told Jackson the minute he becomes a liability, I'm cutting him loose."

Wilcox rubbed at his chin. "I don't know. This is ... way out of bounds. I don't like it."

"I don't either. But it's this or we're done before we've even gotten started. Trust me, Jackson Clay is one guy where you don't call his bluff."

Wilcox grumbled something inaudible.

"I'll explain everything to the team. And I'll offer up my head before any of you so much as get a slap on the wrist. But let's keep this between us. Pitts and the rest of the task force don't need to know about it. At least, not yet." She locked eyes with him until she got the answer she needed.

"Alright."

FOURTEEN

OVER THE NEXT TWO DAYS, Ainsley prepared to leave Arizona. Sophie never sent her so much as a text checking in on her, and her grandmother hadn't called. Ainsley wanted to try to call her (again) but was afraid she'd only get her mother (again).

Still, Ainsley needed her things. Tessa had driven her back to Heber-Overgaard to sneak into her grandmother's house one more time and grab as much as she could shove out her bedroom window and carry in one trip to Tessa's car. Tessa reminded her they needed to travel light.

"All you really need are enough clothes to get by," Tessa had said. "Once we're there, we'll be able to get everything we need, one way or another."

Tessa had also texted her sister to let her know they were coming and if she could help them get a gig at the same place, but Tessa hadn't heard anything back.

Now Ainsley was starting to get nervous. She sat on the edge of slab concrete that served as a back patio of sorts for Tessa's little house, sucking away at a cigarette (a new habit also courtesy of

Tessa). It was late in the day, and the waning sun began to welcome in the cold desert night. The back door opened.

"There you are," Tessa said, stepping out and sitting down next to her. "What's up?"

"Nothing much."

"You worried about going out east?"

"I mean ... how can we do this if we don't know where we're going? Or if we'll even have a job waiting for us out there?"

Tessa leaned in and bumped her shoulder. "It'll all work out. You'll see."

Ainsley wasn't so sure. "We don't even know where we're going."

Tessa sighed. "Yeah, it kind of blows that my sister didn't get back to me." She was quiet for a moment. "I know! Zane!"

Ainsley looked at her, confused. "Who?"

"Zane! He told my sister about the gig out east. I think he might've even hooked her up with the gig. We can talk to him."

Ainsley nodded.

Tessa popped up. "Trust me, it'll all work out."

———

TESSA DIDN'T HAVE a number for Zane, but knew he usually hung out at The Railhouse, a pool hall in the main stretch of town. It had a facade meant to resemble Spanish colonial architecture, but its corrugated metal siding everywhere else, including the roof, gave away its true nature. It was an average dive bar, sparsely appointed with the only real money spent on the pool tables and the televisions hung throughout. Animal heads, old tools, and hunting rifles adorned the empty walls between the TVs. Behind the bar stood a monumental mesa of liquor.

Even for a Wednesday night, the place was crowded. Standing just inside the front doors, Tessa scanned the place, looking for Zane.

"There!" she said.

She grabbed Ainsley by the wrist and escorted her through the crowd of patrons towards a man sitting at the bar. Ainsley had assumed Zane would be roughly Tessa's age, but he was much older. His hair, long and greasy, was graying throughout and the long beard that masked most of his face was smoky white. Ainsley took him to be no younger than sixty.

"Hey, Zane," Tessa said as she came up to him.

Zane turned around, a Bud Light in the clutches of his bony hand. It took him a beat to recognize her, but when he did, he flashed a smile filled with gray teeth.

"Tessa!" he hollered. "Well, goddamn girl, get in here! How long's it been?"

Tessa leaned in and gave Zane a hug. When she came out of his embrace, she reached back for Ainsley. "This is my girl, Ainsley."

"Ainsley, huh? Well, ain't you a desert rose. C'mon in, I won't bite." Zane held his arms open as he chuckled.

Ainsley obliged him, but the hug was uncomfortable. Zane was gaunt and wreaked of gutter whiskey and stale cigarettes. The hug had lasted barely a second before one of his hands began to drop down the small of her back. Ainsley pulled away.

Zane felt her retract and chuckled again. "What are y'all up to? Paintin' the town red on a Wednesday night?"

Tessa flashed a smile as she brushed her braids back over her shoulder. "Something like that. Actually, we came out to see you."

Zane's eyes lit up. "Yeah? Well ain't you two so sweet. Let's get y'all girls a drink."

Ainsley started to say that she wasn't twenty-one but Tessa squeezed her hand, signaling her to remain quiet.

"Hey, Jim! Couple of shots of tequila for my two friends here! And me, too!"

Jim, the bartender, looked at them with skepticism before shrugging off any concerns and lining three shot glasses up on the bar top. Pouring each, he brought them over to Zane. "On your tab?"

"Shit, Tessa here's a big girl. She can pay," Zane said.

Tessa smiled and fished a twenty-dollar bill out of the pocket of her jeans, making a point to arch her back for Zane to notice. "Here you go, Jim. Thanks!"

Jim took the money and disappeared to the other side of the bar. Zane distributed the shots around and then held his up. "Here's to women and horses ... and the men who ride both!" He fired off a raspy laugh.

Tessa and Ainsley toasted him and the three knocked their shots back. Only Ainsley winced as she swallowed.

"Actually," Tessa said. "We were hoping to talk to you. We were thinking of getting out of town."

Zane arched an eyebrow. "Oh, is that so?"

"Yes, sir. And I'd remembered that you helped my sister out."

A wave of caution seemed to come over him. "Maybe I did. And?"

"Maybe you could do the same for us? You still know that place back—"

Zane put a hand on Tessa's hip and laughed so loud it seemed forced. He looked up and down the bar, as if to clock if anyone was listening. "Yeah, course I remember. You know what? I could use a smoke. You want to join me?"

"Sure." Tessa's grin grew.

Zane held a hand up to Jim, signaling that he'd be right back, then led Tessa and Ainsley out a side door of the bar.

The three of them stepped out onto a neglected slab of concrete. A small river birch had started to grow towards the parking lot and hid them from the street beyond. Zane pulled out a pack of American Spirits, plucked one out, and lit it before offering the pack to Tessa and Ainsley. Both of them took one and he filed the pack away.

"So, you want to go work out east," Zane said. He sucked in on his cigarette, bringing the burning end of it to life.

Tessa pulled a BIC lighter from her pocket and lit her cigarette. "Yeah, and meet up with my sister. Have you talked to her recently? She's been ghosting me."

Zane paused before answering. "Oh, sure, yeah. She hit me up a couple months back, I think it was. Thankin' me again for helpin' her out and whatever."

"So it's going good?"

"Out there? Shit, you play your cards right, you can make more money than you've ever seen in your life. That's a fact. We're talkin' like a stack a week. Or more."

"You think you could do the same for us?"

"Sure, yeah. When do you want to go?"

"How fast can you make it happen?"

"I gotta make a couple calls, but I'd think no more than a few days. Gotta find you a ride out east and all that."

"Nah, it's cool. I got a car."

Zane chuckled. "That piece of shit I see you drivin' around in?" He shook his head. "That won't make it to Texas never mind the east coast. No, you find a way to sell that thing and get yourself some cash. Even if I can get you the gig, gotta spend money to make money, ya know?"

"Sure, yeah."

Ainsley was surprised at Tessa's nonchalant agreement to that. She'd imagined them on a road trip across the country together like Thelma & Louise, just without all the crimes and unfortunate ending. She had no idea what Zane meant about finding them a ride.

"Of course," Zane said, as he took a drag from a cigarette. "I need to get mine. I scratch your back, you scratch mine. I do this for you, what are you going to do for me?"

He eyed the two of them up and down. A chill shot through Ainsley as every instinct in her told her to run.

Let's leave, Tessa. This isn't worth it. We can find another way. Let's go back and think of something else.

But Tessa reached back for her braids and brought them over her shoulder as she smiled with her tongue in between her teeth. Ainsley had seen this move before with Dax and Winslow and others. This is how Tessa got what she wanted.

"I don't know," Tessa said, her voice becoming squeaky and playful. "What'd a big man like you have in mind?"

Zane grinned a mouthful of ashen teeth. "Oh, I could think of a thing or two. I got my truck out back."

"Well, why don't you show me and let's see if we can't figure something out?"

Zane's eyes darted to Ainsley. "And her?"

Ainsley was about to say something, but Tessa spoke first. "What? I'm not good enough? Come on, show me where you're parked."

Tessa held her hand out and Zane took it. Together, they turned for the lot behind the bar. Ainsley reached out for Tessa and yanked her back. When it stopped Zane too, he looked back, annoyed.

Tessa giggled and leaned into him. "That your big Ram over there?" She nodded at a white pickup caked in dirt and sand in the corner of the lot.

Zane grunted in the affirmative.

"You go on ahead and start coming up with some ideas for us. I'll be right there."

Zane grinned again and headed for the truck. When he was out of earshot, Tessa turned to Ainsley.

"Don't do it," Ainsley said, exasperated. "You don't have to do this."

"Hon, it's nothing," Tessa replied. "I made sure you didn't have to do nothing. Don't worry, I got this for the both of us."

"You don't have to."

Tessa laughed as if she thought Ainsley was being ridiculous. "Here, take my keys and go on back. I'll get a ride home."

Ainsley didn't say anything.

Tessa giggled again. "Go on. I'll be home soon."

With that, Tessa turned and jogged for Zane's truck. In a trance, Ainsley walked around the little birch and headed for the parking lot out front. She was numb. Everything about this was uncomfortable for her. And yet, it was happening. She hadn't stopped it. Did that make her a part of it now? Maybe she was.

As she walked back to the front, Tessa's words from a couple of days before played in her head. *"Nothing in this life is free, hon."*

FIFTEEN

FOR FORTY-EIGHT HOURS, there was little movement from the resort. Only twice — once midday Thursday and again midday Friday — did vehicles leave the grounds. Each time it was a pair of black Range Rovers that went directly to the airport, at which point an aircraft landed, pulled into the lone hangar and then took off several minutes later. Wilcox had the office in Roanoke pull the filed flight plans for both flights. The plan for the flight Thursday listed a Gulfstream G700 that departed from Teterboro outside New York City with a crew of three and four passengers. The plan for the flight Friday listed a Bombardier Global 5500 that departed San Jose International in California with a crew of four and six passengers.

Because the risk of discovery was too high, the team at the safe house didn't have any surveillance on the airport. They were, however, able to place two cameras and a license plate reader concealed in the trees roadside on the safe house's property. They'd gotten video of the SUV's leaving and returning, but each time the windows were too dark to identify anyone.

Throughout the two days, Bear had more than managed to make himself at home, opting for a couch in the house's living space rather than sharing a bed with Jackson. That meant each morning the team of investigators awoke to the sight of a pantless Bear sprawled out with his legs up on one of the armrests and more empty Miller High Life bottles on the coffee table beside him than had been there when everyone went to bed. When Jackson cautioned he was close to wearing out his welcome, Bear offered a mea culpa and cooked dinner for everyone Thursday night.

But by Friday evening both Bear and Jackson were getting antsy. People were clearly coming and going from the resort and they had yet to even attempt to get in. Jackson truthfully didn't know what he would be doing when he agreed to help Bailey, but he had assumed it would at least be *something*. He stood just outside the screen door to his bedroom, watching a dreary drizzle fall across the valley, when Bailey came out on the deck overhead and shouted down to him.

"Clay! We've got movement!" she said.

Jackson came up and joined her in the dining room where they'd assembled a bank of computers and other equipment on the large dining table. Bailey ushered him over and pointed at the screen of a laptop.

"A single black Range Rover," she said. "It's already past the turn for the airport and headed for the junction with Highway 220."

"You think they're headed to that club?" Jackson asked.

"We'll find out here in a minute."

Bear came up from behind and joined them in watching the screen. "I'm going to need to stop at the bank and get some ones."

Bailey and Jackson ignored his quip. The screen showed an overhead satellite feed focused in on the SUV. A moment later, it slowed at an intersection and turned left.

"That's the way to the club," Jackson said. He turned to Bear. "Get ready, we're rolling."

"They're still miles away from the club," Bailey said. "We don't know for sure that they're going there."

"I'd rather take a drive and find out it was for nothing than to wait and be late to the party."

"Anytime one of us leaves the property, we risk compromising the location. We can't just run out on a whim."

Jackson threw on his coat. "In the five days you've been watching the place, has any vehicle leaving the resort gone north up that highway without going to the club?"

"No, but—"

"We're rolling. How do we communicate with you?"

Bailey scowled at him for a moment as if her glare might give him second thoughts. When it didn't, she reached over for a phone on the table and handed it to him. "With this."

"If it's set up to record, I told you I'm not going in wired. These guys are too smart for that."

"It's not. It's just a boring old smartphone, like you'd have on you if you were anybody else. Registered to your real name and everything."

"Does it got candy crush?" Bear asked.

Again, Bailey and Jackson ignored him.

"What do I do, call 911 and ask for you?" Jackson asked.

"I have my own phone. Privately registered, not with the state police or any other agency. I put its number in your contacts. You text me."

Jackson opened up the Contacts on the phone and saw a couple of numbers put in for him. He assumed most of them went to no one. In amongst them though was the name JENNY CELL with a heart emoji. Jackson turned the screen around to show Bailey and raised an eyebrow.

"We figure if anyone gets nosy, I look just like some girl you're talking to. We'll keep our conversation along those lines."

"You mean speaking in code?"

"You're a sharp guy, I'm a sharp girl. I think we can figure each other out. Use the phrase 'gym time' as a distress call. You text that, we crash the party. Obviously, if we have to do that, the game is over, so don't use it unless you absolutely have to."

Jackson looked down at the contact entry on his phone. "Why not make you my wife?"

Bailey was quiet for a moment. When she answered him, her voice was softer. "I wouldn't do that, Clay." She cleared her throat. "Besides, this works better for us. No hard connections to you."

Bear opened the front door before looking back at them in the dining room. "We rolling or what?" he asked.

Bailey nodded, giving her approval.

"Let's go," Jackson said.

———

JACKSON PULLED into the small parking lot for *Belle Bottoms Gentleman's Club* a half-hour later with Bear (purposely) fifteen minutes behind. The exterior of the club was exactly as the photo he'd seen shown: a windowless building tucked away on a rural highway. Only now a neon sign was illuminated over the lone door out front. The sign had *Belle Bottoms* spelled out in a script font that had gone out of style several decades ago. Next to it, shifting lights were meant to evoke a woman's bottom half bouncing.

Inside, Jackson was hit with a loud wave of disorienting thumping of dance pop music. The sun had set outside, but it wasn't much brighter in the small corridor he'd stepped into. A large man in a blazer and tee-shirt sat on a stool behind a small desk and asked to see his ID. Jackson promptly handed it over.

The man studied it, then handed it back to him. "It's a twenty-dollar cover to get in. You pay here."

Jackson slipped the man a twenty and walked in. The main room of the club was as dimly lit as the entrance, with neon cord lighting piped throughout, accenting the walls and outlining the stages. The room was loosely divided into three sections around three stages. Each stage was circular — the one in the middle being larger — with walkways that disappeared into curtains on the far side. The place reminded Jackson of the three-ring circuses his parents used to take him to as a kid, only, instead of animals and actors, the entertainment was naked women.

Jackson walked over to the far corner and slid into a seat at a small bistro table. Some twenty feet in front of him, a woman in nothing more than a thong and stiletto heels swung herself around a pole on one of the side stages. She cast a glance at Jackson but paid most of her attention to the middle-aged man in a button-down and slacks, standing as close to the table as possible with a handful of cash.

Another woman in a lacy camisole, bikini bottoms and thigh-highs came over to Jackson with a serving tray tucked under her arm.

"Good evening, sweetie," she said. "What would you like to drink?"

"Miller High Life."

"You got it, baby."

The woman left to get his drink. He took in the club around him. There was a smattering of patrons, none looking to be a threat to anyone other than the young women on stage. He didn't see Nick Graves.

A few minutes went by and the waitress returned with Jackson's beer. Behind her, Jackson clocked Bear walking in. Bear spotted him and moved to the opposite side of the room, sliding onto a stool at the bar. Jackson wondered if Bailey had programmed Bear's number into his new phone. He pulled it out and checked. There was no 'Bear', probably for obvious reasons, but there was a 'Bo'. Bear *Beau*champ.

Clever, Jackson thought.

Jackson was just about to text him when two more men walked in. He recognized them immediately. They were Special Agent Wilcox and Investigator Cliff Kavanaugh from the safe house. Jackson felt himself tense up. Bailey had not discussed this part of the plan with him, and he didn't like it. He got the keen feeling they were here to watch over him. It was the kind of micromanagement that risked fucking everything up.

Jackson wanted to text Bailey and tell her to pull them out. But what if this worked, and Graves eventually went through his phone? He couldn't think of a way to say that in coded texting. In any event, two men coming and quickly leaving would be suspicious in its own right. He'd have to play this one out.

Jackson looked over the room again and that's when he saw it. The other waitress — the one working the opposite side of the room — went to the bar to put in an order and then walked past it to a door to the back. The door opened, and the waitress talked to someone before giving him cash. The man, in turn, gave her something small that Jackson couldn't see. The door closed and the waitress walked past all her customers, directly to the woman on the far stage. The dancer crawled over to her on all fours as if it was part of some routine, but when she got close, the waitress handed the dancer whatever the man had given her. This time, Jackson got a clear look at it.

It was a small baggie with two pills in it.

A moment later, the song ended, and the waitress hopped down from the stage and strutted over to a customer that'd been watching her. She whispered something to him with a smile and then led him down a corridor that Jackson figured led to private dance rooms.

Jackson leaned back, putting it all together. Whoever had come here from the resort wasn't here to have a night out, they were working. Just as they had distributed Pepsis to Sean Liles, they were selling the Pepsis here. The girls, in turn, probably sold it to customers at a jacked-up price to take for private dances away from prying eyes.

A moment later, a door opened behind the bar and out stepped Nick Graves. Jackson recognized him at once. Only the butts of his twin pistol tattoos were visible over the collar of his black button-down shirt, but everything else about him was the same from the photos. Brown hair, buzzed short to match trimmed beard, hawk nose and thin lips. Jackson was watching him when his phone began buzzing, breaking his trance. He looked down at it. It was from Bailey under her pseudonym.

Any ideas for tonight?

Jackson parsed the message. She was asking if he saw a way to make a meet with Graves. An idea had floated around in his mind, but he knew it would be problematic. He scanned the club once more, trying to come up with a better play. When he came back to Wilcox and Kavanaugh, he knew there wasn't one. He typed back his reply.

Yeah, but you're not going to like it.

As he hit send, he slipped his phone into his pocket and stood up. Moving along the outside of the room, he made his way past Wilcox and Kavanaugh and took a seat on a stool at the bar on the opposite side of Bear. The bartender was in front of him, twisting open another beer. Graves had his back turned to them both, making himself a drink. As he headed back toward the door he'd come out of, Jackson leaned in and stopped him.

"You know, it's probably none of my business," he said, "but the girls out there are slinging your shit in front of two cops."

Graves shot him a suspicious glance before looking around, as if Jackson might be talking to someone else. "Excuse me?"

"Like I said, probably none of my business. Just thought you'd want to know."

"What the fuck are you talking about?"

"The pills the girls are flipping to customers. They're doing it in front of cops. Probably *to* cops if they're not careful."

Bear eyed the two of them across the way, ready to jump in if it all went sideways.

Graves looked around again and then put a forced smile on his face. "Guy, you don't know what you're talking about."

Jackson cocked his head and raised an eyebrow. "Okay, I don't know what I'm talking about. I definitely don't know what I'm saying about the two cops, main stage, fifty feet back over my right shoulder."

Graves looked in their direction. Whether he'd seen them before or not, Jackson wasn't sure, but now he saw it in Graves' eyes. Graves pegged them for cops, too.

"Maybe it's not you, but someone back there is working the room," Jackson said as he took a sip of his beer. "You might want to let them know."

Graves didn't say anything. He looked at Jackson a beat longer, then opened the door and disappeared. All Jackson could do was hope the seed he planted in Graves' mind did what it needed to do. He turned around on his stool, leaned back against the bar top and took in the club. The woman on the stage closest to him was halfway up the pole, upside down, with her legs over her head. But as the door next to the stage bucked open, she kicked herself upright in alarm.

Two men came charging out of somewhere in the back. Bear reached for his .357 on his hip but the men stormed right past him and Jackson. They were headed straight for Kavanaugh and Wilcox who didn't see them coming until they were right in front of them.

"It's time y'all go!" one of the two men growled.

"What did you say?" Kavanaugh asked.

"What are you, fuckin' deaf?" the other man asked. He slapped Kavanaugh and Wilcox's drinks off their table. "He said it's time to get fuckin' goin'!"

Wilcox put his hands out in front of him. "We're not bothering anyone. What's the problem?"

"The problem is we told y'all to go and you're still fucking here," the first man said.

He went to put his hands on Wilcox, but Wilcox swiped him off. The man came back again, grabbed Wilcox by his shirt, and threw him to the ground. The second man reached for Kavanaugh, who stood and squared up with the man. Now he had both goons' attention. Graves stepped out of the door from the back and watched as his two men moved to flank Kavanaugh. Behind them, Wilcox got to his feet and drew a pistol from the small of his back. He didn't see Graves behind him.

No, Jackson thought, *what the hell are you doing?* He shot off his barstool and headed for Wilcox. Graves drew a gun from his side and started to level it at Wilcox. Before he could, though, Jackson intervened.

"FBI!" Wilcox barked. "Police! Fre—"

Jackson swooped inside Wilcox's stance and grabbed his shooting arm with both hands. He forced Wilcox's hand, gun in its grasp, down before twisting it. Wilcox yelped in pain and dropped the pistol. As it fell harmlessly to the ground, Jackson, still in control of Wilcox's arm, whipped it behind Wilcox's back and thrust upward. As Wilcox stiffened straight up, Jackson threw a sweeping back kick into Wilcox's shins and planted him on the ground face-down. He dropped a knee onto Wilcox's hand, pinning it to the young agent's back, then grabbed the pistol off the ground. He slid the mag out, emptied the round in the chamber, took the slide off the top of it, and placed the pistol, now in two pieces, by Wilcox's shoulder.

He had just finished when a gunshot boomed out from behind him. He turned and saw that Graves had lowered his pistol and fired a round into the floor.

"That's enough!" he yelled. "You." He pointed the gun at Jackson and then waved it to the side. "Step off."

Jackson did as Graves ordered.

Graves then motioned for one of his men to take control of Wilcox. "Get him and his buddy out of here."

The two goons went to grab Wilcox and Kavanaugh when Kavanaugh brushed his man away again. "We are law enforcement! You put your hands on us again and we'll arrest you for assault on a peace officer!"

"And unless you magically produce a warrant, you'll leave right now or your superiors will get a call from a lawyer that bills as much in an hour as you make in a week."

Kavanaugh glowered at Graves, straightening the collar on his shirt, but left without further incident. Wilcox followed him out, but not before turning back and giving a similar scowl. Jackson returned his gaze, emotionless.

"Alright, that's it," Graves said. "Club's closed for the night. Pay your tabs and get the hell out."

The few patrons not involved in the fracas looked around with confusion before following Graves' directions. Jackson pulled a fifty from his wallet and left it on the bar. As he headed for the door, he saw Bear do the same thing.

The front doors to Belle Bottoms opened and a steady stream of everyone inside filed out. Jackson and Bear were the last two customers out, with Graves ushering the group out from behind. As they spilled into the parking lot, they all watched Kavanaugh and Wilcox pull out in the Impala. Figuring the night was a bust, Jackson started to head to his truck when Graves called out behind him.

"You!" he barked.

Jackson turned back and looked at him.

"Yeah, you." Graves motioned for him to come toward him.

Jackson obliged him and joined Graves near the front door to the club.

"Let me see your ID."

"Excuse me?"

"Your ID. Let me see it."

The two henchmen joined Graves in trying to intimidate Jackson with numbers. It didn't work, but Jackson conceded anyway, fished out his wallet, and handed his driver's license over to Graves.

Graves studied it for a moment. "Jackson Clay of Virginia." He pulled out his phone and snapped a photo of the ID before handing it back to Jackson.

"What was that for?" Jackson asked.

"Insurance. You practically broke the arm of a cop back there. If they come back knocking on my door, I want to know where to send them."

"You were about to do a lot more than just break his arm."

Graves pulled a pack of cigarettes out of his pocket, took one, and placed it in between his grinning lips and nodded.

"Which reminds me ... don't make a habit of stepping into my line of fire. It's a good bet that next time it won't work out well for you."

Jackson didn't say anything.

"Nevertheless, *Jackson Clay*, that was some slick shit back there. Where'd you learn to do that?"

"Around," replied Jackson.

Graves arched an eyebrow, but Jackson remained silent. "How'd you make them out to be cops?"

"Two guys dressed like they just came off the links nowhere near a country club?" Jackson shook his head. "It wasn't exactly hard. That Impala screamed law enforcement, too. They might as well have worn badges around their necks."

"I could think of something else I'd like to hang around their necks." Graves laughed. "I haven't seen you around here before."

Jackson shrugged. "Just traveling through, looking for work."

"Is that a fact? I would think a man with the kind of skills I saw back there would be very employable."

"The only people that ever paid me for those kinds of skills was the army, and they paid shit money."

Graves grinned again and nodded. "You got a phone on you?"

"I do."

"Let me see it."

Jackson hesitated for a moment before obliging him. Graves took it and copied down Jackson's number into his own phone.

"Let me guess," Jackson said, "insurance."

"Something like that."

"Do you need anything else ... or can I leave?"

Graves shook his head once as he offered Jackson back his phone. "Have a good night, Mr. Clay. Get home safe."

Jackson took his phone and turned for his truck. As he put it in gear and pulled out of the parking lot, he looked back at Graves and his men. Had he found his way in or blown everything up?

He honestly couldn't tell.

SIXTEEN

JACKSON PURPOSELY DROVE five under the speed limit and circled the small town of Monterey twice, ensuring neither Graves nor any of his men were following him back. After an hour of meandering down the back roads of western Virginia, Jackson was satisfied and headed for the safe house.

He had just thrown his truck into park on the driveway when the front door swung open so hard it bounced off the wall. Out marched Wilcox with Kavanaugh close behind. The two were brick red in the face.

"Turn around right now!" Wilcox barked. "Put your hands behind you! I'm taking you in right now for assault and battery."

Bear appeared in the doorway. "You're going to get your ass kicked for the second time tonight before that happens, bud."

Wilcox ignored him. "I said turn around!"

"That's not going to happen," Jackson said calmly.

"You'll do it or I'll make you do it!"

Bailey pulled Bear back into the house and then stepped out onto the small porch. "Cliff! Timothy! Clay! Get inside right now! We will deal with this in here!"

"Bullshit!" Wilcox shouted back. "I'm handling this right here, right now."

"You are risking compromising all of us. Get in here *right now*!"

"We've already *been* compromised! Our flying under the radar here was just blown to shit thanks to this asshole!"

"*Your* cover's been blown," Jackson countered. "I'm just a guy that looks like he's not a fan of badges."

"And sometimes you can judge a book by its cover," Wilcox turned to Bailey. "This little experiment is over. I'm calling it in."

Bailey stomped out to the driveway, got behind Jackson, and shoved him into Wilcox and Kavanaugh, forcefully shepherding the trio inside. When they were all in, she slammed the door behind her.

"You're not calling anyone until we see how this all plays out," Bailey hissed.

"The hell I'm not!" Wilcox countered. "I'm not going down with you or your jailbird buddy here."

"And what are you going to say, exactly? That you were a part of why your first op went sideways? That you panicked and drew your weapon on a civilian that had every right to bounce you out of a private establishment? Because regardless of what you think Clay did or didn't do, all of that remains true. Your career at the bureau will be over before it ever started."

"Your loose cannon here practically broke my fucking arm, and he knew damn well who I was!"

"And if I hadn't, you'd have a new hole in your head to see out of."

Bailey and Wilcox stopped and looked at Clay, both curious and indignant.

"I'm guessing what Wilcox failed to mention, in whatever debrief you had before I got here, is that Graves drew on him," Jackson explained. "I moved in front of him to take away his shot." He locked eyes with Wilcox. "No thanks needed."

Wilcox's scowl sharpened as he shook his head. Everyone in the foyer could hear the hot air blowing out of his flared nostrils. "And taking me down? What the fuck was that?"

"Me keeping my cover intact."

Bailey wedged an arm between them. "Alright, this is over. Timothy, go take a walk. *Inside* the house."

Timothy didn't move but continued to glare at Clay.

"*Now*, Special Agent," Bailey said, her voice hardening. "This dick-measuring contest is over."

Reluctance in every movement, Wilcox stepped backward before turning and walking away. As he headed into the kitchen, he slammed an open cupboard shut as he passed by it.

"That dude really oughta see a doctor about that stick up his ass," Bear quipped.

Jackson turned to head the other way, but before he could leave, Bailey grabbed him by the shoulder.

"Uh uh," she said, pointing to the stairwell. "Downstairs. I need to have a word with you, too."

Jackson followed Bailey downstairs where she went into the bedroom she was sharing with Cole. When Jackson stepped through, Bailey closed the door behind them. Jackson turned and looked at her. She leaned against the closed door, her arms crossed, looking at Jackson.

"Usually, having a word with someone involves talking," Jackson said.

Bailey shook her head. "I'm not a mother, I'm not a babysitter, and I'm damn sure not an umpire. You don't get three strikes with me, not out here. That shit tonight was your one and only strike, Clay."

"My objective, *the reason you brought me out here*, was to find a way in with Graves. That's exactly what I was doing."

"And you nearly got a federal agent and a sheriff's office investigator killed. I know you well enough to know what you said about Graves drawing on them wasn't a lie. What if he had shot them? What would you expect me to say to their families?"

"You'd probably have to explain how you sent them in there knowing full well what and who was inside."

Bailey clenched her jaw. Her face remained stoic, but Jackson could see the anger and hurt in her eyes.

"You can be pissed at me all you want," Jackson said, his voice emotionless. "The fact of the matter is, we had a game plan, one everyone here agreed to, then, *after* you sent me in, you called an audible without running it by me or letting me know. Wilcox and Kavanaugh weren't the only ones who could've gotten killed tonight. You don't want any surprises on your watch? Fine. Neither do I. You want an answer from me as to what I was thinking, but what about you? What were *you* thinking sending Wilcox and Kavanaugh in there?"

"I was thinking you could use the backup."

"Bullshit. You sent them in there to get a pair of eyes on me and Bear because you got nervous. *You* asked *me* to do this, remember? You came to my house, gave me that little pep talk and everything. If you want me to do this, you need to trust me. And that stunt tonight? That wasn't trusting me."

Bailey stayed quiet a moment longer. Jackson moved to a window across the room. The moon, nearly full, hung low in the night sky, peeking out from the cluster of trees that wrapped around the side of the house. Bailey came over and joined him at the window. When she spoke, her voice was calmer.

"What happened after Wilcox and Kavanaugh took off?" she asked.

"Graves called me over," Jackson answered. "Asked me a bunch of questions. Where I was from, how did I make Wilcox and Kavanaugh, that sort of thing. He took a photo of my driver's license and copied down my phone number."

Bailey looked at him, her brow furrowed. "What do you think that's about?"

"Not sure. Counter-intel would be my guess. Running a background check on me, that sort of thing. It's what I would do if I were him."

"He'll find you're a felon convicted of a violent crime with special ops skills." Bailey chewed her lip, a hopeful gleam entering her eyes. "It might play right into our hands."

"Or he could find I've spent the last decade or so aiding law enforcement in stopping monsters just like him. It depends how far he digs. We don't know what resources he has."

At that, Jackson's phone buzzed in his pocket. He pulled it out and looked at the screen. The caller ID read *Anonymous*.

He answered. "Hello?"

"Jackson Clay," Nick Graves said on the other end of the line. "You know who this is?"

"Yeah." Jackson mouthed 'Graves' to Bailey.

"You said you were looking for work. Are you interested in a job?"

"It depends. I'm not looking to mop up the champagne rooms, if that's what you're asking."

Graves laughed, though Jackson couldn't tell if it was with him or at him. "Let's just say it plays to those skill sets I imagined would be employable."

Jackson took a beat to keep his tone even. "Alright, I'm in."

"Noon tomorrow at the club. Wear something professional." The line went dead.

Jackson slipped the phone back into his pocket. Bailey was eyeing him, an expectant look on her face.

"Noon tomorrow. I guess he just offered me a job."

Bailey nodded. "I'll let the Task Force know we've gotten you in."

SEVENTEEN

TWO NIGHTS after they'd met Zane at the bar, Ainsley and Tessa were invited out to a bonfire at a place Zane called *The Gully*. The day before, a jubilant Tessa had done as Zane had suggested and sold her car for four grand, so Zane picked them up.

Sitting three wide in his Dodge Ram, Zane drove them east out Interstate 40. Behind them, the last rays of twilight shone down the straight stretch of highway. The air, missing the heat of the sun, had already turned cool and gave Ainsley goosebumps as it whipped through the truck's cab. She zipped her hoodie closed over her sundress.

"Next week, y'all will be headed out this way just like this. 'Cept you won't stop. You'll keep going," Zane said.

"Next week?" Tessa asked. "You set it up already?"

"You betcha. Got you a ride out and everythin'."

Ainsley could only imagine it. In her seventeen years on this earth, she'd never left Arizona. She knew the state line wasn't much further ahead — maybe forty miles or so as the interstate cut through the national park and the Navajo Nation — but those forty miles had always felt like four hundred, if not more. She saw the desert all around her as if filled with quicksand, determined to swallow her life whole before she could ever leave. Now she had her chance.

But that would have to wait until next week.

Zane took the exit for Adamana Road and headed south. Ahead of them was nothing but unpaved road and barren desert, an endless wilderness of deadland and scrub brush. Zane drove them further into it until, up ahead in the waning light, it looked like the world simply ended. Zane threw his truck in park and grinned.

"C'mon," he said. "Not too much of a hike from here."

Together, he led them across a set of railroad tracks that cut an iron trail through the desert. On the other side was a steep ravine. As they stepped to it, Ainsley could hear voices below.

"Shit, they haven't started the bonfire yet," Zane said. "Okay, take my hand and watch your step."

Slowly, he guided them down. The earth was nothing but sheared rocks, slippery even when dry. Ainsley lowered herself down on all fours, feeling the way in front of her when *whoosh.*

A massive fireball shot skyward with the kind of roar Ainsley imagined should come down the railroad tracks up behind them. A massive pile of wood afire, burning brilliantly in the dry riverbed at the bottom of the ravine. Dotted around it was a medley of off-road Jeeps and buggies. The people interspersed between them shouted triumphantly. Zane pushed himself to his feet and laughed.

"There it goes," he said. "C'mon, we can see the way down now."

Tessa took Ainsley's hand and together they hopped from rock to rock until they'd joined the others in the riverbed. From the bottom, the fire was an awesome pyre juxtaposed against the dark night sky. As soon as they came up to the fire, a girl Tessa's age with purple hair and a nose ring tossed Tessa and Ainsley each a beer. Tessa pulled out her house keys from her pocket and punched a hole near the bottom of the can before popping the tab, cocking her head back, and draining its contents. When she came back up for air, she simpered with joy and motioned for the stranger to toss her another one. Ainsley opened her own but took only an easy sip.

"Oh, girl," Tessa said in mock disappointment, "Live a little!"

Ainsley laughed and took a larger swig.

Over the next hour, she had two more as she and Tessa joined in the partying. A warm buzz welled up inside her as she danced to the guitar someone was playing. When she closed her eyes and put her head back, everything seemed to drift away. Not just her stress and troubles, but the world they resided in. For the first time since that evening in Sophie's car, she felt free. It was a euphoric feeling. Now that she had it again, she was determined never to let it go.

She opened her eyes and took in the night sky above her. She could see the constellations she'd learned about in school. Ursa Minor, the Little Dipper. Next to it Cepheus and then Cassiopeia. They'd learned about those two in Greek mythology as well. King Cepheus and his vain queen, the woman that offered up her daughter to save herself. Cassiopeia's beauty didn't remind Ainsley of her own mother, but her self-fulfilling actions certainly did.

Ainsley drifted away from the bonfire, following the constellations overhead. As she got further from the bonfire, the stars overhead grew more vibrant. She spun around, watching the Greek figures of tragedy and comedy blend together in a constellational kaleidoscope until she grew dizzy and fell to the ground.

"Whoa, there, tiny dancer. Take it easy," said a familiar voice.

Ainsley looked over to see Zane standing beside the Jeep between her and the party around the bonfire.

"You okay?" he asked.

Ainsley giggled as she brought herself to her feet. "Yeah, no. I'm great," she said. She gave him an unconvincing thumbs up.

Zane grinned. "What's so funny?"

Ainsley shrugged. "Nothing. Everything." She made a sweeping gesture at the riverbed. "All this. It's just funny how things work out."

Zane chuckled himself. "Is that so?"

She walked over to him by the Jeep. "Mmhmm. Tonight was supposed to be senior prom. Instead, I'm here ..." her head panned. "wherever here is."

"Prom, huh?"

Zane came around the Jeep to the far side where she was standing. Something about the way he stepped towards her made her uncomfortable.

"I could still make it a special night for you, you know?" he said.

A chill shot through Ainsley that wasn't from the brisk night air. Now, her smile was forced. "Ah, you know, I should probably find Tessa. She can get into trouble unless I keep an eye on her."

Ainsley went to step past Zane, but Zane put an arm out stopping her and ushering her back.

"Tessa can take care of herself," Zane said. "Lord knows that girl is all grown up." He reached out and put a hand on Ainsley's hip. "But maybe I can take care of you."

"No, that's alright. I should really get back to Tessa, I'm sorry."

She tried to step past Zane again, but this time he used his body to block her. When she stepped into him, his hands reached for her backside.

"C'mon now," he said. "After everything I've done for you?"

Ainsley swiped his hands away from her. Gone was her smile and laughter. Now her tone was sharp. "I said *no*, alright?"

In an instant, Zane's posture changed from that of swooning bachelor to hunting predator. "You fucking *bitch*!"

Before Ainsley could react, his arm had shot out and he had a handful of her hair near the back of her scalp. With it, he swung her around him and threw her forward. Ainsley crashed face first into the Jeep's side mirror, which shattered upon impact. She collapsed in a heap on the ground and Zane came around to stand over her. Ainsley looked over her shoulder at him. Dazed, her image of him was blurry.

"Someone ought to teach you some fucking manners," he growled.

Zane kicked her over, so she was laid out on her back. Ainsley reached out for the earth to try to pull herself away, but it was no use. The alcohol and the blow to her head had sapped her strength. Zane started to undo his belt. She went to scream when someone shouted from the other side of the Jeep.

"Hey, cops!" the voice called out.

Ainsley looked beyond the Jeep's front tires. Two side-by-sides — those vehicles that looked like golf carts on steroids — were coming down the riverbed, their headlights centered on the bonfire. As they rolled up into the light of it, she saw two park rangers dismount from them and corral everyone into a single group.

Zane stepped over Ainsley and approached the officers. As he did, the one closest to him pulled out a flashlight and shone it straight at him.

"Is everything all right, officers?" he asked, his demeanor back to being cordial. "I know we couldn't possibly be disturbing anyone all the way out here."

"No one is out here for you to disturb, because you're on National Park land," the ranger replied. "Do you know that it is a violation of federal law to trespass in a national park?"

Zane let out a nervous chuckle, rubbing the back of his neck. "I'm sorry officer. Honest to God, we didn't know."

"It's also a violation to have an unapproved fire in an unauthorized area of the park."

"I'm sorry about that, too, officer."

The other ranger nodded at a stack of empty beer cans by the fire. "And the same with littering. I hope everyone drinking here is 21."

"Let's see some IDs, folks," the first ranger ordered.

A handful of partygoers stepped forward and produced IDs. Others offered up excuses as to why they didn't have theirs on them. Ainsley used the Jeep to pull herself to her feet. Once there, she leaned against it, to come around to the other side. The ranger with the flashlight shifted it to her. Ainsley winced. Her eye was throbbing from hitting the Jeep's mirror and she was sure a bruise was already forming. She held a hand up to try to shield herself from the harsh glare of the light, but it didn't help.

"You back there," the ranger's tone had an accusing edge, "come here. What are you doing over there?"

"I — I—" As a different kind of fear washed over her, she became paralyzed with the dread of possible legal trouble. Her mouth failed to find the words they were looking for.

"Do you have ID?" the ranger asked.

Despite what had just happened to her, she wasn't relieved to see law enforcement. Just the opposite, actually. Her mind only focused on everything she had done wrong. Ran away from home, skipped school, and now drinking underage. She shook her head.

"What's your name?" the ranger asked.

"Ainsley," she answered.

"Ainsley what?"

"Ainsley Manning." Her grandmother's maiden name popped into her head just in time to lie.

"How old are you?"

"Twenty-three." Another lie.

"What's your date of birth?"

Despite her head throbbing, Ainsley had the foresight to add six years to her real birthday. "June 3, 2001."

Satisfied by her answers, the ranger took a closer look at Ainsley's eye. "What happened to your eye there? That looks fresh."

"I ..."

"Oh, she tripped over herself," Zane stepped in. "I apologize, but as you can see, we've all had a few beers here. And this sand down here. You step funny and, well..."

The ranger shot Zane a scowl. "I didn't ask you, I asked her." He turned his attention back to Ainsley, walking over to her and coming so close that only the two of them could hear each other. He lowered his flashlight just below her eyes, the bottom half of her face still illuminated. "Is that true? Did this happen from a fall?"

Ainsley again struggled to find the words.

"If someone here hurt you, you can tell us. It's okay."

Ainsley's gaze shifted to Zane. Tessa was standing behind him now, and the two of them were looking back at her. Ainsley knew the truth, but she also knew the reality of the situation. If she told them what Zane had done, hers and Tessa's dream of heading out east would be over. Tessa had just sold her car and done God knows what else for them. Plus, telling the truth would almost certainly mean the lies she'd just told would come out, too. She'd be a lying, no-good delinquent and it would be her word against his and all his friends at this party.

"Yeah, no. I was dancing and just fell over." She forced herself to grin. "Clumsy me."

The ranger looked at her a moment longer, as if his wary stare might solicit the truth they both knew she was hiding. When it didn't, he turned around.

"This party is over," the other ranger said. "Pick up all the trash and pack it out of here. Fire department's on their way to put this bonfire out. I want everyone and everything out of here by the time they arrive."

Begrudgingly, the party goers started to pick up after themselves. Ainsley lowered herself down onto a rock, dazed by everything that had just happened. Tessa wandered through the fray of people and came over to her.

"You okay?" she asked.

Ainsley nodded.

Another lie.

EIGHTEEN

THE NEXT DAY at noon on the dot, Jackson pulled back into the Belle Bottoms' parking lot. The front lot was deserted and only a handful of cars were parked around the side of the building tucked away towards the back. Jackson figured that's where the dancers and staff parked. As he exited his vehicle, he spotted a black Range Rover with dark tinted windows parked away from the group of more modest cars.

Stepping through the front door was like entering a cave as he left the bright sunshine of the early afternoon and entered the dim front corridor. Closed for business until later in the day, the building was eerie and quiet compared to the night before. No pop-rock music thumped through the walls nor did any DJ announce dancers as they came out. In their place was only the gusty breaths of the bouncer, the same one that had checked Jackson's ID the night before. The heavyset man said something into a radio and a door opened down the hall opposite the one Jackson had walked through last night into the club. Out stepped Graves, with two men behind him. They were new faces, ones that hadn't been a part of the fracas the night before.

"Mr. Clay," Graves said with a cheerful smile. "Thank you for coming back on such short notice."

"No problem," Jackson replied. "You mentioned a jo—"

Graves held up a hand, stopping him. "Let's step into another room before we continue."

He motioned for Jackson to follow him and, as he did, Jackson noticed the two other men step behind him. Together, the four went back through the door Graves had just come out of. It opened into a hallway, and Graves walked them through another door at the far end. As Jackson stepped into the room, the first thing he noticed was the walls were different — thick, painted cinder block. In the center of the room was a single table with a chair on each side. It reminded Jackson of the dozens of interrogation rooms he'd been in before. The second thing he noticed was the guards hadn't followed them inside.

"Same rules as security in an airport," Graves said. He gestured toward Jackson's body. "Cell phone, keys, wallet, belt, shoes, watch. Anything else with metal. All on the table, please."

Wary, Jackson did as he was asked. When he placed all the items on the table, the two other men entered the room, one with a tray. He put all of Jackson's belongings on the tray and left as quickly as he entered. The other stood in the corner with a wand-like device in his hand.

"You'll get everything back in a minute," Graves explained with an amused grin. "Please, raise your arms out away from you. And spread your legs."

Again, Jackson did as he was asked. The man with the device came over and methodically waved it over Jackson's body. It didn't make a sound, though Jackson wasn't sure if it was supposed to. He glanced at Graves who held his smile.

"I'm sure you understand," he said. "You can never be too careful these days."

Jackson was tempted to ask him what he was looking for but opted to remain quiet. When the man was done, he backed away from Jackson and nodded at Graves. Graves nodded back, and the man disappeared from the room. Graves gestured Jackson toward the chair in front of him.

"Please, have a seat," he said.

Jackson slid into the chair and rested his forearms on the table. A moment later, the first man returned with the tray of Jackson's things. He placed it on the table, then handed Graves a folder and left as quickly as he'd entered. Graves opened the folder and began to finger through the papers inside.

"Can I take my stuff?" Jackson asked. "Or is a cavity search next?"

Graves chuckled. "No cavity search, Mr. Clay. But leave your stuff where it is for the time being."

Jackson imagined Graves' aim was to make him uneasy and therefore more likely to trip up if he tried to lie. Graves laid the folder out flat on his side of the table. Jackson couldn't see the contents over his personal effects. He didn't want to seem too eager to look, so he sat back in his chair.

"Jackson No Middle Name Clay," Graves said, appearing to read off whatever was inside the folder. "You've lived quite the life already."

Jackson remained motionless and didn't reply.

"Enlisted in the Army in 1997. Deployed to Kosovo before completing RASP to become a Ranger. More deployments in Afghanistan and Iraq. Two Purple Hearts, a Bronze Star, Soldier's Medal, and a Silver Star. You were halfway to a bowl of Lucky Charms."

Jackson bit the inside of his cheeks. Graves either had his Official Military Personnel File or DD Form 214 — or both — neither of which he should have as an ordinary civilian.

"Did you serve?" Jackson asked.

"Me? No. No, I had what the Navy called 'disciplinary issues'."

"Half the kids that join up have that."

"But how many of them tried to choke out their RDC?" Graves' grin widened as if he was proud of that.

Jackson bit down harder.

Graves returned to Jackson's file. "Then it looks like you got your honorable discharge in 2017."

"I got my twenty for my pension and got out."

"I thought pensions were terminated in the case of incarceration."

Biting down didn't work anymore. An ironic grin formed on Jackson's face.

Graves returned his expression. "That's right, I have that, too. A bunch of charges here, but the real winner is Attempted Murder."

"I assume you want an explanation."

"I already have that, as well. Apparently, you beat a George Alvanitakis into using a feeding tube for the rest of his life."

"He killed my son and my ex-wife."

"Guys I know would be throwing a parade for the guy that killed their ex."

"I guess I'm not someone you know then."

Graves closed the folder and rested his hands on top of it. He pursed his lips. "You seem like a violent man."

"I can be."

"What I need to know is can you control that violence? I don't have use for hotheads that cause me problems."

"This from the guy that choked out his drill sergeant?"

Graves chuckled again. "Tried to. And that was a long time ago. I've learned my lessons."

I've seen your record, too. It's full of … lessons.

"Your transgression, however, is recent. In fact, it shows you should still be on house arrest."

"I just got off it."

"And now you're here. How'd you put it? 'Traveling through, looking for work'?"

Jackson shrugged. "A man's got to eat."

"You never answered my original question. Can you follow orders?"

Jackson gestured in the direction of the folder. "You have the answer in front of you. I've got twenty years that proves I can follow orders. As for Alvanitakis, don't ask me why I couldn't let my kid's killer run free, and I won't ask you why you think I should have."

Graves rapped his fingers on the table. He studied Jackson, no doubt weighing his answer. "Deal. Do you still want a job?"

"Like I told you last night, that depends on the job."

"Security. Here, at the club."

Jackson tried not to let his surprise or disappointment show on his face. He thought such a deep-dive on his background would surely be for the resort, not to toss out drunks at a strip club. He couldn't let Graves see that, though. The Jackson Clay he needed Graves to buy into didn't know about the resort. At least, not yet. "How much?" he asked.

"We'll start you off at $10 an hour."

Jackson cocked his head to the side. "And I thought the Army gave shit pay."

Graves turned his palms out on the table, spreading his arms to either side. "Take it or leave it. If you prove to be valuable, there's always room for growth within the company, as they say."

"I'm a little old to be swinging on a pole."

Graves laughed. "You're a funny guy. Maybe we should have you host open mic nights around here."

Jackson stared at Graves, straight-faced.

The humor faded from Graves' face. "I'm confident we can find something for you. But for now, it's this or nothing."

Jackson wondered if the strip club might be a trial run for the resort. A way to test out who can be trusted in a lower-risk situation. Either way, it was clear this was the best offer he was going to get. "Alright," he said, "but I want my pay in cash. No W-2's, no taxes."

"I think we can do that, so long as you don't go around driving a Maserati."

"How about a late-model Range Rover?"

Graves laughed again and stood up. "You'll start Monday, day after tomorrow. I'll text you the details."

Jackson nodded. "Monday."

Graves walked out. Jackson gathered his things and put his belt and shoes back on. When he stepped out into the hallway, Graves and the two men were gone.

———

WITHIN A MINUTE of leaving Jackson Clay, Nick Graves was out the back door of the club, into the passenger seat of the Range Rover, and headed out with his men. Coming out this way in the middle of the day just to meet Clay was inconvenient, but it was the only way. He'd done his homework on Clay, as much as his boss' resources enabled him to, but Clay was nowhere near ready to being trusted with The Arcady.

As rustic West Virginia flew by outside his window, Grave's phone buzzed in his breast pocket. He pulled it out and looked at the screen. The number was blocked, but he knew who it was. Only one blocked number ever called this phone.

"Yeah," Graves answered.

"Where are you?" the voice on the other side replied.

Graves could picture his boss now. His slicked-back, graying hair, his pinkish complexion, his facial expression resting in a frown. "I'm headed back now. I had to handle something."

"I'm flying into the airfield. I want you waiting for me at my residence when I get there. We have a problem."

Graves' brow furrowed. "Okay? What's the problem."

"We have an infiltrator."

PART THREE

CONFLUENCE

"Hope is like the sun, which, as we journey toward it, casts the shadow of our burden behind us." —Samuel Smiles

NINETEEN

JACKSON SPENT the next week working his new job as a bouncer
for Belle Bottoms. It proved to be the easiest and most boring work
he'd done in some time. Every day he came to work at six in the
evening and every night he'd leave just after two in the morning.
Whenever he left, he headed out in the opposite way of the safe
house before doubling back when he was sure he wasn't being tailed.

There were no more than a couple times each night when he was
needed, and all but one of those times simply involved escorting
someone who'd had too much to drink out the front door. He
worried about those that stumbled toward their car and chose to get
behind the wheel, but the manager — a slimy, sweaty man with a
bad comb-over named Marv — assured him it was not his problem.
Still, he and Bailey worked out a pre-arranged message (some variation of "I could go for a drink right now") to make sure the local state
troopers knew they could probably catch a quick DUI down the road.

The rest of the time, he sat up front with his fellow bouncer, Gus.
Gus was the one who'd checked Jackson's ID the first night he came
in and was now very excited to have a coworker. Most shifts, he
talked Jackson's ear off about any and every thought that passed

through his enormous head. When he'd found out Jackson was a former Army Ranger, he offered Jackson his favorite war movies, going into graphic detail of his favorite battle scenes. Steven Seagal was an actor very near and dear to his heart.

Bear, eager to back Jackson up, alternated his time between the dance club as a patron — only ever at the bar and mostly just to watch the television — or posted up at a campground a half-mile down the road. When Jackson brought up his concern that he'd become too familiar of a face around the club, Bear was all too happy to lay out the cover story that he was staying with his sister the next town over while he got on his feet.

"It's foolproof!" Bear had exclaimed.

It's full of something, Jackson had thought.

Graves poked his head into the club a handful of times and Jackson got the impression he too was there to keep an eye on him. He always made it a point to check in with him, while never once acknowledging Gus, and every time he spoke with Marv, the two would look over at him.

On his fifth night working there, Jackson had just eased into his seat next to Gus to start the shift when Graves came through the front door. This time, he didn't so much as look in Jackson's direction as he walked past. He opened the door to the private hallway off the club's main room, said something to Marv who nodded, and then shut the door and came back toward Jackson. This time, he looked at him.

"Let's take a ride," Graves said.

Graves' request caught Jackson by surprise, but he tried not to let it show. "Take a ride where?" he asked.

Graves flashed a looming grin. "We're going to go on a little field trip."

Something about the request made Jackson uneasy. He hesitated.

Graves waved a hand. "Come on. I'll have you back in an hour."

Jackson stood up and put on his jacket. He slipped his hand into his pocket, double-checking he had his phone with him in case he needed to give Bailey the distress signal.

As they stepped out of the club, Bear pulled up in his Suburban. A crease in his forehead showed Bear was surprised to see Jackson and Graves leaving. Graves led Jackson not to a black Range Rover, but a Mercedes G63, a boxy SUV that ran for six figures. Behind his back, Jackson made a twirling motion with his index finger, signaling Bear to tail them.

"That's some ride," Jackson said. "Where's the Range Rover?"

"Those grocery getters are for the security team. This one is mine."

"I guess you're getting paid a little more than ten bucks an hour."

Graves grinned as he opened the driver's door. "Door's unlocked," he said.

Jackson walked around to the passenger side and climbed in. Before he had his belt on, Graves tore off.

———

THE BUDDING trees along the two-lane highway were a blurry landscape as Graves and Jackson flew by. Jackson leaned forward to look out the passenger side mirror. They were headed north, away from the safe house and any help beyond Bear. Jackson trusted Bear was following, but he was staying far enough back to remain out of sight. Graves saw Jackson looking and checked his own side mirror.

"Expecting someone?" he asked.

"Just wondering where we're going," Jackson replied. "You going to tell me?"

"You'll see soon enough."

"Will you at least tell me what this is about?" Jackson asked.

Graves gave a slight nod. "You know what I value most in people who work for me? Loyalty."

"That was a little too random and cryptic not to be directed at me."

Graves laughed. "No, the jury is still out on you. But I'm letting you know. That's what I need. To be able to rely on you."

Jackson played his role of a man simply looking for work. "You'll get as much loyalty as my paycheck buys you."

"Surely, a former Ranger such as yourself can appreciate there are other reasons to give your allegiance. Service? Honor?"

Jackson cocked an eyebrow. "Is there honor in tossing out creeps and drunks?"

Grave laughed. They were approaching the town of Franklin when he turned off the highway onto a smaller road. A minute later, he slowed down and pulled over.

"This is it," he said.

Jackson looked around but didn't see much of anything. He wondered if this was a test to see if someone — like Bear — was following them. A pit began to form in Jackson's stomach.

"I don't see anything," Jackson replied.

Graves nodded forward. "Up around the bend there is a mobile home. A guy named Jesse Collins lives there. People call him Nos because he fancies himself a street racer. Really, though, he's just a shitty drug dealer who drives a Honda Civic with every accessory AutoZone stocks."

"Good for him. Why are we here?"

"The same product we offer at the club we distributed out to Mr. Collins, among other local entrepreneurs. For reasons I won't get into, that no longer can be an arrangement we have with him." Graves turned and met Jackson's eyes. "I need you to get our product back."

Jackson read between the lines. "You want me to rip off the drug dealer you sold drugs to?"

"If you want to put it that way, sure."

"Forget it. You don't pay me enough to get my head blown off by some dope pusher."

Graves opened the center console between him and Jackson and retrieved an envelope. "Five hundred dollars cash, as soon as you come back with the product. That's more than a week's pay at your current rate."

Jackson eyed the money. "Why don't you just do it yourself? Save yourself half a grand."

"Because I have you, my shiny new G.I. Joe." He gave a sleazy smile.

Jackson looked forward. He could just see the corner of a building sticking out behind some trees. "Does he live alone?"

"As far as I know."

"Is he armed?"

"That's a safe assumption." Graves reached into his jacket and pulled out a Glock 17. "I wouldn't expect you to go in empty-handed."

"What about something to cover my face?"

"Mr. Collins isn't the type to call the sheriff's office, but if it makes you feel better, I think I still have some N95 masks in the glove compartment there."

Jackson checked and took one. "Your drugs. What are they?"

"They call it Pepsi."

"What does it look like?"

"You saw it at the club."

"Not up close, no. I'm guessing Nos or whoever is in there is selling more than your stuff. I'm going in there exactly one time and you're getting whatever I come out with. If you want it to be the right thing, you should probably tell me what I'm looking for."

"Red tablets with a pair of cherries stamped on them. We sold him a hundred of them two weeks ago. He should still have most of that."

"Any nearby neighbors? Anyone that's going to call the cops if they see or hear something?"

"No one closer than we are here. I'd avoid gunshots, but other than that, you should be fine."

Terrific, Jackson thought. He took the Glock from Graves, slid the magazine out to check that it was loaded, then reloaded and press checked that a round was chambered. He pulled the mask over his face and opened the door.

"Have the car running," he said.

Jackson jogged down the road until he came to the trees that had blocked most of the house. Standing behind a thick trunk, he peered out at the house. It was exactly as Graves described: a single mobile home on a plot of unkempt grass with nothing else around but woods. The long window on the short side of the home facing him had its curtains drawn.

Keeping low, Jackson stalked his way through the tall grass to the front corner. A small staircase made of two by fours led up to a landing in front of the door with a banister along the outside. He ducked underneath the landing. There he found a pile of exposed lumber — likely left over from whoever built the stairs — that had taken a toll from the elements. Stepping around it, he peered up overhead at the landing. The door to the mobile home looked to be made of cheap composite. Jackson's first instinct was to kick it in, going in hard and fast, but a better idea came to him. The door had a small diamond window. Jackson reached down for one of the loose pieces of lumber, grabbed it, and threw it like a javelin at the window. When the glass shattered, he ducked back underneath.

Seconds later, the door flew open.

"What the fuck?" said a voice. Thick footsteps stomped out on to the landing.

In one swift motion, Jackson grabbed the man's legs and pulled them out from underneath him. As the man fell onto his backside, he let out a yelp. Jackson rounded the stair banister, pistol drawn. The man reached for his own gun, but Jackson stomped on his hand. The man hollered again as Jackson kicked the gun off the side of the landing. He placed his knee on the man's chest, pointed the pistol inside the mobile home, waiting a moment for anyone else to come to the door. No one did. Jackson looked down at the man.

"You must be Nos," he said. "Come on and invite me in, we need to have a chat."

Jackson stood up, dragged Nos by the collar of his shirt back inside, and shut the now windowless door behind them. He pulled Nos up to his feet and shoved him onto a sofa in the home's living space. Nos held his hands up to his face, a look of terror on his face.

"What the fuck do you want, man?"

"The shit you're selling."

"I'm not selling noth—"

Jackson took his wrist and twisted it, eliciting a screech from Nos. "We're not playing that game today. The Pepsi. Where is it?"

Nos gave him a confused look. "You want my soda?"

Jackson twisted the wrist harder.

"Argh! In the kitchen! In the kitchen, man!"

"Where?"

"In the cereal box. The Trix."

Jackson let go of his arm. "Sit there and don't move."

Nos obeyed him, cradling his wrist as Jackson moved to the kitchen and started flipping open cupboards until he found the cereal box. When he did, he examined around it first to make sure it wasn't booby-trapped. Then he took it out and dumped the contents into the sink. A half empty cereal bag and a small baggy of red pills fell out. Jackson couldn't count all the pills, but there looked to be about a hundred. He took the baggy and shoved it into his coat pocket before walking back to Nos.

"Turn around, face down on the couch," he ordered.

"Please!" Nos begged.

"Now."

Nos started to tremble as he did what Jackson told him to do. Once he was in position, Jackson took a throw pillow and put it behind Nos' head as if to muffle a forthcoming gunshot. Jackson had no intention of shooting Nos, though, and he knew Glock pistols like the one Graves had given him had a Safe Action System that prevented accidental discharges. His finger off the trigger, he pressed the pistol against the pillow, pointing it at the man's head.

"Listen to me very carefully. This is your retirement party. I don't give a shit what you do, but after today, it isn't selling pills and powder to people. You understand me?"

Nos's sniffles were loud and wet. "Yes! Yes, I understand!"

"I hope you do, for your sake." Jackson took a step back from the couch. "When you hear the door close behind me, count to one hundred and you're not going to so much as turn your head before you do."

A muffled whimper punctuated Nos's reply. "Yes, okay."

Jackson moved to the door, opened it, and left. As he trotted down the ramshackle steps, he looked around, making sure no one had heard nor seen what had just happened. When he got to the road, his eye caught a strange figure along the tree line across the way. He paused for a moment and watched. The figure rose and Jackson saw Bear with a hunting rifle. He was to the right of two large shrubs that hid him from view of Graves in his SUV. Bear gave Jackson a nod. Jackson returned it, and Bear turned and disappeared into the woods.

Thirty seconds later, Jackson was through the tall grass and back to Graves in his G63. Jackson climbed in, shut the door, and tossed the bag of pills onto the dashboard.

"It's done," he said. "Let's go."

Graves' lips curled, his face saying he was impressed. "Not bad." He put the SUV in gear, swung a hard U-turn, and tore back up the road. He tossed the envelope with cash into Jackson's lap. "You earned it."

———

WHEN THEY GOT BACK to the dance club, Graves told Jackson to take the rest of the night off. Jackson did as he was told and, after taking the usual precautions, made his way back to the safe house. A minute after he pulled in, Bear came rumbling down the winding drive behind him. Once parked, Bear climbed out and came over to Jackson, giving him a hearty pat on the shoulder.

"You good, Jacky boy?" he asked.

"I'm good," Jackson replied. "Thanks for watching my back out there."

"No problemo, amigo. I saw the way you took that guy down. Like something out of Wrestlemania." He let out a breathy chortle. "What the hell was that all about, anyway?"

Before Jackson could answer, the front door of the safe house opened and out came Bailey, with Cole close behind. Wilcox hovered in the doorway, the permanent scowl whenever he saw Jackson present on his face.

"What are you doing back so early?" Bailey asked, alarmed. "What happened?"

Bailey and Cole stood shoulder to shoulder, facing Jackson and Bear, a brisk spring breeze blowing between them as birds chattered from the trees along the highway.

"Graves had me run an errand with him," Jackson said.

Bailey's worried look intensified. "An errand? What kind of errand?"

"He had me rip off a drug dealer he sold some pills to."

Bailey raised an eyebrow. "Doesn't he have a bunch of goons for that?"

"He does. Which makes me think this wasn't so simple."

"What do you think it was?"

"I don't know. Maybe some kind of test. To see if I can do what I'm told."

Cole shook her head as she looked down and kicked at a pebble on the driveway. "Let's hope you passed, then."

Jackson acknowledged the comment with a nod. "He seemed pleased. The Pepsi you got off of Liles," he turned to Bailey. "Were they red tablets stamped with a pair of cherries?"

Bailey nodded. "Yeah, how'd you know?"

"That's just what Graves had me take off the drug dealer we went and visited. He told me himself he sold them to the guy. If nothing else, we can link Graves to Liles now."

Bailey drummed her fingers against her thigh. "That's something, at least. But it doesn't make sense. Why bring you in on this?"

"Occam's razor," Jackson offered. "The simplest explanation is usually the correct one. Graves is seeing who he can trust because there's someone he doesn't."

Cole frowned. "But who?"

TWENTY

CODY BUSCH BRACED himself as the side-by-side he was riding shotgun in drove over a downed branch. The back wheels kicked up and over it, shooting him out of his seat. Roscoe, who'd picked him up outside his bedsit, shook his head, embarrassed for the young man.

"Goddamn you're green, boy," he said.

Cody didn't say anything back. Roscoe sort of scared him. He wasn't even sure if Roscoe was the man's first, last, or even just a nickname, and he couldn't bring himself to ask. Cody was new to the crew, having only joined Graves' security team for The Arcady a few months earlier. All in all, it was a pretty easy gig, but he was still getting used to the day-to-day of rural life after leaving the bustling streets of Baltimore.

As Roscoe drove on, Cody wondered where they were headed. To somewhere on the far south side of the resort's property but, in his short time in working for The Arcady, he'd never come out this way. He'd gotten a text from Graves earlier that day saying that the boss wanted a meeting and Roscoe would pick him up. Graves was Cody's boss, so he assumed Graves meant *his* boss, the proprietor of The

Arcady. Cody had heard bits and pieces about the man but had never met him.

Their side-by-side dipped into a sunken field, chasing the setting sun to the horizon. Up ahead were a half dozen more side-by-sides parked in a semicircle. As Cody and Roscoe rolled up, their headlights shined on the mass of people standing at the center. Then Roscoe cut the engine off and the group of people became little more than a shadowy mass.

"C'mon," Roscoe huffed.

They stepped past the vehicles and joined everyone else. The group seemed to be most, if not all, of the security team, only some of whom Cody had met and worked with before. At the head of them were Graves and another man. He was of average build, clean shaven, with slicked back hair. He wore a shirt-jacket underneath a long wool coat and boots that looked like they cost more than what Cody had made in his weeks working at The Arcady.

This must be him. The man in charge of it all.

"'Kay, we're here," Roscoe said.

Graves and the man turned to face the group.

"Good evening," the man said. "I appreciate you all coming out here. I know some of you aren't on shift right now, but we have an urgent matter at hand."

The man fell silent as he scanned the group, eyes stopping on each person's face. Cody wasn't sure if he was supposed to know what the man was talking about. He looked around at the rest of the team and found a handful of others exchanging looks with him. It seemed he wasn't the only one confused.

In the silence, Cody could hear the faintest sound of babbling water. The man turned his back to the men and in the direction it was coming from. He held his hands out to the meadow beyond.

"Do you know where we are? What this is?" he asked.

Again, no one said anything.

"This little stream at my feet here is the source of the South Branch of the Potomac River. Right here, on the grounds of what I have built. You can follow it all the way up to its confluence with the North Branch in West Virginia, then down all the way to our nation's capital." He turned and faced the group once again. "What happens here, at The Arcady, flows down into DC, the most powerful city in the world, and I don't just mean the water at our feet. What happens on these grounds affects and influences more than you could ever imagine, and I will do whatever necessary to protect it."

At that, Graves pulled a pistol from the small of his back and gave it to the man.

The man took it and held it above his head, pointing it to the heavens. "Treason was written into statute for the first time in 1351 by English parliament. In those six hundred-plus years, the offense has always carried the most severe of punishments because it is the most severe of betrayals." He lowered the pistol to his side. "Gentleman, we have a traitor amongst us. Someone that is threatening to undo everything I have built."

Cody felt a wave of fear course through him. Standing on the far edge of the group, he looked at everyone, wondering who the man was talking about. When his gaze came to Roscoe, Cody was surprised to see him sneering back at him.

Before he could process why, a gun shot rang out, followed by an excruciating pain in his left knee. Cody collapsed to the ground, screaming. He looked down at his leg and even in the encroaching darkness, he could see the blood oozing out from what was once a working kneecap. He turned his tear-filled gaze back to the man, bewildered.

"Don't be so surprised, Mr. Busch," the man said. "Like I said, I've gone to great lengths to ensure the integrity of this place. The most powerful weapon has and always will be information. Such as the information that a law enforcement task force has embedded an informant inside my security staff. There's only been one person to recently join us, my dear boy. And that was you."

Cody's mouth hung agape. Nothing made sense, but he couldn't find the words to express it. Informant? Law enforcement? Cody was none of those things. The man was mistaken. But all those thoughts bottlenecked somewhere between Cody's mind and his mouth. In their place, he found only one thing to say.

"No," Cody mumbled.

"Yes," the man countered, his tone and manner mild.

The last thing Cody saw on this earth was the man's cold eyes as he leveled the pistol at his forehead and squeezed the trigger.

TWENTY-ONE

THE THURSDAY AFTER THE BONFIRE, Ainsley and Tessa left Arizona. The transportation Zane had secured for them was riding shotgun alongside a long-haul truck driver named Dex. Dex was thickset with long, silver hair that had waged a losing war with its hairline and had retreated to the back side of his head. The five-day shadow spread across his face was similarly gray.

"If anyone asks, y'all are his kids," Zane had said.

For the most part, Dex seemed alright. He was odd, but otherwise seemed harmless to Ainsley. He had dozens of stories to pass the time and seemed to know every inch of landscape you could see from the interstate. As they crossed into New Mexico, he pointed out the passenger window at a seemingly unremarkable desert landscape.

"You see all that there?" he'd asked. "That all used to be Fort Wingate. It'd been there since just after the Civil War 'til they closed it some thirty years ago. Started out as a fort to keep the natives in their place." He shook his head. "Turns out dope and money worked better than the Army ever did."

Even with her eye swelling to a deep indigo, Ainsley had started to allow herself to enjoy everything again. Zane and what had happened were in the rear view now, and she was bubbly with the prospect of what could be. A part of her worried whoever was waiting in Virginia may not hire her with a shiny black eye, but Zane had said not to worry and that it would clear up before they even got there. He seemed as though he was trying to convince himself as much as her when he said it. Ainsley hated him for failing to take accountability for what he'd done, but didn't dare risk antagonizing him.

Dex slept in his sleeper cab, leaving the two seats for Tessa and Ainsley. They all spent the first night at a truck stop outside Vega, Texas. Though she had been skeptical of the sleeping arrangements at first, Ainsley slept well. Just before dawn, Dex woke her up.

"Sorry to wake ya," he said. "But I gotta hit the head."

Ainsley smiled politely, nodded, and climbed out of her side of the rig. Dex hopped out next and, with the awkward gait of a man that needed to pee, started toward the travel center's rear door.

"Don't let anyone steal my truck now," he called out as he waddled away.

Ainsley climbed back in and shut the door. This early on a spring morning, north Texas was barely above freezing. As she tucked her arms into her hoodie, Tessa turned over in the driver's seat, yawned, and gave Ainsley a good morning grin before peering back into the sleeper cab.

"Where's Dex?" she asked.

Ainsley nodded towards the travel center. "Bathroom."

"Ugh, I've got to pee, too."

"I don't think we should leave the truck alone. Let's wait and we can go when he comes back."

Tessa nodded as she stretched. "And get some grub, too. I'm hungry."

"These places actually have the best breakfast burritos."

Tessa shook her head, giving Ainsley a once over. "Girl, I don't know where you put it all. You don't have an ounce of fat on you."

Ainsley chuckled and felt herself blush.

"I'm jealous. You're going to have guys all over you when we get there."

Ainsley shook her head in disbelief. "You're pretty hot yourself, you know."

"Mmm, not like you, baby doll. And you don't see it. It'll drive the right guy crazy."

Ainsley was quiet for a moment. "Can I ask you something?"

Tessa ran a hand through her hair, working out some knots. "Shoot."

"Why are you so worried about finding a man? Even if it's just us, you heard Zane. We can make more money than we've ever seen before."

"And how do you think we'll do that?"

Ainsley looked at her, confused.

Tessa leaned forward. "Look, baby doll. There are only three things in this world that matter: being pretty, being smart, and being rich. If you don't have any of those, you're shit out of luck. You go through a shitty life until you die. But if you're lucky enough to get one of those three, you have a chance. The bad news for me is I got pretty, which is the only one that comes with a timer on it. That means I got 'til my looks run out to find me one of the other two, and I know we sure as shit aren't on our way to some college or something. Lord knows I wouldn't know what to do there even if we were." She shook her head. "I've got one play. That's the money."

"But even if that's all true, you can make the money yourself."

Tessa shook her head. "Not like someone else. You don't even understand how poor we are. That's what comes with being born in a shithole place like Holbrook or Heber. You're so far down at the bottom, you can't see the top. There are babies being born right now with more money to their name than you or I will make in our entire life. I wasn't lucky enough to be one of those babies. But, if I should have one, *my* baby? I'm going to give my baby that gift. Of being rich.

And a puncher's chance at pretty. Then all they got to do is get smart, and they'll have it made."

Ainsley just looked at her, speechless.

Tessa shrugged. "That's the dream, anyway."

The door to the rig opened behind Ainsley, causing her to jump.

"Mind if I hop back in?" Dex said. "It's cold as balls out here."

"We're going to run in," Tessa said, craning around Ainsely to see Dex. "Use the ladies room and find something to eat. Don't take off without us."

"And miss my payday?" Dex shook his head. "Fat chance of that."

Tessa opened up the driver's side door and disappeared as she hopped down. Ainsley swung her legs out toward her open door and carefully lowered herself down.

"Here, you're doing it all wrong," Dex said. He reached up for her, grabbing her by the hips. "I got ya."

Dex's grasp sent her right back to the riverbed as Zane had grabbed her. She felt her legs go weak. She let go of the rig and hopped down, praying they would catch her. When they did, Ainsley took a deep breath in and exhaled. She turned to find herself in a tight space between Dex and his truck.

"'Scuse me," Ainsley said, her cheeks warming.

Dex's left arm moved up her body and grabbed the step on the rig by Ainsley's head. He leaned against it, coming further into Ainsley's space. He didn't say anything back but bit his lip through a mischievous smile. He was so close now, Ainsley could smell him, a mix of oil and sweat. She stood there, paralyzed.

There's no way this is happening again, she thought. Dex started to slide his right hand up her side when Tessa's voice came from the other side of the truck.

"Ains, let's go. I gotta pee!" she called out.

Dex's shoulder sagged and he let out a breath as if waking up from a spell.

"I better go with her," Ainsley mumbled.

Dex dropped his right arm and Ainsley shimmied sideways out

from underneath him. When she was clear, she jogged around the front of the truck, not stopping when she got to Tessa. She grabbed Tessa's hand mid-stride and continued on toward the travel center.

"What's wrong?" Tessa asked when she caught sight of Ainsley's face.

"Nothing," Ainsley said. "Come on."

She was making a habit of lying about that.

TWENTY-TWO

JACKSON DIDN'T SLEEP MOST of the night, his mind preoccupied with the question of why Graves had used him to rob Jesse Collins. It seemed like Graves had a whole roster of muscle to utilize. What was it about Collins that Graves didn't want to include them?

Bailey had barred anyone from unnecessary excursions from the safe house, and that included runs, Jackson's go-to for burning off pent-up, anxious energy. Instead, just before dawn Jackson stepped out from his bedroom in the basement to use the overhanging deck for pull-ups until his arms were numb. He collapsed into the Adirondack chair just outside his bedroom screen door in a disheveled pile of sweat and workout clothes. The door off the hallway opened and out stepped Bear with two steaming mugs of coffee.

"Heard you out here tryin' to pull the damn house apart with your hands," he said. "Figured this was next."

"Thanks," Jackson replied, taking one of the mugs.

Bear grabbed the Adirondack chair in front of Cole and Bailey's room and dragged it over to Jackson before falling back into it.

"Christ!" he exclaimed. "I hope you're forklift certified to get me out of this fuckin' thing."

Jackson smirked. If anyone had the ability to conjure up a smile from Jackson, a sight rarer than bigfoot, it was Bear.

"I know it might not be any of my business," Bear said, "but I noticed you failed to mention the gun you used in getting to that dealer yesterday."

"Possessing or using any firearms is against my parole," Jackson said. "There are some things Bailey and the task force don't need to know." He turned to Bear. "You good with that?"

Bear raised his mug to his lips. "What gun?"

"And they probably shouldn't know about you providing over-watch, either."

"I don't know what you're talking about. I ran into town to get me a Baconator."

Jackson took another sip of his coffee. He didn't say thanks, and Bear didn't need him to. Their gratitude for each other wasn't something that needed to be spoken to exist.

"You don't really think you're going to get all the way through this thing without needing a boomstick, though, do you?" Bear asked. "One that you and I can't keep from cop lady. I know Graves' type. If they keep asking you to dig, it's only a matter of time before things get ... *kinetic*."

"We'll cross that bridge when we come to it."

The door off the hallway swung open again. This time, it was Bailey who stepped out with a concerned look on her face.

"Don't get your panties in a wad," Bear said. "I'll put the chair back when I'm done with it."

Bailey ignored him. She looked directly at Jackson.

"You need to see this," she said before stepping back in.

Jackson got up out of his chair then gave Bear a lift out of his before following Bailey inside.

"I have Pitts and the Roanoke office waiting on speaker phone," she said before nodding at Bear. "He can't be a part of this."

"The hell I can't," Bear countered.

"He'll be quiet," Jackson offered. "But he listens in."

Bailey shook her head but continued up the stairs without debating it further. She led the two of them into the dining room that had been transformed into a makeshift operations center. Large and elongated with walls on only two sides, the space felt more like a wide hall than a room. A banquette was built into one wall with seating for a half dozen alongside the oak dining table. Around the other three sides of the table were matching chairs. Instead of place settings, the table now held a bank of laptops and other office equipment.

Everyone else in the house was already in the room, either seated or standing along the wall. Bailey nodded at Kavanaugh, reached over and pressed a button on the intercom in the middle of the table.

"John, I have Jackson with me now," Bailey said. "I'm showing him everything."

She moved to stand over a laptop on the table. Jackson joined her. The screen showed an aerial satellite image of what looked like a grassy meadow cutting through a sea of trees. One end of the meadow was speckled with a bunch of dark spots.

"This is aerial satellite imagery taken over the resort yesterday evening," Bailey explained. "It's in the far southwest corner of the property owned by the resort. Near as we can tell, there's no obvious reason for anyone to be out this way. There's no buildings or recreational facilities like the pools or golf course." She punched a key twice and the image on the screen zoomed in. "Here you can see what looks to be a half dozen vehicles surrounded by people. You can tell by their cross section relative to the overhead angle that they're standing."

"They're having some sort of meeting in a field," Jackson said.

"Now, watch. These images are all taken sixty seconds apart from one another."

She poked at the laptop several more times and the images started to play like a flip book. The dots — the people — came together as a group and stayed that way for a moment before most of them headed toward the vehicles and left. Jackson counted five vehicles driving off, leaving just one behind.

"Look here," Bailey said.

She pointed to a spot in the field away from the last remaining vehicle. It was larger than the other dots. As Jackson studied it closer, he realized it was a person sprawled out on the ground.

"One of them is down," he said.

"Yes. Now, keep watching." She punched at the laptop again. "The downed person is carried to the last vehicle and driven off."

"So, one of them got hurt?"

Bailey shook her head. "Not likely. If someone had a medical emergency, why does everybody else leave? Why are only a couple left behind like they're cleaning up a mess?"

"They killed someone."

Bailey nodded.

"Do we know who?"

Bailey reached over to a mouse connected to the laptop and brought up another group of images. "We tracked that vehicle to a building in the northern part of the property. Several minutes later, what appears to be a dark-colored van leaves the building and heads out the front gates of the resort. Only, it heads west on Highway 250, away from the airport and Belle Bottoms and everything else we've connected to the resort."

"And goes where?"

"They cross the state line into West Virginia and drive into the Monongahela National Forest, continuing on before stopping at a remote picnic area here. Then, a few minutes later, they turn back and return to the resort."

"They dumped the body."

"That's what we thought, as well," Pitts said through the intercom. "So, we put in a call. This is where it came in handy to have a federal agency attached to this task force. Forest Service Rangers searched the picnic area early this morning and found a body and were able to ID him. His name was Cody Busch. He'd been shot twice: once in the knee and once execution-style in the head."

Bailey used the mouse again and brought up a mugshot of a young man with boyish features and sandy blond hair cut short. "Twenty-five years old, born in Baltimore. Last address we have for him is in Dundalk, Maryland from a few years ago."

"He has a list of priors that read like a less-accomplished version of the man you met, Nick Graves," Pitts added. "Our theory is he worked in some capacity similar to the men you've seen with Graves. Most likely some sort of muscle for one or all of the places connected to this resort."

"Those other people in the field," Jackson said. "That must have been Graves and his men. Or, at least, some of them."

"We agree. Whether Graves did it himself or not, we think he's behind Busch's murder."

"Okay. So, pick him up. You said it yourself you don't think Graves is running this thing. Flip him for the bigger fish up the food chain."

Bailey leaned toward the intercom. "John, what does the Assistant US Attorney, Weisz, think of all this?"

"Communication with the AUSA has been intermittent as he's been out of the office. It turns out Mr. Weisz is planning a run at the State AG office in four years and has been working on a grassroots project toward that goal. We haven't updated him recently, but I can tell you this is nowhere near enough to threaten Graves with charges. Plus, remember, Weisz is concerned this all a fishing expedition on our part."

Bear made a jerking motion with his hand from across the room.

"What do you want me to do?" Jackson asked. "Start looking for harder evidence tying Graves to Busch's murder?"

"Actually, given this latest development, we're thinking of pulling you."

"Pulling me? Why?"

"If Graves and/or someone is taking out members of his team that are seen as a liability, it's far too dangerous to continue this."

"Hold on, there's a dozen reasons he could kill Busch that wouldn't change what we're doing here. Maybe they caught him skimming money or drugs. Maybe something happened with him and one of their clients. Hell, we could be wrong altogether and he's a trafficking victim himself that got caught trying to make a break for it. We don't know what we don't know."

"That's just it. There are too many unknown variables. We have to reevaluate if we can continue this."

"Shouldn't that be my call? After all, it'd be *my* life on the line."

"Actually, it's my call," Bailey's tone sharp. "You were placed in *my* guardianship. If something happens to you, it's on me."

Jackson turned and looked at Bailey. "We're both adults here. I may technically be in your custody, but I'm not some little kid that needs looking after."

"That's right, you're a source. And I'm not losing another one."

"So, what? We just pack up and go home? Pitts just said it himself. You don't have enough to bring to the US Attorney's Office. What about everything you said to me when you came to my place and got me involved in all this? None of that has changed. There will be another Kristal Hardy if no one does something about it. And another one and *another* one. You're worried about what could happen if we keep going. But what about what *will* happen if we don't?"

Bailey crossed her arms in frustration. She looked at Cole, sitting across the table. Cole didn't say anything, but Jackson saw it in her eyes that she was conceding his point.

"John?" Bailey asked, looking for a final ruling.

There was a brief pause. "It's your call, Jen. I have you running point on the safe house team and you have a better understanding of what he'd be risking than we do here in Roanoke."

Bailey looked around the room again. No one said anything. Even

Jackson acknowledged this was ultimately her call. He locked eyes with her, waiting for a decision.

"Jen? You still there?" Pitts asked through the intercom.

"He's waiting," Jackson said. "Make the call."

Bailey didn't take her eyes off of Jackson as she cleared her throat and answered Pitts. "We're continuing as planned for now. We'll advise you if anything changes."

TWENTY-THREE

THIRTY-SIX HOURS after Busch's death, Graves found himself waiting outside his boss' office in the Lustschloss. The opulent chateau situated atop the highest hill on The Arcady's property and overlooked the rest of the resort. In a playland that catered to the ultra-wealthy and elite, it was a pleasure palace that embodied those two words in every way.

Graves sat in an upholstered chair worth more than the Canali jacket he had on, looking back at his boss's ancestors staring down at him in oil-painting form. It was one of the few places that made him uneasy. Each man had built upon the previous legacy and fortune and had bolstered their resolve to hold on to it. Graves could dispatch a life and not think twice about it, but his boss could erase your whole lineage from history. In his time working for the man, Graves had relearned what it meant to be considered dangerous.

Finally, one of the large oak doors to his boss' office opened and a man in a black suit ushered him in.

"He'll see you now," the man said.

Graves rose and walked into the office that was an ocean of stained wood and gold accents. An exquisite executive desk and upholstered chair sat in the center of the room with floor-to-ceiling bookshelves lining three of the four walls. The fourth wall had large picture windows that looked out at the mountains to the east. Opposite the desk, between it and the windows, were two armchairs bookending a small café table. Graves' boss was at the far side of the room, looking out the large windows.

"Good morning, sir," Graves said. "You requested to see me in person?"

His boss turned and looked at the doors to the office, waiting for the suited gentleman to close them before he spoke. "Your man's body was discovered yesterday morning by forest service rangers."

"Yes sir, I'm aware."

"I told you to make him disappear and you couldn't even keep him hidden twenty-four hours. I've had socks go missing longer than that traitor's body did."

"I don't know what to say. They must've been looking for it. My men told me they marched him fifty yards into the woods and dropped him down to the creek bed there. Only way you would find him there is if you were looking for him."

"And why do you suppose they were looking for him?"

"He was cooperating with authorities, wasn't he? Maybe they expected him to check in or something. But when he didn't?" Graves shrugged.

"But how did they know where precisely to look?"

"I don't know, sir. Didn't your source say a task force has us under surveillance? Maybe they tracked the van. My men know to look for a tail, but it's possible they missed it. Or maybe there was aerial surveillance or something."

Graves' boss looked him up and down once before moving to his desk. "You have an awful lot of 'maybes' and 'I-don't-knows'. I didn't realize that's what I was getting for how much I pay you."

Graves licked his teeth inside his lips. He resented the man for such an unfair assertion, but he knew better than to tell him directly. "I apologize, sir. I'll get you answers."

"I don't want you to be sorry, I want you to fix this damn mess. All of it."

"Well, Busch is neutralized, so he won't be giving them any more information. And if they had anything concrete connecting us to him, they'd be at our front gate right now.

"What if they can prove he worked for you here?"

"Being employed isn't a crime. Busch worked for us and was tragically killed fifty miles away. Like I said, if they had a connection back to us we'd know about it by now. Either from your source inside or law enforcement directly."

Graves' boss lowered himself into the executive chair behind his desk. "So, in your mind, it's handled then."

"Not *in my mind*. It is handled, *period*. But dealing with Busch did put me down a man, and I've told you before I already don't have enough manpower."

"You want to bring someone else on?"

"Right now, I have thirteen men and myself. That's thirteen men to—"

Graves' boss rolled his eyes.

"*Thirteen men* to cover four hundred acres here and another twenty acres at the airport."

"They'd be able to cover more if you didn't have them taking field trips to that strip club."

Graves didn't have a good response to that.

His boss sighed. "I assume, then, you have someone in mind."

Graves nodded.

"And you can vouch for this man? Not that your word means much after this recent mess."

"He's an ex-Army ranger. Quiet, loner, and he's proven he can follow orders. You asked me to tie up loose ends selling extra Pepsi. I used him for a part of that. He can handle himself."

"I don't have to remind you that not everyone would approve of the way we operate here. Being helpful taking out one of your dope-slinging connections is far different than being okay with what we do here."

Graves took a beat, parsing what he wanted to say. "Nothing that I've seen says he isn't ready for this. And if I'm wrong, then we handle it. Just like we did with Busch."

"No, Mr. Graves. Busch became a problem because he slipped past *you*. The same with that mouth-breather, Sugar Bee, I had to put down. That's two strikes. We play baseball rules here. So, if there's a third ..."

"I get it."

Graves' boss leaned forward and folded his hands on his desk. "I want to make sure that you understand, because I'm not saying it out of conjecture. If this next man — this man you say you can vouch for — becomes another problem that you brought in here, it will be two bodies that we're dumping somewhere."

Graves nodded. "I understand."

"I hope that you do." Graves' boss sat back in his chair. "Go get your man, then."

TWENTY-FOUR

AS THEY DROVE through Texas and on into Oklahoma, Ainsley found a way to put Tessa between her and Dex at all times. She'd seen the look in Dex's eye as he cornered her, and she knew what he wanted. It was the same thing Zane wanted down at the river bed: *her*.

When they pulled into a truck stop just over the Arkansas state line for the night, Ainsley insisted they find a motel for just the two of them.

"We only have two more nights until we're there," she'd said to Tessa. "We can spring for it."

Tessa just shook her head. "The truck is fine. And we know it doesn't have roaches. God knows what we'd find in one of those dumps."

Dex, for his part, was nothing but the happy-go-lucky truck driver he had been before the incident. He was charming even, making Tessa giggle with his corny jokes, and not once did he eye Ainsley the way he had at the truck stop. By the time they were cruising through Memphis, Ainsley started to second-guess if she had overreacted to the whole thing, influenced by what had happened with Zane.

When they stopped again in Lebanon, Tennessee, just outside Nashville, Ainsley woke up in the passenger seat feeling spirited. Today was the day they'd make it to Virginia, and her new life would begin. Zane and her mother and all her problems were back in Arizona, a world away. As far as they'd come, it might as well be a different planet. Gone was the endless desert with its arid steppes and cliffs. In its place was lush, verdant forest in spring's full bloom. The trees covered everything, including the mountains, looking like waves of foliage rolling across the earth. This would be the backdrop to her new life.

As she watched the rising sun shine through the arches of the McDonald's sign down the road, she thought about the other Ainsleys in the other multiverses. Had she been on the right path all along and just not known it? Or by leaving her grandma's house and finding Tessa, had she changed the outcome of her own world? Mr. Tucker in history class had talked about Manifest Destiny; Americans' belief that they were destined to expand their budding world out west, taking control of their, well, destiny. Maybe she was doing the same thing, just in the opposite direction. She smiled at the thought of her being some sort of pioneer.

Tessa rolled over, saw the smile on her face, and chuckled. "What's got you so giddy this morning, girl?"

"Nothing," Ainsley said. "Just, you know. We're almost there. It's a fresh start."

"Almost." Tessa took her arms and stretched them out in front of her. When she did, she lowered her head and sniffed herself quickly. "Ugh, but we stink. We can't roll in there looking like rat shit."

"Don't look at me. I said we should've gotten a motel."

Tessa punched her playfully. "There are other ways to clean up, your highness. They just might not be up to your standards."

Ainsley flipped her off and the two of them laughed. The commotion caused Dex, asleep in his quarters, to turn over and right himself.

"Mornin'," he said with a big yawn. "What's so funny?"

"Nothing," Tessa answered, holding a grin as she looked at Ainsley.

"Welp, then let's get some grub. You mind lettin' me out there, Tessa? I gotta hit the head. Probably should wash up, too."

"Yeah, we were just saying we could use a shower."

"They got some in the truck stop here."

"Ains and I better grab one."

"I'll do the same. Here, I can book us each one on the app."

Dex pulled his phone out of his pocket and started punching at it with one thumb as he squinted at the screen. They'd stopped at the same brand of travel stop every night, proving Dex was a frequent patron and a proud supporter of the chain. After a couple more minutes negotiating with his phone, he looked up at the two girls.

"Alrighty, all booked," he said. "We're lucky, they're available right away. That don' usually happen, especially outside a big city like here."

Ainsley followed Tessa out the driver's side of the truck with Dex right behind. The three of them crossed the vast parking lot to the travel center. Inside, Dex led them down a corridor toward the back. It was lined with a half-dozen doors, each with a number pad incorporated into the handle on them. Dex followed the signs on each door.

"Let's see here. Numbers four, five, and six."

Once he found the correct stalls, he opened his phone and punched in a code on each handle. One by one, the doors beeped. When he'd unlocked all three, he stepped back and gestured toward them with his hand.

"Open sesame," he said with a terrible impression of Ali Baba. "Take your pick."

Tessa grabbed a towel from the shelf in the corridor and slipped into the shower nearest her. "Thanks," she said with a smile to Dex as she stepped in.

"No problemo," Dex said, returning the smile.

Ainsley followed suit, and took the next one. She shut the door behind her. The shower room was a full-service bathroom, with a good-sized vanity, toilet, and a walk-in style shower beyond it. The floor walls were lined with uninspired, institutional white tile and the whole space smelled of chemical cleaners. Ainsley took off her clothes, then walked over and started the shower. The water turned warm faster than she expected and she stepped in. Enveloping herself, she closed her eyes and let the flowing water relax her when she heard the electronic beep from the number pad on the door. A final, louder ding signaled the door had unlocked, and the latch opened. Ainsley peered out from behind the shower's wall. No amount of hot water could suppress the chill that coursed through her.

Dex stepped through the door and shut it behind him. Gone was his devil-may-care demeanor and in its place was the look she'd seen the other morning. There was a zeal behind his eyes. A desire to have what was now in front of him.

"You 'n' I been dancin' 'round each other the last coupla days," he said with a menacing grin. "I think it's about time we did somethin' 'bout that."

Ainsley scurried to cover herself up. "What are you doing?" she heard herself say even though, deep down, she knew what this was. "Why are you in here?"

"C'mon now. I see the way you been lookin' at me."

"I don't know what you are talking about. Please, just go!"

Dex took off his shirt. He was paunchier than his clothes let on, with thick chest hair and sporadic tattoos across his torso. "You really want me to go?"

"Yes! Please! I won't tell anyone about this. Just go!"

He unbuckled his belt and pants before bending down and

picking up Ainsley's shirt, discarded on the floor. "That's alright. Truth be told, I was hopin' you'd have a little fight in ya."

Ainsley went to scream, but in a split second Dex was grabbing her, moving with a predatory ferociousness Ainsley hadn't seen in him. Before she could comprehend what was happening, he'd pinned her face-first against the bathroom wall, wrapping her shirt around her mouth to stifle her screams. Ainsley tried everything. First, pushing against the wall back against Dex, then reaching frantically behind her, trying to grab ahold of anything that might get him off her. She dug her nails into his legs.

"Goddamn bitch!" Dex growled.

He used the shirt to slam her head against the tiled wall. Ainsley's world became distant and blurry. She stopped fighting. She felt Dex enter her. With each thrust, her hip smashed against the steel safety railing between her and the wall, making everything all the more painful.

It seemed to go on forever.

Her dizziness formed stars in her vision and her mind transported her back to the night at the riverbed. The constellations spiraling overhead. And then Zane looking down at her. No, it was Dex. No, she wasn't sure. It was an amoebic darkness that she couldn't escape. She felt herself slowly become buried in the riverbed, unable to move, unable to fight. And just as the darkness seemed to take hold, everything became blindingly bright. There were no stars, only the harsh, fluorescent light overhead. It wasn't the sand of the riverbed washing over her, but the shower water. She was on her back on the shower floor.

Dex stood at her feet, looking down at her as he zipped up the fly on his pants. The fervor in his eyes was gone. In its place was a pity. Ainsley hoped it was for himself — some sort of instant contrition — but she knew it was for her. The pitiful thing that couldn't stop him.

"Clean yourself up," he said. "We got to get on the road."

He bent down and instinctively Ainsley retreated deeper into the shower, placing her back in the corner and her arms and legs as a barrier between Dex and her body. Dex just shook his head as he continued to reach down for Ainsley's shirt, now drenched. He balled it up, squeezing the water out of it, then hung it over the bar in the shower.

Ainsley didn't move until she heard the door open and close, and even then, she only sunk her head into arms and began to sob. When she opened her eyes, she saw a single stream of blood, taken by the water around it, circling the shower drain.

TWENTY-FIVE

AINSLEY WAS COMPLETELY numb as she put herself together and emerged from the bathroom. Numb on the outside and even more numb inside. She'd used wadded up paper towels to stem the bleeding, put her underwear, socks, and pants back on, then held her shirt under the hand dryer. She thought she was holding herself together reasonably well until she saw the smudged blood stain just below the American Eagle logo emblazoned across the chest. In a moment, the entire ordeal came rushing back and Ainsley barely made it to the sink before being sick.

Reentering the shopping area of the travel center, she felt like she was sleepwalking; a zombie roaming the earth. Sounds were muted, thoughts were foggy, and it felt like everyone was looking at her, knowing what had just happened. There were looks of pity and disgust on their faces. Was that real, or was she only imagining it? How could they know?

She hadn't been able to fully dry her shirt, so she yanked a gift shop sweatshirt inscribed with the phrase 'Hey Y'all' over the Tennessee state flag off a rack. She didn't know how much it cost and she didn't hear the clerk when he told her at the counter. She reached into her jeans pocket, produced a fistful of money, and left it to the man to make sense of the mess. When he did and gave her the change, she took it and the sweatshirt and skulked out to the truck.

Tessa was leaning against the cab smoking a cigarette, but when she saw Ainsley, she snuffed out the cigarette and trotted over to her.

"Ains!" she exclaimed. "What the hell happened to you?"

Ainsley twitched a finger at Dex's semi. "He ... he ..."

She didn't need to say anymore. Tessa's shoulders dropped as she reached out and squeezed both of Ainsley's arms gently.

"Oh, baby girl," she said. "I'm so sorry."

Ainsley tried to talk to her, but the words came out in fragments. "We need to ... I can't ... you ..."

Tessa looked back at the truck and then again to Ainsley, looking as though she were placed between two impossible decisions. Something in Ainsley's mind saw this and hated her for thinking it was even up for debate. *Fuck him,* a little voice somewhere deep within said. *We're almost there. We don't need him. We'll find a way. Please don't make me face him.*

But Tessa only said one of those things to her. "We're almost there, honey. Do you think ... do you think you can hang on? Just a little longer?"

Ainsley's face was expressionless, but inside Tessa's indifference to what had just happened cut straight through the numbness she'd felt. How could she choose herself — *him* — over them? Yes, they were desperate, but where was the line? And when had they crossed it?

"Come on," Tessa said. "It's just a few more hours. I'll be with you the whole time. Let's just ... get through this, okay?"

When Ainsley still didn't say anything, Tessa put an arm around her and ushered her back to the truck. Inside, Ainsley was screaming. *No! Don't make me go back!* But still she felt herself lumber forward, a passenger in her own body. The zombie, still roaming.

Tessa took her around to the passenger side and climbed in before turning back and helping Ainsley up. She buckled her in, then reached across her for the door and shut it. As she did, Ainsley stared straight ahead, not daring to make eye contact with Dex. Dex gave the two of them a wary look.

"She gonna be a problem?" Dex asked. "I don' need no fuckin' problems."

"She's good," Tessa said. "We're good."

Dex shook his head but turned the ignition anyway and the truck rumbled to life. When it did, Ainsley started to shake. Tessa, feeling it, reached over and embraced her with one arm and held her trembling hands in the other. When that didn't ease the tremors, Tessa reached over into her bag and grab a small pouch. From it, she produced a pair of pills.

"Here," she said to Ainsley quietly. "I scored some Benzos for the trip before we left. Take a couple, they'll help you relax."

Ainsley was too shell-shocked to question Tessa. She took the pills with the Dr. Pepper she'd been drinking the night before and sat back. Soon enough, the numbness returned. This time, though, it was more potent. Chemically-induced.

As they headed down the interstate, Ainsley closed her eyes and drifted off.

———

A GENTLE JOSTLING WOKE AINSLEY. It felt like being adrift on a dark sea, only conscious of the lapping waves. But when she opened her eyes, Ainsley didn't see water; she saw a sea of trees.

"There you are," Tessa said with a smile as she leaned over from the center of the truck's cab. "Wake up, baby doll."

Ainsley squinted, trying to comprehend her surroundings. Woodlands crept up the faces of ragged mountains in the distance. She looked to her right and saw a large warehouse building with a second smaller and fancier building next to it, almost like a large house. It came to her then that she was still in Dex's truck and dared not look his way, but out of the corner of her eye she could see a long, wide strip of pavement that looked as if a runway had been dropped in the middle of a field.

"Where are we?" Ainsley asked.

"The airport for the place," Tessa said.

"Wait, we're going on an airplane?"

"No, this is apparently as far as Dex takes us." Tessa took Ainsley's face in her hand and gently turned it toward her. "You don't have to deal with him anymore."

Ainsley worked up the courage to look past Tessa and was relieved to see only the empty driver's chair. "So, what happens now?"

Tessa's smiled widened. "We wait here. The place is coming to get us."

It didn't feel real to Ainsley. Had they really made it? She'd just been living in the absolute worst nightmare. Could it really end that quickly? A part of her wanted to ask Tessa if they should tell whoever was coming to get them about Dex, but Ainsley decided not to. They'd come this far, and she didn't want to risk anything jeopardizing that. Just getting away from him would be enough.

Five minutes later, a black Sprinter van rolled up next to the truck and out stepped two men in slacks and black polos with wraparound sunglasses. They looked up at the cab of the truck expectantly. Seeing this, Tessa shook Ainsley with excitement.

"Are you ready?" she asked, her enthusiasm infectious.

Ainsley opened the door to the truck and climbed down. As she did, one of the men opened the side door to the van. As she headed towards the van, movement caught her peripheral vision and Ainsely saw Dex at the back of the truck. A chill, sharp and piercing like an icicle, stabbed her chest. But Dex didn't so much as look at her. He stepped toward another man and the two of them began hooking a large hose up from the tank on Dex's truck to a port in the pavement below.

Tessa put an arm around Ainsley's back, causing her to jump.

"Forget about him," Tessa said. "Come on, let's go."

The two of them climbed into the back of the van with their belongings, the door shutting behind them. The two men in sunglasses climbed into the two front seats and together the foursome took off.

Ainsley watched out the window as they sped across the open lot and over to an adjoining road. A gate opened and they passed through it before turning on to a rural highway. Trees like Ainsley had never seen before hugged the sides of the road as it climbed gently up the sloping hillside. They were on the highway for no more than a couple minutes before they slowed and took a right onto a small drive. Across it was a bi-folding gate made of large oaken planks and framed by black metal that joined the large stone pillars on each side. The van crept forward, and the two leaves of the gate swung open, revealing the drive ahead.

Tessa leaned into Ainsley. Her voice was little more than a whisper, but Ainsley could still hear the excitement behind it.

"Welcome to your new life, baby girl."

TWENTY-SIX

JACKSON DIDN'T SEE Graves for three days following their little field trip.

He started to wonder if whatever had happened in that field in Happyland later that day had forced Graves to distance himself. Still, he stuck to his routine and went to work every day. No one there behaved as if anything had changed. It was still business as usual.

Bear stopped visiting the club, opting instead to leave before dawn every morning and use the cover of darkness to post up with his rifle in a hunting blind on the wooded mountainside that overlooked the front of the club.

"No one's taking you for another joy ride without our expressed permission," he'd told Jackson.

As Jackson pulled into the lot outside Belle Bottoms Sunday afternoon, Graves was leaning against the front of his G63. He waited for Jackson to park and step out of his truck before acknowledging him. When Jackson gave him a curt nod, Graves gestured for Jackson to join him.

Graves was halfway through a cigarette, but reached into his suit pocket, fetched a pack, and poked another out. Instead of lighting it, he offered it to Jackson. Jackson simply looked at it and shook his head.

"Those things will kill you, you know," he said.

"Lots of shit in this world will kill you," Graves countered. "Smart money will be one of the things doing me in long before these little guys do."

Jackson noticed Graves' aura was noticeably darker today. He seemed less smarmy and more morose. It made Jackson uneasy.

"So, you've done good here the last couple weeks," Graves said. "Are you still serious about making more money?"

"Why? Do you have another dirtbag drug dealer to rip off?"

Graves flashed a small grin. "No, no more of that. I've got a new gig for you. A permanent one if you want it. Let's call it a promotion."

"To what? Strip club manager?"

Graves shook his head. "Not here. Another place a short drive over the state line."

"In Virginia." Jackson felt goosebumps form on his skin. "Same thing? Bouncing?"

"Not specifically, but the same idea. Making sure things go the way they're supposed to."

Jackson felt his pace quicken with the prospect he was close to getting into the resort. "How much?"

Graves pursed his lips. "I can start you off at two grand a week."

Jackson snorted. "Bullshit. That's more than double I've made anywhere."

Graves shook his head. "No bullshit."

Jackson shook his head. "What's the catch?"

"The catch is this isn't tossing drunks out of a titty bar. You'll need to do *everything* asked of you and not a *single* thing more or less. You have to be a cog in a machine. A well-paid cog, but a cog all the same. No asking questions, no deciding to do things your way."

Jackson felt his heart rate quicken. He had to be talking about Happyland. Had whatever happened with Cody Busch spurred this opportunity, or was this unconnected?

In the end, it didn't matter as long as he was getting a way inside.

He pretended to think it over for a moment. "Alright, I'm in."

"Good." Graves dropped the cigarette and stamped it under his shoe. "Then it's time to take another ride."

As he headed for the other side of Graves' SUV, Jackson looked across the road to the spot on the mountain on which he knew Bear was set up. He couldn't see him, but he knew he was watching. Jackson dropped his hand down low, out of sight of Graves, and gave a sharp wave, telling Bear to stand down.

He climbed into the passenger seat. Graves reached across him, opened the glove box, and produced a dark cloth bag.

"Put this on, please," Graves said to Jackson, gesturing to his head.

Jackson hesitated.

"As I said, you'll need to do everything asked of you."

Jackson took the hood and put it on. It completely blacked out his vision. He heard the SUV engine roar to life as Graves put it in gear and headed out. Jackson closed his eyes and visualized where they were heading. He felt them turn left out of the parking lot. They were headed south, back toward the resort, the airfield, and the safe house. He started to count the minutes in his head. One ... two ... then ten, then twenty. At twenty-three minutes, they slowed and turned right. It was almost certainly Highway 250, still on course to all three places. Another seven minutes ticked by and Jackson knew they'd already gone past the turn for the airfield and the safe house. Then they slowed again and made another right. When the SUV didn't rev back up to highway speeds, Jackson figured they'd turned on to the drive to Happyland. The road wound around lazy bends and Jackson finally lost track of where they were. Still, he kept the clock running in his head.

Three minutes later, they came to a stop. Graves threw the SUV into park, killed the engine, and got out. Jackson waited. A moment later, his door opened. The way the sound echoed told Jackson they were inside somewhere, but a rush of cool, mountain air told him it wasn't fully enclosed.

"Here, step out," Graves said next to him.

Feeling his way, Jackson swung his feet out and let himself drop from the passenger seat. His boots hit hard ground and he could tell they were on an artificial surface.

"Last chance," Graves said. "You can still back out. But if I take the hood off, you're in."

"Then I'm in."

A hand grabbed the hood from the top of Jackson's head and yanked it off. Graves was standing in front of him, silhouetted by natural daylight coming in from beside them. Graves nodded in its direction.

"Go ahead," he said. "Take a look."

Jackson turned and could see now that they'd pulled into some sort of large garage or warehouse. A fleet of vehicles ranging from vans to sedans to the Range Rovers he'd seen Graves and his men drive were parked neatly along one side, while a variety of recreational vehicles — mostly side-by-sides and other all-terrain-vehicles — were parked along the other. In the middle was a large, open bay door.

As he walked out to the opening, a picturesque panorama came into view. Timber frame buildings overlooked large, manicured lawns dotted by the occasional tree. Roads meandered around them, connecting everything together. Just from where he was standing, Jackson could make out a golf course, a complex of swimming pools, and what looked to be horse stables. He'd seen almost all of this from satellite images taken overhead, but they didn't do it justice. The resort was a hidden piece of rustic Americana carved right into the heart of the Appalachian Mountains.

Graves came up beside Jackson.

"Welcome to The Arcady," he said.

PART FOUR
HUNTERS

"I don't think anyone can be more of a predator than a human being." —Robert Rodriguez

TWENTY-SEVEN

GRAVES HELD his hand out to Jackson. "Your phone, please," he said.

Jackson hesitated.

Graves raised an eyebrow. "If I'm going to have to reiterate the 'do-as-I-say' line every time I ask you to do something, this isn't going to work."

Jackson pulled out his phone and handed it over. Graves promptly dropped it on the ground and gave it a hearty stomp with his boot.

"What the hell did you do that for?" Jackson asked.

Graves reached into the breast pocket of his jacket and pulled out a new phone. "Here," he said. "This is your phone now. Your first perk of your new employment."

"I paid half a grand for that one you just smashed."

"If it's a matter of money, I'll have you reimbursed on your first paycheck this week."

Jackson knew it wasn't a matter of money, but he didn't say so.

"This way," Graves continued. "We know how to reach you. And we know where you are at all times."

Frustration welled in Jackson's chest. Graves was sabotaging everything he'd worked out to communicate with Bailey and the safe house. He couldn't decide if Graves was already on to him or not. "If you wanted the address of the motel I'm staying at, you could've just asked."

"Oh, you'll be staying here now. You have your own living quarters with a kitchen, bed, and everything."

Further disrupting my connection with the Task Force. This is what they want. To alienate and isolate people. Graves must've read it all on Jackson's face because he addressed it directly.

"What did you think was going to happen?" he asked. "You were going to commute to work every day with a bag over your head?"

"You still could've told me upfront. What about my stuff?"

"There will be time to get your things. For now, you can find whatever you need here at The Arcady."

Jackson tried to think of another reason to leave. "I'm paying by the week over there. If I don't keep up the payments, they'll clear my room out and throw my stuff away. The lady at the front desk told me as much."

Graves gave him a dismissive wave. "Then we'll handle it all before it comes to that. But your attention should be here now."

Jackson conceded, looking around again. "So what exactly is this place?"

"Exactly what it looks like: a rural retreat for high-end clientèle. Guests are by invite only, handed out by our owner."

Jackson took his shot. "Who is...?"

Graves smiled at him as if he were a puppy shamelessly asking for a treat. "In due time, Mr. Clay. As I was saying, we are by invite only here. We have ten suites in the main manor ranging from two to five bedrooms."

"People bring their families?"

"Often, yes. We're split about half and half usually. Full families and couples, or just singles. Your job will be to ensure their safety and privacy. You'll be expected to be discrete but effective."

"What exactly do they need protecting from?"

"Guests here pay a lot of money to enjoy our refined experience in privacy. Your job is to ensure that happens."

"I can't possibly be expected to watch out for ten different groups."

Graves flashed the same smile. "Of course not. You are part of a team. A little over a dozen personnel right now. Together, you are responsible for keeping the entire grounds here, as well as the private airport we use, from being compromised."

"I can do that. How long am I sequestered here?"

Graves' smile widened. "You're not sequestered, Mr. Clay. You're *employed*."

"Still, people in my life are going to wonder where I am."

At that, Graves raised his eyebrows. "Who exactly will be wondering? I've done my homework on you. Your mother, father, and ex-wife are all gone. You have no siblings, or any other relatives, for that matter."

Jackson felt a flash of anger at the casual mention of Nat, and it took everything in him to suppress it. "I have a girl I'm seeing."

"Ah, well good for you. Luckily, that little black thing I gave you is a phone. It sends messages and everything. It might even make a phone call."

"Messages you'll be reading."

"Not unless you give us a reason to. We're not paranoid, Mr. Clay. We're diligent. If you want to text some random girl and it doesn't interfere with your work here, that's your business."

Jackson decided to quit while he was ahead. "Fair enough. When do I get started?"

"Tomorrow. I'll take you to your living quarters now and you'll have the rest of the day to familiarize yourself with the place. We'll begin at sunup. I'll introduce you to your training officer and he'll show you the ropes."

Jackson looked over the grounds of the resort again, processing everything Graves had just told him. The man had him in a precarious spot. He'd figured all this time the hardest part would be finding a way in. Now he'd done that, getting back out looked as though it was going to be much harder.

Graves tapped his hand against his leg. "Whenever you're ready, Mr. Clay," he said.

Jackson started back for the SUV. "Let's go," he replied.

———

AS EVENING CAME, Jackson settled into the studio-style suite he'd been assigned to. Someone at the resort had already taken the liberty of stocking the refrigerator and pantry with some staple items — coffee, rice, pasta, canned goods — as well as an initial wardrobe. Someone had sized him up well because even the black suit with a white button-down shirt fit perfectly.

Now he was left to decide what to do next. Graves had brought him here with next to nothing. Even worse, he no longer had the phone Bailey had given him with all the contacts in it. All he had was this new one he'd been given, and who knows to what ends its usage was being monitored.

Jackson sat on the edge of his twin bed, eyeing the phone on the nightstand, trying to decide whether or not he could trust it. Even if he wanted to reach out, he hadn't committed Bailey's number to memory. In fact, he'd only memorized three phone numbers in his life: his house phone growing up, Nat's cell phone, and Bear's.

Bear. He tried to think of another play, but none came to him. Whatever message he sent to Bear would have to be coded and even then, it'd be extremely risky. But he had to try.

Jackson reached for the phone and started punching away.

———

IT'D BEEN four hours and thirty-nine minutes since Graves drove Jackson away with a hood draped over his head and Bear's worry was growing by the minute. Truthfully, he wanted to put a 450 Bushmaster round through the engine block of that god awful Mercedes the second Jackson and Graves headed toward it, but Jackson had waved him off. Now, with each passing minute, Bear regretted more and more having yielded to him.

Was it time to let the team at the safe house know? Jackson may be in a risky spot, but their overreaction could only make things worse.

He was mulling all this over, laying prone behind two boulders on the mountainside overlooking Belle Bottoms when his phone buzzed in his pocket. He took it out and checked it. An unknown number had sent him a text message. Bear opened it.

Hey babe, it's me. I got a new gig at work, I'm going to be away for a while. Sorry, for the short notice. Give my best to Jen.

Bear's brow furrowed. "The fuck?"

He was about to dismiss the message as a wrong number or one of those scams when a second message popped up.

Love you. -Jacky Boy

Bear grinned as he understood. Jackson was good, and he was supposed to pass the message along to Bailey for him. Bear typed out a reply.

How long do you think you'll be gone?

A minute later, a response.

I don't know, babe. Could be a while, sorry. Just don't want you to worry. Everything's all good.

Bear rubbed his chin.

Where's this new gig?

A message came back.

Sorry, can't tell you too much. My bosses wouldn't be HAPPY! Just know I'll be thinking about you working out here on the LAND! Got to go. Love you.

Bear read the message, then again a second and third time.

Finally, it clicked.

Bear sent back three kissy-face emojis before calling Bailey.

"What's up?" Bailey asked in greeting.

"Jackson took off with Graves a few hours ago," Bear said. "I just got a message from him under the guise of me being his girlfriend. He's in Happyland."

TWENTY-EIGHT

WHEN BEAR GOT BACK to the safe house, the team was already on the phone with Pitts in Roanoke. Kavanaugh and Wilcox were seated in front of laptops at the table in the dining room/communications center with Cole on the banquette across from them and Bailey standing, hovering over the speakerphone next to them. As Bear walked in, Bailey held her index finger up to her lip, preemptively shushing Bear. Bear extended a finger of his own.

"And how again do we have confirmation Clay is inside the resort now?" Pits asked.

Bailey winced. "Clay reached out to a friend of his," she said. "An Archibald Beauchamp. He contacted us on Clay's behalf."

"Why the hell did Clay bring him into this?"

"Because you pinheads can't take two steps without tripping over your own peckers," Bear said.

"Who was that?!" Pitts demanded.

"That was Beauchamp," Bailey said. "The number Clay reached out on was unlisted, meaning it wasn't the phone we supplied him with. We believe the phone we gave him was taken and, he found another way to reach out."

"Why wouldn't he call you, Jen?"

"We're not sure. Probably because he didn't have the contact info from the phone we gave him and he didn't remember the number for the clean phone I have."

"Why didn't we have Clay commit his only lifeline to memory?"

"I refer you to my two-steps/pecker theory," Bear offered.

"Jen, why the hell is this guy at the safe house?" Pitts asked. "This totally compromises our operational integrity."

"Clay reached out to him," Bailey reiterated. "I had no choice but to bring him in."

An angry sigh came over the intercom. "Fine. So what do we know?"

Bailey pressed her hands against the table and leaned toward the intercom. "Clay is in the resort cleanly. He had an opportunity to send out a distress signal and didn't. He texted Beauchamp under the guise that he was a girlfriend and explained he would be away for work. Obviously, this is a coded message, so whatever this new line is, Jackson doesn't feel it's secure."

"He reached out on someone else's phone at the resort?"

"More likely they provided him with a new one. One that they control."

Pitts cleared his throat. "So, our CHS is embedded in a high-risk situation and his only way to communicate with us is, at best, compromised? Terrific."

"We were prepared to have his communications monitored by the resort. The details have changed some, yes, but the framework of our plan hasn't changed."

"Alright, fine. So what are our next steps moving forward?"

Bailey looked over at Bear. "I suggest we let this play out. Stay in the background and let him work. We maximize opportunities for him to communicate with us. Beauchamp has the number Clay contacted him on, I can reach out now with a coded message of my own and reestablish our initial link. We also know Graves frequents the Belle Bottoms dance club. We can monitor movement from the resort to the club and set-up a face-to-face if we have to.”

The line was quiet for a moment before Pitts replied. “We'll proceed with the operation. But you keep tabs on this Archibald Beauchamp and keep him in check. We don't need this thing going sideways because Clay's buddy lets something slip at the bar.”

“Kiss my ass,” Bear said.

Bailey scowled. “Beauchamp *will not* be a problem. You have my word.”

“I'll brief Weisz and let him know our CHS is now into the resort. Whatever Clay is able to get will need to be reviewed by his office to verify we have enough for a warrant.”

“Sounds good.”

“Also, you should know Agent Nguyen here had the ATF lab do further analysis on the explosives used at the motel outside Winchester. Get this: it's something called MCX-5, a next-gen high-performance composite charge. It was developed for the Department of Defense.”

“By whom? Can they track it?”

“It's made by Touchpoint Systems. We're still working out whether we can trace it or not. Asking questions is bumping up against needing certain security clearances, so it's been slow-going.”

“Alright,” Bailey said. “Understood. Just keep us in the loop over here.”

“You do the same,” Pitts ended the call.

Bailey thought to herself for a moment, then turned and faced everyone centered around the table. “We'll need to make ourselves available to Clay should he need to meet. That means tracking everyone going into and out of the resort.”

“We're already doing that,” Kavanaugh pointed out.

“I know, but now we have to do it in the context of meeting Clay. Look for opportunities in public places, the dance club, that sort of thing.” She looked at Tim. “Reach out to your offices in DC. See if you can get someone to cut through some of the red tape on this Touch-point Systems angle with the explosives."

Bear crossed his arms and leaned against the doorframe over Bailey's shoulder. "You ought to start wondering where that all leads to. Defense means government, government means you all. You better make sure everyone involved in this thing is playing for the same team."

Bailey rolled her eyes before turning and facing him. "And what do you mean by that?"

Bear shrugged as he rocked himself off the door frame. "Watch your back. That's all I'm saying."

TWENTY-NINE

AINSLEY COULD HARDLY SLEEP her first night at The Arcady. She was too anxious, too excited to start her new life here. She'd only seen a portion of the resort on the drive from the front gate to the house where female employees stayed, but it was even better than she imagined. They'd passed a sprawling mansion with large, paned-glass windows framed by stone and wood siding stained a rich mahogany. It looked like one of those European ski chateaus she'd seen on TV. But this wasn't television; it was very much real.

Even the house with her room was far nicer than anything back in Arizona. A brick building painted an immaculate white with large columns, it too was a storybook setting. They were met outside by a woman who introduced herself as Mina.

Mina was tall with a model's physique. She had long, wavy blond hair with tan skin that had been surgically tightened across her face. Ainsley figured her to be in her late forties, but with the work she'd had done it was hard to tell. She met them in an outlaw romper as white as the house behind her and riding boots.

"Welcome to The Arcady," she'd said with only the slightest of smiles. "I'll be your direct point of contact here. If you are the talent, think of me as your manager."

Ainsley had to suppress a grin. No one in her life had ever called her anything even close to talented, and she'd never imagined needing a manager.

Mina led them inside. The interior of the house was much more drab, but Ainsley didn't mind. Girls were paired off, living in small dormitories with bunk beds. The furniture was newer than anything her grandmother owned, but it showed its wear and tear. In each dorm room, there were two dressers and two vanity tables, with one large wardrobe to share. When she saw these arrangements, Ainsley had hoped she and Tessa could room together, but Mina explained that wouldn't be possible. Instead, Ainsley was put with a mousy-looking girl named Mei. Mei was Asian — Ainsley guessed Chinese — and spoke very little English. She said "hi" to Ainsley upon meeting her, but little else.

Dinner was similarly so-so: a small bowl of chicken noodle soup and a bologna sandwich, but it was free, so Ainsley was happy to eat it. After dinner, the excitement returned. She was led away by Mina where she met up with Tessa in a cavernous living room centered around a granite fireplace. Mina took both their measurements before having two large racks of fancy dresses brought in.

"Go ahead, try some things on," Mina encouraged.

Ainsley took a small, form-fitting black dress and a longer navy-blue gown off the rack. When she looked around for a changing room, Mina let out a patronizing chuckle.

"What are you so shy about?" she'd asked. "You don't have anything I don't."

Ainsley looked at Tessa who grinned and winked before pulling her shirt off over her head. Ainsley did the same.

For the next half hour, she was happy. *Truly* happy. She and Tessa danced about the room as they tried on different dresses: a strapless lavender one that reminded Ainsley of the one she'd picked out for prom. A long-sleeve hunter green one that made her feel like a member of a royal family. A high-low hem that she pretended to do the tango in. She was back to being ten years old, not a care in the world as she and a newfound friend played dress-up.

At the end of the half hour, Mina ushered them to make a final decision on a handful of dresses, and Ainsley came crashing back to the here and now. She looked at the pretty dresses she had picked out. Mina didn't say as much, but Ainsley supposed they were hers now. Dresses that were far nicer than any clothes she'd ever owned. This was day one of her new life and it already felt miles better than her old one back in Arizona.

———

THE SUN WAS RISING on her second day in this life as a knock came at her dormitory door. Ainsley opened it and Mina gave her a tray with two bowls of cereal and two granola bars.

"Breakfast," she said. "Be downstairs and ready in an hour. We have some things to go over before the clients sit down for *their* breakfast."

Before Ainsley could ask any questions, Mina was gone. Ainsley brought the tray back into the room and placed it on one of the vanities. She ate quickly, then looked over her new wardrobe. It felt very early to be in something as revealing as the strapless or A-line dresses she'd picked out, so she opted for the long-sleeve green one. Mei slipped on an off-shoulder number that made her look like a doll. She did so with the lethargic reluctance of someone who regretted that it was time to go to work. Ainsley couldn't understand; this was better than any other options she'd had back home in Arizona.

An hour later, Ainsley came down into the living room and found Tessa already there. She was wearing a lacy number that had to be the most revealing thing she'd picked out the night before. Ainsley looked her up and down and marveled.

"You're dressed to kill," she said.

"I'm dressed to *impress*," Tessa countered. "Operation Land-a-Man begins now. Plus, I have to look hotter than my sister when I run into her."

Ainsley had forgotten all about Tessa's sister, Mackenzie, the inspiration for them coming here. A part of her felt guilty for not thinking about Mackenzie sooner.

"Do you know where she is? Is she staying here like us?"

Tessa shook her head. "I don't know, but we'll find her. I'm sure of it."

Mina strode into the room and crossed her arms behind her back.

"Alright, you two, listen up," she said. "The clients will be sitting down to breakfast in the Lodge dining hall in fifteen minutes. You will join the other girls and present yourself the same as them. When a client asks for you, you will go happily. You may partake in anything they offer — including food and drink — but never forget you are expected to maintain certain standards. Those dresses are not forgiving, and I will notice if they stop fitting far before any clients do."

Mina turned her back to them as she walked to an end table next to one of the sofas. When she did, Ainsley looked over at Tessa. Tessa gave Mina's back an eyeroll. Ainsley stifled a laugh.

Mina turned back around and held out two little baggies each filled with three pills. "Take these with you," she instructed. "These are for you to have for your clients should they want them. We don't dictate the price at which you sell them for, but keep in mind we charge you twenty dollars a pill, regardless."

"I'm sorry, I don't have any money here with me," Ainsley said.

Mina chuckled as if Ainsley said something amusing. "It doesn't matter. We take it out of what you are paid, same as everything else."

Ainsley looked at Tessa, then back at Mina, confused. "Everything else?"

"Room and board, your food, clothing rental, if you require medical attention." Mina shrugged. "Everything else."

Ainsley felt a pit form in her stomach. Tessa was right again.

Nothing in this world was free. She wanted to ask Tessa if she knew it would be this way, but she was afraid of the answer; afraid of looking foolish in finding out she didn't know what she was getting into.

"How much does that leave us with?" Ainsley asked.

"That depends on how well you do. Cash gifts from the clients are always a possibility, but remember that the resort takes a third and I take a third of anything as head-of-house."

Ainsley felt her knees weaken, and she thought she might become sick for the second time in as many days.

Mina continued with her instructions and gave Ainsley and Tessa each a baggy with pills. Ainsley looked down at them. They were red with what looked like a pair of cherries stamped into them. She'd never done anything outside of a little weed here and there, so she had no idea what she held in her hands now.

"You are charged for these whether you move them or not," Mina added. "So I'd make sure you don't lose them."

"What are they?" Ainsley asked.

"Pepsis. Don't worry, your clients will be more than familiar with them." Mina checked the gold and leather watch on her wrist. "Alright, it's time to go or you'll be late."

She led them to the back of the house where the main hallway ended at a door. Mina opened it and they continued down a long, windowless corridor. Lacking any sort of insulation, Ainsley could feel the chill of the outside air seeping through the sides and it became clear this was not a part of the house.

The three of them walked the length of the corridor and stepped through another door at the end. They walked past a bar and out to a cavernous room. Large timber beams held up a cathedral ceiling that bisected the room where it joined the chimney of a stone fireplace on the other side. Ainsley's eyes followed it to its base where a warm fire was already burning. Over the mantle was a pair of rifles and a mounted bear's head. The whole room had a hunting lodge feel — making it aptly named — with wooden tables and chairs arrayed neatly throughout. On either side of the fireplace, floor-to-ceiling windows overlooked a pristine lawn and the woods beyond.

"Come on," Mina ushered. "Step forward. It's almost time."

Just off the bar, on the threshold of the main room, Ainsley saw about a dozen girls, lined up and waiting. Most of them were dressed in things much more revealing than the long-sleeve dress she had on. She spotted Mei on the far end, her head down and her arms folded behind her.

Ainsley and Tessa took up positions on the other side, Tessa to Ainsley's right, and another girl to Ainsley's left. She had curly, dark hair with blond highlights. What the strapless little-black-dress she wore lacked, the amount of perfume she had on made up for.

When Mina left, Ainsley turned her head slightly toward Tessa. "Do you see your sister?"

Tessa craned her head slightly each way, then shook it.

Uneasy, Ainsley felt the baggy of pills in her hand. "What are these pepsis?" she asked.

The curly-haired girl on the other side giggled. "The pax love them," she said with a devilish smirk. "It makes them feel like kings when they fuck on them. Makes those that suck at it decent."

"The pax?"

"Yeah. Like, the passengers." When Ainsely didn't say anything, the girl gestured toward the second floor. "You know, the guys. That's what we all call them on account that they always want one thing: to ride us."

The weakness returned to Ainsley's knees, but now she became lightheaded. They were expected to sleep with the clients. If she was afraid to know if Tessa already knew about the money, she was downright terrified, wondering if Tessa also knew about this latest revelation.

"Always?" she found the courage to ask.

The curly-haired girl's tone was matter-of-fact. "All of them. Why and how depends on the pax. Some want the girlfriend experience, some want to imagine you're a random meet-cute, most actually just get off on the hooker thing. But, yeah, at the end of the day, they all want to fuck you."

Ainsley swallowed hard and willed herself to remain upright.

The curly-haired girl finally turned and looked at her. "That's why we're here. To do whatever they want."

THIRTY

THE NEXT MORNING began with a man named Roscoe picking Jackson up outside his living quarters. Roscoe had a thick chest that by comparison made his legs look too small. Balding and clean-shaven, his head looked like a peach-colored egg. He wore cargo pants with boots and a black polo, same as Jackson had been instructed to wear. Sitting behind the wheel of a side-by-side, his wide frame took up more than half the bench seat.

"You must be Jackson," he said.

Jackson nodded. "I am."

"Well, hop in. I ain't got all day."

Jackson came around the front of the side-by-side and wedged himself onto what little of the bench seat remained. As soon as he was in, Roscoe punched the gas. They took a sharp U-turn, nearly unseating Jackson in the process, then descended the winding road to the rest of the resort's campus.

When they got back to what Jackson recognized as the main drive, Roscoe stopped. From there, they had a view of the snug valley laid out before them.

"Alright, now listen," Roscoe said, "because I'm going to tell you stuff you need to know, and I ain't going to repeat it. I don't have the time or patience for dumbasses, so you can pick this shit up or get left behind. I ain't here to hold your hand."

Jackson nodded once. "Got it."

Roscoe pointed to their right, where just the roof of the building Jackson had seen yesterday poked out over the tops of trees. "Down there you have The Manor. That's the main building where most of the amenities are. A tea hall, bar, gym and yoga studio, bowling alleys, and a play area for those that bring their kids. Lawn games and shuffleboard are behind it out back alongside the garden. All of the residence chalets are spread out around The Manor. You don't approach any of the chalets unless you're told to. And you'll only be told to by myself." He pointed to their left at what looked like an old-world chateau mansion. "That up there is The Lustschloss. That's the boss' place. Don't ask me why it's called that 'cause I don't know and I don't give a damn."

"The boss' place? You mean Graves?"

Roscoe snorted. "No, the executive. He owns and runs all this. Graves is directly under him."

"Who's the executive?"

"You don't worry about that. Focus on not fucking up your first day on the job. Just know that's his place. Treat it like you treat the chalets: you don't go near there unless someone tells you to." He gave a vague nod in the same direction again. "On the other side is The Country Club. That's where you got the rest of the client ameni-ties. Golf, swimming, shooting. Equestrian and fishing are just down the hillside from it. They even do falconry out there." He pointed a thumb back the way they'd came. "The row of bunkhouses I picked you up from? We call that The Camp. And the road beyond it ends at The Facilities Barn at the top. That's where Graves took you yesterday."

Jackson looked around as Roscoe explained all this. The main drive slithered in an 'S' shape through the area. To their immediate left, where the drive turned toward The Lustschloss and The

Country Club, he spotted a smaller road that branched off into the woods.

"What's that road over there go to?" he asked.

Roscoe looked to see what Jackson was asking about, then just shook his head. "Like I said, just focus on what I told you about. You got everything I said?"

"Got it."

"Good. Now, we're gonna double back and get one of the Range Rovers to go over to the airfield. We've got clients coming in."

———

JACKSON AND ROSCOE pulled out onto the highway, headed to the airfield, which meant they'd drive past the safe house's grounds. Jackson remembered the team had installed a camera and a license plate reader among the trees that lined the road. He knew they were also probably desperate for any updates on his status. He had an idea.

The Range Rover's windows were tinted too dark to see through. Jackson felt for the button for the window and hovered his middle finger over it. He waited for the telltale bend in the road, where he could spot the turn to the safe house. When it came, he rolled down the window facing the trees, and dropped his hand out the window, holding up four fingers out of Roscoe's view.

"What the hell are you doing?" Roscoe snapped. "Close that window!"

"There was a bug," Jackson explained as he rolled the window back up.

"Quit dickin' around. We're almost there. You're paid to be professional and discreet. Play the part."

Jackson didn't say anything more.

Three minutes later, they took a right onto the private road for the airfield. Here, too, the property was barricaded with a powered gate, but this one was much more industrial. Chain linked with thick steel poles behind for support, the gate slid to the side like a pocket door, and Roscoe and Jackson pulled through. As they did, Jackson clocked two other guys dressed just like them sitting in a side-by-side on the other side of the gate. Likely fellow security assigned to the airfield.

The airfield was just as it looked from the satellite images Jackson had seen. A single runway was centered on a rectangular field cut right into the surrounding boscage. A taxiway at the near end connected to a wide expanse of tarmac, on the far side of which was a hangar big enough for a small airliner. Next to it was a lavish stone-and-glass building that looked as though it had been plucked out of the Adirondacks.

"There's no control tower," Jackson pointed out.

"Not needed," Roscoe said. "Pilots use Visual Flight Rules to take off and land."

Roscoe drove them directly into the open hangar, took a wide 180-degree turn, and came to a stop off to the side.

"Am I missing the plane?" Jackson asked.

"It's not here yet, wise-ass," Roscoe said. "Get out. We wait just in front of the hood on my side."

Jackson got out, came around, and took up a position next to Roscoe. The inside of the hangar had white epoxy flooring that stood in stark contrast to the charcoal tarmac just outside and made the interior of the hangar seem that much bigger.

The distant roar of an approaching jet began to fill the silence between Jackson and Roscoe, getting louder and louder. When he heard the screech of the tires touching down, Jackson looked over his shoulder at the arriving jet. A half-dozen windows dotted the fuselage, leading to a pair of jet engines off the rear. Engaging its flaps, it slowed to a leisurely taxiing speed before turning for the hangar. As it pulled in, the jet's engines, even near idle, were deafening.

Roscoe leaned over to Jackson's ear and shouted over the roaring. "You grab the luggage. It's in the hold behind the wings. Load it all in the back of the Range Rover."

Jackson nodded.

The jet came to a stop and the engines began to power down as the door opened and folded down into a stairway for the passengers to disembark. A flight attendant stepped out first, walked down, and stood beside the bottom of the stairs, all while balancing a tray of water bottles. Next out was a woman in her forties with long, chestnut hair wearing a flowery top, jeans, and oversized sunglasses. She was followed by two little girls Jackson took to be no older than ten. The last out was a man who also looked to be in his forties, with spiky black hair and a trimmed beard. He looked familiar to Jackson but he couldn't place him. The man and the woman each took a bottle of water from the attendant's tray without acknowledging her presence.

"What'd I say?" Roscoe growled. "Get the bags."

Jackson walked around the wing but hesitated when he realized he didn't know specifically where the hold on the plane was. One of the pilots, who had followed the foursome off the plane, read Jackson's consternation, and trotted over to him.

"Don't pull the wrong handle or the whole thing will come apart," he said with a chuckle.

Jackson didn't know what to say, so he just smiled and nodded.

"New to the job?" the pilot asked.

"Is it that obvious?"

The pilot chuckled again. "No worries. Here, this little thing pops out, becomes a handle, and then you just yank it."

A portion of the plane's fuselage flipped up and revealed a large compartment. Inside were four suitcases.

"You grab two and I'll grab two," the pilot said.

"I better get them all. The guy showing me the ropes is eager to chew my ass out."

"All the more reason to let me help you. Trust me, Mr. Karst doesn't like to be held up."

The name and face clicked now for Jackson. Don Karst was the host of a super popular podcast called The Karst Cast. Jackson had never listened to it, but he'd read about Karst's successes. He'd leveraged the show into building a budding media conglomerate based in the New York area. Jackson guessed the woman and two girls were his family.

Jackson let the pilot help him with the luggage, and they each carried a pair of bags to the tailgate of the Range Rover. Roscoe held the left rear door opened for Karst's family. Karst instructed the little girls to go in first and get in the back before letting his wife climb in. Roscoe then trotted around to the other side of the SUV and opened the other rear door for Karst who followed him around and climbed in.

Roscoe and Jackson got back in the SUV and Roscoe began driving them through the airfield gate and out onto the highway, headed back to The Arcady. Jackson could hear Karst typing away on his phone behind him.

"Spotify reached out again," Karst said, seemingly no one in particular. "They're still testing the waters about buying us."

"What did you say?" his wife asked.

"Fuck them. At our growth rate, *we'll* be the new Spotify in ten years. We'll be buying *them*."

"Daddy, don't talk work," one of the girls said from the back. "Work is boring."

"Work paid for that plane you just flew on and this trip," Karst said.

"Why can't we go to Disney World? I want to go to Disney World!"

"Disney is for poor people, Piper. We're not poor."

"Serena's family went to Disney World."

"And I make more in a month than Serena's dad makes in a year."

"Don, stop it," his wife said, laughing. "Ugh, I need a massage first thing when I get in. I hope that woman that was here last year is still here. What was her name? Jane? Jin?"

"You really think they let anyone leave there?" Karst snorted. "In a body bag, maybe."

His wife laughed harder. "Don, *stop!* Not in front of the girls. And *them.*"

Jackson could sense her nodding at Roscoe and him.

"What?" Karst asked. "Do you really think I'm telling them anything they don't know?" He started tapping at his phone again. "Hell, these guys probably pull the trigger."

THIRTY-ONE

ONE BY ONE, guests — all men, of course — came into the dining area of the Lodge, took in the lineup of young girls, and picked one. A handful picked two. Many of the men seemed to have favorites, calling the girls by name as they selected them. Ainsley was one of the last picked. A quiet man with an almost shy disposition took several minutes looking at each of them before coming to Ainsley. He was middle-aged with brown, close-cropped hair and wore a V-neck sweater and slacks. He reminded Ainsley of Ned Flanders from The Simpsons without the mustache.

The man introduced himself as Henry. Henry was part of a trio of guys who had come to The Arcady together. By their interaction with each other, Ainsley figured they were on some sort of "guys weekend". They also dropped several hints that their wives did not know the full details.

Henry's two friends were much louder and more animated than Henry and seemed to be enjoying themselves far more. One of them, Gary — he looked older than Henry by about ten years and had an ample gut and silver hair — had picked Mei and hardly ever took his arm off her shoulder. The other man, Bill — probably between Henry and Gary in age and sporting a thick caterpillar mustache that tried in vain to compensate for his receding hairline — had taken another girl named Amy, a leggy redhead whom Ainsley had never seen before that morning. Bill and Gary dominated the conversation over breakfast, carrying on about their wildest infidelities, while Henry poked at his omelet and laughed along quietly.

Ainsley spent the day as a fixture by Henry's side. He was nice to Ainsley, offering to get her order with every meal they had, and asked her routinely throughout the day if she needed anything. When the group went shooting at the gun range, Henry obliged Ainsley's wish to stand back and watch as the other two forced Mei and Amy to take at least a couple of shots. Ainsley got the impression they were getting off on seeing the petite ladies handle the large rifles. A part of her was thankful for Henry's kindness, but mostly she feared what it would cost her.

In the afternoon, the trio teed off on the golf course. Henry was much better than the other two, though he did drink less as well. Ainsley sat quietly in his golf cart and watched. Of everything they'd done that day, it seemed to be the one thing Henry actually enjoyed.

When they returned to the Lodge for dinner that evening, Gary ordered the most expensive bottle of wine on the menu — a 1989 Krug Clos du Mesnil that went for almost ten grand — and six wine glasses, three for Henry, Gary, and Bill, and three more for Ainsley, Mei, and the redhead whose name Ainsley still did not know.

"Oh, that's okay," Ainsley said shyly. "None for me."

"Don't be a buzzkill!" Gary countered before looking back to their waiter. "Six glasses!"

"I ... I'm not twenty-one."

"Well, shit, honey. I won't say anything if Henry won't!" Gary laughed the hardest at his own joke.

Ainsley gave up her objection. She felt foolish for saying anything at all. These men were well aware what this place was and what they were participating in. A little underage drinking was the least of their worries. She looked at Henry, worried he'd be embarrassed by her. Instead, he looked at her with genuine concern.

A few minutes later, the waiter returned and poured each of them a glass. One by one, they all took a sip, Gary and Bill taking larger ones. Ainsley looked around the room. All the other girls were busy being good company for their clients. She spotted Tessa, practically in her date's lap, taking a shot of something with her head cocked back. Ainsley realized she was at a crossroads. She could either lean in and play the part she was brought here to play or refuse and likely be kicked to the curb. She took a healthy sip of champagne herself. The champagne was warm and bubbly going down. Almost immediately, she felt better, her anxiety and consternation dulled by liquid courage. She took another sip, and then another. Then she finished off her flute.

"Whoa," Gary said with a chuckle. "Take it easy there. That's a thousand dollars' worth of French champagne you just downed."

Ainsley was spurred on by the moment and her intoxication. "Well, I thought we were here to have a good time. Or was I mistaken?"

Gary and Bill looked at her, then Henry, then each other, and then broke out in rambunctious laughter.

"Hell yeah, honey!" Gary said, his beefy arm wrapped around Mei. "That's the spirit. Let's get some shots in here!"

At Gary's request, the waiter brought them all a bottle of Clase Azul. By the end of dinner, it and the 1989 Krug were empty. Ainsley felt warm and tingly. All her pain and anguish was dulled by the libations in her.

This is so much better. This makes everything bearable.

The three men each signed a slip of paper Ainsley assumed was some sort of check. Gary looked over the table.

"Well, I think I'm going to head upstairs," he said. "Goodnight, y'all."

He lifted Mei by her arm as if she were one of his belongings — the way someone grabs their coat when they get up to leave — and led her away. Mei simply looked down at the floor, resigned to what was about to happen. Bill rose likewise with the redhead, and the two pairs headed for the large staircase across the room.

Ainsley looked at Henry. Henry was studying her.

"Well, shall we go, too?" he asked.

Henry said it in a way that felt like he was truly asking. But Ainsley knew he wasn't. She'd come to understand what this all was over the last twenty-four hours. These men did not pay however much they paid to lug them around to shoot guns and watch them golf. Like the champagne and tequila she had, Ainsley knew she was bought and paid for.

"Sure," she said with a sheepish smile, and stood.

Henry led her up the same stairs and down a corridor. It looked like any hallway in a hotel, but Ainsley noticed, instead of numbers, each room was labeled with an animal. Pheasant. Elk. Boar. Deer. Something in Ainsley's fogged mind put together than they were all types of game that were hunted. These men were the hunters. She and every other girl were the game.

Henry came to the third-to-last door on the right, stopped, and opened it without a key. Ainsley looked up at the label on the door. Rabbit. She remembered her grandfather talking about hunting rabbits when he was still alive. He'd said they were some of the easiest game to hunt. That was Ainsley now. The easy prey.

The door beeped and Henry stepped through before holding it open for Ainsley. Ainsley walked in cautiously, taking in the room. It was a cavernous suite, complete with a two-seat dining area, desk, and a pair of armchairs in front of a fireplace. At the center of everything was a California king canopy bed.

"Would you like a drink?" Henry asked.

Ainsley thought about whatever was about to happen, then she thought about the merciful release the champagne and tequila had brought her at dinner.

"Yes, I would," she said.

Henry shut the door.

———

THREE HOURS LATER, Ainsley was tiptoeing down the long corridor back to the center of the Lodge. Henry had fallen into a deep sleep soon after he finished with Ainsley, but she waited another couple of hours to ensure he wouldn't wake, expecting her to still be there. At midnight, she decided it was safe to leave.

Henry had been gentle, if not a bit awkward. Almost nervous. Still, he'd clearly wanted it — *her* — regardless if she wanted to be there with him or not. He acted as though she did, and Ainsley wondered if the misconception of what this all was went both ways.

Her shoes in her hand, she trotted back to the dining hall with the large staircase. She descended it and crossed the main floor over to the bar with the connecting passageway back to her room. She saw a broad-shouldered man standing sentry outside the large windows. He turned back and watched her briefly. *Security*, she thought, but were they keeping outsiders away or insiders from leaving? She didn't dare to find out.

Ainsley closed the door to her room, relishing in the dark. The lights were off and only the subtle bluish-gray glow from a waning moon gave everything inside just enough light for her to see. She shed her dress and collapsed onto her bed, exhausted. The constant tension of fearing every next moment throughout the day had worn her out as much as anything else.

It will get easier.

Staring up at the ceiling, Ainsley's world was an indigo void. Boundless and indefinite, like the universe itself. This was her universe. The timeline in the multiverse she'd chosen. Maybe this had been her path all along. Not Ainsley the starlet or Ainsley the socialite. Ainsley the resort whore. A month ago, she was sure there was nothing worse than being condemned to live out her life in the Arizona desert, going nowhere. Now, with every day that'd passed, she'd regretted leaving more and more. A single tear rolled down her cheek. She brushed it away and closed her eyes tight, trying to stifle a sob, but she heard one anyway. Rolling over, she peered over the side of her bunk bed. Mei was lying in her bed in the fetal position, crying into her pillow.

"Mei," Ainsley whispered. "Are you okay?"

Mei turned and looked up at her. When she did, Ainsley got a better view of her full profile from the moonlight. A chill roiled through her as her eyes began to understand what she was seeing. Dark bruises around Mei's wrists and neck stood in stark contrast to her fawn complexion. Ainsley looked into her eyes and recognized the look in them.

The two of them had finally found a language they were both fluent in: pain.

THIRTY-TWO

AS THE LAST rays of twilight disappeared over the tree line to the west, Bailey stood out on the back deck of the safe house smoking a cigarette. She watched a mother goose lead her goslings across the pond. It circled back twice, rounding up a pair of stragglers.

She's a good mother, Bailey thought.

Those goslings didn't know it, but she was their only safe harbor in a cruel storm that was the rest of the world. She pictured Kristal Hardy, holding her abdomen, wanting so much to be that haven for her own child. Someone out there stole that dream from her, and Bailey was growing ever more convinced those responsible were in the lavish resort just up the road.

The screen door opened behind her and Bailey turned to see Cole stepping out onto the porch. Cole nodded at the cigarette in Bailey's hand.

"You'd told me you quit," she said.

"I had," Bailey countered. She turned back to the pond and the valley beyond.

Cole was quiet for a moment. "This case?"

"This case." She took another drag. "But I guess there will always be another case. Maybe I was kidding myself trying to quit."

Cole came over and leaned her back against the banister. "Maybe you need to quit one thing in order to quit the other."

Bailey turned and gave her an incredulous look. Cole met her eyes, daring her to say she was wrong. After a brief standoff, they both looked away.

"You're worried about Clay," Cole said.

"I am."

"Clay can handle himself. Don't forget you encouraged me to put him on the Parker case. He and his buddy inside took on that whole cult outside of Gretna. Just the two of them."

"I vaguely remember an ATF Special Response Team getting involved."

Cole laughed. "Well ... details."

Bailey shook her head. "In any event, that was before everything that went down with his ex-wife. I had to talk him down from killing that asshole Alvanitakis." She took another drag. "Then, just when he'd started to put everything back together, I talked him into doing this." She exhaled a stream of smoke. "Losing Kristal Hardy was a tough one. But if I get Clay killed ..."

Cole's voice softened. "He's tougher than you're giving him credit for, Jen."

Bailey shook her head again. "Everyone has their breaking point."

The sliding glass doors to the safe house opened again, and this time Bear stepped out.

"We got an update on Jacky boy," he said. "One of your boys in there said it'd be on your phone."

Bailey snuffed out her cigarette on the deck's banister and jerked her phone from her pocket. She opened up the file she'd been sent. A surveillance video from the highway played across the screen and showed a familiar sight: a black Range Rover tearing down the road. This time, though, as it came closer, Bailey noticed the passenger side window was down. Sitting shotgun was Clay. As the car drove by, Clay seemed to look right at the camera.

"Wait, he did something with his hand there," Cole said, looking over Bailey's shoulder. "What was that?"

Bailey ran the video back and played it again, watching Jackson's movement closely. His right hand dropped out the window. With it, he flashed four fingers, his thumb tucked away, before he pulled it in and the window rolled up.

"What was that gesture?" Bailey asked. "Was he signaling something to us?"

The deck was quiet as the three of them thought. Then, a grin flashed across Cole's face.

"Code four," she said.

"What?" Bear asked.

"Code four. He's signaling code four. Patrol radio code for 'Everything is under control and no further assistance is required.' He's telling us he's okay."

THIRTY-THREE

JACKSON WAS BACK in his living quarters about to turn in for the night, when there was a knock on the door. He opened the door only enough to see outside it. Standing there, looking back at him was another man. Jackson took him to be about ten years younger than himself and a few inches shorter, but with the same athletic physique. Even with the watch cap he had on, Jackson could tell his head was shaved bald, which stood in stark contrast to the full black beard that covered the lower half of his face.

"Jackson?" the man asked.

Jackson nodded.

"Name's Beckett. Roscoe told me to get you. Come on, we've got to make a run."

"A run for what?"

"A delivery for the resort. Hurry up, it's colder than a witch's tit out here."

Jackson looked past him and saw a single Sprinter van, empty with the engine running. He thought for a moment about Cody Busch being taken out to that field and executed. He grabbed a chore coat from his supplied gear and followed Beckett out to the van.

Beckett drove them out the main gate and onto the highway. They were headed east, toward everything connected to the resort and away from where Cody Busch had been dumped. Jackson eased.

"Where's the delivery?"

"The load is waiting at the airport. We've got to get it, then bring it to The Manor."

"What's in the load?"

"Food for the kitchen, wine, shit for the spa, could be anything. Doesn't really matter to be honest."

Beckett drove them through the gate at the airport and then into the hangar. At the back of it were two full pallets of boxes stacked six feet high and wrapped together. Beckett turned the van around, then backed up to the load. Both of them climbed out. Beckett opened the back doors to the van, grabbed two utility blades from inside and handed one to Jackson.

"You take one pallet, I'll take the other," he said.

Jackson took his blade and started cutting away at the plastic wrap around his pallet of boxes and leaving it discarded on the hangar floor. When it was off, he began loading the boxes into the van. As he did, he looked over at Beckett and wondered if he'd fill in some blanks Roscoe wouldn't. Jackson took a box off the top of his stack and read what was printed on the side of it.

"Cohiba," Jackson said. "Cuban cigars. I guess Roscoe or Graves would have my ass if I pocketed a few of these."

Beckett didn't stop his work as he answered Jackson. "If you pocketed anything from The Arcady, it'd be the last thing you did."

Jackson wondered if Cody Busch had stolen something. "For real? You've seen that sort of thing happen before?"

"Let's just say the people that run this place aren't the type you mess with."

Jackson took another box off his stack. "Wouldn't it be easier if they just delivered this to the resort directly?"

"No one goes in or out that The Arcady hasn't cleared. Delivery drivers are a liability. That's why we handle most things. Same reason we transport clients ourselves rather than a car service."

"Still, the cooks could pick up their own food, couldn't they?"

"Staff don't leave the property. Ever."

"Why's that?"

"Too much of a risk they'd run or cause a scene."

That sentence stopped Jackson in his tracks. "Why would the staff run?"

Beckett eyed him from behind a large box in his hands. "Do I really have to spell it out for you?"

"What? Are they here illegally or something?"

Beckett lowered the box into the back of the van. "Some are, but that's not why."

Jackson didn't say anything, but just looked at Beckett.

When Beckett felt Jackson's eyes on him, he turned around. "They're all vagrants, man. People the world has forgotten about. Cheap cogs for the machine."

Jackson noted that was the second time someone working for the resort used that metaphor. "You mean like, they're forced labor?"

"Don't be naive. Do they want to get up every day and do their job? Probably not. But neither do most people." Beckett shook his head. "They get a roof over their head, they get food in their belly, they get clothes to wear. They should be grateful is what they should be."

"And they get paid."

Beckett chuckled. "Sure."

————

AFTER THEY'D LOADED everything up, Beckett drove them back to the resort, then took the van a back way to The Manor. When they pulled up to a large loading bay, its door rolled up and out stepped a half dozen men in coveralls. Jackson and Beckett climbed out from the front of the van, came to the back, and opened up its rear doors.

Jackson started to hand the men boxes off the truck, but Beckett stopped him.

"Fuck that," he said. "Let them do it."

From that moment on, Beckett turned from worker to taskmaster. Every few minutes he snapped off some reprimand.

"Come on, I haven't got all night? What are you, fucking stupid? Let's go!"

The men unloaded the truck, misery written on their faces. Jackson wondered how many hours they'd been working.

When the truck was unloaded, Beckett shut the doors and gestured for Jackson to hop back in.

"I'll give you a lift back," he said.

As Jackson got in, he asked, "So, where do you all find them all? The staff?"

Beckett put the van in gear and pulled away. "Shit, all over. China, Mexico, Europe. Even here, stateside. There's no shortage of people looking to come here for one reason or another. Hell, the main chef they got in there? Get this, the dude was on his way up in some fancy restaurant in Peru before a gang put a bounty on his head over gambling debts." He shrugged and nodded over his shoulder. "Now, he's back in there."

"They all work for Graves?" Jackson knew the answer, but wanted to see if Roscoe would give him more.

"Nah, man. Graves doesn't run this place. He may act like his shit don't stink, but he's just middle management. Don't let him fool you."

"So then, who runs it?"

"Corwin Corliss. Man's worth a shit-ton of money."

Jackson couldn't place the name, but he didn't press further. He had what he needed. He or Bailey would be able to figure out the rest.

They got back onto the main drive through the resort and climbed up the hillside. They were approaching the turn for The

Camp when the moonlight caught the pavement of that mysterious drive that disappeared into the woods in the distance.

"Where's that road go up there?" Jackson said. "I meant to ask Roscoe about it."

"That?" Beckett flashed a devilish grin. "That's the other side of the resort, man."

"What do you mean the other side?"

He laughed. "Some of the richest, most powerful people in the world come here. Handpicked guests of Mr. Corliss. You think they all want to just play golf and go fishing? They can do that anywhere. Up that road is The Lodge."

"What's The Lodge?"

"Think the most exclusive bunny ranch in the world. Except, *you* are Hugh Hefner. And any and all the girls up there are for you."

Beckett made the turn for The Camp, but Jackson looked out his window and watched the road to The Lodge until it was out of view. He thought about Kristal Hardy and the other girls that had been at the motel. Was that the connection to Sean Liles? Graves and Corliss were running girls through here?

When he got back to his living quarters, Jackson pulled out his phone and opened up the internet. He searched the name Corwin Corliss. He knew there was a chance Graves or someone was monitoring the phone, but he didn't care. He wanted to know.

The search result showed Corliss's name at the top in bold letters, the way it did when you searched for a public figure. There were several images of him. He was older, looking to be in his sixties, with the same slicked-back graying hair in every shot. He had a hawkish face and pensive eyes. Jackson looked at the title on the search result under his name.

CEO, Founder of Touchpoint Systems

THIRTY-FOUR

CORWIN CORLISS SAT at his desk in The Lustschloss. Centered on the front side of the third floor, facing pine-framed windows that overlooked every inch of The Arcady, save for The Country Club to the north. On late spring mornings like this one, he liked to take his coffee up here and watch the sun rise above the mountains that hid what he had built from the rest of the world.

Corliss had accomplished many things in his life. Taking his startup aerospace and defense company from a one-office operation in Dulles, Virginia to a multinational corporation that had over $40 billion in assets. When he started all those years ago, Touchpoint Systems was mired in the shadows of giants both literally and figuratively. RTX in Arlington. Northrop Grumman and General Dynamics in Falls Church. And Lockheed Martin across the river in Bethesda, Maryland. Ten years ago, no one in their C-suites were returning his phone calls. Now, Touchpoint was competing for the same multi-million-dollar contracts they were and winning more than they were losing.

Still, if Corliss was being honest with himself, The Arcady was his most prized creation. Anybody with half a mind for business could throw together an outfit that could grab some government contracts. God knows the bureaucratic bastards handed them out like mediocre coffee at an AA meeting. No, The Arcady was the crown jewel of his budding empire. He'd managed to create the ultimate retreat that saw the natural pecking order of the way the world should be, the way it *would* be if not for the insipid policies of equality and inclusion. Those were just concepts the weak used to prop up the lazy. Most people despised the rich, but wealth was only a byproduct of what Corwin Corliss really was about: power. He had no interest in rubbing shoulders with athletes or celebrities; they were rich without a purpose, wealthy by happenstance. No, he wanted to be in the same rooms as those with their hands on the levers. And The Arcady gave him the opportunity to do just that.

Corliss was thinking about all this when his phone buzzed on his desk. He looked down at the caller ID, recognized it, and answered. "Good morning."

"Mr. Corwin, are you at your place in the mountains?" the person on the other end asked.

"I am. Why do you ask?"

"We need to meet. That matter we discussed earlier is not resolved."

Corliss's brow furrowed. "I'm sure you are wrong. I was there and handled the matter myself."

"And I'm telling you it is not handled."

"Fine, so tell me."

"No more over the phone. I need you to come to me."

"I'm not wasting half my day going anywhere. If you're in such a fit that you think we have a problem, you can come here."

"Mr. Corliss, we both know why that can't happen. Especially right now."

Corliss sighed as he turned around in his executive chair. Hanging over the mantle behind his desk was a rifle that had belonged to his father. It was an original Winchester 70. Before it'd sat on Corliss's mantle, it had rested against his father's nightstand for over fifty years. In that time, his father had used it countless times to protect their family and the farm they lived on. He'd never forget when he was seven years old and his father shot a coyote fifty yards out as he stood in his bathrobe on their back porch.

"You never hesitate to protect what's yours in this world," his father had told him.

Not many lessons from growing up on the Texas prairie applied to his life today, but that one did. The coyotes looked different in his world, but their threat to him and what he'd built was the same. He had to protect what was his.

"Mr. Corliss? Are you still there?" the person on the other end asked.

"I'll fly out to you," Corliss said. "I have meetings all day, but I can be there tonight. I'll text you what time I'll be on the tarmac. You be there."

"Yes, sir. I will be."

Corliss hung up, wondering what coyotes were prowling in his backyard.

THIRTY-FIVE

ONCE AGAIN, Ainsley hardly slept all night. This time, though, instead of excited anticipation, it was from anxious dread. Every time she closed her eyes, she saw the bruises on Mei as the young girl sobbed beneath her. Ainsley had spent most of the day with her and the man that had picked her as his date, Gary. Gary was a bit obnoxious and a heavy drinker, but otherwise had had a jolly disposition. The kind of switch that had flipped in him when he took Mei upstairs after dinner led Ainsley to wonder just what kind of monsters they were being subjected to.

In her gut, Ainsley wanted to run. To leave this place and never look back. But then she imagined what Tessa would say. She could practically hear it now: *It's been one night. You're being melodramatic.* She felt herself resenting Tessa for a conversation they'd never had.

The day began just the same as the one before: a loud knock on the door with Mina dropping off breakfast and advising them to get ready. Ainsley opened the door wide when she did and pointed to Mei, still in bed.

"I think Mei is not feeling well," she said.

Mina walked halfway over to Mei and looked her over from a distance. Even there, the bruises around her wrists and neck were plain to see.

"I'll get her some Advil," Mina said, emotionless. "Have her cover up those marks with some makeup. Help her if she needs it."

Anger stirred in Ainsley, but she kept it from showing. When Mina was gone, she sat Mei up and helped her into an outfit. On her side of the wardrobe was a long sleeve turtleneck minidress that would cover everything without any makeup.

"Here," Ainsley said softly. "Put this on."

When Mina returned, both of them were ready. They went downstairs and found the other girls milling about in the main room, talking in small cliques. Tessa was with the redhead Ainsley had spent the day with yesterday. Ainsley went over to them and hooked her arm into Tessa's.

"Can I borrow her for a sec?" Ainsley asked with a big, forced smile.

The redhead nodded, indifferent. Ainsley took Tessa and led her to one of the far corners of the room.

"Hey," Tessa said. "What's up?"

"I can't do this," Ainsley said. "This is not what I thought it would be. I want to go."

"What happened? Did the guy you were with ... hurt you or something?"

"No, but I'm not a ..." Ainsley looked around the room. "A prostitute."

Tessa stifled a giggle. "It's just sex, Ains. The only difference is you're getting paid for it."

Ainsley's resentment from their imaginary conversation returned. "It's not just that. We are being used here, Tessa. The guy Mei was with, my roommate? He hurt her last night. And when I showed it to Mina, she couldn't have cared less."

Tessa folded her arms and was quiet for a moment. "I talked to some of the girls here, asking about my sister. They said they haven't seen her, but maybe she works elsewhere in the resort. Apparently, there's a whole other side. I need more time to find her. Maybe, if you don't like it here, we can move over to whatever she does."

"How much time Tessa? I don't know that I can—"

"Look, the stuff during the day isn't so bad, right?"

"I guess not, no."

"So just go with it, be the happy girl-next-door. Then at night, when you guys have drinks, slip them some of these." She pulled out a small baggy from between her breasts. The pills in it looked like the same ones Tessa had given her after Dex assaulted her.

"Are those the benzos?" Ainsley took the baggy and looked at it.

"Yep. They'll knock your guy out just like they knocked you out." Tessa shrugged. "A little trick I learned back in Arizona."

"I don't know."

"Just try it. Maybe it'll get better. But let's wait before we do something we can't take back. If we leave, that's it. It's over."

Ainsley rubbed the plastic bag between her fingers. "What if I get the same guy twice? They'll catch on if they're falling asleep early every night."

"Hon, these guys did not come out to this place in the middle of nowhere to sleep with the same girl over and over again. Most of them are probably here getting away from that."

"Still ... if they talk."

"About what? That they're old assholes that fall asleep before they can get it up?"

Now Ainsley suppressed a laugh. Tessa had a point. Several points, in fact. There was no going back if they left. And, though only imaginative Tessa had said it, it *had* only been one night, one night that wasn't nearly as awful as what Dex or even Zane had done to her. Besides, she hadn't even seen how much money they were making yet. Maybe it was enough, even after everything Mina said they took out, enough to make this all worth it.

"Okay." Ainsley nodded. "Thanks."

"Of course, girl." Tessa reached in and hugged her.

Mina walked into the room and cleared her throat. "Okay, ladies. To the dining hall, please."

Tessa smirked. "C'mon, time to punch the clock."

THIRTY-SIX

JACKSON NEEDED to see the other side of The Arcady. There was no doubt nighttime would be his best opportunity, and he hoped the next day would take him further around the resort so that he could scope everything out and formulate a plan. But when he opened the front door to his living quarters, Roscoe was waiting for him in one of the Range Rovers rather than a side-by-side.

Jackson opened the passenger door. "Where are we going?" he asked.

"The airfield," Roscoe replied. "Today I show you how to work security there."

Jackson tried to think of an excuse for them to stay on the resort grounds, but none came. He climbed in and Roscoe took off.

Just as before, when they pulled through the gate at the airfield, two other guys were sitting in a side-by-side just off the tarmac. Roscoe pulled over to them, then hopped out but left his door open.

"Shift change, boys," Roscoe said. "Go on and get some shut-eye. You're back on tonight."

Jackson recognized them as the same pair that had been there yesterday morning. As he came around the front of the Range Rover, he extended a hand.

"Jackson," he greeted.

Neither man took the offered handshake.

"Goddamn boot," one of the men grumbled back as he passed Jackson.

"Ignore them," Roscoe said. "They just got off twelve hours out here, just the two of them." He sat down behind the wheel of the side-by-side. "Come on. Get in."

Jackson took the passenger seat. They waited for the other two to take the Range Rover and leave. Then, Roscoe fired up the side-by-side and headed for the backside of the buildings.

"I'll take you once around the perimeter," he explained. "Just so you get a look at it. You'll do this once an hour while on duty. The rest of the time, you can monitor everything from the office in the hangar."

The airfield's perimeter was a perfect rectangle save for a chunk cut out of the northeast corner where the road came in through the gate. The entire boundary was marked with a chain-linked fence and barbed wire over top. The airstrip itself sat in the middle of the secure space surrounded by a grassy field. On the outside, thick forest came all the way up to the fence line.

"This is a lot of perimeter for just two people to secure," Jackson shouted over the loud engine as they made their way around.

"The fences have a breach detection system installed onto them," Roscoe shouted back. "Anything breaks the circuit, it'll set off an alarm and tell you where." He rolled to a stop, then pointed at the ground ahead. "Plus, there's a secondary perimeter."

Jackson now noticed little puck-shaped devices sitting atop small stakes just off the ground. "Motion sensors?"

"Yup. Every thirty feet, a hundred feet inside the fence line all the way around. Damn jets set them off as they land half the time."

Roscoe continued on and finished their loop before taking Jackson to the hangar. In the far back corner, tucked away behind shelves of tools and equipment, was a small office with no more than a desk, a computer with two monitors, and a computer chair. Roscoe eased himself into the seat, typed away at the keyboard, and brought up a schematic of the airfield. The fence line had an array of green dots tracing it.

"See, you can monitor the whole system from here," Roscoe explained.

Jackson studied the security system. "Do the resort grounds have this, too?"

"Not the motion sensors, but the perimeter system, yeah."

"Are they interconnected? Can the resort see this and you see the resort system from here?"

Roscoe's eyes narrowed. "You sure ask a lot of damn questions."

"Just trying to understand it all."

"No, the two are separate systems."

Roscoe walked Jackson through how to work everything. He demonstrated a breach by kicking one of the sensors just behind the hangar hard enough to trip it. An alert message flashed across the screen on the computer in the office. Roscoe then came back in and turned everything off.

"The two properties aren't connected, but an alert goes to the entire security team if the alarm isn't deactivated within sixty seconds," he explained. "It's a fail-safe to get backup rollin' in case you can't make the call. So, if one of those damn jets trips the system, make sure to cancel the alert or you'll get everyone goin' for nothin'."

Jackson nodded.

"That's about it. We have airfield duty the rest of the day. Standard procedure is one of us mans the office and the other posts up at the gate. Since you're the rookie, you get outside with the gate."

Roscoe made it seem like it was a lesser post, but truthfully Jackson'd rather be out there than in the windowless box that was the office. He nodded again, walked over to the gate, and took up his watch.

Morning turned into afternoon with little else happening. Once an hour, Roscoe would come by with the side-by-side, pick up Jackson, and the two of them would patrol the perimeter. The entire time, though, Jackson's mind was preoccupied with getting to the other side of the resort. Beckett had insinuated the staff had been trafficked here for labor, but innuendo wasn't strong enough to bring charges and none of it tied back to what happened with Sean Liles and Kristal Hardy. Jackson's gut told him the evidence he needed was up that road that disappeared into the woods.

As the sun began to set, Roscoe came around to pick up Jackson for one last perimeter check. It was just as uneventful as the others, but as they made their way back, a pair of headlights came up to the entrance. When the gate opened, Graves' G63 rolled through.

"How's the new guy working out?" Graves asked Roscoe as if Jackson wasn't sitting right next to him.

Roscoe shrugged. "Not bad."

"Good to hear. Can I borrow him?"

"For what?" Jackson asked.

"I figured I'd give you that opportunity to get your stuff. You said it was at an extended stay motel, right?"

Jackson saw an opportunity to get away and brief Bailey and the safe house. "Yeah, if you don't mind me borrowing a ride, I can go and grab it real quick."

"Don't worry about it. I'll take you."

A pit formed in Jackson's gut. Not only would Graves tagging along complicate a meet-up, he'd expect Jackson to really have a room at a motel with all his stuff.

"I appreciate it, but I don't need to waste your time."

"Nonsense, I don't mind." He paused a beat. "Unless there's a reason you don't want me to go with you."

Jackson didn't need Graves being suspicious. "The more the merrier."

Graves slapped the side of his SUV. "Hop in."

As Jackson got out of the side-by-side and walked to the SUV, his mind raced, searching for a play. One came to him, but it was risky and would put Bailey and the safe house in a tough spot. He trusted her to come through for him.

Jackson opened the passenger door and got out his phone. "I told the girl I was seeing she could stay at the motel if she needed to," he said to Graves. "Let me just see if she's there. Maybe she can pack my stuff while we drive over."

"Make it quick."

Jackson called Bailey.

THIRTY-SEVEN

BAILEY WAS in the safe house's dining room/operations area when her phone rang. She was so hyper-focused on her laptop screen, studying the latest satellite surveillance images from the resort and airfield, that she didn't hear it at first. Kavanaugh seated across from her on the banquette looked at the phone then at her.

"You going to get that?" he asked.

Bailey looked over at her phone on the table. The call was from the number Bear had given her, Jackson's new number.

She answered it, a wary lump forming at the back of her throat. "Hello?"

"Hey, babe," Jackson said. He was in character which meant someone was listening. "Listen, I was going to swing by my room at the motel. Are you there?"

"No," Bailey said. "I'm at my place."

"Ah, okay. I was hoping I would get to see you."

"Do you need to see me?"

"No, I just have to get my things. They're still there, right?"

Bailey was confused. "At your motel?"

"Yeah, the room I was renting at that place in Franklin just off the Highway. Mountain Spring, remember? I need to get my stuff there."

Bailey understood now. He was telling her to take his things and put it in a room as if he'd been staying there. "I, uh, haven't been there in a bit, but I didn't move anything. Your stuff will be there."

"Okay. Thanks, babe. Love you."

Bailey gave a "love you, too" back for the sake of appearances before ending the call. She turned and called out to the house. "Alright, listen up."

The rest of the team filed in from the kitchen and living room beyond.

"We have to move fast," Bailey announced. "Jackson needs his stuff at a room at the Mountain Spring Motel in Franklin over the state line in West Virginia."

Kavanaugh punched away at the laptop in front of him. "That's the small town just north of the strip club. Our cameras put Jackson at the airfield earlier today. They're closer than we are."

"We have to find a way to beat them there. And obviously we can't just race past them on the road."

"Why not? The only vehicle of ours they've made is the Impala."

"No, it's too risky."

Cole walked over to Bailey. She pulled up the map app on her phone, studied it, then showed the screen to Bailey. "Here, this road just west of here. It joins Route 640 which loops around to 220, the highway up to Franklin, just before the state line. It's the long way around, but if we can beat them to that junction, we'll be ahead of them."

"They'll have to go through the town of Monterey to get to 220," Wilcox added. "That should slow them down at least a little. It gives you a chance."

"And we're taking it," Bailey said. "Angela, get the Explorer. Bear, help me pack enough of his stuff to make this work."

"Let me go in the Suburban," Bear said, walking in from the

foyer. "I'll head toward Monterey, see if I can't get eyes on and find a way to slow them down."

Bailey thought for a moment. "Okay, go. Cliff and Timothy, you give me a hand then."

Everyone broke from their huddle around the table and went their separate directions. Bear hopped into his Suburban and took off as Cole pulled the Explorer out of the garage. Four minutes later, Bailey came running out with Jackson's duffel bag. She jumped into the passenger seat of the Explorer as Cole hit the gas.

They got out onto the highway, drove a mile to the bypass Cole had found on the map, and gunned it. Bailey reached over her shoulder for her seatbelt and clicked it in.

"No faith?" Cole said with a grin behind the wheel.

"I can read the headline already," Bailey said. "Local detective kills decorated special agent."

The suspension on the Explorer went slack as they crested a hill, all four wheels barely holding onto the road. Bailey put in an ear bud and called Bear.

"Hyello?" Bear answered.

"Where are you?" Bailey asked.

"I'm rolling into Monterey now."

"Do you have eyes on Jackson yet?"

"Not yet." Bear paused. "Wait, hold on. You've got to be shitting me."

"What? What is it?"

"I'm at the turn for 220. There's a black G63 here, on 220, at the same light. That has to be them, right?"

"Can you confirm? Can you see?"

"No. Damn tinted windows."

"We'll have to assume that's them."

"I'm five cars back, I'm not going to make the turn before they do. Unless— hold on."

Bailey heard a series of car horns blare in the background followed by Bear laughing.

"Bear, what's going on?"

"I cut through a gas station at the corner to get onto 220. I'm ahead of them now."

Bailey grabbed the handle overhead as Cole took a turn at an intersection of their own at speed. The back of the Explorer fishtailed before Cole straightened them out.

"Alright," Bailey said. "We just got onto 640. I need you to slow them down anyway you can."

"No problemo. I'm letting a whole parking lot full of people turn out in front of me." Another car horn sounded in the background. "Kiss my ass!"

640 arced and cut through open fields, making it easier for Cole to see the road ahead and pick up speed. They flew into an unincorporated community, rattling the 35 MPH Speed Limit sign as they tore past it. The open fields turned into homes and business hugging the road. An elderly couple stepped onto the sidewalk in front of a bank, inches from the road.

"Easy! Easy!" Bailey yelped.

"I see them," Cole said.

Coming out the other side of the locality, the road came up parallel with a wide creek and together the two cut between two mountains.

"We're almost to the highway," Cole said.

"Bear, we're almost to 220," Bailey relayed. "Where are you?"

"Just outside Monterey. I'm driving five under the speed limit, but the G63 is fixin' to pass me."

Bailey turned to Cole. "This doesn't work if they see us."

"It'll be close."

"I hear y'all," Bear said. "I got this."

Bailey heard what sounded like tires squealing before more car horns. Bear laughed heartily again.

"Bear, what's going on?" she asked.

"I decided this stretch of road was the perfect time for me to turn around. I'm doin' a piss poor job of it, blockin' both lanes." More horns blared. "Hey! That's not very ladylike!"

Bailey smiled. Bear had mostly been an unnecessary headache to her, but she couldn't deny he had his moments.

A moment later they turned onto 220. Bear's impromptu roadblock ensured they had nothing but open road ahead. Cole raced them on into West Virginia. Ten minutes later, they pulled up to the office for the Mountain Spring Motel & Apartments. Bailey flung the door open and ran in. A pimply teenager looked up at her, startled.

"I need a room," Bailey said. "Right now."

———

"WHAT THE HELL is this jackass doing?!" Graves hissed.

Jackson was stone-faced but inside he was smiling. *Atta boy, Bear*, he thought.

He'd seen Bear cut through a gas station in the town of Monterey to get ahead of them on the highway and figured he was there to slow them down while Bailey could get things in position. This was confirmed when Bear spent the ensuing couple of miles driving conspicuously slow, allowing more traffic to get ahead of him and them. Now, Bear pulled out his coup de grace and was blocking both lanes of the road as he made the most lackadaisical U-turn possible.

"Oh, for fuck's sake, come on!" Graves yelled.

Bear finally couldn't keep the act up any longer without it becoming overly suspicious and he righted his Surburban onto the road going the other way. Graves flipped him off from behind tinted glass. Jackson doubted Bear could see it, but he was sure Bear was laughing as they passed him all the same.

Traffic ahead got back up to speed and Graves and Jackson continued on to the motel unimpeded. As they did, Jackson's phone buzzed with an incoming text message in his pocket. He looked at his phone. It was from Bailey.

The Powerball was #17 this week. I almost won! #17!

She was telling Jackson the room number. He sent a heart emoji in reply and put his phone away. Two minutes later, they pulled into the parking lot for the Mountain Spring Motel & Apartments. It was comprised of two buildings, each two floors with the outer corridor and doors overlooking the parking lot. White with black trim, it was a mid-century building that had clearly just gotten a fresh paint job.

"You going to need a hand?" Graves asked.

"I can manage," Jackson said. "Just give me a sec."

Jackson went into the motel office where a pimple-faced teenager looked at him with a dumbstruck expression.

"Evening," Jackson greeted. "My friend and I just checked in and I lost my key car—"

"Jackson? Jackson Clay?"

Jackson was caught off guard for a moment. "Yeah."

The teenager reached over and slipped him a key card. "Your friend said you'd be by. She asked me to give you this."

"Thanks."

"You hittin' that, bro?"

Jackson shook his head.

"She's smokin', bro."

"I don't think you're her type. Thanks for the key."

Jackson left.

Room #17 was on the second floor in the building the office was attached to. Jackson trotted up the stairs and down to the room. He slipped the key card in and the door opened with an electronic beep. He walked in and shut the door behind him. No lights were on inside and the shades were drawn, giving the whole room a dark, golden hue.

"Bailey?" Jackson called out. "You in here? It's just me."

Bailey stepped out of the bathroom in the back. "I didn't know if you'd be bringing your friend or not." She nodded at the bed nearest her. "There's your bag. We threw in as much as we could."

"Thanks. They've provided most things I've needed. He sprung this little field trip on me last-second."

"Could it be another test?"

Jackson shrugged. "Could be." He stepped to the window and peaked out behind the window shade. Graves was still behind the wheel in the Range Rover. "If it was, he seems satisfied."

"Where are you at with Happyland?"

"The Arcady, actually. That's what it's called. They have me working security. We picked up a client that flew in yesterday. It was Don Karst, the podcaster. Him and his family. There might be an angle there to lean on him, depending on what you can dig up?"

Bailey folded her arms. "We'll look into it. Is Graves calling the shots?"

Jackson peeked out the window, checking on Graves. "No. Another guy named Beckett took me on a supply run with him last night. He told me Graves is basically middle management, in charge of the security staff. The guy behind everything, according to him, is Corwin Corliss. I googled him he's—"

"The CEO of Touchpoint Systems." Bailey's voice lowered to a whisper. "Son of a bitch."

Jackson looked back at Bailey. "What is it?"

"The ATF did an analysis on the explosives from the motel outside Winchester. It was a proprietary type of plastic explosive designed by Touchpoint."

Jackson shook his head. "You said all along that whole thing was too big time for a guy like Sean Liles. Corliss and The Arcady must've been behind it, probably by way of Graves."

Bailey nodded. "Yeah. That's good, Clay. Pursue that angle. See if you can get a more concrete connection."

"I'll work on it."

"You get anything else useful so far?"

"I'm not sure. The Arcady is spread out in separate parts. There's a main building and each guest has their own standalone residence. Then there's other facilities like a country club, gun range, et cetera. This Beckett guy basically insinuated all the staff are trafficked labor, but it's just hearsay at this point. Karst's conversation in the car with his wife made it seem like they know how the place makes the sausage, so to speak. That may be more opportunity to flip them. But I think there's more to it."

"What do you mean?"

"There's a road that branches off from the rest of the resort. I asked this guy, Roscoe, who seems to be some sort of senior member among the security guys and he told me not to worry about it. I asked Beckett later and he made it sound like they're running girls for prostitution over there."

"That might be another connection to Liles. A high-level trafficking op like this wouldn't normally be connected to a street level thing like Liles was running but—"

"Pepsi. The pills. Graves had me rip off that kid, Collins, saying he needed to take the stuff *back*. Maybe Graves was distributing the stuff but when things went sideways with Liles he decided to cut out anyone else that could be a problem."

Bailey nodded again. "If that's true, Collins was lucky he was only stolen from and not killed."

"Not killed yet, anyway. We still don't know how Cody Busch's murder plays into all this."

Jackson's phone buzzed in his pocket. He took it out and saw Graves was calling him.

"Yeah, I'm on my way out," he said.

"Hurry up," Graves said. "We've got to go. Something's going down back at the properties."

Jackson ended the call and looked at Bailey. "I've got to go. He said something's going on."

"Okay. Go. Be careful."

Jackson grabbed his duffel bag and left.

THIRTY-EIGHT

AINSLEY'S CLIENT for the day was a man who introduced himself as Stephen. Stephen was a portly man who looked at least sixty but might've been younger and hadn't aged well. He had a round face and wide nose with tiny eyes. His hair — or what was left of it — was toffee brown and combed across the top of his head.

Stephen barely acknowledged her presence, even once. He hadn't picked her out so much as waved in her general direction and offered little more than his name. Ainsley gathered from the conversation he and his colleagues had over breakfast that each of them was head of a bank. Not like a local branch, but the bank overall. The other three engaged with the girls they'd picked — none of whom Ainsley had gotten to know yet — off and on, but Stephen practically pretended Ainsley wasn't there. It gave Ainsley time for her mind and eyes to wander. She found Mei, sitting with a younger man that was more focused on his phone than her.

Maybe it would give her an easy day, she thought.

Then she saw Tessa across the room and her heart sank. Tessa was sitting with Gary, the man that had given Mei her bruises. She knew Tessa could take care of herself, but Gary was at least a head taller and probably had a hundred and fifty pounds on her.

Stephen and his peers paid for their breakfast and stood to leave, Stephen hardly even looking over to see if Ainsley would be joining him. Ainsley did get up, but as she did, she made sure her hand knocked over a glass. The loud clink got almost everyone's attention in the Lodge.

"Oh, I'm sorry," Ainsley said.

Stephen made a noise that sounded like a growl. "Clumsy girl."

Ainsley looked over and met Tessa's eyes. Gary wasn't watching them, too taken with whatever story he was telling his friends. "Be careful," Ainsley mouthed with raised eyebrows, but Tessa just grinned and winked at her.

Stephen continued to pay little attention to Ainsley throughout the day. After breakfast, the group went to the pool. Ainsley didn't have any swim suits, but found several options available in the communal bathroom. The other three girls shed their clothes in front of the men as if that was normal, and the men either gawked or came over and put their hands on them. Stephen stood in the corner, changed into a pair of swim trunks, and walked out to the pool.

The one thing the man did care for, though, was his alcohol. Ainsley had noticed he'd had three bloody marys with breakfast and immediately had Ainsley get him a beer at the pool. The drinking continued on into the afternoon, where he had four gin and tonics over eighteen holes. That night at dinner, when they returned to the lodge, he finished off a seven-hundred-dollar bottle of merlot himself and two more Irish coffees for a nightcap. By the time he was ready to take Ainsley upstairs, he was listing side to side.

He took Ainsley to the Boar Room, leaning heavily on her as they went, and stumbled in.

"Would you like another drink?" Ainsley said, stepping again into her role.

"Mmm, yeah, sure," Stephen mumbled as he fell into an uphol-stered chair.

"What would you like?"

But Stephen didn't answer. Ainsley looked over. Stephen was out cold. She went over and placed the back of her hand under his nose to see if he was still breathing — a trick she'd been unfortunate enough to learn after her mother had drunk herself into a similar stupor enough times — and he was. *Thank God.*

Figuring her night was over, she kicked off her heels and plopped onto the bed. All she'd have to do was hang out a couple hours, then slip out just as she did the night before. She looked around. The room had a television, but that risked waking Stephen. Stephen had a phone — something she hadn't had since Mina took hers when they'd arrived — but trying to sneakily use it brought the same risks as the television, if not more. So, instead, Ainsley lay there quietly as Stephen snored away in the chair, a bit bored but content not to have the husky man on top of her.

She had nearly fallen asleep herself when she heard some sort of commotion in the hallway. The doors to the rooms were thick, but Ainsley strode over and put her ear to it. She could hear Tessa's voice out in the hall.

Ainsley cracked the door open. "Tessa?"

"Ainsley!" Tessa said in a hushed stammer. "I've been trying to find you!" She ran over to Ainsley in bare feet and dropped her voice to a whisper. "We have to go, now!"

The door to the Elk Room across the way also opened, and a pair of suspicious male eyes glared out at them. Ainsley grabbed Tessa, pulled her into her room, and shut the door. She looked towards Stephen, but he was still passed out.

"What are you talking about?" she asked.

"The thing with the benzos I told you about," Tessa said. "I couldn't stand this guy all fucking day, so I dropped a few in the drink he had me fix him. Ains, he more than passed out. He *stopped breathing.*"

"What?!"

"We have to go! Now, before everyone else finds out!"

"What about CPR? Try to wake him or something?"

"And say what? Sorry about drugging you? No, Ains, we have to *go*! If he's dead—"

"What about your sister?"

"It won't matter where she is if they find out I *killed* someone. Please! I'm leaving! Come with me!"

Ainsley thought she was going to pass out herself. This couldn't be happening. She'd wanted to leave but not like this. Still, what was the alternative? Stay here? Alone?

"Okay, we have to go get our stuff," Ainsley said.

"No, Mina will be lurking around there. If we run into her, it's over."

"But Tess, we don't have literally *anything*."

"I took this off the guy." Tessa reached between her cleavage and pulled out a wad of cash, all hundred-dollar bills."

"Oh my god. You just *took* it? How much is that?"

"I counted. It's over five grand and taking it is the least of our problems right now. But it's enough for us to figure things out. We just have to get out of here."

Stephen started to stir behind Ainsley.

"Like *now*," Tessa said.

"Okay. But how?"

"We make a run for it. Back down the road they brought us in on. Back to the rest of the resort and then down to the front gate. We hop it, and we're out of here."

Tessa made it sound far easier than Ainsley knew it would be, but she nodded without a reply. Tessa took her by the hand and the two of them trotted down the hall back to the center of The Lodge. Tessa turned for the French doors that led out front, but Ainsley resisted.

"Wait," she said. "There was a guard posted up out that way last night. He's probably there again."

"Then where?"

Ainsley thought. "What about through the kitchen? There's must be a back door."

"No, if the kitchen staff see us, they could tip off security same as Mina."

The two of them stood on the threshold of the hallway, Tessa's brow furrowed and Ainsely racking her brain.

"My room!" Tessa said. "One window overlooks the woods out back. We lower ourselves down, go along the back side, and get down to the road."

"Back with … his body?"

"Unless you have a better idea? We're running out of time."

Ainsley shook her head, and Tessa took her back to her room. It was the last one on the left and Tessa had left it unlocked. She opened the door and shut it behind them. There, on the bed, was Gary. Lifeless, he'd already turned a shade of blue.

"Oh my god," Ainsley said. "He's really dead."

"I wasn't lying. Come on." She went to a large wardrobe on the other side of the bed. "The son of a bitch wanted to tie me up. I guess it was his thing. But the rope in here could help us."

Tessa threw everything on the ground at the foot of the bed. There were several short ropes and one longer one that had to be at least ten feet.

"Help me tie some of these little ones to the big one," Tessa said. "That should give us enough to drop down."

Ainsley did as she asked and, in a matter of minutes, they had one even longer rope. Tessa went to the back window, opened it, and started feeding the rope out. When there was just a little left, she tied it to the leg of the armchair next to the window.

"You go first," Tessa said. "I'll hold it. If it's going to give, it'll give on me. I can take the hit."

Ainsley swung one leg out the window, then the other, and grabbed the rope with both hands.

"Lower yourself down," Tessa said. "Hand over hand."

Ainsley tried to, but her grip slipped each time. The rope was burning in her hands. She bit her lip as she slid down, fighting the urge to scream. Finally, her feet found the knots they tied and gave her some leverage. She lowered herself down inchworm-style until her feet found the ground. Her hands and the insides of her thighs were stinging in pain, but she was down.

"Okay, come on," she said.

Tessa came out the same as she had but was much more adept at handling the rope. She'd get a grip, let herself drop, get a new grip, and repeat. She was nearly to Ainsley when the chair groaned up above and the rope went slack. Tessa let go of it, hit the ground, and rolled on to her side.

"Tessa!" Ainsley ran over to her. "Are you okay?"

"Yeah." Tessa winced as she got up. "Come on. We have to go."

The two of them ran along the enclosed breezeway at the back side of The Lodge, and the house where their rooms were. When they came to the other side, the road to the rest of the resort was just fifty feet away. They stopped at the front corner of the house and peeked back. The guard was there, just as Ainsley had warned, but now they were past him. If they stayed in the shadows, they might be fine.

They crept forward until the road turned, and The Lodge was out of sight. There, Tessa broke into an all-out sprint. Ainsley ran after her, but struggled to keep up. They made it back to the bigger road that wound through the resort, but instead of turning for The Country Club as they had each day before, they ran headlong down the hill toward the front gate. They ran harder, faster, the downward incline propelling them towards freedom. The final big turn was just ahead. Then the big building they'd driven past when they first came in, then the gate.

Ainsley started to think they might make it when two flashlights shone on them from the road ahead.

"Hey! Stop right there!" a male voice barked.

"Shit!" Tessa said.

She pivoted away from the lights and started running back the way they'd come. Ainsley nearly tripped as she turned to keep Tessa in sight, a stitch forming in her side.

"Wait!" Ainsley called out between pants. "We can't go back. Not now."

"We're not going back! We're finding another way."

"I've got the two AWOL girls on the main road between The Manor and The Lustschloss. They're dressed like they came from The Lodge," Ainsley heard a voice shout behind her.

The men had already been out looking for them. Someone somewhere must have seen them. Ainsley's heart sank with the realization they were never as close to leaving as it had just seemed.

When they got back to the first big turn, Tessa's head turned at the sight of a smaller road that branched off the other way. She took it and kept running, Ainsley still on her heels.

"Where does this go?" she asked.

"Don't know, but it's away from them!"

The road climbed up before flattening out on a small plateau. It turned into a large gravel lot with a row of small, one-room cabins connected to each other on the outside. A few of the doors started opening and out stepped more young men. They were different from the clients. Rougher-looking. A few of them yelled at them, ordering them to stop.

Tessa just ran past them, Ainsley desperate to keep up. The road climbed again and on the horizon was what looked to be a large barn.

This has to be the end. Let this be the end of the property.

But as the ground evened out again and Ainsley could see everything around them cast in the eerie glow of the pale moonlight, her heart fell into her stomach. The barn sat just feet from a sheer cliff. There was no going through or around the barn, and there was nowhere else to go. There was only the cliff or back the way they'd come, which was now swarming with a small army of angry, half-dressed men.

"What do we do now?" Ainsley asked.

Before Tessa could answer her. The throng of men separated, revealing a pair of headlights.

———

GRAVES MONITORED the comms from the resort the whole way back. A guest had made his way back to The Lodge's dining room for a night cap, when he heard a commotion above. He followed the noise to an open door at the end of the hallway. There, he discovered a man unconscious and a window open with a rope hanging from the sill. He'd immediately gone and called security.

Jackson prayed whoever it was would escape, but Graves' team was playing it smart. A perimeter had been established while they got more manpower to the area. The comms had been quiet for several minutes as Graves and Jackson arrived at the front gate when a strident voice burst forth.

"I've got the two AWOL girls on the main road between The Manor and The Lustschloss. They're dressed like they came from The Lodge."

Jackson recognized the voice as Beckett. When the gate was open, Graves gunned through.

Another voice came over the comm. "They just turned for The Camp and The Facilities Barn. Everyone converge. We'll have them cornered."

Graves roared past The Manor and took the long, swinging turn up the hill, the tires screeching underneath them as he did. He shot off the main road and onto the turn for The Camp without slowing down. As the SUV bobbed up and down, its headlights settled on a pack of half-dressed members of the security team.

"What the hell is this bush-league bullshit?" Graves asked.

Hearing the SUV behind them, the men divided, and Graves pulled through. At the front were Beckett and Roscoe. Their pistols were drawn, leveled at two small figures at the edge of the cliff. Jackson climbed out of the G63, he could see it was the two young girls.

"Get on your goddamn knees right now!" Beckett was shouting.

The girls did as they were told. Neither of them could've been much older than twenty. Jackson's heart sank as he took in the girls in front of him. One of them, a half-head taller, was lanky and angular, with a head full of brunette hair wrapped into tight braids. The other looked younger and had long blonde hair that was now slightly disheveled. Tears streaked her mascara down her cheeks. Both of them looked terrified, though the one with braids was doing a better job of putting on a brave face. Neither of them had anywhere to go.

Roscoe looked at Graves as he stepped forward. "Got them, boss," he said. "What do you want to do with them?"

Graves looked at the girls, both of whom were shaking.

"They killed one of the clients!" Beckett pressed. "That shit can't go unchecked."

Graves raised the radio he had brought from the SUV up to his lips. He keyed the mic.

"Is anyone at The Lodge?" he asked.

"This is Carter," the radio came back. "I'm here."

"What's the status up there? Is there a client down?"

"Hold."

Everyone waited in silence.

The radio crackled. "I've got one down in the Deer Room. His ID says Gary Hoskins," Carter said.

"He's a guest," Beckett said again.

Graves ignored him. He keyed the mic on his radio. "Confirm status? Do we need to get Medical?"

A pause. "Negative. He's dead. Confirmed."

"You see!" Beckett said. His eyes were as wide as saucers as he placed one hand around the pistol on his hip. "They're goddamn junky killers. That shit can't slide."

A man in only sweats and a tank top pipped up, "Let's run a fuckin' train on them. That'll teach 'em their place."

A few others laughed with approval.

Jackson couldn't stand doing nothing. "Boss," he said to Graves under his breath. "We shouldn't do anything we can't undo. Maybe we need to run this up the flag pole."

"No." Graves drew his pistol. "There's only one way to handle this."

He stepped past Beckett and the other man and pointed his pistol at the blond.

"No! Wait!" The one with braids threw herself in front of the other girl. "It was me, and it was an accident. Please, you have to believe me! He asked if I had anything besides the Pepsis. I told him I had some benzos. He asked for them, so I gave them to him. Next thing I know, he's passed out. I was scared. Ainsley was only trying to help. But it was me. It was an accident."

Graves lowered his pistol. His eyes darted between the two girls before they settled on the blond.

"Is that true?" he asked.

The blond gave several erratic nods. "It was — accident," she sobbed.

Graves paused for a beat longer. "Fair enough."

Before Jackson could even react, Graves took a step toward the girl with braids, leveled his pistol at her head, and squeezed the trigger. The blond let out a blood-curdling shriek as she was splattered with blood and brain matter. The other girl collapsed to the ground, dead.

Graves motioned for the others to come forward.

"Take this one back to The Lodge," he said, nodding at the blond. "Have Mina get her cleaned up."

Beckett and another man took the blond girl, the one the other had called Ainsley, by the arms and dragged her away. As they did, she locked streaming eyes with Jackson. Jackson recognized the helplessness they held. The pain, the fear. He'd seen it in a dozen other victims. He'd come to all their aid, one or another.

Now he just stood there, watching the girl.

He was outnumbered, ten to one. If he made a move now, it'd be the last thing he ever did. So, he stood there, watching the blond girl as they took her away.

He promised himself right then that he would get her out of this place.

THIRTY-NINE

CORLISS WAITED inside his plane as it sat on the tarmac outside the fixed-based operator at Roanoke-Blacksburg Regional Airport. His tendril was late.

Corliss had several tendrils. It's what he called the various men and women he had backed professionally in exchange for their loyalty. He had tendrils all throughout government and law enforcement, up to and including three members of the house of representatives and one sitting senator. This particular tendril was not quite of their stature — not yet, anyway — but was no less important, especially since he learned a multi-agency task force was investigating what he'd built at The Arcady.

Finally, the tendril arrived. He opened the door from the terminal and jogged out to the plane. A moment later, he was on board and seated in front of Corliss, trying to catch his breath.

"You're late," Corliss said.

"I know," the tendril replied. "I'm sorry. I couldn't get away from the off—"

Corliss held up a hand. "Just get to it. What is this problem?"

The tendril reached into the briefcase he'd brought with him and pulled out a manila folder. "The infiltration at The Arcady is still active. The asset you uh, *eliminated* wasn't the problem."

"The asset was *eliminated* based on the intelligence you provided. That means *you* screwed up."

"I was told they'd placed a source within your team. They'd meant he worked for Graves. I assumed that meant he was inside The Arcady, but that was incorrect. However, that's changed now. Now, he *is* there. At The Arcady."

Opening the folder, he showed the files inside to Corliss. At the top of the first page was a booking photo. It showed a man in his forties with a trimmed, brown beard that was graying on the edges and close-cropped hair.

"His name is Jackson Clay. We missed him initially—"

"*You* missed him," Corliss corrected without taking his eyes off the files.

"*I* missed him because he's never been in law enforcement. At least, not officially. But I have confirmation now he is the source that was inserted by the task force."

Corliss was quiet for a moment as he reviewed what was in front of him. "How close are they to building a case?"

"It's hard to say. They tied the explosive used on the woman in Winchester to Touchpoint, but any connection to The Arcady is tenuous at best." The tendril nodded at the folder. "But this Clay guy is inside. And he's seeing whatever is going on out there."

"He's on Graves' security detail?" Corliss asked.

"That's my understanding, yes."

"And he's the only source they've placed? We're sure?"

"Yes, sir."

Corliss sighed. "Fine. Stay on top of it. We'll handle things on our end."

"Yes, sir."

Corliss waved his hand. "Go. Get off my plane."

The tendril got up and left. As soon as they did, Corliss had his stewardess tell the pilots to fly them back to the airfield immediately, then fix him a drink. If there was one thing he hated in this world, it was incompetence. Graves and this tendril failed to do their jobs and now there were coyotes in his backyard. Or, more accurately, one coyote. Corliss looked down at the files again.

The coyote's name was Jackson Clay.

Now he had to put him down.

PART FIVE

GOING DARK

"Strength does not come from physical capacity. It comes from an indomitable will." —Mahatma Gandhi

FORTY

AINSLEY COULDN'T STOP SHAKING.

It had set in as the two men took her away from the cliff and put her in the back of an SUV. It had continued as she was dropped off at the girls' bunkhouse, and Mina forced her into a shower, washing Tessa's blood off her before changing her into a baggy cover up. Now, as she sat in a room in the basement of the bunkhouse — a basement she hadn't known even existed — with the door locked from the outside, she couldn't suppress the tears that fell in sync with her trembling.

Tessa's final moments played on a loop in her mind. There one minute, defending Ainsley, and gone the next. Slumped over on the ground, lifeless. In so many ways, Ainsley wished it had been her. This all had been Tessa's dream first and foremost. A dream that had turned into the most unfathomable nightmare. Laying on the canvas cot in the pitch-dark windowless room, Ainsley started to wonder what would come next for her.

Would they force her back to work? Would they kill her? As much as she didn't want to die, the thought of this nightmare ending was comforting.

She reached out into the darkness for the dress she'd had on that day. Mina had thrown it in with her before shutting the door. It was a starry sequin lace dress Ainsley had fallen in love with that first night they'd arrived. It reminded her of the night sky and the constellations. But that was before it'd become diffused with Tessa's blood, turning the starry sequins into a field of bloody asteroids. Ainsley found it on the floor below the cot and pulled it close to her, clinging to whatever she could of her friend.

Running her fingers over the lacy fabric, she felt a bump. Confused for a moment, she remembered it was the pills — the Pepsis — in the dress' pocket. Ainsley slid her hand into the pocket and pulled out the baggy.

The three tablets slid and shifted inside.

Not once since Mina gave them to Ainsley did she consider taking them herself, but she imagined the escape that might await inside them. It didn't matter if it was real or just chemical reactions in her brain, Ainsley was desperate to be anywhere but here. She opened the baggy and swallowed all three tablets dry. Then, she rolled on to her back and waited.

Minutes went by. Ainsley didn't know how long it was supposed to take, but she started to doubt they were real. Maybe they were just another lie this place peddled. A promise that never materialized, just like all the others.

Ainsley had all but convinced herself this was the case when a euphoric warmth welled up inside of her. No, not inside her. It was *all around* her. Inviting and enveloping, like slipping into a warm bath. Her senses came alive. The canvas cot was an intricate tapestry she couldn't stop running her hands across. Bands of color started to wave through the darkness before raining down around her. Tessa's laugh singsonged through the room as though she was right there with her.

Ainsley closed her eyes and left the gloomy room. She floated higher and higher, The Arcady and all its problems getting ever smaller below her. She looked up and saw the night sky stretched out across the filigree pattern of the lacy dress, the constellations she'd memorized ahead of her. She flew amongst them. She became one with them. She was Andromeda, sacrificed by her mother Cassiopeia and cast out to the rock, but saved by Perseus and made his queen. It was everything she wanted in that moment: to be saved from this dark corner of Appalachia.

Ainsley kept ascending, never looking back.

FORTY-ONE

JACKSON COULDN'T GET the young blond girl out of his head. The expression of pain and hopelessness she had given him was seared into his mind. The other girl had sacrificed herself for her without any hesitation. There was no doubt in his mind that they knew each other. Were they close friends? Sisters?

Graves had killed the one in front of the other and didn't think twice about it. It was cold and matter-of-fact, as if he didn't see the girl as a person. Jackson had come across some truly heartless people in his new life of helping those who had fallen through society's cracks, but Graves was one of the worst.

Jackson wondered where they were keeping the blond girl. They must not have plans to kill her — at least not yet — or else they would have done so out on the cliff. Likewise, they surely couldn't trust her to continue to work. She'd already proven to be a flight risk, and who knows what kind of mental state she would be in after tonight.

More importantly, though, if there were those two girls, there had to be others. Jackson had to see what was up that road through the woods and end this before anyone else got hurt.

He was lying in bed mulling everything over, when an engine roared up the road outside. A moment later, tires skidding to a stop on the gravel drive sounded so close outside he could head pebbles hitting the side of the house. Jackson got up and looked out the window. Graves and three men got out of a black van and moved quickly toward his front door. Jackson scrambled to get his phone off the dresser, but the men kicked in his door and filled the room. Jackson squared up to them.

"What the hell are you doing, Graves?" he asked.

"Take him," Graves ordered.

The other three men closed in. As one reached out for him, Jackson took the man's arm, swung him around, and twisted it behind him. The man yelped as he fell to his knees. Jackson shoved him at one of the others, forcing that one to step over his buddy. The third came around and tried to put Jackson in a rear naked choke, but Jackson threw a hard elbow into his abdomen and then mule kicked him into the wall.

The first two now came back at him. As one telegraphed a punch, Jackson ducked and launched into his midsection, tackling him against the dresser. The second guy tried to pin Jackson's legs, but Jackson rotated around and landed a kick to the man's jaw.

Jackson got to his feet and started back for the third guy, who'd recovered from Jackson's mule kick, when a gunshot cracked off like thunder. Jackson flinched and turned to see Graves had fired a round into the floor. Now, the gun was pointed at Jackson.

"Enough," Graves said.

Jackson saw in his eyes Graves knew the truth about him. He looked at Jackson as though he'd just caught vermin rooting around in his trash cans. There was no use keeping up the charade.

"You going to shoot me like you shot that girl?" Jackson asked. "It's easy to feel big when you're the only one with a gun, isn't it?"

Graves didn't say anything. Instead, he grinned and lowered the gun.

Then Jackson felt something hit him from behind and his world went black.

———

WHEN JACKSON CAME TO, he found himself sitting in a chair with his hands bound behind him and his legs taped together at the ankles and at his knees. The chair swiveled beneath him and Jackson almost toppled out of it before a pair of beefy arms grabbed him from behind and sat him back upright.

Jackson took in his surroundings. He was in the middle of The Facilities Barn, with the large bay door and the early morning sun rising in the sky to his left and the back wall to his right. In front of him was the row of fleet vehicles. Leaning on the front fender of a Range Rover twenty feet in front of him was Graves. Spread out across the barn on either side of him were another half-dozen members of the security team including Roscoe and Beckett. Graves was leering at Jackson, disdain written in every line of his face. Gone was the smug tough-guy act. In its place was sheer vitriol.

"Tell Mr. Corliss he's awake," Graves said, without taking his eyes off Jackson.

Roscoe talked into a cellphone off to Jackson's left, then looked over at Graves and nodded. "He's on his way up."

"You all are making a mistake," Jackson said.

"Is that so?" Graves replied. "What mistake are we making?"

"Killing me."

"You don't look dead to me."

"Stop with the games, Graves. We both know what this is."

Graves shook his head and folded his arms. "You? Accusing me of playing games? You're out here playing one big game with all of us."

"I never lied to you. Not once. You even had my real DD 214."

"So you're saying you're not an informant for the police?"

"I never said I wasn't. You never asked."

An Audi sedan pulled up out front and Corwin Corliss got out of the rear passenger-side door. He was taller than Jackson expected, but other than that, he was just as he looked in the picture Jackson had seen of him online: clean-shaven and rosy-cheeked, with hair slicked back and to the side.

Graves was locked onto Jackson. "You think this is funny?"

"I don't," Jackson countered. "I think you're bad at your job."

"I agree," said Corliss, walking over to them. "Luckily, I have multiple layers of people and security insulating me. And the police are not the only ones with sources." He dropped a manila folder at Jackson's feet. "Jackson Clay, a confidential human source placed among us courtesy of the newly formed Western Virginia Human Trafficking Task Force. You had us chasing our tails there for a little while — I even had to neutralize another team member we thought was our leak."

Cody Busch, Jackson thought. That's why they killed him. Busch wasn't some sort of liability. They thought he was a mole.

"Fortunately, we've got everything figured out now. You, our little infiltrator, and that safe house a little ways down the road."

Jackson met his eyes.

Corliss laughed. "Yes, we know it all now. How else do you think a place like this exists? Not to use a tortured cliche, but the best defense is a good offense. I identify the threats and eliminate them."

"The Task Force knows I'm in here. If I disappear, do you really think they'll just pack up and go home? The only thing cops hate more than a truly evil asshole like you is a cop killer. You'll have every agency in the state coming for you."

"A cop killer? That would presume you're law enforcement, which you're not."

"If you think they'll make the distinction, you're dumber than you look."

Corliss reached his hand out, palm up. Roscoe came over to him and placed a pistol in it.

"They can try to come after me if they want," Corliss said. "That won't stop me from cleaning house. Of *all* my problems." Corliss leveled the pistol at Graves.

Graves froze. "What the fuck is this?"

"I told you. Baseball rules, Mr. Graves, and you're out of strikes."

A sneer spread across Graves' face. "You just said it yourself. Busch didn't slip past me. He was clean. *You* killed him."

"I told you time and time again to end that little drug operation you had on the side, but you wouldn't. You couldn't, because you're greedy. And greedy people can be bought. They have no true loyalty. Look what it brought in here? Into what *I've* built. *Him*." He nodded at Jackson. "Please restrain Mr. Graves."

Roscoe pulled a pair of zip cuffs out from behind him and stepped toward Graves.

Graves shook his head. "So, what? You're his lap dog now? You don't think he'll get rid of you just like this one day?"

"I ain't you," Roscoe said.

He stepped toward Graves and reached out for one of his arms. When he did, Graves grabbed Roscoe's wrist instead and twisted it. He put Roscoe between him and Corliss, drew his own pistol off his hip, and pointed it at Corliss.

"Yeah, you're a lot bigger and dumber," Graves hissed. Controlling Roscoe's wrist, he used the husky man like a shield.

The other men inside the barn also drew their pistols, but seemed unsure who to point them at.

"Come on, now," Corliss said. "You all can't be that shortsighted. Who do you think cuts your paychecks? If you want to continue to get one, you'll put Mr. Graves down."

"Or they could kill you and loot five years-worth of salary from this place in less than an hour." Graves pulled on Roscoe's wrist harder, causing the big man to grunt in pain. He eyes each of the men standing there. "Either way, if you come for me, you have to go through Roscoe here, who I'm assuming Corwin has lined up to be your next boss. How long do you think you last under this fat fuck after shooting him?"

Graves, still holding Roscoe, backed up against the row of vehicles and started moving sideways toward the open bay door. All the other guns in the room had their sights set on the two of them, but no one fired.

"That's right," Graves said. "You're going to let me go, and then you all can figure the rest out." He walked backward out of the bay door. "You don't mind if I borrow your car, do you, Corwin?"

Corwin sneered but didn't say anything. Graves stepped out of the barn and came around to the driver's door of the Audi. He opened it and ordered the chauffeur inside to get out. Graves now had two men to use as shields, and he wedged himself between them.

"One last thing, Corwin," Graves said. "Go fuck yourself."

Graves fired a shot that went wide of Corliss and shattered a van's windshield over his shoulder. Everyone with a gun inside the barn returned fire as Graves ducked into the car. The driver fled down the road. Rounds plinked and plunked off the body of the sedan. Fractured spiderwebs of cracks began filling the windows, but no round got through.

The sedan is armored, Jackson thought.

Graves continued to fire blindly into the barn and the team inside fired back. Jackson used the confusion to kick the computer chair backward and roll into the relative safety of the parked side-by-sides. One of Corliss's men moved around him and used the off-road vehicle nearest Jackson for cover. Jackson got his feet under him and launched himself into the back of the man who grunted as he became pinned between Jackson and the side-by-side.

Something on the chair broke and snapped the zip cuffs around Jackson's wrists. His legs were still bound but with his hands free, Jackson dropped the lower half of his body onto the man's legs, pinning them, then wrapped his arm around the man's neck and squeezed. The man slammed into the ground, dropping the gun and clawing at Jackson to try to break his choke hold. Jackson squeezed tighter. Seconds later, the man went limp.

Someone saw this and fired at Jackson. Jackson fell back, pulling the unconscious man's body on top of him. More shots were fired at him and Jackson felt bullets hit the man on top of him. If he wasn't dead already, he'd bleed out in seconds. Jackson tried but couldn't reach the gun on the floor. He started patting down the man on top of him for anything to use. On his belt was a knife, and in his pocket was a phone.

That would have to do.

Jackson slid on his back, carrying the now dead or dying man with him, until he was behind one of the side-by-sides and into relative cover. He got the knife and cut his legs free. Then he opened up the phone. This time around, he'd memorized Bailey's number.

Bailey answered. "Hello?"

"Gym time," Jackson said.

There was a chaotic mix of noises of people scrambling on the other end of the line. "Jackson, where are you?"

"The Facilities Barn. It's a large warehouse-style building on the south side of the resort, up a cliff." A bullet whizzed by just over Jackson's head. "My cover is blown, but Corliss turned on Graves. Now I'm in a firefight between the two of them and Corliss's men."

"Copy. Hang tight. We're coming. We're rolling right now!"

"Graves is in an armored Audi sedan. He's going to make a run for it. I'm going after him."

"No. Jackson, hang tight. Help is com—"

Jackson ended the call and tucked the phone away. He needed a gun, and he needed a car. He peeked out over the back of the side-by-side he was using for cover.

Corliss and his men were spread out on either side of the barn, but their attention was on Graves. Keeping low, Jackson made his way between the rows of vehicles to the back of the barn before coming to the open space down the middle. Beckett was behind everyone else. Jackson waited for Graves to stop firing, then he moved.

Springing up, he dashed across the open middle area and threw himself at Beckett, hitting him in the midsection like a human javelin. Beckett's gun went sliding. He tried to move to defend himself, but Jackson was too fast. He got on top of Beckett, placed his knees on the young man's arms and punched him square in the jaw. A second time and Beckett was out cold.

Somewhere to his left, Jackson heard the engine of a car roar to life. Graves had had enough of the shootout and was making a break for it. Jackson got Beckett's pistol then flung himself at the door of the Range Rover next to him, yanked it open, and scrambled inside. He pushed the ignition on the SUV's engine, praying the key fob was somewhere in range. The eight-cylinder engine roared to life.

Jackson closed the door, but the sound of the Range Rover got everyone's attention. Half the men turned and started firing at Jackson. Unlike the Audi, the SUV was not armored and round after round came through a splintered windshield. Jackson kept low, put the SUV in gear, and gunned it.

The SUV swerved out of its spot and headed for the open bay door, forcing Corliss and his men to jump out of the way or get run over. Jackson didn't slow down. He tore down the gravel road past The Camp and chased Graves onto the main drive. The shot-up Audi was several hundred feet ahead and headed for the front gate. Jackson tried to make up ground, but the firefight up on the cliff had drawn clients and security staff alike out to investigate. Now, they dotted the road, forcing Jackson to slalom through them. It wasn't until he got to the front of The Manor that the road cleared and Jackson got up to speed.

Coming around the final bend, he saw up ahead Graves was already through the front gate and it was closing behind him. Jackson pressed the gas pedal as far down as it would go. The SUV bucked high and shot right for the closing gate. At the last moment, Jackson saw he wasn't going to clear it, but it was too late. There was a thunderous boom as the SUV slammed through the narrowing gap. Every airbag inside deployed as the two gate doors tore into the Range Rover like a pair of giant can openers.

The SUV made it through, but just barely. It rolled onto the highway.

Jackson was woozy from the impact. He tried the gas pedal again, but it didn't respond. The Range Rover coasted to a stop, blocking both lanes. Jackson opened the door and got out, but his legs gave out underneath him.

He collapsed onto the pavement. Off in the distance he saw Graves headed west for the state line, disappearing out of sight. Seconds later, the Impala and the Explorer rolled up, led by Bear in his Suburban.

Bear got out and trotted over to Jackson, his .357 in hand. "Jacky boy," he called out. "You alright, brother?"

Bailey slammed her car door behind her and ran over to them.

"Go, go. I'm fine," Jackson said, waving them off. "Graves is headed West. We can't lose him."

"I've got nothing to charge him with, Jackson," Bailey said.

"He shot and killed a young woman right in front of me. Murder one, Bailey. Get him."

Bailey looked back at Kavanaugh and Wilcox in the Impala. "Go!"

They got back in, drove around Jackson and the smashed Range Rover, and sped off. Bailey pulled out her phone, punched a few buttons, and put it to her ear.

"This is Special Agent Jen Bailey with HTU," she said. "I need a BOLO put out for a Nicholas Graves. Last seen traveling west on US 250 toward Hightown in an Audi sedan, likely visible gunshot damage. He's wanted on suspicion of murder and should be considered armed and dangerous. Advise West Virginia State Police and local agencies in central West Virginia, as well." She ended the call and looked down at Jackson. "Come on, let's get you to a hospital."

"I'm fine. Kavanaugh and Wilcox will need backup."

"And they'll get it. But I'm getting you in front of a doctor."

Bear and Bailey helped Jackson up and walked him to Bear's suburban. As he limped along, Jackson looked over his left shoulder. Behind the wreckage of the front gate, parked on the main drive was a convoy from The Arcady. Corliss and a half dozen men stood there, watching him.

In his mind, Jackson begged them to make the stupid move and engage them. But they resisted the temptation. No more than a hundred yards apart, but in that moment, each party was as unreachable to one as the other.

Bear loaded Jackson into his Suburban and took him away.

FORTY-TWO

JACKSON SAT UPRIGHT on a hospital bed in the Emergency Department of Roanoke Memorial with his feet hanging over the side. To his left, monitors and medical instruments surrounded the head of the bed. A TV played cable news to Jackson's right, but he paid it no mind. He held a thousand-yard stare through the sliding glass doors to the room in front of him as he replayed the shootout in his head.

A nurse was taking his vitals for the third time in as many hours. As she squeezed the inflation bulb repeatedly, the blood pressure cuff tightened across his biceps. She let out some of the pressure and a pneumatic hiss filled the enclosed room.

"One thirty-five over eighty-eight," the nurse said. "A little high. Do you take blood pressure medication?"

"No," Jackson replied.

"Have you been under any unusual stress?"

"I drove a two-and-a-half-ton vehicle through an iron gate while getting shot at. Does that count?"

The nurse's face was deadpan aside from a raised eyebrow, indicating she wasn't amused with his sarcasm. She undid the cuff around his arm. A knock came on the plate glass of the sliding door. From the other side, Bailey showed her credentials to the nurse and slid the door open.

"Can we have the room for a moment, please?" she asked.

The nurse nodded. "I was just wrapping up." She looked at Jackson. "The doctor will be in to talk over discharge instructions soon."

Bailey gave the nurse a polite smile as she left, sliding the door shut behind her. Bailey took a seat in a chair opposite Jackson.

"Sounds like you'll be getting out of here soon. What's the word?"

"Just banged up. Might've sprained my wrist. I'll live."

Bailey nodded. Jackson gave her the rundown on everything that had happened since he left the motel in Franklin. He told her how two girls, almost certainly trafficked, had tried to escape and Graves had killed one execution-style. Told her how Graves came for him early the next morning only to have Corliss show up and turn on Graves, which brought about the ensuing shootout.

"Graves is in the wind," Bailey said. "We have a BOLO out as far as all neighboring states and the FBI and US Marshals are assisting."

"I figured as much."

"He's alone, on the run, with limited resources. He'll turn up."

Jackson nodded. A quiet fell between them and Bailey picked at a fingernail with her teeth. The only sounds were that of the staff and patients outside, muffled through the closed door. Finally, Jackson spoke.

"Are we going to talk about the five-hundred-pound gorilla in the room?" Jackson asked.

Bailey folded her arms. "What's that?"

"You have a mole in your task force."

Bailey looked at him for a beat. "That's a serious allegation."

"Not an allegation, it's a fact. When Graves killed that girl on the cliff side, I was one of the guys on the inside. He did it right in front of me without hesitating. Not six hours later, he's rolling up on me with a car full of goons. Corliss showed me the file, Bailey. They had everything."

"Corliss is the head of one of the biggest defense contractors in the country. There are dozens of ways he could've gotten that information."

"Not without someone giving it up from within."

"The Task Force was put together without even knowing Corliss or his resort were the target. A dozen investigators handpicked from almost as many agencies. How could Corliss possibly ensure his mole got on the team?"

"That's what you need to ask yourself."

Bailey shook her head. "It doesn't matter. The investigation is FUBAR. That's why I came here. I just got the official word: they're shutting us down."

"The whole thing?"

"Not the task force, but the op on The Arcady, yes."

"There are still people in that place, Bailey. The girls, the staff, and God knows who else. They're in more danger now than ever because of us. We can't just abandon them."

"What do you want me to say? You told us yourself they know about the safe house. They know about you."

Jackson shook his head. "I don't accept that. There's got to be another way."

Bailey stood up and came over to him. "I'm not saying we're done pursuing this. We know what's going on up there and it's well within the task force's charter to investigate. But your cover is blown with them. Even if I wanted to keep you on, there's nothing more you can do. If you go back to The Arcady, they'll kill you as fast as they can. You know that."

Jackson didn't say anything.

"I have a meeting across town at the Task Force's offices, but I'll come back after. The team will bring anything that is yours from the safe house. I'll have Roanoke PD bring you over to the offices when you're done here. Then I'll drive you back to your place."

Jackson remained silent. Bailey turned and walked to the door.

"I'm sorry this didn't go how we wanted it to. But like I said, it's not over."

Bailey slid the door open and left.

Jackson flopped back on his pillow and stared at the ceiling tiles. He couldn't let it go. He was right about there being a mole in the task force. As long as there was, anything they tried to do would be compromised. It didn't matter that he trusted Bailey. If she was a part of the task force, she was compromised, too. He'd made a promise to himself on that cliff side last night that he'd get that young girl — and all the others — out.

If he had to do it without the help of Bailey and the task force, so be it.

He looked over at the counter across the room. The cellphone and knife he'd had in his pockets sat on top in a plastic bag. Jackson knew Bailey or the Task Force would want to log it as evidence and that they hadn't already was surprising. The phone was his only direct connection back to the resort. He'd need it if he was going to get back into The Arcady.

When the doctor came five minutes later to give Jackson his discharge paperwork, the room was empty.

And there was nothing on the counter.

FORTY-THREE

JACKSON LEFT the hospital and headed north into the heart of the city, taking a pedestrian bridge across the Roanoke River. As he did, he called Bear with the phone he'd taken with him. Bear answered on the first ring.

"Jacky boy, you still at the hospital?" he asked. "I've got some of your stuff. I was going to head your way."

"I just left," Jackson replied.

"What do you mean?"

Jackson waited for someone walking the other direction to pass him by. "Bailey and the Task Force are shutting everything down. She wants to send me home." Another pause as someone else walked past him. "Look, I'm going dark on this one. I get it if you can't come with me."

"Where are you now?"

"It's probably best I don't say unless you're in."

"Brother, for you, I'm always in. You know that."

Jackson got to the other side of the bridge and headed into a parking garage. "I'm headed north from the hospital. Just crossed the river. I'm staying out of sight from surface streets."

"I'm on my way."

Jackson used the phone to look up a map of the surrounding area. "There's a park a quarter mile from the hospital on the river bank. I'll be there."

"Roger."

Jackson ended the call. He made his way through the parking garage, across a small parking lot on the other side, and over to the park. It was little more than a long, grassy knoll with a small boat ramp at one end. By the stairs that led down to the river was a small picnic table, with bench seats on either side. Jackson eased into one of the benches and waited for Bear. He'd been there less than five minutes when the phone rang. It was a blocked number.

"Hello?" Jackson answered.

"Clay," Graves voice came from the other end of the line. "I thought I saw you take Carter's phone off him back at the resort. You and I need to talk."

"Cold-calling numbers in hopes that the one guy who wants to put you away the most picks up? You must really be desperate."

"Yeah, well, you fucked me pretty good."

"You fucked yourself. I just facilitated it."

"And now you're going to un-facilitate it."

"Why would I do that?"

"Because I can give you Corliss. That's what you really want, right? The Arcady."

Jackson thought for a moment. "Okay, I'm listening."

"You're working with the police, right? I want to come in. Immunity and protection in exchange for what I know."

"How do I know what you have is worth that?"

"Believe me. I have enough to string up Corliss and then some."

"We need to meet up. You show and tell me what you have, then we'll see if I believe you."

There was a pause on the other end. "Fine. Where?"

"The club. Belle Bottoms."

"Fuck that, Corliss will have that place staked out. I'll only meet you some place not connected to the resort."

Jackson scanned his surroundings. "Roanoke."

Another pause. "Where?"

He turned around. A giant steel star stood atop the mountain across the river, looking over the city. He knew the landmark well. "The Mill Mountain Star. At the overlook. How far away are you?"

"A few hours."

"The overlook at the star in three hours." Jackson ended the call.

————

THIRTY MINUTES LATER, Bear pulled into the park's parking and Jackson hopped in.

"We better get you out of Dodge before Bailey and co know you're missing."

"We're not going much of anywhere. Graves called me while you were en route. We have a meet."

"Graves called you? How?"

"He saw me take the phone off one of the goons back at the resort. Took a flyer on me still having it."

"Why'd he reach out to you?"

"I'm guessing he did the math between Corliss and every agency in the mid-Atlantic looking for him and didn't like his odds."

Bear chortled. "So what does he want?"

"Immunity and protection in exchange for information on how to bag Corliss."

"And you told him yes? Without checking with Bailey or anyone?"

"We're not giving him shit. We're taking him and making him talk."

Bear's laugh deepened with pleasure. "Brother, I like your style."

————

BAILEY WAS in a meeting with the J-Team back at the Task Force's offices when her phone rang. She excused herself, then stepped out of the conference room to take the call.

"Special Agent Bailey," she said.

"Hello, ma'am. This is Corporal Ramirez with the Roanoke Police Department."

"Hello, corporal. What can I do for you?"

"Well, ma'am, I'm down here at Roanoke Memorial. I believe your office requested a transport for a Jackson Clay, but I haven't been able to locate him."

"I was just there with him a couple hours ago. He should be in the Emergency Department. Did you ask the hospital staff?"

"That's just the thing, ma'am. They said they can't find him, either. They believe he's AWOL."

A cold shiver washed over Bailey. "What do you mean 'they believe he's AWOL'?"

"Apparently the doctor came in to talk to him and he wasn't there. He didn't sign himself out and they can't locate him."

"Thank you, Corporal. There must've been some sort of mix-up, I apologize. I'll take care of it."

"You sure, ma'am? I can keep looking."

"Yes, thank you. Why don't you do that and I'll call you back."

"Sure thing."

Bailey ended the call. From inside the conference room, Pitts saw the look of consternation on Bailey's face and started toward her. Bailey pulled out her phone and started scrolling for Clay's number when she remembered his phone had been taken at the resort. The only phone he'd had on him when they checked him into the ER was the one from which he'd called in the distress signal. That phone might not have been taken in for evidence and, if it hadn't been, she wondered if Clay had taken it with him. She opened up her call log and called the phone back. It went to a generic voicemail.

Bailey's chest tightened. "God dammit, Clay!"

Pitts stepped out of the conference room. "What's wrong?" he asked. "Who just called you?"

"Roanoke PD," she answered. "Clay isn't at the hospital anymore."

Pitts' expression darkened. "What do you mean? Where is he?"

"No one knows. I just tried the cell phone he'd called us on. Nothing."

Pitts was silent for a beat. "You told him he was done?"

Bailey nodded. "I said I'd have Roanoke PD give him a lift back here, and I'd take him home."

"What are the chances he's gone rogue?"

Bailey raised an eyebrow. "Are you asking me what the chances are that *Jackson Clay* has gone off-script?"

"Christ." Pitts took a deep breath in and sighed. "You know what you have to do, right?"

Bailey shook her head. "We don't know what this is yet. Not for sure. Give me some time to find him."

"He's a parolee in the wind, Jen. There's no room for discretion here. You have to call it in."

"What if something happened to him? We call this in now, and there's no walking it back. It could seriously fuck Clay. And after all he just did for us?" Bailey shook her head again. "Let me find him."

Pitts took a deep breath in and sighed. "Fine, but do it quick."

FORTY-FOUR

THE ROANOKE STAR, or Mill Mountain Star, was erected atop Mill Mountain in 1949. Almost ninety feet tall, it was designed as a beacon to bring tourism and trade into the commonwealth's tenth largest city. Now, Jackson sat underneath it, waiting for Graves to arrive. Bear was posted up in the back of his Suburban in the parking lot, yards up the curving walkway to the overlook. They each had a Bluetooth ear bud so they could talk to one another.

"Any sign of him yet?" Jackson asked.

"Negative," Bear replied. "I'll let you know."

Jackson and Bear had used the time until the meet-up to draw up a plan. If it worked, Graves didn't know what he was about to walk into and would have no choice but to cooperate with them.

Now late in the afternoon, the sun headed for the horizon on the other side of the city, shining at a sharp angle on the overlook. Jackson's face was a silhouette underneath the visor of his ball cap. It was a weekday, and the overlook had few visitors. An elderly couple looked out from the edge of the deck as a young boy struggled with the coin-operated viewer off to the side. A woman around Jackson's age, undoubtedly the boy's mother, was chatting and laughing with someone on her phone.

"Hold on," Bear said. "I might have him. A white Toyota Camry just pulled in. Single guy fitting Graves' age and build."

It figured Graves would find a way to switch cars. The Audi had been shot to hell and would draw attention. If this was Graves, it was a smart play. Silver or white Camry's were among the most common cars on the road.

"He's looking around," Bear said. "He's checked each mirror on the car twice."

"It's got to be him," Jackson replied.

"Hold on, door's opening." A pause. "Yep, it's him. Confirmed." Another pause. "He's heading for the walkway now."

"Copy. Stay on him. You know what to do."

"Yessir, he's coming your way. You should see him ... just about ... now."

Almost in unison with Bear's words, Graves came around the bend on the walkway. Jackson didn't move and waited for Graves to spot him. When Graves did, he took slow steps toward Jackson, looking around them.

"You look jumpy," Jackson said.

"Fuck you, I'm here," Graves replied. "I didn't see any police driving up. Where are they?"

"Standing by, I'm supposed to take you to them." Jackson stood up from the ledge he was sitting on and brushed his jeans off. He nodded back to the walkway. "Shall we?"

Graves followed him, though his every move was reluctant. They walked by the woman on the phone who gave them little more than a cursory glance.

"I meant what I said," Graves said. "I'm not saying shit without immunity and protection."

"I believe you."

"You better have gotten them to agree to that, or you're just out here wasting your time."

"I doubt that."

They walked back up the walkway and came to the parking lot. Jackson led them until they were in clear view of the back of the Suburban, then stopped. Jackson turned and faced Graves.

"So, there's been a little change of plan," Jackson said.

Graves stared daggers at Jackson. "I told you," he said, shaking his head. "I'm not talking without a deal."

"There's not going to be a deal, Graves. You're going to come with me and we're going to take a little ride. I have a nice place where you can decide if you really want to talk after all."

"And why the hell would I do that?"

"Now, Bear."

A red laser sight appeared on Graves' shirt. Jackson nodded to it, and Graves looked down and saw it. He looked up and found the source of the laser coming from the back of an old red Suburban whose back section had been blacked out and the rear windshield lowered.

"Because if you don't," Jackson said. "My friend over there is going to put a large bore round through your sternum. You'll bleed out before someone can even call 911."

Graves' scowl deepened. "You wouldn't get away with it."

"Putting a monster like you in the ground? I wouldn't want to." Jackson motioned toward Graves's Camry. "Your car's right over there. Go ahead, call my bluff. You think you can make it?"

Graves's eyes bore into Jackson, but the man didn't move. He took a deep breath in then let out a hissing sigh. "Fine."

"Smart move. Now, we're going to walk straight to the Suburban, and you're going to get in the rear on the passenger side. Deviate at all and you know what happens."

Graves didn't move. He continued to glare at Jackson.

"Now, please."

Graves walked just slow enough to show he was doing so under duress. The two of them crossed the parking lot and went to the Suburban. Jackson opened the rear passenger door and ushered Graves in. Then, he came around and climbed in behind the wheel.

Bear leaned over the middle seat from the back of the Suburban with a pair of zip tie cuffs.

"Good afternoon!" he said, his tone cheerful. "Welcome aboard! May I have your hands, please?"

Graves put his hands out in from of him.

Bear bent closer, grinning. "Pardon my reach." He slipped the cuffs onto Graves's wrist and tightened them.

"Kiss my ass," Graves growled.

"We good back there?" Jackson asked.

"Good as gold, Jacky boy," Bear said.

Jackson fired up the Suburban, backed out, and started down the mountain. When he got to the bottom, he turned on to Highway 220 and headed south.

"Will you at least tell me where you're taking me?" Graves asked.

"Martinsville," Jackson said.

"What the fuck is in Martinsville?"

Bear patted Graves on the shoulder. "Home, my guy," he said.

FORTY-FIVE

JACKSON AND BEAR co-owned an outdoor recreation store in Martinsville called Piedmont Ammo & Supply. More accurately, Bear owned and operated it with Jackson as his silent partner. After swinging by Bear's house just long enough to switch cars — with Jackson on the lam, it wouldn't take the police long to come check if Bear was harboring him — they headed to the Piedmont. They pulled up to the store in Bear's utility bodied Forest Service Green F-350 fifteen minutes before six that evening. Jackson and Bear waited with Graves for Lenny, the lanky kid Bear had left to mind the store, to lock up and leave for the day. When he was gone, they pulled into the back alley and let themselves in.

"We'll need to find a more permanent place," Jackson explained to Bear as the two of them got out of the truck, "but that'll take time. Right now, I need to know if Graves knows who the mole is on the Task Force."

The back door opened into a storeroom. Jackson grabbed a chair from the adjacent office while Bear got Graves out of the truck. The two marched inside and Bear sat him down. Jackson duct taped Graves's cuffed arms and torso to the backrest and each of his legs to a leg on the chair. Once he was secured, Jackson grabbed another chair and sat down opposite Graves.

Bear disappeared into the store's front for a moment then came back out with a ball cap. He tossed it to Jackson.

"You just don't look right without one on," he explained.

Jackson looked at the front of it. It had an eagle, wings spread, clutching a musket embroidered on to it. Below it read 'Piedmont Ammo & Supply'.

"Had a couple dozen of those made up," Bear said. "Been meanin' to give ya one."

Jackson put it on, his eyes locked on Graves from underneath its bill.

"So, what?" Graves said. "Is this the part where you threaten me with torture until I talk?"

Bear leaned against a stack of boxes behind Jackson. "Oh, buddy," he said. "This here's our hunting supply shop. We got all kinds of fun stuff we could use on you."

"It's a thought," Jackson said. "But there won't be any need for that. Because you're going to answer all our questions without it."

Graves chuckled. "Yeah? And why would I do that?"

"Because the other option is I hand you off to Corliss or law enforcement—whoever gives me more for you—and I let them deal with you."

"Meaning Corliss kills you," Bear added. "Or you go to prison where Corliss probably will find someone to kill you."

"Do you think I'm stupid? I answer your questions and what? You promise to let me go?" He shook his head. "I don't think so."

"Maybe, maybe not. Or maybe I let Bear here do some product research at your expense."

"No, I know your type. Principles and morals and shit. You couldn't bring yourself to allow that."

"For just anyone off the street? Sure. But for truly vile people like you, I wouldn't lose a minute of sleep."

Graves's signature scowl reappeared.

"Luckily for you," Jackson said, "I think our interests are aligned at this moment. We want to take Corliss down, and you wouldn't mind seeing that."

Graves shrugged his shoulders as much as Jackson's tape job would allow him. "Okay?"

"Someone gave me up," Jackson said. "One minute you were committing murders in front of me, the next you were trying to put me in a body bag yourself. You didn't suspect a thing until someone told you. Who was it?"

Graves tried to shrug through the duct tape. "One of Corliss's guys. I don't know."

"Bullshit. You were head of his security team."

"He keeps each part insulated from one another. That's how he protects himself. We may have been his right hand, but that doesn't mean we know what the left was doing, much less know who they are."

"You do realize your life expectancy in this moment is directly tied to how useful you are to me?"

Graves groaned. "What do you want me to say? He's got people all throughout government and law enforcement. I don't know who any of them are. Hell, I don't even know that whoever gave you up is the same person that got it wrong in the first place."

Jackson's brow furrowed. "What do you mean?"

Graves met his eyes. He realized he'd over-shared, but it was too late to backtrack. "Someone told Corliss there was a rat in our unit before you. We had to take care of it, but, considering the real rat was you, I guess they were wrong. Poor bastard."

Jackson put the pieces together. "Cody Busch."

Graves nodded. "Corliss's source said that a newly formed task force had just gotten a rat into the resort, working security as his cover. We'd brought Busch on not too long before, so he was the only one that fit. Ironically, taking care of him brought you into the fold for real."

Jackson thought a moment. Anyone in the task force would've

known when exactly he got into the resort. Why would they first feed Corliss the wrong information? It didn't make any sense.

Jackson checked his watch. They'd been at the store for nearly half an hour. The sun would be setting soon, and then they'd have the cover of darkness. He stood up and put his chair back in the office, then came back with a knife to cut Graves free.

"We have to move," Jackson said to Bear. "If they come to check if you're helping me, it won't be long after they check your house that they come here."

Graves laughed. "Well, I'll be damned. You two are on the run yourselves. What'd you do, Ranger?"

Jackson ignored him as he cut the tape. "Stand up and walk. We're moving."

"What happened to letting me go?"

Jackson gave him a shove toward the back door. "I haven't decided anything yet."

FORTY-SIX

THE SOUND of a key unlocking the door bolted Ainsley back to reality. The knob turned and the door opened. Ainsley curled into the fetal position, expecting to see the same man that had shot and killed Tessa, but instead Mina's slim frame stood in the doorway. Taking a step in, she lowered herself to a crouch. Ainsley didn't say anything and neither, at first, did Mina. Her eyes looked Ainsley up and down, taking stock of her.

"Come," she said. "Let's have a chat."

Ainsley knew she didn't have a choice, so she followed Mina. Anything would be better than that windowless room, anyway. Mina led her upstairs to the main floor, then through the breezeway and in to The Lodge.

It was deserted inside.

Mina escorted her into the dining room where only a single table still had its tapered candles lit. Pulling out a chair, she gestured for Ainsley to take a seat. When Ainsley did, Mina came around and sat opposite her.

Again, Mina paused, assessing Ainsley. Ainsley met her gaze. The flames of the candles reflected in Mina's amber irises.

"How about a drink?" Mina suggested. "I'm sure you could use one."

Ainsley assumed in this too she didn't have a choice, so she nodded.

Mina snapped her fingers, and a waiter appeared from the kitchen with a bottle of vodka. Ainsley didn't recognize the brand, but the bottle looked like a piece of modern art.

"Are you going to take this out of my pay, too?" Ainsley asked, her voice flat.

Mina let out an amused chuckle. "This is, as they say, on the house."

The waiter placed a crystal rocks glass in front of Ainsley and poured two fingers worth, then did the same for Mina. Ainsley took a sip. It tasted awful, but she tried to hide her displeasure. It must've been in vain, because Mina grinned as she swallowed it.

"Is this some sort of last meal?" Ainsley asked. "Are you going to kill me, too?"

"*I* have no desire to kill you," Mina replied.

"That man then."

"Nobody wants to kill anyone here. But your friend broke some major rules here. She violated our trust. And once you lose our trust ..." Mina's voice trailed off.

"You have to take us out back and shoot us. Like dogs."

Mina cocked her head as if Ainsley had said something amusing. "When I was five years old, my mother and father fled our town. The fallout from Chernobyl smothered where I was born with its fallout. We were on the train to Slavutych when a man cornered my mother and tried to rape her in the bathroom. My father was a teacher. He never so much as laid a hand on us when we'd misbehaved. He was a kind and gentle man. But when he heard my mother's screams, he came running. I watched as my father got his hands around that man's neck and squeezed until the man stopped moving. He killed that man without a single thought." She took a sip. "People will do whatever to protect theirs. Your friend Tessa threatened what we've built here. And let's not forget she killed someone herself."

"That was an *accident*. You all killed her in cold blood!"

"What was done was necessary. And now it's over with. The question is what are you going to do now?"

"I just want to go home."

Mina took another sip. "This could be your home. If you let it be. Twenty years ago, I was you. I'd lived my whole life never knowing a home. When I was a teenager, my parents sent me to the US, hearing about all the opportunities, but I never made anything of myself until I came *here*."

"I have a home, though. Back in Arizona. Please, just let me leave. I'll find my own way ho—"

"And what? We just lose all the money we've spent on you? We brought you and your friend here from across the country. We gave you fancy clothes and food and a roof over your head. And what have you given us in return? Nothing but problems."

"Then tell me how much it is and I'll get you the money. But just let me leave."

"What do you think you are doing, working here? You are paying off what you owe."

Ainsley's head dropped. It took everything within her to fight back the tears. This nightmare refused to end.

"Then, at least let me do something else." Ainsley looked up into Mina's face again. "I'll work in the kitchen and wash dishes or clean or something else. Anything else."

Mina shook her head. "It doesn't work like that. You were brought here to do one thing. We have no use for another person that does something else."

"You did for Tessa's sister. She came here before us, the same as we did. But Tessa said she hadn't seen her with the other girls. So, you all must've given her something else to do."

Mina raised her eyebrows. "Her sister?"

"Yes, her name was Mackenzie."

Mina nodded as if suddenly it all made sense. "Mackenzie doesn't work somewhere else in the resort."

"Where is she then?"

"I'm afraid she's no longer with us."

"You let her leave?"

"No. I mean she's no longer *with us.*"

It took Ainsley a minute to understand, but when she did, the reality of it all hit her squarely in the chest. So much so that she felt like the wind had been knocked out of her. Her breath became shallow as panic set in. She'd never met the Tessa's sister, but now she felt her loss all the same.

"Wh-what happened?" she asked in little more than a whisper.

"An unfortunate accident. She took too much of one thing, more than she should have of another, and she was gone."

A shiver roiled through Ainsley. "When?"

"I don't know. About a year ago."

Ainsley gripped the sides of the chair. She felt if she didn't, it and the rest of the earth would fall out from under her. The reason Tessa wanted to come here had been a lie. An illusion to hide the reality of this place, one put on by Zane and Dex and everyone else that coaxed them along the way. She and Tessa had spent the last two weeks chasing something that had never existed.

Mina leaned forward and placed her elbows on the table. She looked like one of those praying mantises Ainsley had seen on Animal Planet.

"But you," Mina said. "You're still here. And you need to decide what you are going to do."

———

THAT NIGHT, Mina let Ainsley sleep in her old room. She moved Mei to bunk with another girl, giving Ainsley the room to herself.

Laying on her back on the top bunk, she looked out the window at the night sky. It was dark enough that the stars shone. She studied them, wondering where she had gone wrong. She'd been so sure this all was fate, her taking control of her path in the multiverse, giving herself a life that otherwise wouldn't have come her way. Now, Tessa was dead and Ainsley was a world away from anything that she could call home. She was trapped.

Ainsley had already decided hours ago sleep wasn't going to come tonight. Mina's words danced through her restless mind. *You need to decide what you are going to do.* What choice did she really have? Mina already said they weren't just about to let her leave. But the thought of staying felt equally impossible. She'd been there all of two days and everything had been miserable when it hadn't been downright terrifying.

A tear formed in the corner of Ainsley's eye and she let it roll down her cheek. She wished Tessa was still here. She would know what to do. Tessa was a fighter, and she'd fought to the end. She had come all this way not knowing her sister was no longer here. Maybe somewhere in the heavens above they were reunited now; up in those stars and looking down on her. She hoped so.

The thought made her feel more lonely.

Ainsley wanted to leave this place. Tessa and her sister had succeeded even if it had cost them their lives. Wherever they were now, they were free. A part of Ainsley wished Tessa had never stepped in front of her on that cliff side. She hated it, but she couldn't deny it. Death couldn't be as awful as this place.

And in that moment, Ainsley made up her mind. It didn't matter if it was dangerous or if she doubted she could pull it off. She had to try. Staying in this place forever was unacceptable. She was going to run. Resist. *Fight.* It no longer mattered to her if they killed her in the process.

One way or another. Ainsley was getting out of this place.

FORTY-SEVEN

BAILEY HAD DRIVEN BACK to the hospital and walked the entire
Emergency Department herself. She checked every adjoining stairwell and each bathroom on the floor. Jackson was nowhere and the
phone he'd had with him was missing. She tried calling it repeatedly.
Each time, it went to an automated voicemail. Jackson Clay was officially in the wind.

The phone call she did get, however, was from Jackson's parole
officer. Someone must have alerted him that Jackson was unac-
counted for. Bailey had cursed Pitts for not giving her more time.

"It was a highly stressful day," she'd told Marvin Thompson. "I'm
sure our wires just got crossed."

"This is exactly what I was worried about," he'd replied.

"I will find him. I'm just asking you to please not do anything
that'll hurt his parole status."

Now, the sun was set and the offices for the Western Virginia
Human Trafficking Task Force were deserted. Only Pitts and the J-
team, working on trying to find Graves, remained.

Bailey sat alone in the conference room where she'd been
working on her laptop, not wanting this business of finding

Jackson to distract the rest of the team, when Pitts came in. He shut the door behind him and folded his arms as he leaned against the wall.

"Weisz knows about Clay being AWOL," he said. "He's pushing hard to issue a warrant."

"What did you say?" Bailey asked.

"I told him we shouldn't be rash and we should allow some time for things to clear themselves up, but I don't know how much longer I can hold him off."

"We brought Clay in on this, John."

"I get that, but he's also a parolee that's violated his terms. I can't blame Weisz for wanting to cover his ass on this one."

Bailey shook her head but didn't say anything.

"I can get you another twenty-four hours. After that, if we don't have a twenty on him, I'm letting Weisz go ahead with a warrant." Pitts pushed off the wall and left.

Bailey leaned back in her chair, closed her eyes, and rubbed her temples. Twenty-four hours. This whole thing had turned into a clusterfuck and she doubted it would all fix itself in the same time frame. She came back to the table, picked up her cell, and tried the missing phone again. No answer. This time, though, when it went to voicemail, she left a message.

"Clay, I know you have this phone. It's me. They're giving me twenty-four hours to bring you in before they issue a warrant. You *need* to contact me. Please."

Bailey ended the call. She racked her brain for another angle to pursue. Jackson didn't have any family still alive, and he wasn't the type to pal around with friends. In fact, the only person that could probably call him a friend was …

Bear Beauchamp. Bailey had been so hyper-focused all afternoon on finding Clay that she hadn't realized that Bear too was MIA. The last she'd heard, he was supposed to get Clay's things from the safe house and bring them to Roanoke. If he hadn't been able to find Clay, he would've reached out. Bailey sprung from her chair and marched out of the conference room to the bank of cubicles where the rest of the J-team was working.

"Have any of you heard from Bear this afternoon?" she asked.

A medley of shrugs and shakes of the head interspersed with side glances was her only reply.

"Son of a bitch," she muttered.

She trotted back to the conference room and scrolled through her call log for Bear's number. She tried it.

"Hyello?" Bear's voice bellowed after several rings.

"Bear, it's Bailey," she said. "I can't get a hold of Jackson. Is he w—"

"Ah, I'm just fuckin' with ya! I'm not here right now, but you know what to do!"

Bailey raised the phone over her head only to will herself not to slam it onto the floor. After a deep breath in and out, she dropped it onto the table.

So, Bear had disappeared, too.

Now it was only a question if the two were missing together. She opened up her laptop and ran a check on Bear. His last-known address was a Martinsville listing. That was only an hour away.

Again, Bailey trotted out of the office and came over to the J-team. Cole was the only other member of the task force that had any kind of history with Clay and Bear. She looked over at Cole and nodded toward the office doors.

"Want to take a ride with me?" she asked.

Cole grinned. "Let me get my coat."

———

BAILEY AND COLE took Highway 220 south. As they drove, Bailey read her in on Jackson going AWOL.

"Why do you think Clay is dodging us?" Cole asked.

"He's not happy that he's being benched," Bailey replied.

"Can't say I blame him. To come all this way just to not be able to see it through?" Cole shook her head.

"It's out of my hands."

A minivan up ahead was adhering to the speed limit. Bailey swerved across the double yellow line on the road to pass it.

"How do you think The Arcady found out about Clay?" Cole asked.

Bailey shrugged. "I have no idea. Clay seems to think we have a leak."

"Could we?"

"I don't know. In general, I don't like looking sideways at fellow badges. I know I wouldn't appreciate it if someone were doing it to me."

"I get that." Cole paused. "Still though, it would explain a lot."

Bailey didn't say anything more on the matter.

Bear's address took the two of them down a narrow, wooded drive that ended at a quaint Bungalow-style house. It sat at the head of a large, oval-shaped plot of lawn several acres in size and surrounded by trees. Only the headlights on their unmarked Explorer made it possible to see.

They got out of the car and took in the area around them. Bailey went to the tailgate, opened it, and grabbed two flashlights. She handed one to Cole who clicked it on and shone it at the dark corners of the driveway.

"Doesn't look like they're here," she said.

"Clay would know better than to leave their vehicle out in plain view," Bailey countered. "Let's take a look around."

Each of them walked down opposite sides of the driveway toward the house. When the headlights on the SUV timed out and shut off, they could only see what was in the beam of their flashlights. Bailey moved to the corner of the house and looked down the side of it. The house, showing no life, was eerie in the harsh, concentrated light.

"Jen, over here," Cole called out.

Bailey turned back and crossed the driveway over to her. Cole was focusing her flashlight on a section of grass coming off the pavement.

"Look, the grass is matted down here," she said. "Two lines, each about a foot wide, like someone recently drove over this way."

She directed her light to the corner of the property the tracks headed. About fifty yards from the house was a large equipment shed. Walking side by side, they followed the tracks in the grass. Sure enough, they led right up to the bay door on the shed. They each scanned portions of the structure with their flashlights.

"I don't see any windows," Cole said. "No way to see inside."

"I don't even see another door," Bailey said. "Just this big one."

She walked over to the right side of the bay door and studied it. The whole thing was held closed by a large sliding bolt that was padlocked shut.

"Hold on," Bailey said.

She trotted back toward the driveway and their SUV. Bailey opened the tailgate once more, grabbed something else, and came back. She held the tire iron up for Cole to see.

"What's that for?" Cole asked.

"We can't cut through that padlock, but the metal around the mechanism looks pretty flimsy. I bet with a little leverage I can pry it off.

"You're going to *break in*?"

"I'll buy him a new latch. But we need to find them before they get themselves in even more trouble."

Cole shook her head but didn't stop Bailey. Bailey slid one of the arms of the tire iron into the hole the padlock latched onto, then levied the arm against the rest of the door and pulled. Sure enough, the portion of the sliding bolt ripped off the door. Bailey smiled.

"Congratulations, you pried off the fourth amendment," Cole quipped.

Bailey ignored her, pulled the damaged bolt free of the door and lifted it. Just inside was Bear's suburban, parked nose-in, the back half facing Bailey and Cole.

Something was off about the vehicle. Bailey stepped closer and examined the rear quarter glass windows. They had been blacked out, and the window on the tailgate was partially down. Bailey peeked through the opening and saw a rifle tripod set up.

"That makes one hell of a mobile hide site for a shooter," Cole said. She shone her flashlight further inside the shed. "Bailey, check it out."

Bailey stepped back from the Suburban and looked at the end of Cole's flashlight beam. Stacked in a messy pile were a bunch of equipment cases. She recognized a couple on top of the stack. They were Pelican cases for rifles. All of them were empty.

Bailey bent down and picked one up. "What the hell are you planning to do, Clay?"

FORTY-EIGHT

JACKSON DROVE HIM, Bear, and Graves to a Budget Inn outside the town of Lexington, thirty miles south of The Arcady. It was the kind of place very few questions would be asked. Jackson paid cash for a room and he and Bear had escorted Graves in with a jacket draped over the zip-tie cuffs on his wrists.

It was almost midnight. A weather system had blown in and the three men, quiet in the motel room, could hear the rain doing paradiddles on the roofs of cars in the parking lot outside. Graves had dozed off in an armchair and Bear was nodding off as he watched Roadhouse on TV, but Jackson sat at the little bistro table, plotting their next move.

He stood and smacked Bear's foot.

"Get him up," he said.

Bear rolled out of the left side queen bed and smacked Graves awake. "Wakey wakey, sunshine," he said.

Jackson came over and sat down on the edge of the other bed in front of Graves. "Corliss," he said. "How do we get to him?"

Graves shook his head again. "Corliss still has nearly a dozen guys, most real killers, on that security team. It's just the two of you here. You *can't* get to him."

"Let us worry about the numbers. Corliss must have something that can damn him. Records of who stays at The Arcady or how much they've paid him. *Something*."

"He runs it all through a company called Alleghania Travel. On paper, it's based out of Delaware for tax purposes, but it's all run out of the Arcady."

"Where specifically?"

"His residence."

"The Lustschloss."

Graves nodded.

"The Lust what?" Bear asked.

Jackson ignored him. It made sense that Corliss would keep everything there, secure with the rest of his secrets, but that meant it wouldn't be easy to get to.

"Alleghania Travel have staff at The Arcady?"

Graves shook his head. "No, but it's all there. There's a server room in the cellar. Alleghania Travel exists on there."

"But they must have someone running things day-to-day."

"Probably somewhere, but Touchpoint has offices all across the country. Hell, there are at least ten just in Virginia. He could have a secret staff housed in any one of them. It would take months and more resources than you two idiots have to figure it out."

"But the servers are in the Lustschloss at The Arcady."

Graves nodded. "The servers and the black book."

Jackson paused. "What's the black book?"

"It's an external hard drive he keeps offline. His insurance policy against any cyber attacks. It has a ledger of everyone who's visited. When and for how long, how many times, all of it. He logs it all himself. He doesn't even trust his security team with it."

"Is it in the cellar, too? In the server room?"

"No. In his private office on the top floor. He keeps it locked in a drawer safe in his desk. Biometric lock, only he can access it."

Jackson stood and began to pace. He moved to the window and peeked out the drapes. Against the charcoal rainy sky, a pair of red and green strobing lights glided down as a regional jet descended to land at the nearby airport.

The airfield, Jackson thought.

He turned sharply and came back to Graves. "The front gate to The Arcady," he said. "It always opened automatically. What or who operates it?"

"The vehicles we use have a transponder under the hood. When it gets within so many feet of the gate, the gate opens automatically."

"All the vehicles there have that?"

"Not the side-by-sides, but anything street legal, yes."

"And this doesn't trip the perimeter system?"

"It alerts that a vehicle opened the gate, but that's it."

Jackson thought took a beat to think. He needed one of The Arcady's vehicles. "The Audi you fled in. Where is it?"

"I ditched it at a little league field outside Huttonsville, West Virginia. Cops probably have it now."

Jackson kept thinking. "When is there another pickup at the airfield? When do the next people come in?"

Graves took a moment to think. "Tomorrow. Late morning. Beck Galway and his wife. He's some hedge fund manager from New York."

Jackson stepped back toward the window, but this time he pulled the phone he'd taken out. There were a dozen missed calls and voicemails from Bailey.

Bear came to his side, turning his back to Graves. "What are you thinking?"

"We're going back into The Arcady. Tomorrow," Jackson replied. He scrolled to the latest missed call from Bailey and called her back.

"The two of us? What about him?" Bear nodded toward Graves.

"I have an idea for that, too."

Bailey picked up the phone. "Clay?"

"It's me. We need to meet."

PART SIX

EXIGENT CIRCUMSTANCES

"Better to fight for something than live for nothing." —George S. Patton

FORTY-NINE

BAILEY AND COLE walked the length of Bear's property before leaving to check out the hunting shop he co-owned with Jackson downtown. Both were deserted and the only sign that they had been to either spot—assuming Bear was with Jackson—was Bear's Suburban left in the equipment shed.

Fresh out of ideas, Bailey and Cole drove back to Roanoke. Before calling it a night, they decided to stop and grab a late-night dinner at a pizza joint off Williamson Road, one of the few places downtown still open at this late hour.

They were seated next to one another at a high-top table sharing a pepperoni pie when Bailey's phone buzzed in her pocket. She pulled it out and read the caller ID before swallowing hard. It was the number she'd been trying to reach Clay on all day.

"Clay?" Bailey answered. Cole looked up.

"It's me," Jackson replied. "We need to meet."

Bailey did a one-eighty on her stool, turning her back to the interior of the restaurant. "Clay, where the hell have you been?"

"Working. We need to meet."

"Yeah, no shit we need to meet. You went AWOL on me. Do you

remember you were placed in *my* guardianship? This isn't spring break for you."

"You left me little choice."

"As you with me. Pitts has given me twenty-four hours to bring you in before he reports you absconded. That means a warrant goes out for your arrest. Do you understand? They will pull your parole. You'll finish your sentence back behind bars."

"This will all be over in twenty-four hours if I can help it. I have a play, but we need to meet."

"If we meet, you're coming back with me. I don't care if I have to handcuff you to me."

"Then I'll do this on my own."

Cole wiped her mouth, looking at Bailey with intrigue.

Bailey sighed and rubbed at her face. "How do you know I'm not tracing your call right now and putting it out to troopers on patrol."

"The same reason you've held Pitts back from putting out a warrant yet. You know I can close this."

Bailey shook her head, irritated that Clay was right. "What's the play?"

Cole went to the counter and asked for a box for the rest of their pizza. She brought it back to Bailey and started packaging their leftovers up.

Jackson paused. "Not over the phone. Like I said, we need to meet. Are you still in Roanoke?"

Bailey looked at Cole, then out the window. She wouldn't put it past Jackson to be tailing her to test if he can trust her. "Yeah. Where are you?"

Jackson cleared his throat. "Lexington."

"Okay, so where do you want to meet?"

"Natural Bridge State Park. The parking lot for the Visitor Center."

"We'll look suspicious out there after hours."

"Good point. You think they'll call the police?"

Bailey sighed again. *Asshole*, she thought. She looked over at Cole who was ready to roll. "I'm bringing Cole with me."

"Fine. One hour."

———

JUST AFTER ONE in the morning, Bailey and Cole pulled into the parking lot for Natural Bridge State Park. Shaped like a large arrowhead with a colonial-style visitor center at its base, the lot was deserted save for a large truck in the far corner. A man was standing in front of it.

As they rolled up to him, Bailey could see it was Clay leaning against a utility truck painted in the U.S. Forest Service's colors. Bailey nosed up to him in an unmarked Explorer, opened the door, and got out.

"Please tell me you did not steal a Forest Service vehicle," she said in greeting.

Jackson waved his hand. "You want to run the VIN, be my guest."

Cole got out and joined the two of them at the fender of the truck.

"Okay," Bailey said, folding her arms. "We're here."

"I have Graves," Jackson said.

"What? Where?"

"In a safe place for now."

"Somewhere in Lexington."

Jackson didn't say anything.

"If you want justice for the girl he shot, you have to turn him over to the authorities, Clay."

"I do and I will. But not yet."

"When then? You said you had a plan to end this all in twenty-four hours."

"Later this morning. I'll give you a location and you pick him up. But it has to be you. No one else from the task force."

"This is still about the mole, isn't it?"

"If you haven't found them yet, then you still have one. I'm not turning Graves over to someone that'll set him free. Or worse."

"How do you know I'm not the mole?"

"You've run point on this thing. You wouldn't have brought me into this just to have Corliss kill me." Jackson looked at Bailey. "Plus, I trust you."

Bailey appreciated him saying as much. She nodded to her right. "What about Cole?"

"I'm guessing she was already with you when I called, which left me little choice. But, no," Clay nodded to Cole. "I don't think it's you either."

"So, you'll turn over Graves in exchange for what?"

"I need you two to back Bear and I up."

"Back you up how?"

"We're going into The Arcady tomorrow."

"Yeah, there's a thing called the fourth amendment that might have a problem with that."

Cole raised her eyebrow at Bailey, but didn't say anything. "Just be in position at noon tomorrow," Clay said. "Outside the front gate. I'll get you your exigent circumstances to go in."

Bailey shook her head. "This is reckless, even for you."

"What do we already know about Corliss? He's quick to eliminate loose ends. Graves is in the wind, and I slipped through his fingers, too. He's going to want to insulate himself from risk. And if he can't get to us, he'll take out the people he can."

Bailey's voice was soft. "Shit. Everyone inside."

Jackson nodded. "Graves told us Corliss has everything about The Arcady stored on servers in the cellar of his private residence there. That and a digital ledger he keeps on a hard drive offline. Either should be enough to take him down, but we have to get it before he decides to go scorched earth. Bear and I are going in with or without you. But we could use your help."

"I think you're overlooking a major problem with this plan of yours. Right now, you're the only one that can finger Graves for the girl's murder. If you give us Graves just to turn around and die up on that mountain, Graves walks."

"Then I guess you better back us up."

Bailey and Cole exchanged a look. Cole paused for a moment, then nodded. Bailey turned back to Jackson.

"Fine," she said. "We're in."

Jackson lurched off the fender and headed for the driver-side door. "Expect a text 9 AM where you can find Graves. Then, get into position. Noon. Don't be late."

Jackson climbed into the truck, fired it up, and rolled out.

FIFTY

WHEN JACKSON GOT BACK to the motel room, he walked in on Bear in the corner opposite the door, attempting to play cards with a bound Graves at the little bistro table. Jackson was holding a shopping bag from a drugstore. He went over to the nearest bed and dumped an assortment of things onto it.

"Get him up and into the armchair in the other corner," Jackson said.

"I'm sitting on pocket rockets here," Bear protested.

"Now."

Bear folded his hand and moved Graves to the other chair. Jackson took a cheap pair of sunglasses and a roll of black tape from his pharmaceutical bounty and applied a thick layer of tape over the lenses. He handed them to Bear along with the roll of tape.

"Put these on him," he said. "Arms and legs taped to the chair."

Bear took them and did as he was told.

"What the fuck is this bullshit," Graves griped.

"I got stuff for a gag, too," Jackson said. "Will that be necessary?"

Graves didn't say anything more.

Next, Jackson opened up a pair of Bluetooth headphones. He gave those too to Bear.

"Pair it with your phone," Jackson said. "Give him something to listen to."

Bear chortled as he nodded. He punched at his phone for a minute and then came over to put the headphones on Graves head.

"Why don't you take some time and enjoy the musical stylings of Tila Tequila," Bear offered.

A muffled pop beat seeped out from the headphones around Graves's ears. Jackson sat down at the bistro table and Bear came over and took the other seat.

"Alright," Jackson said. "Bailey and Cole are in. We go into The Arcady later this morning."

"How do we do that?" Bear asked.

"We need to get a hold of one of the resort's vehicles. Graves told us guests are arriving later today. They'll send a car probably with two guys from the security team. There will likely already be two more on site at the airport securing the perimeter. The fence line is protected by a two-pronged disturbance detection system, one hard-wired into the fence itself, and a battery of motion sensors just inside. If they're tripped, it sends up an alert, but Roscoe, who seems to be something of a sergeant for the security team, told me the system is so sensitive that planes landing or taking off often trip it."

"Meaning, we go in as the plane lands. And they'll think the plane tripped the alarm."

Jackson nodded. "Exactly. There's a road south of the airfield that winds its way up the mountains to the west. At the closest turnoff, it's just a quarter-mile hike to the airfield. We use handheld GPS to guide us to the backside of the hangar and breach the perimeter there. If they look at it closely, they might see it's not the plane, but their focus will be on the arriving clients. *And* they'll bring the vehicle to us where we only have to handle four possible shooters instead of the whole squad."

Bear scratched at his chin. "What about the plane's crew and these guests? One of them makes a phone call, it could turn into a very bad day for us."

"We move hard and fast and take control of the hangar strong-arm style. We don't take out anyone we don't have to, but if they give us no choice, we drop them."

"So, we take the hangar and the security at the airfield, then Trojan horse our way into the resort itself."

Jackson nodded again. "Right. We'll take two security guys and put them up front to keep up appearances. We keep things quiet as long as we can. We'll get made eventually, but the key is to minimize how far we have to fight our way in."

"We're going after the servers Graves told us about?"

"And the black book." Jackson pulled out his phone and brought up a satellite image of the resort property. "This main drive snakes its way through the front half of the property. We need to get by The Manor at the front, and the turnout here for what they call The Camp. That's where all of Corliss's hired guns live out of." He pointed at a square next to the winding road. "This is The Lustschloss, Corliss's private residence. That's our objective. Take that with Corliss in it and dig up the skeletons in his closet."

"That's great and all, but how do we get out, especially if we've been made going in?"

"After we're in, Bailey and Cole are going to post up outside the property. Once we have Corliss or what we need to take him down, the calvary rolls in."

Bear shook his head. "I hate to burst your bubble, Jacky boy, but they're not going to go in there without a warrant. And they won't be able to get that unless *we* get them what we find inside."

"They can go in if we give them the exigent circumstances that allow it."

Bear's brow furrowed in confusion for a moment until he put it together. "We get the party started, and then they crash it."

Jackson nodded.

Bear chortled with glee. He leaned back and placed his hands on his ample belly. "There's only one problem." He cocked his head to the side. "What do we do with Tila Tequila's newest fan over there?"

"I told Bailey and Cole we had Graves and that I'd give him up tomorrow. As we roll out, we tell them where they can find him. We keep him like a mushroom until then and he won't know we've screwed him until it's over."

"Keep him like a mushroom?"

"In the dark, feeding him shit."

Bear's gut jiggled as he laughed. "When do we get started?"

"We're on the move at nine, so get some rest while you can. I'll take first shift watching Graves."

FIFTY-ONE

WHEN MINA CAME to check on Ainsley the next morning, Ainsley was ready for her. She opened the door wide, revealing herself to be fully dressed. She wore a white-and-navy vertical striped jumpsuit with a plunging neckline and cream-colored loafers with her hair pulled back in a tight ponytail. Even Ainsley knew she looked fantastic. She deliberately chose something she could move quickly in.

Mina couldn't help but to marvel. "My," she said with a sly grin, "look at you."

"Shall we?" Ainsley asked.

Mina seemed caught off-guard by Ainsley's initiative. "Don't you want breakfast?"

"I'll eat with my client at breakfast." She stepped out and closed the door behind her. "I'm sure they will offer." She started for the stairs.

Mina followed her. "I guess this means you thought about our talk last night."

Anger and resentment flashed across Ainsley's face, but since Mina was behind her, she couldn't see it. "Uh huh."

"And you've decided to work. No more problems?"

"It's the best option you've given me, so I'll take it."

"Smart girl."

The two of them descended the stairs, crossed the common room to the breezeway, and made their way over to The Lodge. There, the rest of the girls were already standing shoulder-to-shoulder in their line. Ainsley hurried over to the end and joined them. A moment later, the clients filed in.

Ainsley scrutinized each of them, identifying her best target. She needed one older and out of shape that gave her the best advantage physically if she needed it, but they also couldn't be so close to an invalid that they'd want to loiter around The Lodge or other central places all day. She needed one that would want to go somewhere more remote. The shooting club wouldn't work for obvious reasons, but the golf course or fishing creek would do nicely.

Among the second half of the group of men ambled in a man that wasn't white so much as he was red. Clean-shaven, with a jowly face and a head of white hair, he was easily fifty pounds overweight. However, he also had on khakis and a pastel blue polo that screamed a day on the links. When she saw the visor sticking out of his back pocket, she knew he was the one.

As other men took their turns selecting from Ainsley and her peers, Ainsley did what she could to make herself seem undesirable. Shoulders sagging, looking off into the distance, disinterested. A couple of men paused on her, making for close calls, but ultimately, she was passed over by every one of them. Then came her man's turn. Ainsley straightened her posture and put her chest out. When the man looked at her, she met his eyes and gave her best playful smile with a wink. The guy couldn't help but grin in pleasure as he nodded at her.

Step one completed.

Ainsley came over and joined the man. Five minutes later, they were seated at a table in the dining room. Another man came over and joined them. Mei was wrapped around his arm. Ainsley felt her pulse quicken. She'd figured at least one other client and their date would be joining them, but she hadn't expected Mei. Ainsley had never shaken the way Mei looked at her that night sobbing in her bed with bruises around her neck and wrist. She hated this place as much as Ainsley did. As Mei and her date sat down at the table, Ainsley met her eyes. *You and me, girl,* she thought. *We're going to get out of here today.*

When the waiter came to take their order, Mei's date ordered for her and a pit formed in Ainsley's stomach, fearing her client would be inspired to do the same. That wouldn't work. Thankfully, the ruby-hued man rattled off his order, then looked over at Ainsley expectantly.

"Would you like somethin', honey?" he asked with a thick southern drawl.

"The filet mignon benedict, please," Ainsley said with a wide smile.

The man's eyes opened wide as he chuckled. "Whoa," he said. "That's quite the meal for such a little lady."

"Well, I think I'm going to need my energy today." Ainsley winked again.

The man actually giggled with delight.

Breakfast and the cocktails that followed took nearly an hour. In that time, Ainsley learned her date's name—Barrett, as well as Mei's date's name—Clarence. She also learned they were two oil executives from Dallas. Each of them had a pair of Irish coffees and then Barrett had a third, just forgoing the java. When he was done, he pulled the napkin from his lap, wiped at his mouth, and dropped it onto his plate.

"Well," he said. "We should get goin'. We leave now, we can get a beer at the clubhouse before our tee time."

"I always knew you were a smart man," Clarence said with a laugh.

As they rose from the table, Barrett and Clarence paid Ainsley and Mei little mind, almost expecting them to follow like loyal subjects. Ainsley had counted on this, too. The pieces were falling into place. The ideal client, a midday appointment on the links, and now his indifference to her as they left. They'd be whisked away in a golf cart and taken to the country club. Then, when they were isolated, Ainsley would look for the right moment. Not just for her, but now for Mei, as well.

With Barrett and Clarence's backs turned, Ainsley grabbed the steak knife the waiter had brought her for her breakfast and slipped it into the pocket of her jumpsuit.

Step two completed.

FIFTY-TWO

COLE AND BAILEY agreed to meet out in front of their hotel at eight the next morning and head up to Lexington, figuring Jackson was keeping Graves nearby. When Cole walked out, Bailey was already in the unmarked Explorer, waiting. Cole climbed into the passenger seat.

"Morning," she said.

"It is," Bailey replied. "I got you a coffee. Black, two sugars."

"You know me so well. Ready to roll?"

Bailey didn't put the SUV in gear or give Cole an answer. Instead, she looked at her.

"Best case scenario, we're about to bend a few rules here. Worst case," she shook her head. "I don't even know. I don't want to put you in a position you don't want to be in. You can go back in the hotel right now and act like last night didn't happen. I'll say I went alone."

Cole met her eyes as she reached behind her. Bailey thought she was reaching for the door handle and, truthfully, couldn't blame her. But her arm kept going back until it grabbed the seat belt, brought it around her, and clicked it in.

"Ready to roll," Cole said. This time it wasn't a question.

Bailey grinned. She slipped on her sunglasses, put the SUV in gear, and pulled out.

———

JACKSON WOKE up to the sharp rays of light ripping through the dilapidated motel curtains. Bear was on the other bed watching SportsCenter. He looked over at Jackson as he slowly rose and stretched.

"Mornin'," he said.

"It is," Jackson replied.

Bear looked back at the TV. "Braves got their hats handed to them last night. That rookie pitcher didn't make it out of the first inning."

Jackson ignored the sports report. He turned and looked over at Graves who was out cold with the headphones and makeshift blindfold still on him. Bear clocked his glance and shifted his morning brief accordingly.

"He asked to take a piss around five," he said. "I walked him over and let him do his business. Dude stared at me like I was gonna hold it for him." He shook his head. "Other than that, he hasn't been a problem."

Jackson reached over and pulled on a shirt. "Still listening to Tila Tequila?"

"No, I've got him on a steady diet of Yanni and Kenny G now. My Spotify Wrapped is going to be crazy this year."

Jackson went to the window and peeked around the curtain, checking that no surprises had come while he was asleep. "Take a shower, get ready. Whatever you need to do. I'll watch him."

Bear rolled out of bed and headed for the bathroom.

An hour later, they were both dressed and ready to go. Graves had stirred but didn't seem to clue in to the fact that they were about to leave. As they moved to the door, Jackson and Bear looked back at him.

"Should I give him a kiss goodbye?" Bear asked with a chuckle.

"Leave it for Bailey and Cole," Jackson replied.

"My phone's going to go out of range when we leave. His music will cut off."

"That's fine. I checked his wrists and ankles. He's not going anywhere, anytime soon. Besides, if I know Bailey, she's already in the area. She and Cole will be here before he knows what's happened.

Jackson and Bear opened the door to the motel room and left.

As they settled into the truck, Jackson sent Bailey the text.

————

BAILEY AND COLE killed their coffees on the way to Lexington and agreed they could use another. They got a second round at a Sheetz off Route 11 near the center of town and waited in the parking lot. At 8:59, Bailey's phone buzzed with an incoming text. It was Jackson.

Graves. Budget Inn in Buena Vista. Room 18 on the far west side.

"That him?" Cole asked.

Bailey punched the info into her maps app. "Yeah, Budget Inn in Buena Vista, not here."

"Classic Clay."

"It's just outside of town. We're ten minutes out. Call it in."

Cole called the task force. "John, I'm with Jen. We have a possible twenty on Graves. He's at a motel in Buena Vista, just outside Lexington. We're rolling, get local PD to back us up."

Bailey and Cole tore down Route 11. As they rolled up, they killed their lights and siren. Bailey pulled into the parking lot, foregoing the office, and went straight to the west side of the motel. As they got out, they could hear sirens in the distance. Back up was on its way, but Bailey wasn't waiting. She moved to the front door, posting up beside it. She motioned Cole to cover around back before rapping hard on the door with her knuckles.

"Virginia State Police! Open up!" she ordered.

She listened. Nothing came from inside.

Cole came back to her. "No way out on the back or side," she said.

Now Bailey pounded the door with her fist. "Virginia State Police! Come to the door, or we're coming in."

Again, nothing. She nodded to Cole who was on the side of the door with the knob. Cole reared up and kicked hard backwards, placing the heel of her shoe just below the door knob. The frame splintered as the door swung open.

Bailey moved in fast, gun drawn. The room was empty save for a bound Nick Graves, duct taped to an armchair with some sort of blindfold and headphones on him. Cole moved past her, and cleared the bathroom, then came back to Bailey's side. Bailey stepped toward the man and pulled off the headphones and blindfold.

Though the inside of the room was dark, Graves squinted up at her, wincing at what little light came through the broken open door. "Who the fuck are you?" Graves asked.

Bailey gave Graves her most professional smile. She holstered her pistol. "Mr. Graves, I'm Special Agent Jen Bailey with the Virginia State Police. You're under arrest."

"Arrest? What for?"

"Suspicion of first-degree murder."

FIFTY-THREE

JACKSON AND BEAR turned off Highway 220 and onto the road that would take them as close to the airfield as they could get without being seen. It was unpaved and the grass growing across it told Jackson it was seldom used, but both his maps app and satellite imaging assured him it was there. As it left the highway, the road climbed and carved a single-lane path through the thick forest ahead. Venturing into it, towering oaks and maples passed by just inches from their windows.

Jackson's phone buzzed with an incoming text message.

Graves in custody. Don't get dead.

Bear read the message over Jackson's shoulder before he set the phone down. Jackson kept on driving.

"You going to reply?" he asked.

"When it's time," Jackson said.

The road snaked its way straight up the mountainside for about a quarter mile before the grade became too steep. There, it took a sharp right north toward the airfield and continued climbing at an angle. Before long, they were at the road's first switchback. Jackson slowed as if he were going to make the tight, hairpin turn but instead eased the truck off onto a flat piece of earth between two massive silver maples.

In tandem, Jackson and Bear got out of the truck and started gearing up. Ballistic plate carrier, tactical vest, backpack, radio, throat microphone, leg holster, and a full suite of other goodies. Bear came around to the driver side with their rifles.

"For today's adventure, we have for you M-4 rifles," Bear said in his worst fake fancy voice. "Complete with electro-optical sights, foregrips, and of course, suppressors."

Jackson took one, loaded a magazine, and chambered a round. "Do I even want to know where you got these?"

Bear chortled. "Don't ask, don't tell." He slapped Jackson on the arm. "Just like your army days, brother."

Jackson shook his head but couldn't help grinning.

Bear opened the back passenger door on the truck and pulled out another case. "For a sidearm, we have—"

"I've got mine covered."

Jackson leaned into the cab of the truck and came out with his M9 Beretta, his late son's initials engraved into the custom grip. A small, knowing smile appeared on Bear's face as he nodded. When they were finished putting their gear on, they closed all the doors and Bear locked the truck for good measure.

"Ready?" he asked, turning to Jackson.

"Ready," Jackson replied.

He pulled out his phone and shot Bailey a text.

Moving now. Remember, noon at the front gate.

He was about to put the phone away when a thought came to him. He sent a second message.

Everything by the book on your end. What we get has to stick to Corliss.

Jackson put his phone away and pulled out his handheld GPS.

"Airfield is a quarter-mile northeast," he said, pointing. He checked his watch. "The plane should land in thirty."

"On you, brother," Bear said.

Together, they left the truck behind and headed deeper into the woods. Somewhere ahead was the airfield. And beyond it, The Arcady, with the girl Jackson had seen dragged away two nights ago. However many others there were, Jackson just needed them to hold on a little while longer.

He and Bear were coming.

And they were going to end this.

———

BAILEY HAD Graves in cuffs in the back of the Explorer and stood sentry just outside the rear door, smoking a cigarette. The parking lot of the motel was now filled with patrol cars, mostly those of Buena Vista and Virginia State Police, but no one was getting access to Graves without Bailey's personal approval. She watched as another unmarked Explorer pulled in. Out climbed Pitts who made a beeline over to her.

He tried to see past Bailey into the rear window. "He in there?" he asked.

Bailey nodded. "You better believe it."

"And where is Clay?"

"You're really more concerned about him than a cold-blooded killer?"

"No, I'm concerned about both. Especially since one seemed to be a little birdie, tweeting in your ear, that led to the other."

Bailey shrugged. "We work off of anonymous tips all the time."

"Come on, Jen. We don't play out of bounds like this. Clay doesn't have a badge, and if you keep going at this like this, you're putting your own at risk."

"Let me worry about that. Consider your ass sufficiently covered."

Pitts sighed, then looked around. He nodded in Graves's direction. "How come he's not in the back of a Buena Vista cruiser?"

"Ours work just as well as theirs."

"Still on about the mole?"

Bailey didn't say anything.

Pitts sighed again. "He's going to have to go to Buena Vista's station for booking. You can't hold him forever."

"But I can facilitate how and when it happens."

Pitts shook his head. "It does us no good if he walks because you violated his rights. Just get him booked, okay? Then, get back to Roanoke. Your boy Clay has only a few more hours to come in."

Pitts walked past Bailey to a group of state troopers huddling near the motel's office. Cole, who had been going through Graves's things as they were splayed out on the hood of a nearby patrol car, watched Pitts walk away before coming over to Bailey.

"He seemed oddly grumpy considering we just bagged a Man One suspect," she said.

"Yeah," Bailey agreed, looking off into the distance. She pulled a cigarette from a pack in her pocket and lit it. "And we don't even get good enough medical for him to remove that stick up his ass."

Cole nodded at the tinted rear window masking Graves. "What do you want to do with him?"

Bailey took a drag from her cigarette. "Get him booked at Buena Vista's station. Tell the desk sergeant no one sees him except you and I or his lawyer. And if it's his lawyer, they better check his ID and bar card before letting him in."

"You know, a better friend might say you're being paranoid."

"Then I guess it's a good thing you're a shit friend."

Cole grinned. Bailey's phone buzzed in her pocket. She pulled it out and checked it.

"Clay?" Cole asked.

Bailey nodded. "He and Bear are making their move now." She let the cigarette drop from her mouth and stomped it out on the pavement. "Come on, we have to hurry."

FIFTY-FOUR

WHEN JACKSON and Bear got within sight of the airfield, they went prone and crawled the remaining fifty feet. The tree line ran about a yard from the fence. Jackson and Bear came up to the edge, tight against opposite sides of a thick tree trunk. They were directly behind the airfield's hangar near the corner with the door just off the small office Roscoe had shown Jackson.

Bear checked his watch. "Five minutes," he whispered. "Hope they didn't come early."

"They didn't." Jackson replied. "Look."

He pointed north at the main gate. Almost on cue was a black Range Rover rolling up to it. Two members of the security team rolled up in a side-by-side to meet it. Jackson pulled out a night vision monocular.

"Night vision?" Bear asked. "I hate to state the obvious, but it's the middle of the day."

"Near-Infrared," Jackson explained. "Works during the day and, more importantly, sees through glass. Even tinted glass." He used the monocular to watch the main gate. "Two in the Range Rover. Two more in the side-by-side."

"Just like you said."

The gate slid open, and the Range Rover pulled through with the side-by-side following it. The two-vehicle convoy went around to the front of the hangar and disappeared.

"Looks like they'll all be in the hangar," Jackson said. "Easier to take them there than if two stayed out on the perimeter."

Bear nodded. "Now all we need is the plane."

Jackson watched the horizon to the south. After several minutes, a black silhouette appeared against the blue backdrop of the sky. As it got closer, Jackson could see it was a small jet.

"Plane inbound," he said.

Jackson didn't know enough about planes to identify the make or model, but it was a mid-sized private jet with two engines attached to the rear of the fuselage like other jets Jackson had seen come to the airfield before. Jackson rose into a crouch.

"Get ready to move," he said.

Bear followed suit. Jackson pulled out a small circular saw and handed it to him. They waited until the plane was just seconds from touching down.

"Now," Jackson said.

Bear stepped to the fence and started making a vertical cut into it. The fence put up little resistance against the saw, the landing jet and its engines drowning out the noise it made. In a matter of seconds, Bear had made a human-sized slit. Jackson slipped through first, and Bear followed.

They moved quickly to the back corner of the hangar, checking all the windows of the adjacent building and seeing no one. He peered around the corner to the side. Also clear.

The side door was closed. Inside the hangar, Jackson could hear the muffled whir of the jet engines powering down. Jackson tried the side door's handle, finding it unlocked. He signaled to Bear to get ready to go in. They posted up on either side of the door. Jackson counted to three with his fingers, then Bear opened the door. Jackson moved in first, gun up. Out of the corner of his eye, he saw Roscoe in the little office but left him for Bear. Roscoe reached for a pistol on the desk, but Bear leveled his rifle at him.

"That'd be a dumb move, buddy," he said.

Jackson went deeper into the hangar toward the front of the plane. A security team member standing next to the Range Rover saw Jackson first and went for his pistol.

"Don't do it!" Jackson ordered. "Hands, now!"

The man ignored Jackson. He barely got his pistol out of its holster before a round hit him square in the chest. The two security personnel sitting in the side-by-side, started for their guns, but stopped when Jackson swung their way.

"Try it, and you'll end up like your friend," Jackson barked.

The men gave up and raised their hands. Jackson moved to the man he'd shot and kicked the gun out of his hand. From there, he had a good view of the plane's door. Standing in the open doorway was one of the pilots, looking at him with terror.

"Everyone out of the plane, right now!" Jackson ordered.

Bear marched Roscoe over at gunpoint. He ordered him and the other two from the security team to lie face down with their hands out in front of them. Left with no other choice, they complied. When they were down, Jackson turned to clear the inside of the Range Rover.

As the two pilots, Beck Galway, and his wife filed out of the airplane, Bear told them to lie down the same way the security guards had. Beck, the last one out of the airplane, paused on its stairs.

"What the fuck is this?" he asked, worry lacing every word.

"Arcady Concierge," Bear said. "You have a midday appointment for our signature hog-tie treatment. It'll do wonders for your joints."

The Range Rover cleared, Jackson switched his attention to Beck atop the jet's stairway. "On your stomach, hands out, like everyone else," he said.

Beck came down and did as he was told.

"Watch them," Jackson said. "If anyone moves, you know what to do."

He ran back to the office, quickly disabled the alarm, then came back to everyone on the ground. He patted each one of them down, taking any cell phones or weapons and tossing everything else across the hangar. He dropped seven cell phones, three pistols, and two knives at Bear's feet, then grabbed a handful of zip cuffs from his bag and worked his way through the Galways, the two pilots, and one member of the security team. Each one of them got a pair of cuffs on their wrists and ankles, then a third connecting the two. Lastly, he shouldered his rifle again and pointed it at Roscoe.

"You and the other guy, load your third guy into the tailgate of the Range Rover."

"God damn rat!" Roscoe stammered.

"The name's Bear, actually," Bear said. "Now, do as he said."

The two men pushed themselves to their feet, then picked up their bound team member, carried him over to the Range Rover, and lifted him into the back.

"Gold star!" Bear quipped.

"Go fuck yourself," Roscoe growled.

"I've tried, but it's harder than it looks."

Jackson nodded toward the front of the SUV. "Get in, hands on the wheel."

Roscoe again did as he was told. Jackson got out two open-ended zip ties and bound Roscoe's hands to the wheel. Bear ordered the last man into the passenger-side seat and bound his hands and ankles, then strapped him in with the seat belt. When they were done, they got into the back of the Range Rover and shut the door. Jackson got out his Beretta and pressed the business end of it against the back of Roscoe's neck.

"Now," he said. "You're going to drive exactly where we want you to drive exactly *how* we want you to drive. If you try to gun it, veer off course, wreck us, or do anything in general we did not tell you to, the dashboard will get a nice fresh new coat of you. Understand?"

Roscoe didn't move or say anything. Bear brought his own side arm up and pointed it at Roscoe's head.

"And I'll paint the side window," he added.

"Fine," Roscoe said.

"Atta boy," Bear said. He holstered his pistol, then reached over and pressed the push ignition on the SUV and put it in gear. "Then away we go."

"Where am I going?"

"Back to The Arcady," Jackson said.

The Range Rover rolled out of the hangar and left the airfield.

FIFTY-FIVE

BARRETT AND CLARENCE teed off on the first hole as a twosome just after eleven that morning. They were both several drinks in and their play suffered as a result. Ainsley had seen enough golf the past two days to understand neither of them was particularly good. It took them seven and eight shots respectively to finish the opening Par 4 and another six each to nail the subsequent Par 3. Still, Barrett and Clarence seemed to be having too much fun to notice.

The first holes of the course made their way down the mountainside, with holes three and four nestling the same creek the resort used for fishing. Running nowhere near the greens, even a mediocre golfer could easily avoid the water hazard, but Barrett and Clarence's abilities had descended far below mediocre. Barrett teed off on the third hole and sent a shot downrange that sliced hard and disappeared around a copse of trees near the creek.

"Ah, son of a bitch!" he griped.

Clarence followed suit by hooking one the opposite way before it came to rest in some rough grass several yards off the fairway. Barrett came over and plopped into his golf cart next to Ainsley.

"Welp, see ya in a minute," he hollered towards Clarence's cart.

Barrett drove him and Ainsley down the fairway then hung a sharp right around the copse of trees. The woods thickened along the creek, so Barrett stopped several feet short and walked the rest of the way. Ainsley watched as the rotund man tepidly plodded his way to the water's edge all while scanning for his ball. After a moment, his head dropped and hung in defeat. Then, he looked up at Ainsley.

"Hey, come here a minute, would ya?" he said.

Ainsley did as she was asked and joined him next to the creek. With his club, he pointed at a lump of rocks a few inches in. There, his ball was pinned by the current of the gently flowing stream.

"Say, reach in there and get my ball," he said.

"I don't know if I can," Ainsley replied. "I don't really have the shoes on for it. I don't want to fall in and get all wet."

"Better you than me. Come on, sweet cheeks. Be a doll." He grabbed her back-side.

Ainsley looked at the ball, then Barrett. This was it. This was the line. She wasn't going to be pushed any further. "No," she said, pushing his hand away. "You can get your own ball."

Barrett's jaw hung slack. Dumbfounded by the mere idea that Ainsley would resist him, he said, "I'm not askin', honey, I'm tellin' ya. Get in there and get my ball!"

"And I told you no. If you don't want to get wet, work on your swing."

Barrett let out a befuddled snort. "You got a mouth on ya, don't ya?" He closed the gap between them. "Maybe I ought to show you how to use it right."

That was it. Ainsley's breaking point. She reached into her pocket for the steak knife and drove it hard into Barrett's thigh. Barrett hollered in pain. She pulled it out and swung again.

And again.

And again.

Rage over came her as Barrett screamed through the repeated stabbings. He fell into the creek where Ainsley pounced on top of him and drove the knife into him several more times. She didn't stop until her hands felt like lead weights. She let them drop into the cool water running against her legs. Her chest heaving, desperate for oxygen, she watched as blood oozed out of the man. His face was just above the water and his breaths were shallow. All the anger inside Ainsley had been unleashed on the man. It told her to finish him, but now the knife felt as though it weighed a hundred pounds in her hand.

Barrett gurgled as water trickled into his mouth. He was mere centimeters away from not being able to breath. Ainsley found the strength to lift her arms up to Barrett's head and drop them like anchors where they pinned his face against the creek bed. Barrett squirmed with what life was left within him, any attempt to call out for help muffled by water. And then, after several seconds, nothing. Barrett lay lifeless in the middle of the creek.

Ainsley sat on top of him, catching her breath and recovering her strength. She heard a faint shout in the distance. It was Clarence.

"Barrett? Barrett, you okay?" he called out. "What happened down there?"

Ainsley's breathing slowed, but her heart still thumped hard in her chest. She pushed herself to her feet, turned, and made her way out of the creek. She climbed on all fours, back out of the woods. Clarence was halfway across the fairway when he saw her. Ainsley's jumpsuit was torn and wet and stained with blood. Her hair disheveled and thrown to the side, she marched at Clarence with purpose. The lanky gentleman didn't know what to make of the sight now before him, his mouth unable to form words. Then, he saw the knife in her hand.

It was too late. Ainsley threw herself at him and knocked him down. Clarence was too stunned to mount any real defense. Ainsley brought the knife over her head and drove it down into his chest. Clarence tried to grasp at it, but Ainsley held her grip. She pushed down, putting all her weight behind it. His eyes met hers, pleading with her to stop.

She wouldn't. She couldn't. She didn't.

When Clarence stopped breathing and his body went limp, Ainsley looked across the way at Mei. She'd balled up into the fetal position in the golf cart Clarence had been driving. Ainsley got up and made her way to her. As she approached, Mei tried to make herself even smaller, pulling her hands over her head as she sobbed out of fear. Ainsley opened her arms up wide and embraced her, hugging her tightly. She dropped to her knees and gently ushered Mei's head up to look at her.

"Let's get out of here," Ainsley said softly.

Mei had never given any kind of indication she spoke English, but the look she gave Ainsley said she understood her. It was a message communicated in the different language they were both fluent in.

Ainsley came around to the driver's side of the cart and slid in. She steered them toward the next hole, away from the resort and closer to what she imagined had to be the end of this place, when what she saw up ahead stopped her. The cart path crossed a small bridge across the creek. Standing on the bridge were four men that had been playing ahead of Barrett and Clarence. They must've heard Barrett's screams because they were looking at Ainsley and Mei with heavy suspicion.

Ainsley looked around. Thick forest bordered the golf greens on all sides and these men were not like Barrett and Clarence. They were much younger and looked fit. They looked back at her curiously, each with a girl on their hip. Ainsley doubted she and Mei could outrun them on foot, but there were only two ways the cart could go: across the bridge or back toward the resort.

Ainsley didn't have a choice. She hung a sharp U-turned and sped back toward everything she was trying to flee.

FIFTY-SIX

JACKSON HELD his gun steady against the back of Roscoe's neck as the SUV eased toward the front gate of The Arcady. This was the moment of truth. Jackson knew Graves could be lying about how vehicles entered, but he had no way to verify. If their SUV didn't open the gate, Jackson and Bear would have to fight their way to Lustschloss.

The SUV came to a stop. For a moment, nothing happened. Jackson reached for his door handle, ready to leave Roscoe and his men behind, when the gate started to slowly glide open. Jackson let out a deep breath.

"Drive," he told Roscoe.

Roscoe did. They came around the first bend in the road and saw The Manor directly ahead.

"Where exactly am I supposed to go?" Roscoe asked.

"Keep on the main road," Jackson said. "Drive normal."

"As soon as we don't pull into the Manor people will know something is wrong."

"Just drive."

They cruised past The Manor. Out front was another member of the security team. Jackson saw Roscoe look over at him.

"Give any sort of distress signal and it'll be the last thing you do," Jackson said. "Keep driving."

He watched the man outside as they drove past The Manor. Like Roscoe warned, he became suspicious of the SUV when it didn't pull in. He started walking toward where the road turned and ascended further into the resort. Jackson and the SUV circled and climbed, coming around behind The Manor. The man outside kept eyes on them, then keyed the mic on his radio.

"Roscoe, where are you going?" his voice said through a radio up front. "Do you have the clients with you?"

"Don't answer him," Jackson said.

They continued to ascend up into the resort. The SUV passed the turn for The Camp when another message came through.

"Beckett, Roscoe's gone silent. He's headed up the drive your way. He's supposed to have clients with him."

"Copy, I'll stop him and see what's up," a second transmission said.

"Things are getting squirrelly, Jacky boy," Bear said. "If it comes to a fight, we're going to want to throw the first punch."

"Thirty more seconds and we're there," Jackson said.

They came around the second large bend in the drive. Jackson and Bear could see Corliss's private residence. On the road ahead was a side-by-side. Beckett was behind the wheel, and he was driving straight for them.

"Whatever you do, don't stop," Jackson ordered.

"I'm not going to play fucking chicken with him," Roscoe said.

"That's exactly what you'll do and you'll run him off the road if you have to. Keep. Driving."

Beckett got to within a couple hundred feet of the approaching SUV and swerved to a stop, blocking the roadway. He climbed out and held out his hand, telling Roscoe to stop the Range Rover.

"Keep going," Jackson repeated.

"I ca—"

"Do it!"

Roscoe panicked and gunned it. The roaring engine gave them away. Beckett drew his pistol from his hip.

"Shit," Jackson said.

He brought his M4 up over Roscoe's shoulder and fired several shots through the windshield. A round clipped Beckett in the shoulder and spun him around. The SUV hit him at speed before colliding with the side-by-side, pinballing off, and careening straight into The Lustschloss. Before Jackson or Bear could react, the vehicles smashed into the front corner of the building.

Jackson slammed his head on the driver's headrest.

Everything became blurry as a ringing in his ears drowned out the other noises. He was vaguely aware of people screaming over the radio. Bear reached over and shook him. Jackson looked at his mouth. It was moving, but no words came out. Jackson couldn't make head or tails of what he was saying.

Then, as quickly as they'd hit the building, his senses came flooding back to him.

"You good?" Bear was yelling. "You hurt?"

"I'm good," Jackson replied.

He looked at Roscoe and his fellow goon up front. Roscoe was writhing in pain and bleeding profusely from his face. His cohort was awake and alert but was still pinned in by the zip ties and seatbelt. Jackson checked the man in the tailgate. He wasn't moving.

"We have to move. Now!" Bear said.

He threw his shoulder into his door and tumbled out. Jackson climbed out after him. They could see men from below running up after them. The front door to The Lustschloss was only a few yards away.

Jackson and Bear ran for it and tried the knob. It was unlocked. Bear opened it and they both tumbled through. Across the open floor, another security team member was trotting down a large staircase. When he saw Jackson, he brought a semi-automatic rifle up to his shoulder, but Jackson fired first. The man tumbled down the remaining stairs and spilled out onto the landing, lifeless. They cleared each connected room around the outside of the main space and came to the staircase on the other side.

"Second floor," Jackson said. "Go, now."

They moved as a team, Bear covering Jackson as he took the rifle from the dead shooter and slung it over his shoulder. The stairs came to a long hallway on the second floor that ended at a pair of large French doors.

"I'll bet you anything that's the asshole's office," Bear said.

But before Jackson could reply, one of the doors swung open and a man leaned out with a shotgun. Jackson and Bear jumped to opposite sides of the hall as the man started shooting. Jackson fired back, hitting the man twice. The man fell, blocking the door from closing shut again.

Jackson moved quickly, covering the rest of the hallway in a matter of seconds. He kicked the ajar door.

There, standing by the window, was Corliss on his phone.

"Drop the phone right now!" Jackson ordered.

Corliss did as he was told, then voluntarily raised his hands in the air. Jackson came to him, took the phone, then patted him down.

"Remember me?" Jackson asked.

"Yes. The rat," Corliss said.

"The one and only." When he was finished checking Corliss, he stood back and pointed to the floor. "On your knees."

Again, Corliss did as he was told. Bear came into the room, pulled the dead man's body away from the door, then shut it.

"Who's this?" Corliss asked.

"Just another dude here to ruin your day," Bear answered.

Jackson took two zip-tie cuffs from his backpack, slipped them around Corliss's wrists and ankles, then pushed him from behind so he fell to his stomach. He dragged Corliss to his desk, checked the drawers, and found the one with the biometric safe. He looked down at Corliss.

"I'm opening your safe," he said. "It'll be a lot easier on you if you cooperate."

"I'm not helping you do a damned thing," Corliss said from the floor.

Jackson went over to Bear and grabbed the circular saw they'd used to cut through the chain link fence at the airport. He turned, crouched, and held it in front of Corliss's face.

"Last chance," Jackson said. "That safe is getting opened one way or the other. It's only a matter of how many digits you lose in the process."

"You wouldn't," Corliss hissed.

"I would."

Jackson dropped a knee onto Corliss's back and pulled the man's right thumb away from his hand. He engaged the saw and pressed the blade into the base of Corliss's thumb. Blood sprayed onto Jackson and the back of Corliss who cried out in agony. It took no more than a couple seconds for the saw to cut clean through the finger. When it was off, Jackson stood and took it to the desk, leaving Corliss sprawled in a crying heap on the floor. He looked at Bear.

"Make sure he doesn't bleed out," he said.

Bear went over, pulled a trauma kit out of his backpack, and went to work on Corliss's hand. Jackson took Corliss's thumb and pressed it onto the biometric scanner on the safe. With a nasally beep, it opened.

There was only one thing inside: a small, black external hard drive.

Jackson grabbed it and it held it up for Bear to see.

"We've got it," he said.

FIFTY-SEVEN

BAILEY AND COLE rolled up to the front gate of The Arcady. It was closed, and no one was in sight, just as Bailey had imagined. She checked the time on her phone. It was two minutes to noon. She opened up her messages and reread the last text Jackson had sent her.

Everything by the book on your end. What we get has to stick to Corliss.

She looked around again for some sign from Clay or a reason to be here. There was nothing but the woods, the gate, and the highway. Bailey reached over, grabbed her radio, and keyed the mic.

"4417," she said. "Show me Code 6 with CAR143 near 7734 Mountain Turnpike. 10-76."

A reply message acknowledged her as she opened her door and got out. Cole followed suit, looking over at Bailey as she did.

"What 'debris in roadway'?" Cole asked, referring to the 10-code Bailey had called in.

Bailey cocked her head and shrugged in reply. The two of them had prepared for a full-on confrontation at The Arcady, strapping on their Kevlar bullet-resistant vests that identified them as police.

Now, though, everything was quiet.

Bailey walked to the middle of the road and kicked a stick out of the way before turning to smile at Cole. She came back to the highway shoulder and took in the mountainside The Arcady was nestled on. She could just make out the pointed roof of a building in the distance.

"Alright, Clay," she murmured. "We're here. What's your big plan?"

————

AINSLEY, with Mei sitting shotgun, drove as fast as the luxury golf cart could go. They crossed back across the first two holes, past another foursome that had just teed off. When they got to the club-house at the top of the hill, Ainsley didn't stop. She couldn't. The array of other golf carts parked at the top led to an open-air equipment shed. Ainsley saw the open road on the other side and swerved head on into it.

"Hang on!" she said to Mei.

A handful of people inside dove out of the way as she sped through. In a second, they were in and out the other side. They were past The Country Club and onto the main drive.

This might work, Ainsley thought. *This might really work.*

But as they crested the incline on the road, Ainsley's heart sank. There, in front of the garish mansion she'd seen a half-dozen times coming and going from the golf course, was a mass of those security guards; the same ones that had killed Tessa. One of their vehicles had wrecked into the side of the mansion and now a whole squad of them blocked the roadway with large guns.

What was this? The four men on the bridge must have found Barrett and Clarence and reported them driving this way. But how could they have reacted so fast? Ainsley took her foot off the pedal and let the golf cart coast to a stop. The men on the road saw her now and seemed to have their attention split between her and the mansion itself.

That was it. Her great escape was over before it'd even really started. She'd killed two men and now the security team would kill her just as they killed Tessa.

Ainsley closed her eyes, grabbed Mei's hand, and waited for the inevitable to happen.

————

BEAR CAME to the large windows that overlooked the resort. Below them, the rest of the security team had surrounded the front of the house, all now armed with assault rifles. He turned and looked back at Jackson who was examining the hard drive.

"It's starting to get real hairy lookin' out there, Jacky boy."

Jackson came over and joined him by the windows. He counted eight in total, including Roscoe and the one they'd strapped into the passenger side of the Range Rover. All of them were looking up at Jackson and Bear. Two against eight was tough math no matter how you looked at it. Having two more on their side would be a lot better. Jackson checked his watch. It was three minutes past noon. He hoped Bailey was in position.

Jackson detached the suppressor from his M-4. "Let's give the girls in blue their exigent circumstances," he said.

Bear grinned as he did the same. The two of them shouldered their rifles, picked a target, and fired.

————

BAILEY PACED BACK and forth alongside the unmarked Explorer. Noon had come and gone with nothing changing. It was dead quiet out by the road. She was about to check her phone again when a burst of gunshots cracked through the air. Both Bailey and Cole instinctively ducked. Crouching, they met each other's eyes and understood. This was it.

"4417," Bailey said into her radio, "10-33. Multiple shots fired, my location. Request additional units, Code 3!"

Bailey got a running start at the stone wall bordering the fence, grabbing the top of it and pulling herself up. "Come on, let's go!" she shouted back to Cole.

She was down and onto the other side of the wall when the back half of the Explorer came smashing through the gate. It swerved right, swung around, and came to a stop facing the looming drive into The Arcady. Cole looked at her from behind the wheel.

"Exactly," she said. "Let's go!"

Bailey ran over and jumped in the passenger seat. "What if that hadn't worked?"

Cole shrugged. "It's your cruiser."

Bailey shook her head, stifling a grin. "Go."

————

AINSLEY JUMPED and screamed as sudden gunfire erupted from the large mansion. The security guards out on the road fired back. Ainsley grabbed Mei and shoved her out of the golf cart, taking her to the ground and covering her with her body. When they survived the first few seconds, she looked over her shoulder to see what was happening.

The men on the road were in some sort of shootout with people inside the mansion. Ainsley and Mei were caught out in the open. Their escape to the rest of the resort was cut off by the ensuing battle, and Ainsley wasn't about to retreat back to The Country Club. Whoever was inside that mansion was against the people running this place. That made them her and Mei's best chance to get through this. She rolled to her feet and grabbed Mei underneath her arms.

"Follow me," she said.

FIFTY-EIGHT

JACKSON PUT down one of the security team members outside and shifted left. He had a second pinned down behind a large boulder across the road when he caught movement out of the corner of his eye. He shifted, bringing his gun around, but it wasn't Corliss's men.

A young blond-haired girl was guiding a young Asian girl to the relative safety of the side of the mansion. When the blond dropped the arm covering her head, Jackson got a good look at her face. It was the girl from the cliff. She was still alive, but now, somehow, she was caught in all this.

"We've got two of the resort's victims outside," Jackson called out to Bear. "I'll get them in and cover the cellar. Make sure the server room is secure. Cover me from up here."

Bear nodded as he loaded a fresh magazine into his M-4. "I got you. You just get them to safety."

Jackson left the office, ran down the hallway, and took the stairs two at a time. The girls were on the north side of the building. He needed to find a way to get to them and going out the front wasn't an option. He moved from room to room, looking for a window or door on the north side. In the third room he tried, he found three windows in what looked to be some sort of study. Jackson dashed to the one furthest away from the shooting and smashed out the window. Then he stuck his head out.

The two young girls were huddled on the ground against the house fifty feet from him.

"Hey!" he called.

Their eyes darted to him, pupils dilated.

Jackson slung his rifle over his shoulder. "Come here! It's okay, we're here to help."

The blond girl grabbed the other by the hand and led them over to Jackson who helped them through the open window and then further into the room for cover.

"Are you guys alright?" he asked, quickly checking them for injuries. "Were you shot or anything?"

"No, I don't think so," the blond replied.

"What are your names?"

"I'm Ainsley. This is Mei. She doesn't speak much English, if any."

"That's okay. My name is Jackson."

Ainsley studied his face then her eyes widened as if she saw something familiar in it. She tried to lurch away from him.

"No!" she cried. "You're one of them! You were with the guy that killed Tessa!"

Jackson raised his hands, placating. "I'm working with the police! I'm sorry I couldn't save your friend, but I'm going to help you two. I promise."

Ainsley hesitated. Jackson looked into her eyes, trying to convince her he was telling the truth. That no matter how many people here had lied to her, he wasn't one of them. The tension in Ainsley's arm loosened.

"Please, we just want to get out of here," she said.

"That's the plan, but right now I need to get you two to safety."

Ainsley nodded.

Jackson moved to the door leading into the hall, calculating his options. He could send them up to Bear or down into the cellar with the server bay. Either had its risks but upstairs provided added safety if Corliss's men got inside.

Jackson keyed his throat mic. "Bear, I've got them inside. Two young girls, Ainsley and Mei. I'm sending them up to you. I'll cover down here."

"Copy!" Bear radioed back.

Jackson looked at Ainsley and Mei. "My friend is upstairs. You'll be safer up there. When I move, you take those stairs there up to the second floor. Go all the way down the hall. My friend is in the office at the end of it."

Ainsley was shaking, but she nodded, putting an arm around Mei.

"Go!"

Jackson placed himself between them and the front door and fired. Ainsley and Mei made a break for it.

———

AS BAILEY and Cole sped up The Arcady's main drive, people started to run in an attempt to flee the shootout happening at the top of the property. Panicked, they darted across the road, forcing Cole to brake or swerve to avoid them.

"God dammit!" Cole grunted. "Are the lights or siren still working on this thing?"

Bailey reached over and flipped a pair of switches, but nothing happened. They continued to bob and weave their way through people until the flow of fleeing jaywalkers strewn in pastel vacation wear ebbed just before a fork in the road.

"Right, right," Bailey said. "The gunfire is coming from up there."

"I've got it."

The road rose and turned again before plateauing out onto a scene of absolute chaos. A group of men in security garb had a large mansion partially surrounded and were firing at it. None of them looked like Jackson or Bear, which left Bailey to assume they were somewhere inside being shot at. She kicked her door open, drawing her pistol.

"Virginia State Police!" She called out. "Drop your weap—"

Several of the shooters pivoted and began firing at them. Cole and Bailey moved to the damaged rear of their SUV and took cover.

"4417," Bailey said into her radio, "Signal 13! I've got multiple subjects 10-71. Myself and CAR143 are taking fire. Tell arriving units shooters are in front of a large residence at the top of the property."

Bailey got on one knee and started shooting back.

———

BEAR COULDN'T HELP but grin when he saw help arrive. As soon as they rolled up, though, Bailey and Cole came under fire. Bear moved positions and fired on the men shooting at them. He took two of them down before the rest got cover. He ducked under cover and began loading a new mag when Jackson's voice came into his ear.

"Bear, I've got them inside. Two young girls, Ainsley and Mei. I'm sending them up to you. I'll cover down here."

"Copy!"

Thirty seconds later, Ainsley and Mei came running through the open French doors and looked as they were going to go straight through the open windows across the room. Bear dropped his rifle and put his arms out, catching them.

"Whoa, whoa. Okay," he said. "Let's stay away from the windows as they're a bit bullet-y at the moment.

Bear escorted them over to Corliss's desk. He flipped it over, placing the thick mahogany top facing the windows.

"Here," he said. "You all take cover behind here. You'll be safe as long as you keep your head down."

The blond girl brought the other into a tight embrace between the large legs on either side. Bear returned to the window and started shooting at the men outside. Every few seconds a round would whiz in overhead, forcing Bear to take cover. When one shot splintered the window frame next to his head, he dropped all the way to the ground.

Bear checked himself then looked back to see if the girls were still okay. The blond one had her eyes locked on Corliss. He was lying on his stomach just feet from her. Bear watched as anger began to burn in Ainsley's eyes. By Corliss's feet was the dead security team member and the shotgun he'd wielded. Ainsley rose, impervious to the danger of gunfire. She walked over and picked up the shotgun, sliding her finger around the trigger, and pointed it at the man.

"You," she said, tears forming in the corners of her eyes. "Is this your place?! Did you do all of this to us?!"

Bear keyed the mic on his radio. "Uh, Jacky boy? We've got a problem up here."

"What is it?" Jackson radioed back.

"One of the girls has got Corliss at gunpoint."

No reply came back. Bear could only hope that meant Jackson was on his way. Calmly, he approached Ainsley and put a hand out toward her.

"Whoa, easy there," he said. "Careful with that."

Ainsley didn't hear him. Her focus was on Corliss. "Answer me!" she shouted.

———

JACKSON TOOK the stairs two at a time back up to the second floor, then sprinted down the hallway. When he got to the open French doors, he stopped and took in the situation.

"Bear, cover downstairs," he said. "I've got this."

"You sure?"

"I'm sure. Cover downstairs."

Bear hesitated a moment longer before stepping around Jackson and disappearing down the hall. A moment later, Jackson could hear him returning the gunfire of the men outside.

He didn't move. His voice was calm and soft. "I need you to put that gun down for me. Please."

"Why? It's him, isn't it? The one behind this place."

"Yes, he is."

"Then he deserves to die! He should be dead, not Tessa and her sister, and God knows who else!"

"If you kill him, you let him off easy. We're here to make sure he answers for everything he's done. But killing him when he's unarmed and defenseless like this isn't the answer."

"Then untie him! I don't care! I'm not afraid!"

"I know you're not. You're better than him. And that's why I can't let you do this. I can't let you fall to his level. Not too long ago, I was in your shoes, facing someone who killed people I loved more than anyone in the world. I wanted him to die just the same as you want this man to die. But I had a good friend stop me, and I've been thankful every day since that they did that for me."

Ainsley stood there, eyes never leaving Corliss.

"Ainsley, look at me," Jackson implored.

She didn't.

"Please."

After a small eternity, Ainsley's head turned. Her eyes met his.

"I need you to trust me. Put the gun down. Don't do it for him. Do it for you."

Ainsley's finger lingered on the trigger, but she didn't pull it.

Jackson extended a hand. "You're not him. You're not a killer. You're just a kid. He's taken so much from you, but you still have your whole life to live. Don't let him take that from you, too."

Ainsley began to sob. The gun dropped from her hands, now impossibly heavy.

Jackson stepped toward Ainsley. He picked up the shotgun with one hand and brought Ainsley close to him with the other. "You made the right choice," he said quietly.

Corliss laughed, lying at their feet. Jackson put one of his boots on Corliss's neck. Corliss groaned.

The sound of gunfire filled the room when a whirring in between the shots caught Jackson's ear. As it got louder, Jackson realized it was a helicopter. Through the windows across the room, he spotted it. It was converging on them. Could Bailey and Cole have gotten air support here that quickly? It seemed unlikely. Then Jackson remembered the moment he and Bear first entered the office. Corliss had been on the phone.

Jackson looked down at him. Corliss had a menacing grin plastered on his face as he looked over at the approaching chopper. His thumb and his phone lay on the ground near where Bear had overturned the desk. Jackson reached over, grabbed the thumb, unlocked the phone, and opened up the call log. The last call had been placed at 12:03 p.m., just as everything had kicked off outside with him and Bear in the Range Rover. He looked back at Corliss. His grin was even wider now.

"Who the hell did you call?" he asked.

Before Corliss could answer, machine gun fire poured in from outside.

FIFTY-NINE

LEAD ROUNDS the size of double-a batteries tore through the second floor of The Lustschloss. Jackson grabbed Ainsley and dove for cover behind Corliss's desk, but not before a searing pain ripped through his calf.

He took cover behind the desk with the girls, keeping his bloody leg outstretched. As he looked around for Corliss, a stabbing pain erupted in his shoulder, and he cried out in renewed agony.

Corliss stood above him, holding a bloodied letter opener. The broken pieces of zip ties lay at his feet. Jackson drew his pistol with his good arm, but Corliss grabbed his wrist and slammed it against the floor. Jackson's pistol clattered out of reach.

Corliss made a run for the pistol. Ainsley, at Jackson's feet, took the shotgun once more. She pointed it at Corliss and pulled the trigger but cried out in frustration when nothing happened. Jackson had engaged the safety on it.

Jackson got his M-4 out from underneath him just as Corliss got to the pistol. The two fired at each other almost simultaneously. Jackson felt a round splinter the wood of the desk leg next to his head. He aimed his rifle at Corliss again, but Corliss was gone down the hall.

Jackson keyed his throat mic. "Bear," he groaned.

"Jacky boy," Bear radioed back. "What the hell is going on up there?"

"Corliss has a chopper outside laying down fire for him. He's coming your way. He's got my pistol."

No reply came back. The barrage of machine gun fire drowned out anything happening deeper inside the mansion. Jackson crawled to the office door, then pulled himself up onto his good leg. He motioned for Ainsley and Mei to follow him.

"Keep your head down and stay behind me," he said.

As Jackson started to hobble down the hall, Ainsley grabbed Mei and came up beside him. She slipped herself underneath his arm, shouldering some of his weight. The puncture wound in his shoulder hurt like hell, but with his other arm Jackson shouldered his rifle. Together, they made their way back to the staircase, but not knowing what was happening downstairs made it too dangerous for Ainsley and Mei to come any further. He took his good arm back from Ainsley and tried the knob for one of the last rooms before the stairs. It opened into a palatial bathroom.

"In here," Jackson motioned. "Lock the door and get in the tub. Don't open it for anyone except Bear or me or the police."

Ainsley and Mei did as they were told. Jackson got halfway down to the first landing on the stairs only to see Corliss in the middle of the room, pinning down Bear with gunfire as he backed his way to the front door. Jackson raised his rifle and fired but missed. Corliss pivoted and unloaded the rest of the pistol's magazine in Jackson's direction, forcing Jackson to drop and take cover. When the shooting stopped, he came back to the railing only to see Corliss slip out the front door.

"Bear!" Jackson shouted. "He's going for the bird!"

The two of them got to the front door at the same time only to be brushed back in by gunfire from what remained of the security team outside. Beyond them, they could see flashing lights coming up the wooded drive from below.

"Calvary's coming," Bear said to Jackson on the other side of the open doorway.

"Not fast enough," Jackson countered.

The two of them weren't going through the front door any time soon. But they had to try to stop the helicopter. He thought of the window he had pulled the two girls through.

"Cover me!" he called out to Bear.

Bear nodded as he loaded a fresh magazine into his rifle. Jackson broke across the open floor of The Lustschloss to the study near the back corner. Tottering as fast as he could, he crossed the room and got to the window. The helicopter had touched down on the road toward The Country Club. Its gunner was out of the helicopter and escorting Corliss back to it. Jackson rested his rifle on the window sill to steady his shot. He took a deep breath in then out and squeezed the trigger.

He hit the gunner square in the chest and the man collapsed onto the road. Jackson shifted to Corliss, but he was already in the helicopter. The powerful rotors sped up and lifted it off the ground.

Jackson shimmied out the window and fired at the helicopter as it climbed into the sky. But it only got higher and smaller and harder to hit. Then it banked north and headed out of the area. Jackson felt the adrenaline start to drain from him. He collapsed against the side of the house, utterly exhausted.

He had his hands on his knees when a silhouette rounded the front corner of the house. It was Bailey. As soon as she realized it was Jackson, she lowered her service weapon and jogged over to him.

"Christ! Are you okay?" she asked.

"I'll live," Jackson replied.

"You're shot." She examined him further. "And stabbed."

"Not really stabbed, it was a letter opener."

"Does that make it hurt any less?"

"More, actually." Blood ran down Jackson's forearm and over his hand where it seeped on to his pant leg. "You need to find a way to track that helo."

"We're already on it. "

"There are two girls in a bathroom upstairs. One was on the cliff and witnessed that other girl's murder the other night. I'm guessing there's more up the road back there."

"We've got back up coming. We're going to go over every inch of this place."

Jackson reached into his pocket and pulled out the external hard drive, holding it up for Bailey to see. "Then there's this."

Bailey took it from him and held it in her hand. "What is it?"

"Corliss's little black book. Names and dates of everyone who's been here."

Bailey grinned. "You did good, Clay."

"There are servers in the cellar, too. They should have everything on it you need."

"We'll take care of it. *You* need a medic, though. For real."

"I told you I'll be fine."

Bailey ignored him and grabbed her radio. "Get me an EMT to the north side of the mansion. I've got one down over here with a GSW and a puncture wound."

Jackson slid down the side of the house until his backside found the earth. His eyes focused on the helicopter in the distance, watching it until it disappeared.

SIXTY

SIX HOURS LATER, Ainsley found herself in the offices of the Western Virginia Human Trafficking Task Force in Roanoke. She was sitting in the cubicle of a young, black woman that had introduced herself as Detective Angela Cole.

Ainsley sat in the spare chair in the corner, drowning in a pair of FBI sweats two sizes too big for her. Cole came back to her cubicle with a cup of coffee and sat down. She gave Ainsley a kind smile.

"I'm sure you can agree it's been a long day," she said.

Ainsley gave a half smile and nodded as she brushed her hair behind her ear.

"Would you like a cup of coffee as well?" Cole asked.

Ainsley shook her head. "No, thank you. I don't like coffee."

"Water? A soda?"

"I'm okay."

"Alright, well, you just let me know." Cole opened a file on her desk and flipped a couple of pages in. "You're from Arizona, right?"

"Yes, ma'am."

Cole smiled again. "You calling me 'ma'am' makes me feel old. Please, just call me Angela."

"Okay. Yes, Angela."

"You came here with a friend. A ..." Cole checked the file. "Theresa Wilson of Holbrook, Arizona."

Hearing her name, a flood of emotions crashed into Ainsley. She bit her lip, trying to stifle what was coming, but she knew she couldn't. As tears welled up in her eyes, she dropped her head into her hands and began sobbing. A second later, Angela had an arm around her and was placing a box of tissues in her lap.

"I can't imagine how hard this is," Angela said.

"*Wilson*," Ainsley said. "I followed her all this way—threw my entire life away—and I didn't even know her last name. My god, I didn't even know her *actual* first name. I'm so damn stupid."

"No. Listen to me. Everything that happened? It's not your fault. *None* of it. People lied to you. People took advantage of you. And now, we're going to make sure they face justice."

"They killed her. Tessa."

"And we have that man in custody. He's not going to hurt anyone else."

"What about the others? What about Mina?"

Cole again consulted the files on her desk. "Assimina Ivakin. Is this her?" She held up a booking photo of Mina.

Ainsley nodded.

"We have her in custody, too. We're going to get them all, Ainsley. Everyone who worked there. Everyone who knew what was happening there. *All of them.*"

Ainsley lifted her head back up and took a tissue, blowing hard into it. When she was done, she balled it up and held it in her hands. "So what happens to me now?"

"Well, we'd like to talk to you some more, but that wouldn't take more than a few days. You're still a minor, so after that, you'll be placed back into the care of your guardian. I understand that's your grandmother."

Ainsley shook her head. "My mother's there. I can't go back. She's the reason ... I left."

"Yes, you told my colleague that, so we checked it out." Cole flipped a couple more sheets over. "Your mother was arrested a week ago."

Ainsley felt a spark of hope. "Arrested for what?"

"From what it says here, DUI, domestic battery, and assaulting a peace officer. Her bond's been set at three hundred grand. So far, it hasn't been posted, which means she's still in lock-up."

Ainsley shook her head again. "She doesn't have that kind of money. None of us do."

"Then, I'd imagine she'll remain in jail for some time."

Ainsley didn't say anything.

"That means you can go back to your grandmother. Go back home. Is that what you want?"

More tears streamed down Ainsley's cheeks. "More than anything."

"Then we'll make sure that happens. But for now, we're going to find you a place to rest tonight. Someplace warm and safe."

Ainsley nodded. "That sounds really good right now."

Cole closed the file. "Perfect. I'll get to work on that. Do you have any other questions for me?"

Ainsley shook her head.

She was relieved this was all over. Somehow, she'd managed to escape the hell that was The Arcady. Tessa and her sister hadn't been so lucky. How many more like them were there? The man. The one on the cliff that had watched her with pain in his eyes as she'd been taken away. He was the same one at the mansion that had come for her and Mei.

"Actually, I have one," Ainsley said. She wiped a tear from her cheek and looked up at Cole. "The man today who came for us. Who was he?"

———

DOWN THE ROAD, Jackson Clay was back at Roanoke Memorial Hospital. Back in an ER examination room with his feet dangling over the side of the bed as he sat surrounded by monitors and medical instruments. This time, though, his left leg and right shoulder were heavily bandaged and a Roanoke deputy was posted outside his room.

The glass door to the room slid opened. He looked up, expecting to see a doctor or nurse, but it was Bailey. She tossed him a water as she stepped into the room. He caught it with his left hand.

"Smart," Bailey said as she slid the glass door shut behind her before dropping into a chair at the foot of the bed. "Not using your bad shoulder. Maybe you're not as hardheaded as I thought."

"Don't get soft on me just because I got shot."

Bailey snorted and shook her head.

"We got Corliss," she said.

Jackson nodded. "The officer outside told me. Apparently, it's all over the news."

"That helicopter took him to the executive airport in Leesburg. He was boarding a private jet when a small army of law enforcement came to arrest him."

"And you have Graves?"

Bailey nodded. "Graves, the security personnel that survived the shootout, and everyone else who was responsible at The Arcady."

Jackson turned, bringing his good leg up onto the bed to look at her. "Good."

"Haven't found any connections to a possible leak in the task force, though. I know it's still early, but—"

"I've been thinking about that. I think I know who it is."

Bailey raised her eyebrows in surprise. "Well? Do you mind sharing with the class?"

"Not yet." He looked her in the eyes. "I need a favor."

"What?"

"Another twenty-four hours."

Wariness flooded Bailey's face, and she shook her head. "Pitts isn't going to go for that. He gave me the leeway to bring you back in quietly once, he's not about to risk you going AWOL again."

"I promise you, twenty-four hours. This time tomorrow, I'll be at my house just like I should be. I just need you to cover for me in the meantime."

Bailey hesitated. "How do you know they're not going to keep you here overnight?"

"I've already signed out, AMA. Against Medical Advice. They're bringing me the form right now to sign."

Bailey sighed. "Clay …"

"Didn't I deliver you Corliss and Graves—not to mention myself —like I said?"

Bailey didn't answer him.

"Last night, when you asked how I knew you weren't the mole, I told you I trusted you. That trust goes both ways. You brought me into all of this to finish it. So, let me do that. Finish it. This final piece."

Bailey folded her arms. "I suppose you won't let me tag along on."

"You can be there. This time tomorrow. At my house, with me. I promise."

Bailey nodded. "Okay."

When the doctor returned, Jackson signed his discharge paperwork. Bailey, relieving the officer, walked him out of the hospital. She had her state-issued unmarked Explorer parked curbside.

"Your truck is still at the dance club," Bailey said. "I'll take you to it. Get in."

Bailey got behind the wheel. Jackson opened the passenger door and climbed in.

"For the record, I do trust you."

Jackson nodded. Bailey fired up the SUV and left the hospital.

SIXTY-ONE

JACKSON SAT in the darkness of the mole's living room. The armchair, rich leather with sculpted wooden legs, was comfortable and supported his recuperating shoulder well.

Betraying your oath had its advantages.

Just before eleven, a key clicked into the deadbolt on the front door. Then, the lock on the knob clicked, and the door opened. The outside porch light cast the mole in a long shadow as his silhouette stepped into the house. He shut the door behind him, and for a moment, Jackson and the mole were bathed in darkness. Then Jackson switched on the lamp beside him.

Assistant US Attorney Chris Weisz jumped. He braced himself on the credenza in his foyer, looking at Jackson. Jackson waited, watching the man's eyes as he identified him.

"You," he said in between heavy breaths. "What the hell are you doing in my house?"

"It's not fun, is it?" Jackson asked. "Finding what you thought was safe compromised."

"I asked you a question. What are you doing here?"

"I always wondered what it would take, the dollar amount to betray everyone around me."

"If you're insinuating I somehow am—"

"I'm not insinuating anything. I'm telling you I know."

Weisz was quiet.

"It didn't make sense at first. Why would a mole inside the task force first out the wrong guy, especially when doing so put me *closer* to Corliss? And that's when I figured it out. The mole wasn't in the task force, they were adjacent to it."

"I don't know what the hell you're talking about."

"Don't you? Bailey reported it up the line that I'd gotten in with Graves at the club. But in a classic game of telephone, the message got skewed, and you understood that a mole was *in* Graves's security team inside The Arcady. That's when they killed Cody Busch. It was only later that you learned your mistake and reported back to Corliss they'd gotten the wrong guy. That I was the real source the task force had placed inside."

Weisz took a step into the room, tossing his keys onto the table. "That's certainly an interesting theory. Of course, you can't prove any of that."

"I can't, you're right. There's no paper trail of any of it. But there are for other things." Jackson pulled out his phone. "You've been laying the groundwork to run for State AG. The first stepping stone on the way up the political ladder, I'm sure, for an ambitious guy like yourself. I'm also sure you know all political contributions are a matter of public record. Graves told me Corliss ran the business for The Arcady through a shell company called Alleghania Travel. So, imagine my surprise when that very company is listed as having contributed almost half a million to the super PAC you established to aid your campaign. That's quite the coincidence. What do you think happens when it comes out your campaign was funded by human trafficking?"

Weisz still didn't say anything.

"When Graves was feeling me out for a spot on his squad of

goons, he asked me if I was a violent man. I told him I can be. That was the truth and there are half a dozen men dead on a mountainside just outside Monterey that attest to that fact."

"You wouldn't be here unless you wanted something, so what is it?"

"You're right that I can't prove you were Corliss's mole, and the feds are never going to cut him any sort of deal worth giving you up. So, here's what's going to happen. You are going to go into the office tomorrow and resign as Assistant US Attorney. You are going to shutter your campaign for AG and release a statement that you are ending your time in public service. Say it's because you want to spend more time with your family, that the stress of the job has weighed on you, whatever. You can say you're ill, and it wouldn't be so far from the truth. I don't care the reason, but as of tonight, your place in any position of power or influence is over. Because if you continue, I will make sure all sorts of interested parties connect the dots on your campaign finances." Jackson paused. "Then I'll come back here for good measure. And you'll learn what a violent man I can be."

Jackson gingerly got himself up out of the armchair and headed for the door. Weisz gave him a wide berth as if he were an animal that might turn and attack.

When he got to the door, Jackson looked back at him.

"I look forward to hearing about your resignation tomorrow," he said.

Then, Jackson turned and walked into the night.

SIXTY-TWO

A MONTH to the day she hitched a ride out of Heber-Overgaard, Arizona, Ainsley returned. Seated in the passenger seat of an FBI sedan, she fidgeted with her hands as the baby-faced agent that had picked her up from the airport in Phoenix now pulled onto the dirt road that led to her grandmother's house.

As he pulled up to the house, Ainsley's heart lurched into her throat. There were no cars in the driveway. She'd feared seeing her mother's truck but never imagined *no one* being here. Had something happened to her grandmother? What would happen to her if that were the case? Ainsley's mind was about to spiral when the side door to the house opened. Her grandma took a wobbly step out with her cane.

Ainsley opened her door before the car had even stopped and ran to her. Her grandma wrapped her in a tight embrace, tears cascading down her cheeks.

"I'm so sorry, grandma," Ainsley sobbed. "I'm so, so sorry."

"Oh, stop that!" Her grandmother said. "I'm just glad you're safe."

"But I left. I ran away and I left you here. I didn't tell you where I was. I can only imagine—"

"But you're home, now sweet girl. You're home now."

At that, Ainsley cried harder. Juxtaposed to the cruel, brutish world she'd just endured, her grandmother's loving forgiveness was overwhelming. They held each other like that for what seemed like hours. And when they were done, Ainsley got her bags from the agent and went inside.

Coming back was like stepping into a memory. Everything was just as it had been, not that she really expected much to change. It was she who had changed. She looked down at a photo of herself — her school photo from just this year, taken only eight months ago — and didn't recognize the girl smiling at her.

That girl was blissfully naive. Innocent.

Ainsley hoped to get much of what she'd lost back over these last few weeks, but that innocence was forever gone. She couldn't undo the pain she'd endured. The fear she'd felt. The hopelessness that had threatened to swallow her whole. All she could do was carry all of that with her now and never look back.

Ainsley opened the door to her bedroom. Things were still scattered about from the way she'd quickly ransacked the space with Tessa waiting in her car outside. Thinking about it caused a profound sadness to wash over her. Not the kind where she got upset — God knows there had been enough of those moments the last few days. This was a tearless sadness. A deep ravine of guilt and regret carved through her. She and Tessa had left Arizona together. They hadn't imagined returning, but Ainsley did. Tessa or her sister Mackenzie no longer could. Ainsley could only imagine how many Tessas that awful place had preyed upon. Ainsley never considered herself a particularly spiritual person, but she hoped somewhere now the two of them were reconnected. And they were safe.

She hoped she might be reconnected with Tessa again too, but not right now. No, right now she was here. *Alive.* She had to build a life, not just for herself but for Tessa and her sister and everyone else who no longer could; everyone who had been lured to that place trying to find just that: a better life.

Ainsley set her bags down and began unpacking.

———

TWO THOUSAND MILES AWAY, Jackson sat on the front steps of his timber frame home on Bull Run Mountain, watching a similar sedan pull into his driveway. Special Agent Jen Bailey opened the driver-side door and got out.

She walked up to Jackson, looking him over.

"You've healed up in the last few days," she said. "How's the leg feel?"

"Kind of like a bullet went through it," Jackson said.

Bailey laughed. She took off her sunglasses and sat down next to him. "Techs cracked that server in Corliss's basement. It's damning stuff. So much so that the AUSA isn't even offering Graves a deal to turn state's evidence."

"The *new* Assistant US Attorney, that is." "Yeah, that was a strange one, Weisz abruptly resigning like that. He even ended his campaign for state AG." Bailey looked over at him. "I'm guessing you wouldn't know anything about that?"

"Threatening a government official, even a crooked one, would be a federal felony and a violation of my parole. Anyway, I came straight home from the hospital, remember?"

Bailey shook her head and grinned. "We never did find any evidence of a mole at the task force."

Jackson shrugged. "I guess I was mistaken. Paranoid in my old age."

"Your instincts aren't often wrong."

"I guess there's a first time for everything."

Bailey's grin disappeared as if it were blown away in the breeze. She looked down at the monitoring bracelet back on Jackson's ankle. "Listen, I've been in touch with the Governor's office. I pushed hard and called in just about every favor I could, but they feel the optics of pardoning someone convicted of a violent felony, the circumstances aside, just aren't great right now."

Jackson nodded, keeping his eyes on the woods ahead.

"I'm sorry. I know I promised you—"

"You didn't promise me anything. And I didn't help you out for my sake."

Bailey's voice was soft. "I know. I'm just ... I'm sorry, anyway." She cleared her throat. "But they did promise to expunge your record once your sentence is served out. Provided you don't get into any more trouble."

"That depends. Are you going to ask me to?"

Bailey chuckled. "That's fair. But do you think you can tough it out?"

"Six more months up here on my own land? I think I'll manage."

"There are worse places to be trapped. Like that god awful hell they called a resort." She snorted. "'Happyland'. If there was ever a more ironic moniker."

"There's going to be more Happylands out there, though. You know that, right?"

Bailey nodded.

"I guess that's something the new Special Agent *In Charge* of The Western Virginia Human Trafficking Task Force will have to run down."

Bailey's cheeks reddened. "You read about that, huh?"

"We do get internet even out here in the sticks. What did Pitts say when he heard you were replacing him?"

"He got his own promotion, liaising with the FBI in DC."

"Good for him, I guess. And congrats."

"Thanks." Bailey stood up and brushed her pants off. "I've got to get back, but I'll be in touch."

Jackson nodded. "Sounds good."

Bailey put her sunglasses back on and looked at Jackson's yard. "I see you finished the fence."

"I did."

"Maybe now you can get that dog."

Jackson looked over his shoulder and whistled. A loud bark came back in reply. A second later, a large yellow labrador retriever came barreling around the side of the house. It ran up to Bailey who held her hands out and let it sniff them.

"Well, look at you, Clay," she said.

"Bear found her. She's five. They were about to put her down."

Bailey crouched down and let the dog lick her face. "Not that you'd know a thing or two about a new lease on life."

Jackson raised a shoulder.

"You give her a name yet?"

"Josie."

Bailey looked at him, one eyebrow raised.

"Short for Josephine."

Bailey smiled and nodded, then wiped at something in the corner of her eye. She stood up. "Well, I'll leave you and Josie to it. There's a joke in there somewhere about teaching an old dog new tricks."

"Somewhere. Someone ought to go find it."

Bailey nodded again. "Maybe someone good at that kind of thing."

Jackson raised a hand and waved. "Drive safe."

Bailey walked back to her car and got in. Jackson watched her back down the dirt drive and leave. When she was gone, he stood and stretched. Josie barked at him. He looked over at the tennis ball on the stairs.

"You know I only have one good shoulder at the moment, right?" Jackson asked.

Josie barked again, shifting her gaze between him and the ball.

Jackson sighed. "Alright."

Grabbing the tennis ball, he reared back, and threw it as far as he could. Josie tore after it and brought it back. Jackson threw it again. He climbed the steps up to his porch and slipped into one of the Adirondack chairs there. When Josie came back, he threw it again.

And again.

They continued to play fetch until the sun set.

———

The story continues in *Safe Harbor*, click here to order your copy now or keep reading for a sneak peek!

https://a.co/d/bOcVnyK

Join the B.C. Lienesch reader family and stay up to date on all the latest news!

https://www.bclnovels.com/newsletter

SAFE HARBOR: PROLOGUE

STEPHIE MEACHEM STOOD on the dock watching the fireworks overhead. Mortar shots fired into the late evening twilight burst into red, blue, and yellow chrysanthemums. She could feel the explosions as they rippled through the air and onto the water beneath her. It was late July 1999, and the hot, humid air hung on to the smoke from the pyrotechnics with a vice-like grip. She brushed her blonde hair off her shoulder and picked at the peeling sunburn there. At seventeen, she was quickly growing into her leggy body, one that had darkened from sunning over school break, but remembering to put on sunscreen was a habit she was still working on.

The dock stood on the far tip of the Meachem family's property on Chincoteague Island, where Oyster Bay joined Assateague Bay, tucked up behind Assateague Island. When Stephie's English ancestors had settled the plot of land in the mid-seventeenth century, Chincoteague itself had been a Virginia barrier island. The earth had changed over centuries, but the Meachems remained a constant. Stephie wondered if that would still be the case once everyone learned the truth about what had happened.

A pontoon boat wrapped in neon lights sailed through the bay between the two islands, pop music thumping. Today had been the pony penning, an island tradition and tourist attraction where Chincoteague's firefighters got on horseback and corralled Assateague Island's wild pony herds, swimming them across the channel for some to be auctioned off in order to manage the population on the island. The town's population ballooned from thirty-six hundred to over forty thousand in the days around the swim. The boaters whooped and hollered as more fireworks exploded overhead. Everyone nearby always enjoyed the show Stephie's father put on, even if it wasn't entirely legal. She doubted the chief of the small town's police force would ever discipline one of his poker buddies.

Stephie wrapped her hands around her belly, cradling the secret within her. She turned, looking back at her family's property. Three large houses—some of the largest on the island—stood on their squat, wide foundations and glowed like ornamental lanterns on the flat grasslands, each with a much more substantial dock running out to a small flotilla of personal watercraft. One McMansion for each of the three siblings. Together, the family was having their own pony penning celebration, and Stephie could see little black silhouettes moving in between windows or underneath the lights on the wraparound decks.

She watched the dark shadows move back and forth like ants when she heard the rapid pitter-patter of running feet in flip-flops. More fireworks burst overhead, and now Stephie saw her brother, Zach, sprinting toward her, his figure changing in the sporadic, colorful flashes.

"Stephie!" he shouted. "Stephie!"

Zach ran full speed as he hit the dock, then pulled up just feet short of his sister. Stephie flinched as if he were about to knock two of them into the water. Zach doubled over, dropping his hands to his knees, trying to catch his breath.

"Russell's here," he said in between heavy breaths.

Stephie felt her heart lurch into her throat. She stared at Zach, hoping this was some sort of joke. But Zach just stared back at her, his chest heaving under his tie-dyed tank top. Sweat matted the edges of his short, sandy hair, dropping in beads across his angular face.

"Did you hear me?" Zach asked. "I said Russell's *here*."

Stephie shook her head. "Dad..."

"Dad knows." Zach took another gulp of air. "He knows about all of it. Steph, when I saw him, he was going upstairs to get his gun."

Stephie could barely hear her own voice. "Oh, God. We have to stop him."

"I know. Come on."

Zach held his hand out, but Stephie just looked at it. Her feet were like cinder blocks beneath her.

Zach huffed in through his nose. "Steph, you have to be brave now. There's no more hiding this. You have to face it. I'll do it with you, but we have to do it *now*. Before the wrong people get hurt."

Stephie nodded. She reached out and took Zach's hand. Together, they began running for their house nestled between the two others. The mortars across the way began firing off their grand finale. In rapid succession, starbursts of every color painted the dark world around them, strobing with their flashes. Green, white, red, blue, red, yellow. Stephie's legs began to burn, but she pushed the pain out of her mind. Zach was right. She had to stop this before it went too far. They reached the first house and kept going. Their cousin, Adam, stood on the deck corner nearest them, two stories up.

"Hey!" he called out. "Where you all off to? A hot date? You know that family thing is frowned upon now." He cackled at his own joke.

Stephie thought she was going to be sick. Not from the morning sickness, which had started a couple of days earlier. From the fear that clawed at her insides. Fear of the truth that was about to come out. Fear of what it would do to her, to her family. Fear of what the town would think when they heard. The rumors, the gossip. Most of all, she feared her life as she'd known it was seconds away from ending.

They crossed the footbridge over the swampy marshes between

their aunt and uncle's house and theirs. Amidst the thunderous bombardment of fireworks came another pair of blasts. They were sharper and snare-like.

Gunshots.

"Oh, god," Stephie cried out.

"Come on!" Zach shouted.

Over the tall marsh grass, Stephie could see Russell's red Dodge Dakota in their driveway. She collapsed to her knees, fearing the worst, and began sobbing.

"Get up!" Zach begged. "We can't stop! You have to get up!"

The cab light on the Dakota clicked on as the driver's door opened. Stephie stared, mouth gaping, relieved to see Russell unharmed.

Russell looked over at them, his eyes narrowed and brow furrowed. "Stephie? What the hell is going on?!"

Before Stephie could find the words to answer, her father stepped out onto the driveway with a shotgun nestled under his arm.

"Russell!" Stephie screamed. "Go! Please!"

"Not until you tell me what is going on."

Over the fireworks, a third gunshot rumbled into the night.

SAFE HARBOR: CHAPTER ONE

JACKSON CLAY DROPPED his head and looked down the sights of his Benelli Super Black Eagle shotgun. He watched his target until it was inside the forty-yard marker he'd placed, moving fast. Jackson estimated it to be thirty-seven yards. *Definitely a makeable shot.* Following the target, he took a deep breath in, held it, then let it out. His heart rate slowed to the optimal sixty beats per minute. *Good to go.* Jackson slid his index finger down from the body of the shotgun and onto the trigger.

A metallic snap came from over his right shoulder, followed by a thud.

"Sonofabitch!" Bear grunted.

Jackson turned and looked just in time to see Bear fall off the back end of the duck blind and into the water below. He turned back to his shotgun. The duck had banked left and flown back out to Calfpen Bay. Jackson frowned and lowered the gun.

Bear began splashing somewhere beneath. "Help me up, dammit!" he said. "I'm not a strong swimmer."

"It's three feet of water, Bear," Jackson said. "Stand up."

Bear stopped floundering and got his feet underneath him. "Goddamn chair snapped on me."

Jackson snorted. "You don't say. Use the ladder to pull yourself up."

Bear reached out for a wooden rung built into the blind and hoisted himself up. The blind itself was crudely constructed but effective. A two-foot-by-four-foot platform stood a couple of feet over the shallow bay, with a wooden pen on the back end big enough to slip in a small to medium-sized boat. Harvested vegetation and branches camouflaged the structure on all sides.

The blind itself was tucked away on a tiny estuary called Will's Creek on the north end of Assateague Island, where it cut into the thin strip of land like a sickle-shaped knife. Tall southern pine trees shot up from the marsh grass and lowlands on either side, creating the perfect corridor for waterfowl to swoop down into.

Jackson took off his Piedmont Ammo & Supply ball cap and ran his fingers through ash-brown hair that was just long enough to show its natural curls. A lot longer than it had been during his Army Ranger days, or even in his time as a father and a husband. Those were completely different lives from the one Jackson lived now.

Putting the hat back on, he scratched at his beard, watching Bear struggle to climb out of the empty boat pen. Jackson was in his forties, but his athletic frame made him look ten years younger. The tapestry of scars that covered his body, however, told the true story of a life lived harder than most.

Beneath him, Bear had managed to get himself onto the ramshackle ladder. He'd just begun to climb it when the rotted rung holding his foot gave way and sent him back into the bay.

"Godfuckingdammit!" Bear stammered.

Bear was a few years younger than Jackson but looked older with his six-and-a-half-foot frame and bourbon-barrel physique. His legal name was Archibald Beauchamp, but he embodied his "Bear" nickname in every way. From his unkempt chestnut hair and his long, bushy beard to the way he had a habit of growling when he got excited, one could be forgiven for thinking he'd descended from the population of black bears that called the Old Dominion State home. They'd met five years ago as Jackson tracked a missing girl across Virginia. Bear had backed him up in a bar fight, and the two had watched each other's backs ever since.

A staticky voice came from a radio in one of Jackson's coat pockets.

"Jackson? Bear?" the voice said. "I see y'all moving around out there, didn't hear a gunshot, though. Y'all got a bird down?"

It was their boat driver and hunting guide, Captain Terry Yarbrough. He waited a quarter mile away, on standby, with the twenty-foot Carolina Skiff they'd ridden in on.

Jackson pulled the radio out and keyed the mic. "Negative. Bear fell in the drink."

"He fell in? How?"

"He's talented."

Bear huffed as he took a second go at climbing the wooden ladder. "Let me get back up there and I'll show ya talented."

Captain Terry radioed again. "Well, y'all have been at it ten hours now. What do you want to do?"

Jackson looked at the sun dipping over Chincoteague Island to the west. They had a half-hour more of daylight tops.

He keyed the mic again. "Yeah, we better call it. Get Bear here into some dry clothes."

"Copy that, I'm on my way."

Bear got the top half of his body up to the platform, then flopped forward and rolled onto it.

Jackson scooted his own camping chair out of the way. "You look just like a fish I caught once."

Bear rolled onto his back, his camouflage waders and drab green hoodie dripping wet, and gave him the finger. "Help me up."

Jackson did as Bear asked. Minutes later, Captain Terry came gliding down Will's Creek and eased the boat into the hunting blind. The paunch-bellied skipper had gray hair and a clean-shaven face as round as his gut. He pulled a pair of glasses out of the breast pocket of the plaid flannel shirt he had on and examined the damage Bear had done to his blind.

"I'm going to have to run to Ace and get me some two-by-fours to fix that ladder," he said.

"Make sure you send Bear the bill," Jackson said.

"I din' do shit," Bear countered. "Those boards were rottin'!"

Captain Terry's belly jiggled as he chortled. "I'd have to agree with you there."

A few minutes later, Jackson and Bear had their gear in the boat, and the three men pulled out of the duck blind. As Captain Terry whisked them down the Assateague Channel, Jackson took in the wildlife refuge to their left. The squat white oaks dotting the marshlands reminded him of the fig trees he'd seen on the Serengeti when he and a couple of Army buddies backpacked across Tanzania a lifetime ago. The brisk autumn air whipping into his face, though, reminded him of anywhere but Africa.

Captain Terry cruised wide of a small island. On the other side, a ramshackle cottage nestled on one of the several fingers of land that jutted into the channel. Jackson looked back at Captain Terry, then nodded at the cottage.

"What's that?" he asked over the roar of the engine.

"Old hunter's club cabin," Captain Terry said. "Back in the day, the guys who owned it would come out here with a month's worth of supplies and hunt to their heart's content." He shook his head. "Been abandoned for a coupla decades now."

It took another forty-five minutes to get back to the small harbor on the extreme south end of Chincoteague Island. No more than a few hundred feet wide, with fishing trawlers, tour boats, and personal yachts bobbing in slips laid out in a square horseshoe. Beyond it on all sides was a vast blacktop for trucks and trailers. Captain Terry eased them over to the dock they'd left from. On the other side of it, a handful of men were unloading one of the fishing trawlers. Captain Terry waved to one of the men, dressed in orange waders and a long-sleeved tee. The man waved back.

"How's it going, Bert?" Captain Terry said.

"Not bad, how 'bout yourself?" Bert replied.

"Oh, can't complain."

Jackson tied a line around one of the dock posts before he and Bear grabbed their gear. Bert stood over them on the dock. He was tall and slender with a sharp jawline and salt-and-pepper hair.

"You boys been out fishing? That's what they pay me for, you know," he said, chuckling.

"Hell no," Bear said. "I ain't got time for some damn pole and string."

Bert nodded back at his thirty-foot trawler and grinned. "Same."

Jackson stepped out of Captain Terry's boat. "Duck hunting, actually."

Bert's eyebrows lifted. "Bag anything?"

"Few of them." Bear held up the day's take.

Captain Terry laughed as he climbed out of the boat as well. "It cost them a chair in the process, though."

Bear huffed.

"It buckled under my friend here," Jackson explained. "We own an outdoor rec store in Martinsville. Figured we could put some R&R on the company card as long as we do some product testing while we're out here. I guess we won't be recommending that chair."

Bert laughed. "Where you all staying?"

"We have a rental over on the west side of the island," Jackson said.

"Very nice. You boys here all week?"

Jackson nodded. "Got a couple more trips with Captain Terry here on the calendar, including tomorrow."

Captain Terry finished securing the boat and joined them. "Not if I can't get that ladder fixed early tomorrow morning." He checked his watch. "Shoot, I got to get over to Ace before they close."

One of Bert's crew members stepped off the fishing trawler but slipped and knocked into Captain Terry. Captain Terry caught the young man and righted him.

"Whoa, easy there," Captain Terry said.

The man looked back at the group. "My bad," he muttered sheepishly before heading toward the parking lot.

Bert rolled his eyes before turning back to the others. "Sorry about that. New guy." He shook his head. "I don't think they come any greener than that."

"New guy? You lose another member of your crew?" Captain Terry asked.

Bert nodded. "Sam Cutter. A crabbing crew out of Norfolk lured him away."

Captain Terry shook his head. "Ah, that's too bad."

Bert shrugged. "Can't say that I blame him. Fishing here isn't what it used to be. I don't recognize half the faces on the boats these days. I'm just lucky to scrounge together enough warm bodies at this point."

"Ain't that the truth." Captain Terry checked his watch again. "I really do gotta get to Ace, though." He waved at Bert and then Jackson and Bear before heading up the dock.

"See you tomorrow," Jackson said. He turned back to Bear. "Ready to roll?"

Bear grabbed his shotgun and the day's take. "If I hear one more quip about the damn chair, you're cleaning the birds."

Jackson ignored him and smiled at Bert. "You have a good night."

Bert smiled back. "You all do the same."

SAFE HARBOR: CHAPTER TWO

THE BULL SHARK stalked his victim as morning dawned, watching the man slip out of the harbor in the early light. He'd heard others call him Captain Terry, a doughy geezer that earned his keep ferrying tourists around. The Bull Shark had watched him for days. Now it was time to hunt.

Of course, The Bull Shark had a real name of his own. He wasn't, in fact, a sleek-bodied fish, swimming around with fins and gills. He was a person. A man, seemingly like any other, but The Bull Shark had always been different. Yes, he had a name, but it meant nothing to him. Nothing more than a random assortment of letters, as foreign to him as the people who gave it to him. A moniker claiming no lineage or ancestry. A permanent reminder of the discarded bastard he was.

But ever since The Awakening, that night two weeks back, he'd come to know himself as The Bull Shark. It was representative of his newfound purpose in this world. Bull sharks were notoriously aggressive, lone hunters that could live in fresh and saltwater alike. They adapted to their environments to survive. No, to *thrive*. They hunted not just to nourish but because they could. Because they were good at it. That was what The Bull Shark was doing here. Who he was. He chased his prey until he caught it. Because he had to. Something in him wouldn't let him quit, like a primal instinct.

He waited until Captain Terry turned north up the channel, then put his own boat in gear. Following him from a distance, they passed under the bridge over to Assateague Island and continued all the way to Will's Creek. When Captain Terry pulled into a duck blind just off the inlet, The Bull Shark killed his engine and waited. The blind was like several that dotted the waterways around Chincoteague, a boat slip and an elevated shooting platform covered with branches and brush. Only carrying his serrated hunting knife, he wondered if the hunting blind meant the boat captain was armed.

Minutes went by, and Captain Terry never appeared in the blind above the boat slip. This piqued The Bull Shark's curiosity. Slowly, he approached. His engine little more than idling, he floated up to the boat slip and found Captain Terry kneeling over the side of his boat near its bow, hammering away at the base of the duck blind. Inside the boat, at his feet sat a bin full of hardware supplies. As if sensing his presence, Captain Terry turned, startled at the sight of him.

"Good heavens!" Captain Terry said, falling onto his backside and clutching his chest. "You damn near scared the piss out of me."

The Bull Shark flashed his teeth, but with his head buried inside a hoodie and ball cap, he doubted Captain Terry saw it. "Sorry about that," he said. "I was going by and saw you deep in here. Wanted to make sure everything was okay."

"Ah, yeah, just fine." Captain Terry rolled back over onto his knees. "I took a coupla guys out hunting yesterday. Big fella did a number on my ladder here. Just trying to fix it up before I take them back out again today."

The Bull Shark got up from the outboard motor on his boat and put a foot on Captain Terry's. "'Early bird gets the worm', as they say."

"Yup, that's what they say."

"You need a hand with that?"

Captain Terry shook his head. "Oh, no. Just nailing a coupla planks is all. Wish the sun wouldn't take its damn time rising, though." He hammered at a nail, missed it, and clipped his thumb. "Ow! Dagnabbit!"

"You sure you don't need a hand? I don't mind."

Captain Terry looked over his shoulder, studying him for a moment. "Alright, sure. Go on and just hold the boat steady there if ya don't mind."

Stepping completely onto Captain Terry's boat, he got behind the steering console a few feet from the stern and gripped the outer post of the blind, holding the boat in place.

Captain Terry finished nailing in one rung, then replaced the one just above it. The last one needing work was the top one just before the platform deck. He got a fresh two-by-four and a handful of nails from the bin at his feet, then stood to finish the job. When his weight shifted, the boat rocked underneath him.

"Hold her steady," Captain Terry said. "I'm almost finished here."

Not saying anything in response, The Bull Shark looked down at the steering column. The keys were in the ignition. He had everything he needed to strike. He turned the key and the console beeped. The engine rumbled to life.

"Hey!" Captain Terry said. "What are you doi—"

The Bull Shark jerked the throttle back, and the boat jutted in reverse. Captain Terry lost his balance and fell backward. His rear hit the front lip of the boat and his momentum carried him over the bow. Tumbling backward, his upper half flipped over into the water. The Bull Shark shoved the throttle the other way and the boat shot forward, slamming into Captain Terry and pinning him upside down underwater.

Grinning, The Bull Shark watched as Captain Terry's legs kicked erratically in the air, trying desperately to right himself. The shark had to give the boat captain credit for being a fighter, even if it was all in vain. At this point, it was simple physics. With that much force pinning him in place, Captain Terry didn't have the strength to fight it. After almost a minute, the splashing stopped. His legs gave one last kick of spasmodic protest, and then Captain Terry was gone, his life washed from his body in the ebbing tide.

The Bull Shark cut the engine and looked out at Calfpen Bay, listening. Only the tall grass, rustling in the early morning breeze, mourned the life the shark had just snuffed out. The bay was tucked away in a corner of Assateague Island, with Will's Creek a separate nook off of that. At the busiest times of the year, this place could still pass for secluded. But here, at the dawn of a mid-autumn day, it might as well be on a different planet.

The Bull Shark stepped back over to his own boat, fired up his outboard motor, and twisted the throttle. The boat bucked high as it cruised out of Calfpen Bay, leaving Captain Terry's body and boat behind.

When the sun finally rose over the small dunes of Assateague Island, not a living soul was around.

———

Enjoying *Safe Harbor*? Click here to order your copy now!

https://a.co/d/b0cVnyK

ACKNOWLEDGMENTS

Six years ago, I sat down and began writing my first novel, The Woodsman, with the dream it would find a home with a publisher. Over the past half-decade, that dream was delayed and deferred as I navigated the publishing industry. In that time, I released The Woodsman and my next two novels under my own imprint. This novel, Happyland, published from its inception with Liquid Mind Publishing, is the culmination of that journey.

I owe a legion of peers and colleagues I've met along the way for supporting me. Far too many to name here but you know who you are and how much I appreciate you.

Thank you to my friends – most notably Austin, Jess, Madeline, Greg, and Rosi. You have been nothing but cheerleaders for me and winds in my sails. To that end, a special thank you to Zach Lamb and Amy Dewey who read early versions of this book and provided invaluable feedback. This is a better story because of your efforts.

Thank you to my family, especially my mother, who have been steadfast in their support of me and this adventure from its inception. I am so grateful to have your support.

Thank you to Pam Elton, whose expertise and insight were integral to shaping and telling this story. I could not have written a book like this without your guidance.

Thank you to L.T. Ryan for taking a chance on me and believing in my vision for the Jackson Clay & Bear Beauchamp series, ultimately giving it the publishing home it deserves. To that end, thank you to the entire Liquid Mind Publishing/Liquid Mind Media team –

Nicholas, Nicolette, Fiona, Holly, Walter, and Suzanne – for all their efforts in bringing this book to fruition. This is as much your work as it is mine.

Thank you to my editor, Christyn West, for taking my manuscript and turning it into something that looks like I knew what I was doing all along. One day I will repay you for whatever gray hairs I have given you.

But most importantly, thank you to my wife, Meg. I am in awe every day of your ability to unapologetically support and believe in me, even on those days when I stop believing in myself. This book, at its core, is a story about finding a home in others when your own home becomes a stranger to you. Wherever you are, wherever we are together, I am home.

ABOUT THE AUTHOR

B.C. Lienesch is an award-winning mystery, thriller, and horror author hailing from the nation's capital.

A former freelance writer, featured columnist, and editor for guysnation.com, he is an author-member of the International Thriller Writers and the recent recipient of three 2024 LitStar Book Awards including Outstanding Book Series for his Jackson Clay & Bear Beauchamp Series.

Born in Washington, D.C. and raised in Northern Virginia, he now lives in the same area with his wife, Meg, and their feline overlord, Hitchcock.

Join the B.C. Lienesch reader family and stay up to date on all the latest news!
https://www.bclnovels.com/newsletter

facebook.com/bclnovels

x.com/bclienesch

instagram.com/bclienesch

threads.com/@bclienesch

tiktok.com/@bclienesch

bsky.app/profile/bclienesch.bsky.social

JOIN LIQUID MIND PUBLISHING'S MAILING LIST

Follow the link to join our newsletter and stay up to date with Liquid Mind Publishing!

https://BookHip.com/GTQPXSQ

You'll receive a **free** copy of

A Dangerous Game: A Jackson Clay Prequel.